OVID

METAMORPHOSES

OVID

METAMORPHOSES

Translated by Stanley Lombardo

Introduction by W. R. Johnson

Hackett Publishing Company, Inc.
Indianapolis/Cambridge

Copyright © 2010 by Hackett Publishing Company, Inc.

23 22 21 20 19   3 4 5 6 7

For further information, please address
    Hackett Publishing Company, Inc.
    P.O. Box 44937
    Indianapolis, Indiana 46244-0937

    www.hackettpublishing.com

Cover design by Brian Rak and Elizabeth L. Wilson
Interior design by Elizabeth L. Wilson
Composition by Agnew's, Inc.

Cover art: *They Snaked Together* (*Cadmus and Harmonia*) by Micheline Klagsbrun.
Reprinted by permission of the artist.

Library of Congress Cataloging-in-Publication Data

Ovid, 43 B.C.–17 or 18 A.D.
    [Metamorphoses. English]
    Metamorphoses / Ovid ; translated by Stanley Lombardo ; introduction
by W. R. Johnson.
        p. cm.
    Includes bibliographical references.
    ISBN 978-1-60384-307-2 (pbk.) — ISBN 978-1-60384-308-9 (cloth)
    1. Fables, Latin—Translations into English. 2. Metamorphosis—Mythology—
Poetry. 3. Mythology, Classical—Poetry. I. Lombardo, Stanley, 1943– II. Title.
    PA6522.M2L66 2010
    873'.01—dc22   2010019307

Contents

Metamorphoses

Analytical Table of Contents

Tales and episodes related in the poem are indicated below. Tales told by a character (as well as epitaphs and descriptions of works of fine art) are indicated by indentation. Unless otherwise indicated, narration is given directly by the poet.

Introduction

The History of Everything

Who among Ovid's first readers could have predicted that this master of numerous short comic poems, just at the midpoint of his poetic career, would undertake and complete a long and complex poem that would come to rival the *Aeneid* (and perhaps outdo it) in its influence on the literature of Western Europe? He had begun with publishing five volumes of lighthearted love elegies (later harshly winnowed and reduced to three volumes). He had then turned to witty, sometimes poignant representations of legendary ladies writing letters to the men who had absented themselves from their felicity (the *Heroides*). After this splendid compilation, he had written a poem in three volumes, giving cynical and shamelessly sexist (and hilarious) advice to men who needed help in obtaining the consent of the women they lusted after, the *Ars Amatoria,* a sort of seducer's manual. This poem (which may have earned him the intense displeasure of Emperor Augustus and his permanent exile to the Black Sea) was followed by the *Metamorphoses,* an immense poem in fifteen volumes, which took as its chief theme a paradox to which Heraclitus had given its essential form: "all things flow," "you never step into the same river twice"—in short, it is changing realities that constitute the only real permanence in the universe.

Ovid may have been drawn to this particular theme because it gave him warrant to retell stories that he happened to like, stories drawn from Greek myths that focused on (and explained) how given entities came into existence, in particular how certain beings, both semidivine and human, were transformed into animals, vegetables, and minerals. This seemingly limitless source, a narratological paradise, offered the storyteller all the material he needed to construct vivid characters, dramatic conflicts, and surprising outcomes. The major problem facing the poet who found this treasure house irresistible was how to impose on this delicious welter some semblance of intelligible order. (One of Ovid's masters, the Alexandrian poet Callimachus, had found a solution to this problem, but his *Aitia* [*The Origins*] exists for us only in fragments, and we have no real notion of how much help Ovid may have gotten from his great predecessor as he set about trying to devise a shape for, a pattern to, the tales of transfigurations he wanted to narrate.)

Ovid found the answer to his problem in history. To be more precise, in the history of the time he was living in. Like most of his contemporary inhabitants of the Mediterranean world, he felt that he was living at a moment of *weltwende,* of radical change in the world's destiny. Seventeen years before he was born, Julius Caesar had begun his conquest of Gaul and was preparing to invade Britain; six years before he was born, just as the Roman republic entered upon its implosion, Julius Caesar crossed the Rubicon and began his struggle to secure for himself absolute control of Rome; finally, in the year in which Ovid donned the toga of manhood (30 BCE), Octavian, Caesar's heir, defeated Antony and Cleopatra and was well on his way to becoming emperor of the Roman Empire. The nature of these events and the metamorphosis of Rome's political, economic, and military institutions they produced were quickly understood by some and gradually understood by everyone living in the Roman Empire.

But a writer born in the generation before Ovid's, Diodorus of Sicily, undertook to provide a remarkable representation of that knowledge and the feelings that it engendered. He wrote a universal history of the known world, beginning with the Middle East and India, going down through the Trojan War and the history of Greece to Caesar's invasions of Gaul and Britain. Substantial portions of his work remain, but much of it is fragmentary. We can surmise from his preface however that he was convinced that the successes of Julius Caesar—he was writing his history during the early years of Octavian-Augustus' reign—had marked a significant alteration in the history of the (known) world. It is perhaps not too much to say that he saw the history of the nations that he examined as being elements in a progression leading to the establishment of Rome's permanent hegemony or that he felt (he would not be alone in the feeling) that Caesar and Augustus had between them saved the world from its long zigzag patterns of law and disorder: there broods over Diodorus' preface a sort of intuition that what he and his first readers are witnessing is the end of history. That sense of a triumphant finale for history and its nations, one provided by Augustus and his role model, provides the frame for Ovid's great counter-epic. Augustus is emphatically (and wittily) alluded to early on in Book 1, and he and Julius put in a sudden and splendid joint appearance at the very end of Book 15. But before turning to these passages and the ironic world-historical frame they impose on Ovid's diverse and disparate tales of mutability and impermanence, it might be well to see how Ovid begins his poem.

Ovid's Cosmology

Unlike Diodorus, Ovid does not begin with Egypt and other ancient civilizations. Instead, like Hesiod's *Theogony,* he begins with Chaos, but he replaces Hesiod's primeval Void with a vision of the world's origins that smacks of something like atomic theory. Ovid's Chaos is "a crude, unsorted mass, / Nothing but an inert lump, the concentrated / Discordant seeds of disconnected entities" (1.7–9). This unpromising mess is gradually transformed into ordered entities by "Some god, or superior nature" (1.21), whichever god it was "who had sorted out this cosmic heap" and "divided it into parts" (1.32–33). We are here near the realm of Spinoza's *Deus sive Natura,* God or Nature. This god that is nature or this nature that is god is as much a product of the scientific imagination as it is of metaphysical speculation. The purpose of this surprising fusion of Epicurus' world-constituting atoms and the all-pervasive, all-governing god of the Stoics is to remove the true matrix of Ovid's stories from their usual playground, the one that Hesiod and Homer combine to design when they give Zeus (in this poem Jupiter) and his Olympians their permanent poetic identities. Jupiter and his Olympians will indeed dominate many of the stories in the first two-thirds of the *Metamorphoses,* but the poem and its stories is not about them. It is rather about the world in which human beings live and love and suffer. In initiating his poem in a space-time outside the realm of religious mythology that the stories he retells inevitably inhabit, Ovid makes clear that this is going to be a poem about nature and her progeny—even if the exact means by which the human beings who enact Ovid's stories come into existence is uncertain:

> Man was born, whether fashioned from immortal seed
> By the Master Artisan who made this better world,
> Or whether Earth, newly parted from Aether above
> And still bearing some seeds of her cousin Sky,
> Was mixed with rainwater by Titan Prometheus
> And molded into the image of the omnipotent gods.
> And while other animals look on all fours at the ground
> He gave to humans an upturned face, and told them to lift
> Their eyes to the stars. And so Earth, just now barren,
> A wilderness without form, was changed and made over,
> Dressing herself in the unfamiliar figures of men.
>
> (1.79–89)

The awkward and no doubt vexatiously intended mythological linking of Epicurus (seen here in the world's shared material substance, down to the divine seed from which humans are fashioned) and the Stoics (seen here in the gods who govern all, down to the orientation of the human face) gains in a provocative indeterminacy what it loses in clarity. But in this passage the two strains of thought conspire to provide nature (here Earth) and humankind (in its noblest aspect) with a unity that can be seen independently of the traditional mythologies that religion and politics nourish and depend on.

Heaven's King and His Earthly Double

Having accounted for the world and the creatures in it, the poet now turns to the description of the early history of humans: the Four Ages—Gold, Silver, Bronze, and Iron. The happy Golden Age is ruled over by Jupiter's father, Saturn, but "after Saturn was consigned to Tartarus' gloom / The world was under Jove, and the Silver race came in" (1.115–16). This means that the stories that make up the poem, from this moment on, take place in the Iron Age over which Jupiter holds dominion.

The first challenge Jupiter must deal with is the rebellious Giants, whom he easily defeats. In retaliation, Mother Earth creates a race of violent humans from their blood, and this "incarnation," which "also was contemptuous / Of the gods" (1.164–65) makes Jupiter very angry, so angry that he summons a council of the gods. Unlike Hesiod, his chief model up to this point, the poet does not relate how Saturn had seized power from his own father (Uranus) just as he has had his power wrested from him by his own son. By representing the creation of humans and their early history (the Four Ages) in such detail and by very briefly sketching Jupiter's seizure of power in a couple of verses, Ovid avoids explaining how Jupiter and his fellow Olympians came to possess the immense power they will wield throughout the rest of the poem. In doing so he avoids implicitly dwelling not only on Rome's implosion as a republic, its rise to empire, and its bloody history of civil war but also on the Olympians' earthly counterparts themselves. But the angry entrance of the king of Olympus into the poem creates a different and disturbing impression. Still irate with the Giants and now furious with their replacement (and doubtless with Earth who had given birth to all of his recent enemies), Jupiter summons a council of the gods and lays bare his plan to destroy mankind (1.186–203). The Olympian gods hasten by way of the Milky Way "to the royal palace / Of the great Thunderer" (1.174–75). The lesser (plebeian) gods live elsewhere, "but the great / All have their homes along this avenue. This quarter, / If I may say so, is high heaven's Palatine" (1.178–80). Ovid's blasphemous (and witty) equation of Olympus with the Palatine where Augustus lives is hardly mitigated by the ostentatious timidity of Ovid's "if I may say so."

Jupiter's is not a constitutional monarchy, and the council of the gods has not been summoned to debate or to advise. Nevertheless, when Jupiter singles out "infamous Lycaon" (1.203) as the worst of the humans whom he intends to destroy, the gods instantly demand his death.

> So it was when a disloyal few
> Were mad to blot out Rome with Caesar's blood,
> And the human race was stunned with fear of ruin
> And the whole world shuddered. The loyalty

Of your subjects, Augustus, pleases you no less
Than Jove was pleased.

(1.205–10)

Here Augustus is formally identified as Jupiter's earthly counterpart, and these verses might, save for the wry irony that suffuses this passage, be reasonably judged as the copious flattery of a court poet. Some readers will decide against an ironic reading of this passage, but what cannot be denied is that the first story in the poem represents Augustus as Jupiter's human double and depicts Jupiter as a capricious tyrant, since despite what we have been told about those who live in the Iron Age, it is by no means clear that the majority of human beings are as wicked as Lycaon is purported to be, much less that all of humankind merits annihilation.

This emphatic linking of Jupiter and Augustus recurs in yet more spectacular form in the poem's final pages. When Ovid's history of everything that matters is almost complete, he concludes his poem with the apotheosis of Julius Caesar, whose supreme achievement, surpassing all his conquests and triumphs, turns out to be his having fathered the emperor Augustus: "For in all Caesar has done, / Nothing is greater than this, that he became / The father of our emperor" (15.834–36). Augustus, of course, was in fact the great-nephew of Julius, and Julius had only adopted him as his heir. But because Augustus has to be divine, it is necessary that his "father," Julius, be himself transformed into a divinity: "And so, that his son not have a mortal father, / It was necessary for Caesar to become a god" (15.846–47). When Venus realizes this, knowing that Julius, blood of her blood and her direct descendent, is about to be assassinated by his enemies on the Ides of March, she appeals to the other gods, but they are as helpless as she is against the decrees of the Fates. Then Jupiter calms and consoles his anguished daughter by revealing to her the splendid destiny that awaits her Roman progeny after Julius is murdered and deified (15.911–55). Once Julius has taken his fated place in heaven, his (adopted) son will perform his glorious deeds throughout the known world and, having gifted it with enduring peace, he will furnish it a model for morals, with an eye to its future, and he will pass on his name and reign to his stepson, Tiberius, and then follow Julius into godhood in the heavens:

And when peace has been bestowed on all these lands
He will turn his mind to the rights of citizens
And establish laws most just, and by his example
Guide the way men behave. Looking to the future
And generations to come, he will pass on his name
And his burdens as well to the son born to him
And to his chaste wife. And not until he is old
And his years equal his meritorious actions
Will he go to heaven and his familial stars.
                                        (15.933–41)

Having finished this prophecy of Augustus' restoration of the
Golden Age, Jupiter instructs Venus to rush down to Rome and
snatch up the soul of dying Julius and bear it up to its heavenly destination and final home. This she does, clutching it to her breast, but
its heat is such that she is forced to let go of it and it speeds off on
its own, traversing the sky as a glorious comet until it becomes a star.
It is from this vantage that Caesar comprehends the real meaning of
his former life on earth:

And now he sees
All his son's good deeds and confesses that
They are greater than his own, and he rejoices
To be surpassed by him. And though the son forbids
His own deeds to be ranked above his father's,
Fame, free and obedient to no one's command,
Puts him forward, only in this opposing his will.
                                        (15.954–60)

So had Atreus yielded in glory to Agamemnon (a dubious comparison), and Aegeus to Theseus, and Peleus to Achilles, and Saturn to
Jupiter. Jupiter reigns in heaven, and Augustus, surpassing his "father," reigns on earth: "And as Jupiter is in control of high heaven /
And the realms of the triple world, the earth / Is under Augustus, as
both ruler and sire" (15.965–67). Having said so much, Ovid prays
to several of Rome's special guardian gods, those to whom a vatic
poet may offer his supplication, that after a long life on earth Augustus may go to his heavenly reward and, once there, give ear to
the prayers of the Romans he left behind (15.968–80).

Once he has testified to the imminent divinity of Augustus in ful-
some measure (deftly pilfering from Horace, *Odes* 2.20, 3.30), Ovid
proceeds to claim deathlessness for himself, one that rivals the emperor's and in certain ways may surpass it (15.981–92). This immortality will be proof not only against fire, sword, and time but also
against the anger of Jupiter. If, as seems as likely as not, this closing
challenge to oblivion and power was composed after Ovid had arrived at his bleak destination on the Black Sea, he here underlines,
again, his comparison of Augustus to Jupiter. In any case, thus far the
poet has been right about both Augustus and himself. The emperor's influence on Western Europe and its various offspring is enduring if fragmentary. The poet's has been and continues to be as
hardy as it is fertile. And his masterpiece, that strange omnium-
gatherum of fragments, is whole and intact.

Augustus and the Prophecy of Pythagoras

Curiously, there is one more reference to Rome's and Augustus'
supremacy, one that seems intended to reinforce the poem's Augustan frame. Toward the beginning of Book 15, Ovid introduces
a long speech by the philosopher Pythagoras (15.69–515). This
speech, part philosophical explication and part sermon, is peculiar
in several ways. It takes up nearly half the book in which it appears,
contains no story, and thereby awkwardly interrupts the easy, steady
flow of narrative transitions that the poem has up to this point
maintained. But incongruous as they may at first seem, the figure
of Pythagoras and his lengthy discourse serve Ovid's design in a
number of ways.

First, Pythagoras, exponent of the transmigration of souls, allows
Ovid to brush aside, with his customary sleight of hand, the centuries of Roman history that separate the death of Romulus from
the triumph of Augustus (Ovid hardly has any space for them, and,
in any case, the coming of Augustus and his Peace render them all
but irrelevant).

Second, Pythagoras' doctrine (his explanation of the nature of
things) provides the entire poem, just as it is hastening to its closure, with a very powerful counterperspective, one which completely

ignores—and in so doing disavows—the theological underpinnings that provide the Olympians and their stories with much of their verisimilitude. Sounding something like Lucretius and something like the Hesiodic voice with which the poem opens, Pythagoras argues for a world governed by an unending and dynamic mutability (15.184–96), one in which souls migrate forever from body to body, both the spiritual and the physical realms being subject to transformations without end. This speech, then, provides Ovid with a new and complex warrant for this representation of the world as metamorphosis. But, in a strategy of self-ironization that suits this poet perfectly (deliberately hoist with his own petard), it abolishes the Olympians who figure so prominently in the stories he has been telling. Pythagoras is by no means an enemy of the divine: he worships nature (15.278–85) which (or who) is clearly associated with (if not identical to) the earth. In his view, nature and earth are wholly benign and wholly opposed to the slaughter of animals for food (15.88–159, 492–515).

Finally, we come to the essential reason for Pythagoras' strange intrusion in a poem that would not seem to want him. Just before his final plea for a vegetarianism that is both merciful and pious, he had extended his doctrine of the unfailing mutability of things to history itself. "Times, too, change; we see some nations grow strong / And others decline" (15.459–60). After the fall of Troy, Sparta, Mycenae, Thebes, and Athens flourished for a while, but they are now little more than names (15.464–66). It is now Rome's turn in the spotlight of history:

> And now we hear Dardanian Rome is rising,
> Laying her foundations with monumental effort
> On the banks of the Apennine-fed Tiber River.
> She changes form by growing, and, one day,
> She will be the capital of the boundless world.
>
> (15.467–71)

So even the mystic proponent of moral vegetarianism cannot resist repeating a prophecy he has chanced to hear, namely, that with Augustus the history of humankind and its nations will have reached its final goal:

> . . . one born of the blood
> Of Iulus will make her mistress of the world,
> And when the earth has made use of him, heaven
> Will enjoy him, and the sky will be his final abode.
>   (15.484–87)

Pythagoras is not much interested in the swerve his logic takes from philosophic disquisition to a validation of Augustan propaganda. But Ovid and his readers, the lines about Sparta and Mycenae and Thebes and Athens still echoing in their ears, may find themselves wondering if Rome is immune to decline and fall, if Augustus has in fact brought history to its stop. Heard in one way, this is the poetry of praise, as eloquent in its reverence as, say, Anchises' prophecy of Augustus in *Aeneid* 6. But heard in another way, in a speech that refuses permanence to anything or anyone and that excludes any possibility of "divine right," the eloquence seems stained with irony.

The Olympians

Ovid's gods seem at first glance to be identical with the gods of Homer. On closer inspection, however, they diverge radically both from their Homeric models and from the Roman versions of those models (as we find them, for instance, in Virgil). Homer's divinities manifest human emotions, and their motivations are for the most part transparently clear. More importantly, their actions are closely monitored by Zeus, who, for all his power, is himself subject to the dictates of both Justice and Fate. Justice and Fate have little place in the *Metamorphoses,* and Jupiter himself, in most of his appearances in the poem, is as capricious and as vindictive as the other gods whose behavior he ought to be supervising. When Ovid's gods encounter human beings they are likely to rape, maim, or murder them (usually by transforming them into some lower, uglier entity). Blessed with enormous powers as well as with immortality, they are beyond good and evil, they have little acquaintance with reason, and it is mostly whim and cruelty that govern their activities. Taken all in all, the impression they make is that of malicious children whose favorite playground is the human world.

This sustained defabrication of the Olympians constitutes one of the chief strategies of the opening books of Ovid's poem (roughly from Book 1 through Book 9 or more than half of it), and its purpose would seem to be a dual one. On the one hand, this attack on the Roman Olympians (in their Augustan avatars) is a part of Ovid's criticism, throughout his poem, of the idea of epic and of its indispensable theological foundations. On the other hand, the gods as he represents them here function as symbols of the mysterious causes of evil in the world, as a way of imagining (and protesting against) the suffering that marks the human condition, most specifically the suffering that human beings endure when they are confronted with power in its various guises. The Olympians represent, both in their poetic and their political representations, the power and glory that epic poetry exists to celebrate (Homer and Virgil, in their different ways, offer objections to the idea of epic, but from Ovid's perspective they are nevertheless complicit in propagating its fundamental untruths). Ovid's cartoons of the Olympians (in their Homeric and Virgilian guises as well as in their political representations) are not fair-minded and are not intended to be. What shapes them is an irony that is rooted in sarcasm and satire. What sets them in motion is a determination to speak truth to power.

Jupiter's and Apollo's rapes need little in the way of comment. It is ludicrous (not to mention, wicked) when Jupiter, during his inspection tour of the damage caused to the earth by Phaëthon's fiery crash, transforms himself into a replica of his chaste daughter, Diana, before raping Callisto (2.473–81). It is equally ludicrous (and hardly less wicked) when Apollo gains access to Leucothoë by assuming the appearance of her mother and then raping the terrified girl once he has restored himself to all his godly beauty (4.244–61).

But these crimes of the heart (or the groin) seem almost trivial when compared with what happens when the gods are bent not on rape but on revenge. Sometimes the revenge seems to have some basis in human wrongdoing, as is probably the case with Jupiter's anger at Lycaon (though it is possible that Lycaon angered Jupiter because he protested Jupiter's rape of his daughter Callisto). But, even when it is in some degree merited, divine vengeance is often extravagantly cruel. Certainly, in the case of Niobe, her arrogant claim that her fourteen children, seven boys and seven girls, gave her warrant to challenge the fertility of Latona (who could boast but two children, Apollo and Diana), was asking for trouble (6.183–231). And trouble comes when Latona goads her son and daughter to punish Niobe's stupid boast, and they, in one of the poem's most devastating scenes (6.250–345), obey their mother by performing on Niobe's innocent offspring a piece of baroque mayhem (and epic pastiche) that ranks with similar set pieces in the poem (Perseus 5.1–270; Lapiths and Centaurs 12.247–615).

Worse is the punishment of innocence, as when Actaeon comes upon Diana when she is bathing with her nymphs in her grove (3.184–201). He catches only a fleeting glimpse of her—if he does—because she is taller than the nymphs who try to hide her from his gaze. But he is doomed. She splashes him with water from her bath, and, in a lengthy, elaborate, and utterly gruesome passage which is perhaps preeminent among the poem's frightening pictures of divine murder, transforms him into a stag which his own hunting dogs tear to pieces (3.202–67).

The Gods of Nature

These selfish, ruthless Olympians intrude themselves into many if not most of the stories that make up a little more than the first half of the poem. Their arrogance and malicious contempt for human beings are thrown into sharp relief by another, admittedly smaller, group of deities whose virtues far outweigh their vices. Demeter and Dionysus were not admired by Homer and his noble patrons, and their visits to Olympus seem to have been infrequent and unmemorable: they are gods of the earth, they are, respectively, Bread and Wine. Their Roman counterparts, Ceres and Bacchus, resemble them closely in the functions they perform and, above all, in the benevolence that motivates their behavior. In Rome, Ceres and Liber (Dionysus), along with his female aspect, Libera, shared a temple and worship, and they enjoyed ardent devotion by the *populares,* the common people. (For fascinating observations on Dionysus as Liber, and his crucial place in Roman religion, see T. P. Wiseman's *The Myths of Rome* and *Unwritten History.*)

The spirits of Bread and Wine have little to do with law and order, which seems to be a major concern for the Olympians. By con-
trast, the spirits of Bread and Wine cherish peace and plenty; their
chief concerns are for nature's health and fertility and for the welfare of the human beings who revere them and thank them. They are
the deities who foster the horn of plenty. As emblems of the opera-
tions of nature they will find their ultimate validation, in this poem,
in Pythagoras' impassioned testament to the goodness of Nature.

On the other hand, they are quick to punish those who deny
their divinity or show ingratitude and contempt for the bounty that
they and nature provide them with. During her long search for her
missing daughter, Proserpina, a grieving and weary Ceres transforms
the nasty brat who mocks her into a spotted lizard (5.516–33). In a
long passage (8.832–990), when impious Erysichthon chops down
her sacred oak, Ceres arranges to have him taken over by an insane,
ravenous hunger that drives him, when he has consumed everything
he can lay hold of, to devour himself. Ceres is in fact an avatar of
Mother Earth, as her frenzied search for her daughter (resulting in
earth's renewal in spring) clearly shows. Her rare outbursts of anger
cannot blemish her essential goodness.

The acts of revenge committed by Bacchus are far more extensive and far uglier than those of Ceres. But in each case, modeled on
Euripides' *Bacchae,* Bacchus' cruelties are fueled by the rejection of
his godhead by arrogant men and women who reasonably (and foolishly) demur at embracing a new object and new style of worship.
The tale of Pentheus' crime and punishment is told at 3.562–810,
but it is interrupted by the parallel tale of the god's angry transformation of the impious Tyrrhenian pirates at 3.641–765, which is the
origin of one of Pound's most brilliant passages (*Cantos II*). Bacchus'
angry revenge on the daughters of Minyas (transformed into bats)
is represented in 4.1–11, 425–54; unlike the Pierians, whom we will
shortly encounter, they are punished not for the kind of stories they
tell but for their refusal to accept the divinity of Bacchus (who seems
not in the least bothered that one of the sisters relates the story of
Venus' adultery with Mars, 4.189–211). Ceres and Bacchus equal the
Olympians in their swift anger and contempt for their victims, but
differ from them in that the punishments the former inflict are never
on the innocent but only on the guilty, on those who despise these

givers of the precious bread and wine without which humankind could not live.

Earth (Hesiod's Gaia) and her surrogates counter the Olympians' rage for order with a passion for fertility and variety. Earth gave birth, as we have seen, first to the Giants and then, from their blood, to a new race of humans whom Jupiter hated and sought to destroy with the flood. Two humans alone, Deucalion and Pyrrha, survive Jupiter's wrath, and when they approach the shrine of Themis and beg her help, she instantly grants it, telling them to scatter the bones of their mother as they walk on (1.332–34, 388–96). The bones, of course, are rocks that are transformed into men and women. Themis is in fact an earth goddess, and it is her bones that they cast behind them, so it is the Earth Mother, not Jupiter, who has saved the earth and mankind. This event is paralleled in the next book when Earth cries out to Jupiter to end the conflagration that was caused by the crash of Phaëthon's chariot and that is about to destroy the world. Jupiter listens to her and puts out the fire (2.296–328). Here, as in the matter of the flood, it is Earth, not Jupiter, who is responsible for the salvation of nature and mankind.

Possibly, the earth mother puts in another appearance, this time as Isis, when the girl Iphis begs the goddess to change her into a boy so she can marry her beloved Ianthe (9.888–915). And possibly it is also the earth mother who is the nameless and mysterious deity (seconded by other nameless gods) who hears the plea of the grieving, incestuous Myrrha and transforms her wretchedness into something beautiful, a myrrh tree (10.529–50). In any case, these moments of compassion, rare and dwindling though they are, offer an undersong, sometimes poignant, sometimes tragic, to the tales that reveal the injustice and savagery of Olympian power. In so doing, they help define Ovid's grieving perspective on the condition of humankind.

Ovid's Heroes

While Ovid gives his gods generous exposure, he provides his readers with only a few random snapshots of his heroes, and those brief glimpses represent them in unflattering, sometimes comic, postures. This odd parsimony may be best explained in two ways: first, like the gods (whose children they are), the great Greek heroes flourish in the world of epic, the very genre Ovid is committed to deflating; second, Ovid begins to notice the Greek heroes only when they are about to enter "history," that is to say, when they exist on the verge of or take part in the Trojan War. Up until the time when the Greek heroes start making their appearances in it, the poem has made ample use of a vague chronology. But with the advent of the war at Troy and of Aeneas, one of the few Trojans to escape his city's fiery ruin and Rome's founding father, Ovid gradually turns his attention to Rome, its evolution, its "history" and its myths. He is getting ready to prepare his readers for the splendid epiphany of the Caesars with which his poem will reach its closure and its goals: on one level, the triumph of Augustus, and, on the other, the perfection of the poet's ironic meditations on how myths become epics.

We have noted how Ovid enlisted Perseus to enact one of his epical pastiches (5.1–270). Theseus fares little better, whether reduced to being rescued from the Minotaur by Ariadne, whom he quickly deserts (8.203–12); or saved by his father from Medea's poisoned cup and then serenaded by the citizens of Athens with songs that scantily sketch his heroic deeds (7.453–503); or noted only in passing among the opponents of the Calydonian boar (8.348–49); or even depicted briefly and bloodily as initiating the Battle of the Lapiths against the Centaurs (12.272–89). Hercules garners the opening passages of Book 9 (1–304) for himself, but it is the tale of how, poisoned by the Centaur Nessus, he comes to his agonized and glorious apotheosis that Ovid focuses on (147–304). There would be no point in Ovid's trying to compete with Homer, so, ironically, Achilles is permitted his biggest moment when he meets Cygnus on the field of battle and is the instrument of his foe's translation into a swan just at the moment when he prepares to strip away the armor he has won (12.81–172). And he is the luckless subject of the long and funny (mostly grandiloquent) debate that Ajax and Ulysses engage in when they attempt to demonstrate which of them has the better claim to the armor of the fallen Achilles (13.1–460). It is this debate that replaces (and all but effaces) the Trojan War.

Retrieving himself and his nearest kinfolk from the immediate aftermath of the Greek triumph and rapine, Aeneas is ready to step into the pages of history (13.752–63). But again, Ovid is loathe to compete with Virgil and his *Aeneid,* so he decides to break up the journey of Aeneas toward his goal, the founding of Rome, with a variety of interwoven tales, until, when his war with the native Italians is ended, he can enjoy his own special apotheosis. When Venus orders the river Numicius to wash her son clean of his mortality and render unto her what of him is deathless, he becomes, like his remote descendant Julius, heaven-bound (14.691–99). Then, with Aeneas safely gathered up among the Roman Olympians, Ovid quickly transfers his attention to Romulus, greatest of Rome's indigenous founding fathers, until the coming of Augustus and his great-uncle. It is these *Roman* heroes the world has been waiting for.

The Perils of Artists and the Perils of Lovers

(i)

It is no surprise to discover that Ovid is partial to artists or that he is fascinated (and proud) of the power of art. But he combines his celebration of artists and their art with a vivid awareness of the dangers artists tend to encounter when their art challenges the official version of reality. At times, reading these stories that focus on the perils of art and on what happens to artists when power speaks power to truth, one senses that Ovid had a presentiment of his own destiny. (But of course we know neither when Ovid wrote that final coda to the *Metamorphoses* nor what revisions he might have made to his portraits of luckless artists once he had settled into his exile.)

The ugliest of these tales of artistic crimes and their punishment is the one that sketches with chilling brevity the fate of Marsyas. Ovid dispenses with the scene that depicts the contest between Apollo and this satyr (who had apparently challenged the god's preeminence as a flautist) but instead we are instantly confronted with his repentant screams as the victorious god has his skin flayed from his body:

> As the satyr screamed
> His skin was peeled from his body's surface
> And he was one massive wound. Blood flowed
> All over the place; his muscles were laid bare;

His veins throbbed and quivered without any skin;
You could count the pulsing entrails; the fibers
Of his lungs showed clearly through his chest.
(6.441–47)

Any feeling we might entertain that, however great his virtuosity, Marsyas gets what he deserves for his arrogance in daring to vie with the god of music is instantly effaced by the response of the crowd of onlookers who weep so abundantly at his suffering that the Earth can gather their tears and transform them into the clearest stream in Phrygia (6.448–57).

In yet another story Apollo is again challenged to a musical performance (once again, on the flute), this time by Pan, who has some claim to being a virtuoso on this instrument; his music is described as "foreign," but when we keep in mind that he is a follower of Bacchus, we can regard this contest as one being one, almost à la Nietzsche, between the official music of Olympus and a rival music, wild, primeval, and ecstatic, that constantly threatens to replace it. Mt. Tmolus in Lydia (a suitable place for Pan and his music) acts as judge of the contest. He listens first to Pan, whose music pleases King Midas, and then to Apollo, who takes the stage gorgeously and every inch a star:

Phoebus Apollo's golden head was wreathed
With laurel from Parnassus, and his mantle,
Dyed deep Tyrian purple, swept the ground.
In his left hand was his lyre, inlaid with gems
And Indian ivory, and his plectrum
Was in his right. His very pose was an artist's.
(11.190–95)

Tmolus decides in Apollo's favor, a judgment unanimously approved by the audience—except for Midas, who protests that the judge's decision is unfair. Apollo severely punishes him for expressing the opinion he does, but that does not mean that his judgment of Pan's performance is wrong. The glittering grandeur of the Olympian contestant and the pomposity that it reveals may fool Tmolus and the audience but they fail to take Midas in.

Artistic arrogance meets with retribution once again when the daughters of Pierus, nine in number, offer to compete in song and story with the Olympian Muses (5.342–57). The nine Muses accept the challenge, and, with nymphs as judges, the competition begins. The leader of the Pierians sings a song, briefly described, wherein the Giants war with the Olympians, whose deeds are trivialized: they flee in terror from Typhoeus, transforming themselves into various animals to escape detection (5.373–86). (Bacchus is incongruously numbered among these cowards, for he had no place in traditional war with the Giants, being born after it was concluded.)

Calliope, representing the Olympian Muses, undertakes to answer these blasphemies with a long tale which centers on Ceres' grieving search for her daughter, Proserpina, whom Pluto had abducted and taken as his wife in hell (5.396–766). Her song begins with a vivid picture of the punishment of Typhoeus and ends (after the interpolated tale of Arethusa, 5.659–740) with Ceres' restoring to earth the fertility that, in her grief and anger, she had deprived it of and with her establishing the Eleusinian mysteries in Athens (5.741–766). Interestingly, Calliope doesn't bother refuting the Pierian's brazen tale of Olympian shame but instead ignores the Olympians to celebrate an earth mother whose true home is not among the Olympians. Since we do not hear the Pierian song we cannot say for sure whether the nymphs fairly judge Calliope to be the victorious singer. Yet, with the evidence of the next story clearly in mind, we may be tempted to think that, as was the case with Marsyas and Pan, the Pierians were perhaps cheated of victory and that their transformation into chattering magpies has more to do with revenge than with justice (5.767–87).

There is no doubt that Arachne is guilty of an inordinate artistic vanity which drives her, despite Minerva's stern warnings, to persist in challenging the goddess to the weaving contest that will prove to be Arachne's undoing (6.30–50). The question is whether she loses the contest (if she does) because her skills are inferior to those of the goddess who transforms her into a spider. Rooted in a naïve egotism, the tapestry of Minerva centers on her victory over Poseidon when the two vied with one another over the naming of Athens while the Olympians watch their rivalry and approve her triumph (6.80–92). And to remind her opponent of what happens to fools who fail to acknowledge the power and glory of the Olympians, in the four corners of her tapestry she depicts exemplary miscreants and the severe chastisements the Olympians inflict on them (6.95–112). To frame her square, ultraconservative, and purely Academic work of art, Minerva chooses her signature vegetation: "She bordered it all with peaceful olive wreaths / And with her own tree brought the work to an end" (6.113–14).

Arachne's composition differs from the goddess' in several ways. She represents nine of Jupiter's rapes, six of Neptune's, the various disguises of Apollo and his rape of Isse, one of Bacchus' rapes, and one of Saturn's. As a frame for her elegant representation of divine crimes, she designs a spare, swirling pattern of flowers and ivy intertwined, one that is as unobtrusive as it is beautiful. Once again, the artist is primarily interested in countering the propaganda and alibis of the Olympians, but the hostile content is no more crucial to the excellence of her art than its exquisite style. In the first of her pictures, the rape of Europa, a combination of deft, vivid image and exact psychological detail bespeak an artist as sophisticated and sensitive as she is talented:

> Arachne depicts Europa deceived by the false bull,
> But you would think the bull real, and the water too.
> She looks back at the shore and calls her friends,
> And, afraid of the waves, tucks up her dainty feet.
>
> (6.115–18)

Arachne, like the tapestry she produces, is Ovidian in feeling and in form, and her art may be easily read as Ovid's statement about his own artistic credo.

Naturally, Minerva's response to her opponent's accomplishment goes well beyond displeasure. She knows great art when she sees it, and reacts to the humbling experience of being bettered by an arrogant human by transforming her successful rival—the picture of the transformation is horrendous—into a deathless spider, condemned to repeat the making of its meaningless, ugly web forever. From the Olympian perspective, Arachne may be read as the culprit in an indelible cautionary tale about people who are tempted to quarrel with the reigning ideology. For other readers, she, like her creator as he sat staring at the Black Sea and pondering his career and his fate, is an emblem of the power of art and of the risks that sometimes confront artists whose temperament and genius are such that they cannot refrain from scrutinizing the myths that power lives by.

(ii)

Orpheus, to whom Ovid devotes Book 10 in its entirety, is far from being a critic of power. He is instead a lover who happens to be a poet as well, and it is therefore not by chance that most of the stories he sings are about the ups and downs (but mostly the downs) of the amatory life. We first encounter him when, here as in Virgil's *Georgics 4,* he descends into hell to win back from the dead his beloved Eurydice whom a snakebite killed.

He charms the rulers and the denizens of hell with his song and his wife is returned to him. When summoned she comes limping from her wound, a nice touch of parody (10.51–52) that arouses our suspicion—if it has not stirred before—that Ovid's Orpheus will not be immune to Ovid's penchant for ironic send-ups of "classical" icons.

After Orpheus loses his wife again, he returns to the upper air, desolate and bitter. He swears off women, introduces pederasty to Thrace, and resumes performing his poetry to an appreciative audience of trees, among whom is the cypress. This tree reminds Orpheus of the beautiful boy Cyparissus, much loved by Orpheus' father, Apollo. This boy doted on a stag which he adorned with lots of jewelry (the parody here of Silvia's stag in *Aeneid 7* is gorgeous in its malice). But unfortunately Cyparissus killed the stag with a random cast of his javelin, and then, broken by a grief that Apollo himself could not console, faded away into a funeral tree.

The mocking sentimentality that drenches this tale finds an echo in yet another tale of Apollo's attraction to handsome adolescents. This time Apollo forsakes his usual pastimes (music and archery), and spends his days in rough Spartan athletic activities with his beloved Hyacinthus (10.153–60). But an unlucky discus throw hits Hyacinthus in the head. Unable to revive the stricken young man, Apollo addresses him a lengthy, somewhat operatic monologue and watches as the boy's blood becomes a lovely flower (10.185–227).

In one of Orpheus' most famous stories, that of Pygmalion and his Galatea, the singer turns from sad and sentimental pederasty to heterosexual fulfillment. Pygmalion, another artist, disgusted with women as nature has made them, refuses to marry, and, repressing his sexual instincts, sculpts for himself his ideal woman from ivory. He soon falls in love with his creation, adorns its, fondles it, kisses it, and ends by taking it to his bachelor's bed. What happens in that bed Ovid refrains from telling us but we do learn that on one of Venus' festal days, the sculptor, who has been smitten with his own creation, shyly begs the love goddess to help him. Knowing that he wants his statue for his wife, beneath his ardent caresses, she promptly transforms the cold dream girl into a living, breathing woman (10.306–25). This clever and very influential tale is capable of various interpretations, but the reader who senses, beneath its soft erotic shimmer, not a little sour misogyny ironically prettified may be close to the truth of Pygmalion. It is the sort of "happy" love story that Ovid's Orpheus might contrive.

A child born from this lucky marriage is Cinyras, whose daughter is Myrrha, and she, a paradigm of perversity, falls in love with her father. Orpheus is shocked by the story that he is somehow compelled to narrate and he warns his listeners, especially fathers and daughters, to put their hands over their ears while he performs this vile history:

> My song is dire. Daughters, stay away; and fathers, too.
> Or if my songs charm you, do not believe this story;
> Believe instead that it never happened,
> But if you do believe it, believe the punishment too.
>
> (10.334–37)

This story is among Ovid's longest and very best, and one sometimes gets the impression while reading it that two storytellers are simultaneously engaged in devising it. Orpheus, who warns us not to experience it, is as prurient as he is puritanical, and he delights, almost like a voyeur, in each detail his conflicted imagination can concoct. But Ovid concerns himself with Myrrha's dilemma, and his sympathetic study of her thoughts and feelings is sophisticated and persuasive, not least when he represents her complete contrition and her exquisite transformation (10.560–75).

Orpheus expends all his gifts for combining easy pathos with rich ornament (and a touch of schadenfreude?) when he closes his recitations with two more tragic and perhaps cautionary tales about unsuccessful heterosexuals (Adonis and Venus, Hippomenes and Atalanta). We are not surprised when, at the opening of Book 11, a mob of women tears him limb from limb (11.23–44).

The love stories Ovid tells without the assistance of his Orpheus offer a wide spectrum of lovers, one that ranges from the luckless to the lucky, from the selfish and cruel to the generous and humane, but sorrow far exceeds joy, and it is sorrow that triumphs in the most complex and most memorable of these stories. The horror story that Tereus, Procne, and Philomela enact represents the pathology of eros at its worst (6.472–780). With Ceyx and Alcyone, by virtue of Ovid's rare fusion of empathy and skill, a tale of happy marriage and true love shifts imperceptibly and plausibly from melodrama to pathos to tragedy (11.481–862). Since the *Metamorphoses'* central inspiration is the poet's intimations of the world's suffering, it is not surprising that one doesn't need all the fingers of one hand to count its happy love stories: Deucalion and Pyrrha (1.324–431), Baucis and Philemon (8.697–817), Iphis and Ianthe (9.812–915), Vertumnus and Pomona (14.716–803, 883–90). His major concern is with young people who encounter the attractions and the dangers that eros brings with it. A variety of young lovers come to ruin in a variety of ways, victims of powers both inside them and outside them that their innocence and inexperience expose them to. Narcissus (3.371–561), Hermaphroditus (4.321–424), Medea (7.12–113), Scylla (the one enamored of Minos, 8.12–183), Byblis (9.503–764), Iphis, and Myrrha are all of them hurled suddenly into passions that they cannot comprehend and cannot shake themselves free of. Medea, though she initiates this pattern of young despair and provides it with its major rhetorical tropes, finally releases herself from her infatuation with Jason, and Iphis is rescued by the intervention of Isis from tragedy and reassigned to comedy.

But these exceptions prove the rule, which is that under the sign of eros humans who fall in love (no less than victims of divine rape) fare no better than artists. Like everyone else in the poem, the innocent and the guilty alike, they exist in a universe whose only constant is mutability. Change sometimes happens for the better (for some human beings to be transformed into a flower, a tree, or a fountain is preferable to the suffering or the humiliation they find they are unable or unwilling to endure), but more often metamorphosis provides only an endless prolongation of suffering: For unrelieved horror, Arachne's fate is hard to match, but those of Scylla (14.20–80), Dryope (9.366–445), and Aesacus (11.863–922) come close. In any case, Ovid's lovers are rarely rewarded, and his artists almost always punished.

The Author and His Authors

Ovid's poem glories in its perpetual ambivalence. On the one hand, it offers an ironic promise to provide its readers with a grand narrative that will let them view the world, in all its complex unfoldings, from a stable perspective. Starting from utter chaos it ends with the perfect order that Augustus imposed on human history (which seems always to have been working its way, however hectically, toward the salvation that he alone could proffer it). On the other hand, in the wide gap between its abrupt and opaque beginning and the clarity of its salvific conclusion, the poem consists both of a fascinating jumble of people, places, and things and a deceptively smooth, yet ultimately disturbing series of broken images, a seemingly plausible representation of intelligible realities that are caught up by and disappear into the incessant, incoherent, purposeless flux that the poem posits as the really real. In the clash between these two strategies it is the grand narrative that is swallowed up into the myriad fragments that compose it and that it sought to compose. This peculiar design, at once pastiche epic and self-consuming artifact, invited, indeed required, a system of storytelling that is as original as it is complex and beguiling.

From time to time, Ovid or his chief narrator delegates his duties to roughly thirty surrogate narrators. In his primary models, the two Homers and Virgil, some of their characters undertake storytelling, but these interruptions of the chief narrative voice (the omniscient epic narrator) are for the most part few and far between (the obvious exception to this rule is Odysseus, a born raconteur). The two Homers and Virgil control their grand narratives from beginning to ending, but they permit their surrogate narrators to temporarily replace them when these substitutions serve the interests of their plots and furnish a welcome variety of tone and perspective. Ovid's purpose and his task differ from theirs. Since, despite his hints to the contrary, he really has no grand narrative to control, he is not required to invent and maintain a traditional omniscient narrator. Instead, he can construct a sort of unreliable pseudo-omniscient narrator who, after establishing his credentials early in the poem, is free to pop in and out of the poem as his whim chooses and to play ventriloquist when his imagination has fastened on a new tale or a new protagonist and it seems proper for a new character to tell his or her own story or someone else's story. This freedom may make for some degree of disorder, but it fosters a pleasing variety of voices and vantages, and in addition to releasing him from the onerous duties which a traditional omniscient narrator would impose on him it permits him to choose whatever tone suits him in any given tale (dispassionate, skeptical, judgmental, empathetic) without worrying much if this variation in attitude does damage to a unified persona or to its coherent moral code and its omniscience. Such freedom does not mean that the inventor of this narrative strategy is committed to flippancy (ever the *poeta ludens,* the poet at play) or that he places himself beyond good and evil. This narrator cares deeply about injustice and corrupted power and inexplicable suffering, even if such concerns are never explicitly announced but instead lie veiled beneath the flux and the flow of the stories told by him or the storytellers who replace him. This freedom from omniscience means, moreover, that Ovid can concentrate on sharpening his technical skills, that he can focus his attention on inventing the short story, or, if that seems too wild a claim, on perfecting the idea of the short story.

What Callimachus did with the short story is lost to us, though we can perhaps see some of his achievements reflected in Catullus' poem on Ariadne or in Virgil's on Orpheus and Eurydice. But when we turn to Ovid it is in the range of his experiments in the representation of personality (his efforts to make his human beings as verisimilar as possible) and in the variety of his themes and tones and shades that we can see already in existence what Dante, Boccaccio, Chaucer, Shakespeare, and Milton found in Ovid's stories, found and loved and strove to imitate and outdo. The task that Ovid set himself—outside that of commenting on the injustices and sorrows of the world and celebrating some of its joys—was to try to figure out how, in the best possible ways, to concentrate plausible (verisimilar) representations of important, universal human experiences in a few thousand words or less. He saw that big emotions and exemplary events could be compressed into small forms in which they could, paradoxically, sometimes become more resonant, more vivid, than would be the case if they were given larger canvases. (He might well have admired *The Satyricon* and *The Golden Ass,* but it is hard to imagine him showing much patience with the Greek novel.) He was eloquent about the human heart and its woes and blisses, he was ferociously hostile to what meddles with human happiness, but conjoint with moral passion was dedication to the succinct tale and the precise artistry it requires. (That artistry, it should be stressed, is equally in evidence when Ovid finds room for short stories in his *Ars Amatoria* and in the *Fasti,* his unfinished poem about the Roman calendar.)

"A big book is a big bore," said Callimachus. In Ovid's version of this prescription for stories that elude boredom, the briefer the tale, the more vivid the core of its design, and the more vivid that core, the closer comes the tale to truths about the human mind and heart that it has fastened on. The scores of brief stories that combine to make up Ovid's sad and funny counter-epic satisfy Poe's recipe for a successful short story: in their economy of detail and minute particulars and in the stylized compression that marks their exposition and resolution they provide "a unity of effect or impression" (as when the arrow pierces the bull's-eye). This doesn't mean that we should be willing to give up the *Iliad* or *Paradise Lost,* that we can get along without *Moby Dick* or *War and Peace.* It means rather that Ovid (and Poe) offer us alternative styles of pleasure and cognition, that they furnish us with perspectives that can challenge the wider, larger realms of feeling and form that epic and the novel open up to us.

This formula (compression, concentration on a simple, vivid impression into which all the elements of the entire narrative are gathered and firmly knotted) works its magic even when the tale turns out to be, on rereadings, complex and ambiguous. The hero Cephalus tells some strangers the story of how he lost his wife Procris and then won her back and then lost her again, this time forever. This is a tragic tale of jealousy and infidelity, one in which Cephalus' efforts to relate what really happened to him and his wife seem to unfold with admirable simplicity and impeccable honesty. Early one ordinary morning, two months after his marriage, Cephalus went out to hunt (his favorite pastime), and was seen and seized (raped) by Aurora, goddess of the dawn (7.768 ff.). The goddess has her way with him, but, faithful to his Procris in mind if not in body, he keeps singing her praises to Aurora. She becomes irritated with this pillow talk, and sends him back home, but not before she has planted doubts in his mind (so he claims) about his wife's fidelity. Having decided to test her, he slips into a disguise and attempts to seduce her by promising generous monetary rewards. At last he names a price that makes her hesitate to say no again (or so he thinks). When he reveals himself in triumph, she leaves him (out of shame, he thinks) and goes off into the mountains to become a devotee of Diana, goddess of the hunt and of chastity. Having become remorseful (how long it took for him to become so is left vague), he asks her forgiveness and begs her to return to him. Won over by his pleas, she goes home with him and gives him two marvelous gifts that Diana had given her: a hound that cannot be outrun (7.834–36) and a javelin that goes "Straight to the target, no luck involved, / And comes back bloodied all on its own" (7.748–49). After her return, husband and wife enjoy several years of wedded bliss when, one ordinary day, Cephalus begins hunting once again. He gets into the habit of finding himself a shady place to relax when tired out by the hunt and of speaking with fervent gratitude to the breeze (Aura) that refreshes him. Someone overhears this passionate speech and reports it to Procris. After first refusing to believe what she has been told, she ends by going off to see for herself the truth of the matter. She hears him speaking like a lover to Aura. He hears the rustle of falling leaves coming from the place where she has concealed herself and hurls his javelin at the animal that he thinks lurks there. She cries out, and he, recognizing her voice, rushes to her as she tries to pull the javelin from her breast. As he attempts vainly to staunch her wound, she begs him never to replace her with Aura. Grief-stricken, he understands how she came to confuse the breeze with a goddess (Aura/Aurora), and watches her expire:

> While her eyes could still focus on something,
> She looked at me, and breathed out on my lips
> Her unfortunate spirit, but as she died
> Her face at last seemed to be free from care.
>
> (7.953–56)

It would seem she bestows on him a final, dying kiss. Is it possible that he imagines she is smiling up at him?

It is hard not to take from this tangled tale the comforting, satisfying image of this grieving, unfortunate, and *innocent* young husband. That image blossoms vividly from the final scene when Cephalus embraces the corpse of Procris, faithful, loving, but jealous. This is the definitive picture that this teller of his own tale has of himself, it is the idea (the truth) toward which all the events of the story *as he selects and judges them* have been inevitably propelled. If we are not moved (as Ovid tries to move us) to reread and rethink this teller and his tale, this image–truth is what our memory may well recall of it.

But that final (unique, simple) image is deceptive. For all Cephalus' efforts to make sense of what he has done and what has happened to him, when we examine the discrepancies in the tale he tells, we begin to suspect that this apparently reliable narrator is utterly incapable of telling it "the way it really happened." Supreme among the author's substitute authors, he is not unreliable because he is lying; he cannot be trusted because he has revised and refurbished his alibis so frequently (the technical term here is *confabulation*), he has told and retold his story so often for decades, that he now believes it absolutely. He did enjoy his rape by Aurora (and how long did it go on?); he did not manage to shake Procris' fidelity (she left him in anger at his duplicity and mistrust); and, strangest lapse of all, he did not remember that the unerring javelin had not stayed stuck in his wife's wound but had instead returned to him, dripping with blood, as it always did, as it was always fated to do. What actually happened was: hearing her cry, his magic javelin in his hand, he rushed toward the voice he recognized, and he could not bear what he found. Still less could he endure what he afterward came to see as he pondered that image of himself and his wife and uncovered, beneath it, the pattern of egotism and selfishness that produced it and that destroyed her life and ruined his. Out of his sorrow, guilt, and self-hatred he had evolved a story, an elaborate alibi, that he could almost live with and could not stop retelling. The tale of Cephalus could easily have been told by the omniscient narrator, but that direct version would entirely lack the complex ironies of Cephalus' efforts to retell, to revise, and to hide his real story. Placed in the mouth and mind of Cephalus, his story combines Ovid's gift for designing the simple, single effect with his equally fertile capacity for the ironic deconstruction of simplicities (sometimes the stories retain their simplicities, sometimes they yield their simplicities to the poet's ironic scalpel).

What it shares with all his stories is his handling of character. Cephalus, like all the characters in all the stories, is constructed from a careful selection of plausible psychological details, so exact in their probings that a Schnitzler or a Wharton might envy them. No less crucially, we believe in the conflicted, complex voice of Cephalus (as we believe in Medea's or Byblis' or Myrrha's) because its rhetorical precision and the illusions that it creates are at once psychologically convincing (this is, in accordance with Aristotle's prescription, the kind of thing such a person would say in such a situation) and artistically beguiling (this person is saying things with a sort of elegance, clarity, and passion that is *not* what we are likely to hear in life, in the real world). That oxymoronic fusion of the real and the imaginary is near the heart of fiction, and, in the creation of his people and their voices, Ovid is among its supreme masters.

W. R. Johnson
University of Chicago

Translator's Note

It was Ovid's technical virtuosity in his *Metamorphoses* that first tempted me to try to capture his endlessly modulated, brilliant voice, his wit, and his wordplay in English translation. His sense of utter ease and fluidity amidst the tensions and complexities of his artistic medium—Latin hexameter verse—is, I believe, essential to Ovid's process as a narrative poet. His verse has a forward momentum that belies the sophistication of its internal structure, as the narrator serenely but briskly leads the reader through the often monstrous, frequently poignant, and sometimes darkly comic vicissitudes of his characters without ever breaking stride. It is just these Ovidian sensibilities of pace and tone that I have tried to capture in crafting this translation.

In the process I have come to appreciate the subtle depths below the bright, shifting surface of these stories told in verse, subtleties into which W. R. Johnson has initiated us in his introduction to this volume, as it admirably lays out the general thrust of the entire poem. Ever since the publication of his *Darkness Visible,* he has been one of my heroes, and I respectfully dedicate this translation to him.

I am deeply indebted as well to David Fredrick and Gail Polk, both of whom suggested numerous improvements and corrections to the translation; and to Brian Rak, my editor at Hackett, whose oversight and detailed suggestions have again proved to be both generous and invaluable. I am grateful also to Liz Wilson at Hackett for her work as project editor in transforming raw manuscript copy into a finished book.

I have profited from conversations about Ovid's poem with Anthony Corbeill, Pamela Gordon, Jonathon Roitman, Garth Tissol, and Tara Welch. William Levitan has my sincere thanks for reading an early draft of part of the translation and offering his advice and encouragement.

Cara Polsley has earned my gratitude for compiling the Glossary, as has Michael Pulsinelli for compiling the Catalog of Transformations.

I had the good fortune of teaching the *Metamorphoses* in Latin to a splendid group of undergraduates at the University of Kansas as I was revising this translation and wish to thank them for their insights and enthusiasm as well as for their patience.

And I wish to express my gratitude to my wife, Judy Roitman, for her support and encouragement over the course of this work.

Stanley Lombardo
University of Kansas

Note on the Text

This translation is based on G. P. Goold's revision of F. J. Miller's edition in the Loeb Classical Library series (1977). I have also consulted R. J. Tarrant's Oxford Classical Texts edition (2004) and adopt his readings in preference to Goold's in a number of instances, including the following that have a significant impact on the translation (line numbers refer to the Latin text):

1.2: *illa* instead *illas*
6.582: *germanae* instead of *fortunae*
7.61: *natorumque* instead of *matrumque*
7.770: *coetum* instead of *centum*
15.515: *guttis manantia* instead of *cannis latitantia*

At 4.388, I read *incerto* with W. S. Anderson's Teubner edition [1977] rather than *incesto* with Goold/Miller and Tarrant.

I have been conservative in retaining lines and passages bracketed for various reasons by one or another of these editors.

Suggestions for Further Reading

Barkan, Leonard. *The Gods Made Flesh: Metamorphosis and the Pursuit of Paganism.* New Haven: Yale University Press, 1981.

Bate, Jonathan. *Shakespeare and Ovid.* Oxford: Oxford University Press, 1993.

Brown, Sarah Annes. *The Metamorphosis of Ovid: From Chaucer to Ted Hughes.* New York: St. Martin's Press, 1999.

Du Rocher, Richard. *Milton and Ovid.* Ithaca: Cornell University Press, 1985.

Fantham, Elaine. *Ovid's Metamorphoses.* Oxford: Oxford University Press, 2004.

Forbes Irving, P. M. C. *Metamorphosis in Greek Myths.* New York: Oxford University Press, 1990.

Galinsky, Karl. *Ovid's* Metamorphoses: *An Introduction to the Basic Aspects.* Berkeley: University of California Press, 1975.

Hardie, Philip. *Ovid's Poetics of Illusion.* Cambridge: Cambridge University Press, 2002.

Hardie, Philip, ed. *The Cambridge Companion to Ovid.* Cambridge: Cambridge University Press, 2002.

Martin, Christopher, ed. *Ovid in English.* New York: Penguin, 1998.

Martindale, Charles, ed. *Ovid Renewed: Ovidian Influences on Literature and Art from the Middle Ages to the Twentieth Century.* Cambridge: Cambridge University Press, 1988.

Otis, Brooks. *Ovid as Epic Poet.* Cambridge: Cambridge University Press, 1970.

Segal, Charles. *Landscape in Ovid's Metamorphoses.* Wiesbaden: Franz Steiner Verlag, 1969.

Solodow, Joseph B. *The World of Ovid's* Metamorphoses. Chapel Hill: University of North Carolina Press, 1988.

Tissol, Garth. *The Face of Nature: Wit, Narrative and Cosmic Origin in Ovid's* Metamorphoses. Princeton: Princeton University Press, 1997.

Wheeler, Stephen M. *A Discourse of Wonders: Audience and Performance in Ovid's* Metamorphoses. Philadelphia: University of Pennsylvania Press, 1999.

Wilkinson, L. P. *Ovid Recalled.* Cambridge: Cambridge University Press, 1955.

For

Ralph Johnson

METAMORPHOSES

Book 1

Invocation

My mind now turns to stories of bodies changed
Into new forms. O Gods, inspire my beginnings
(For you changed them too) and spin a poem that extends
From the world's first origins down to my own time.

Origin of the World

Before there was land or sea or overarching sky,
Nature's face was one throughout the universe,
Chaos as they call it: a crude, unsorted mass,
Nothing but an inert lump, the concentrated,
Discordant seeds of disconnected entities.
No Titan Sun as yet gave light to the world,   10
No Phoebe touched up her crescent horns by night,
Not yet did Earth hang nested in air, balanced
By her own weight, and Amphitrite had not yet
Stretched her arms around the world's long shores.
Yes, there was land around, and sea and air,
But land impossible to walk, unnavigable water,
Lightless air; nothing held its shape,
And each thing crowded the other out. In one body
Cold wrestled with hot, wet with dry,
Soft with hard, and weightless with heavy.   20

Some god, or superior nature, settled this conflict,
Splitting earth from heaven, sea from earth,
And the pure sky from the dense atmosphere.
After he carved these out from the murky mass,
In peaceful concord he bound each in its place.
The fiery, weightless energy of the convex sky
Shot to the zenith and made its home there.
The air, next in levity, was next in location,
Then the denser earth attracted the heavier elements
And was pushed down by her own weight. The circling sea   30
Settled down at her edges, confining the solid orb.

Then, the god who had sorted out this cosmic heap,
Whoever it was, and divided it into parts,
First rolled the earth, so it would not appear
Asymmetrical, into the shape of a great sphere;
And then he ordered the sea to flood and swell
Beneath high winds until it lapped the planet's shores.
He threw in springs and immense wetlands,
Lakes and rivers, which he channeled in sloping banks
So some are absorbed by the land itself, while others cascade   40
Into the sea, where received at last into open water
They beat no longer against banks but shores.
He also ordered the prairies to stretch, the valleys to sink,
The woods to take leaf, rocky mountains to rise.
And as two zones belt the sky on the right,
Two on the left, and a fifth burns in the middle,
This providential god marked the globe beneath
With these same five zones, so that of the earth's regions
The middle is too hot for habitation,
Deep snow covers two, but the two wedged between   50
Have a climate that tempers heat with cold.

Hanging above is the air, as much heavier
Than fire as water is lighter than earth.
The god ordained mist and clouds to form there,
And thunder that would make human minds tremble,
And winds too, gusting with thunder and lightning.
The World's Fabricator did not allow the winds
Free rein in the air. He barely controls them now,
When each must blow in his own tract of heaven,
Else they would shred the world with their fraternal strife.   60
Eurus receded to the East and the Nabataean realms,
To Persia and its ridges bathed in morning light.
Evening, and the shores warmed by the setting sun,
Are nearest to Zephyrus. Bristling Boreas
Invaded Scythia and the Arctic stars. The land
Due south drips with Auster's constant mist and rain.
Above all these he put the liquid, weightless
Aether, which has nothing of earthly dregs.

The deity had just finished zoning off everything
When the stars, which had long been smothered   70
In dark vapor, peeked out and glowed all over the sky.
And so that no region would be without living things
Of its own, constellations and the forms of gods
Possessed heaven's floor; the sea allowed itself
To swarm with glistening fish, the land became
A wild kingdom, and the air teemed with wings.

Still missing was a creature finer than these,
With a greater mind, one who could rule the rest:
Man was born, whether fashioned from immortal seed
By the Master Artisan who made this better world,   80
Or whether Earth, newly parted from Aether above
And still bearing some seeds of her cousin Sky,
Was mixed with rainwater by Titan Prometheus
And molded into the image of the omnipotent gods.
And while other animals look on all fours at the ground
He gave to humans an upturned face, and told them to lift
Their eyes to the stars. And so Earth, just now barren,
A wilderness without form, was changed and made over,
Dressing herself in the unfamiliar figures of men.

The Four Ages

Golden was the first age, a generation   90
That cultivated trust and righteousness
All on its own, without any laws, without fear
Or punishment. There were no threatening rules
Stamped on bronze tablets, no crowds of plaintiffs
Cowering before judges: no one needed protection.
Not a pine was cut from its native mountain
To be launched on a maritime tour of the world;
Mortal men knew no shores but their own.
Steep trenches around cities were still in the future;
There were no bronze bugles, no curved, blaring horns,   100
No helmets or swords. Without a military
A carefree people enjoyed a life of soft ease.

The inviolate earth, untouched by hoes, still
Unwounded by plows, bore fruit all on its own,
And content with food unforced by labor
Men gathered arbute, mountain strawberries,
Wild cherries, blackberries clinging to brambles,
And acorns that fell from Jove's spreading oaks.
Spring was eternal, and mild westerly breezes
Soughed among flowers sown from no seed.   110
Even uncultivated the soil soon bore crops
And fields unfallowed grew white with deep grain.
Rivers flowed with milk, streams ran with nectar,
And honey dripped tawny from the green holm oak.

After Saturn was consigned to Tartarus' gloom
The world was under Jove, and the Silver race came in,
Cheaper than gold but more precious than bronze.
Jupiter curtailed the old season of spring
And by adding cold and heat and autumn's changes
To a brief spring, made the year turn through its four seasons.   120
For the first time the air, parched and feverish,
Began to burn, and icicles now hung frozen in wind.
People now took shelter; their houses were caves,
Dense thickets, and branches bound together with bark.
Cereal seeds now lay buried, sown in long furrows,
And for the first time oxen groaned under the yoke.

The next and third generation was Bronze,
Harsher in its genius and more ready to arms,
Not wicked however.
                        The fourth and last is Iron.
Every iniquity burst out in this inferior age.   130
Shame and Veracity and Faith took flight,
And in their place came Duplicity and Fraud,
Treachery and Force, and unholy Greed.
They spread sails to the winds still a mystery
To sailors, and keels that once stood high in the mountains
Now surged and bucked in unfamiliar waves.
The cautious surveyor now marks off the fields

Once held in common like the sunlight and air.
And the rich earth is not only required to produce
Crops and food: now her bowels are tunneled, 140
And the ore she'd sequestered in Stygian darkness
Is now dug up as wealth that incites men to crime.
Iron with its injuries and more injurious gold
Now came forth, and War, equipped with both of these metals,
Brandishes clashing weapons in bloodstained hands.
Plunder sustains life; guest is not safe from host,
Or a father safe from his daughter's husband;
Gratitude is rare even among brothers. Husbands
Can't wait for their wives to die, wives reciprocate,
Frightful stepmothers brew their aconite, and sons 150
Inquire prematurely into their father's age.
Piety lies beaten, and when the other gods are gone,
Virgin Astraea abandons the bloodstained earth.

The Giants

And, so the lofty sky would not be safer than earth,
They say the Giants went after the kingdom of heaven,
Piling up mountains all the way to the stars.
Then the Father Almighty shattered Olympus
With a well-aimed thunderbolt and blasted away Pelion
From Ossa beneath. When the Giants' dread corpses
Lay crushed beneath their own bulk, they say Mother Earth, 160
Drenched with her sons' blood, reanimated
Their steaming gore, and to preserve the memory
Of her former brood, gave it a human form.
But this incarnation also was contemptuous
Of the gods, with a deep instinct for slaughter,
And violent. You could tell they were sons of blood.

The Council of the Gods

Jupiter, seeing this from his high throne, groaned.
He recalled, too, the sordid dinner parties of Lycaon,
Too recent for the story to be well-known, and conceived

In his heart a mighty wrath worthy of the soul of Jove.   170
He called a council, and none of the gods were late.

On a clear night you can see a road in the sky
Called the Milky Way, renowned for its white glow.
This is the road the gods take to the royal palace
Of the great Thunderer. To the right and the left
The halls of the divine nobility, doors flung open,
Are thronged with guests. The plebeian gods
Live in a different neighborhood, but the great
All have their homes along this avenue. This quarter,
If I may say so, is high heaven's Palatine.   180

So, when the gods had been seated in a marble chamber,
The God himself, enthroned high above the rest, leaning
On his ivory scepter, shook three times, four times,
The dread locks whereby he moves land, sea, and stars.
And opening his indignant lips, he spoke in this way:

"I was not more concerned than I am now
For the world when the serpentine Giants threatened
To get their hundred hands on the captured sky.
Although the enemy was brutal, that war at least
Stemmed from a united body and single source.   190
But now, wherever old Nereus' ocean roars,
The human race must be destroyed. By the river
That glides through the underworld grove of Styx,
I swear that I have already tried everything else,
But gangrenous flesh must be cut away with a knife
Before it infects the rest. I have demigods to protect
And rustic deities—nymphs, fauns, satyrs,
And sylvan spirits on the mountainsides.
Although we do not deem them worthy of heaven,
We should at least let them live in their allotted lands.   200
Do you think they will be safe there, I ask you,
When even against me, who rule you gods,
Snares are laid by the infamous Lycaon?"

The gods all trembled and zealously demanded
The traitor's head. So it was when a disloyal few
Were mad to blot out Rome with Caesar's blood,
And the human race was stunned with fear of ruin
And the whole world shuddered. The loyalty
Of your subjects, Augustus, pleases you no less
Than Jove was pleased. With word and gesture   210
He stilled the crowd, and when the clamor
Had been suppressed by his royal gravitas,
Jove once more broke the silence, saying:

"He has paid the penalty—of that you can be sure—
But listen to what he did, and hear his punishment.

Lycaon

The infamy of the age had reached my ears,
And hoping to discover the report was false, I slipped down
From Olympus, a god disguised as a human,
And crisscrossed the land. There is not time to do justice
To the catalog of iniquity I found everywhere.   220
The report fell short of the truth. I had traversed
Mount Maenala, its thickets bristling with animal lairs,
Crossed Cyllene, and Lycaeus' cold pine forests,
And was coming up to the Arcadian tyrant's
Inhospitable hall as the late evening shadows
Ushered in the night. I gave a sign that a god had come,
And the common people began to pray. Lycaon
Started by mocking their pieties, and then said,
'I'll find out if this is a mortal or a god. A simple test
Will establish the truth beyond any doubt.'   230
The test of truth he had in mind was to murder me
While I was fast asleep. And not content with that,
He slit the throat of a Molossian hostage,
Boiled some of his half-dead flesh and roasted the rest.
As soon as he set this delicate dish before me,
My avenging lightning brought down the house
On its master and his all-too-deserving household.

He fled in terror, and when he reached the silent fields
He let loose a howl. He tried to speak but could not.
His mouth foamed, and he turned his usual bloodlust   240
Against a flock of sheep, still relishing slaughter.
His clothes turned into a shaggy pelt, his arms into legs.
He became a wolf, but still retains some traces
Of his former looks. There is the same grey hair,
The same savage face; the same eyes gleam,
And the same overall sense of bestiality.
Only one house has fallen, yet more than one
Has deserved perdition. Erinys, the wild Fury,
Reigns supreme to the ends of the earth. You would think
They were sworn in blood to a life of crime! Let them all   250
Pay quickly the price they deserve—this is my edict."

Some of the gods voiced their approval and even
Goaded him on, while others playacted their silent consent,
But they all winced on the inside at the impending loss
Of the human race and wondered out loud
What the world would be without men. Who would bring
Incense to their altars? Was Jupiter planning
To deliver the world to the depredations of beasts?
The master of the universe told them to let him
Worry about all that, and he promised them a new race,   260
Different from the first, from a wondrous origin.

The Flood

He was poised to hurl volleys of thunderbolts
All over the world, but he backed off in sudden fear
That the conflagration might kindle the sacred aether
And set the long axis on fire from pole to pole.
He recalled, too, that a time was fated to come
When land and sea and heaven's majestic roof
Would catch fire, and the foundations of the world
Would go up in flames. So he laid aside
The weapons forged by Cyclopean hands   270

And chose instead a different punishment:
To overwhelm humanity with an endless deluge
Pouring down from every square inch of sky.

So he shut up the North Wind in Aeolus' cave
Along with every breeze that disperses clouds.
But he cut loose the South Wind, which scudded out
On dripping wings, scowling in pitch-black mist,
His beard sodden with rain, his white hair
Streaming water, clouds nesting on his forehead,
And dew glistening on all his feathers and robes.   280
The flat of his hand presses low-hanging clouds
And rain crashes down from the sky. Then Iris,
Juno's rainbowed messenger, draws up more water
To feed the lowering clouds. Crops farmers prayed for
Are beaten flat; years of hard work are all blotted out.

Jove's wrath was not content with his own sky's water,
So his sea-blue brother rolled out auxiliary waves.
The Rivers jumped to formation in their tyrant's palace
And he gave his command:
                    "My brief to you is to pour forth
Everything you have. This is a crisis. Open wide   290
Your doors and dikes and give your streams free rein!"

The Rivers returned, uncurbed their springs,
And tumbled unbridled down to the sea.

Neptune himself struck the Earth with his trident;
She trembled, and split mouths wide open for geysers,
And the Rivers spread out over the open plains,
Sweeping away orchards and crops, cattle and men,
Houses and shrines and the shrines' sacred objects.
If any houses were able to resist this disaster
And still stood, the waves soon covered their roofs,   300
And towers were submerged beneath the flood.
And now sea and land could not be distinguished.
All was sea, but it was a sea without shores.

Here's a man on a hilltop, and one in his curved skiff,
Rowing where just yesterday he plowed. Another one
Sails over acres of wheat or the roof of his farmhouse
Deep underwater. Here's someone catching a fish
In the top of an elm. Sometimes an anchor
Sticks in a green meadow, or keels brush the tops
Of vineyards beneath. Where slender goats once browsed   310
Seals now flop their misshapen bodies. Nereids gape
At houses, cities, and groves undersea,
And dolphins cruise through forest canopies,
Grazing the oak trees with their flippers and tails.
Wolves swim with sheep, tawny lions and tigers
Tread the same currents. The boar's lightning tusks
And the stag's speed are useless as the torrent
Sweeps them away. With no land in sight, no place to perch
The exhausted bird drops into the sea,
Whose unbridled license has buried the hills   320
And now pounds mountaintops with unfamiliar surf.
Most creatures drown. Those spared by the water
Finally succumb to slow starvation.

Deucalion and Pyrrha

Phocis is a land that separates Boeotia
From Oetaea, a fertile land while it was still land,
But now it was part of the sea, a great plain
Of flood water. There is a steep mountain there
With twin peaks stretching up through the clouds
To the high stars. Its name is Parnassus.
When Deucalion and his wife landed here   330
In their little skiff (water covered everything else)
They first paid a visit to the Corycian nymphs,
The mountain gods, and Themis, who was the oracle then.
There was no man better or more just than he,
And no woman revered the gods more than she.
When Jupiter saw the whole world reduced
To a stagnant pond, and from so many thousands
Only one man left, from so many thousands

Only one woman, each innocent, each reverent,
He parted the clouds, and when the North Wind   340
Had swept them away, he once again showed
The earth to the sky, and the heavens to the earth.
The sea's roiling anger subsided, as Neptune
Lay down his trident and soothed the waves. He hailed
Cerulean Triton rising over the crests,
His shoulders encrusted with purple shellfish,
And told him to blow his winding horn
To signal the floods and streams to withdraw.
Old Triton lifted the hollow, spiraling shell
Whose sound fills the shores on both sides of the world   350
When he gets his lungs into it out in mid-ocean.
When this horn touched the sea god's lips, streaming
With brine from his dripping beard, and sounded the retreat,
It was heard by all the waters of land and sea,
And all the waters that heard were held in check.
Now the sea had a shore, rivers flowed in channels,
The floods subsided, and hills emerged into view.
The land rose up; locales took shape as waters shrank,
And at long last the trees bared their leafy tops,
Foliage still spattered with mud left by the flood.   360

The world was restored. But when Deucalion saw
It was an empty world, steeped in desolate silence,
Tears welled up in his eyes as he said to Pyrrha,

"My wife and sister, the last woman alive,
Our common race, our family, our marriage bed
And now our perils themselves have united us.
In all the lands from sunrise to sunset
We two are the whole population; the sea holds the rest.
And our lives are far from guaranteed. These clouds
Still strike terror in my heart. Poor soul,   370
What would you feel like now if the Fates
Had taken me and left you behind? How could you bear
Your fear alone? Who would comfort your grief?
You can be sure that if the sea already held you,

I would follow you, my wife, beneath the sea.
Oh, if only I could restore the people of the world
By my father's arts, breathe life into molded clay!
Now the human race rests on the two of us.
We are, by the gods' will, the last of our kind."

He spoke and wept. Their best recourse was to implore   380
The divine, to beg for help through sacred prophecy.
So they went side by side to the stream of Cephisus,
Which, though not yet clear, flowed in its old banks.
They scooped up some water, sprinkled their heads and clothes,
And made their familiar way to the sacred shrine
Of the goddess. The gables were stained with slime and mold,
And the altars stood abandoned without any fires.
When they reached the temple steps, husband and wife
Prostrated themselves, kissed the cold stone trembling,
And said, "If divine hearts can be softened by prayers   390
Of the just, if the wrath of the gods can be deflected,
Tell us, O Themis, how our race can be restored,
And bring aid, O most mild one, to a world overwhelmed."

The goddess, moved, gave this oracular response:

"Leave this temple. Veil your heads, loosen your robes,
And throw behind your back your great mother's bones."

They stood there, dumbfounded. It was Pyrrha
Who finally broke the silence, refusing to obey
The commands of the goddess. She prays for pardon
With trembling lips, but trembles all over   400
At the thought of offending her mother's shades
By tossing her bones. Stalling for time,
The pair revisit the oracle's words, turning them
Over and over in their minds, searching out
Their dark secrets. At last Prometheus' son
Comforts the daughter of Epimetheus
With these soothing words:
                    "Either I'm mistaken

Or—since oracles are holy and never counsel evil—
Our great mother is Earth, and stones in her soil
Are the bones we are told to throw behind our backs."   410

Pyrrha was moved by her husband's surmise,
But the pair still were not sure that they trusted
The divine admonition. On the other hand,
What harm was there in trying? Down they go,
Veiling their heads, untying their robes, and throwing stones
Behind them just as the goddess had ordered.
And the stones began (who would believe it
Without the testimony of antiquity?)
To lose their hardness, slowly softening
And assuming shapes. When they had grown and taken on   420
A milder nature, a certain resemblance
To human form began to be discernible,
Not well defined, but like roughed-out statues.
The parts that were damp with earthy moisture
Became bodily flesh; the rigid parts became bones;
And the veins remained without being renamed.
In no time at all, by divine power, the stones
Thrown by the man's hand took the form of men
And from the woman's scattered stones women were born.
And so we are a tough breed, used to hard labor,   430
And we are living proof of our origin.

Earth herself spontaneously generated
Various other species of animals.
The sun warmed the moisture left from the flood,
Slime in the swamps swelled with the heat,
And seeds of life, nourished in that rich soil
As in a mother's womb, slowly gestated and took on
Distinctive forms. It was just as when the Nile,
With its seven mouths, withdraws from the flooded fields
Into its old channel, and then the Dog Star bakes   440
The plains of soft muck, and farmers turning over the clods
Find many animate things, some just on the verge
Of new life, some unfinished and just budding limbs,

And sometimes they see in the very same body
A part living and breathing, and a part still raw earth.
For when heat and moisture combine, they conceive,
And all things are born from their blended union.
And though fire fights water, moist vapor is fecund,
And this discordant concord is pregnant with life.
So when Mother Earth's diluvian mud   450
Again grew warm under the rays of the sun,
She brought forth innumerable species, restoring some
Of the ancient forms, and creating some new and strange.

Python

She would have rather not, but Earth begot you then,
O Python, greatest of serpents and never before seen,
And a terror to the new people, sprawling over
Half a mountainside. The god of the bent bow
Destroyed him with weapons never used before
Except against does and wild goats on the run,
Nearly emptying his quiver of arrows,   460
And venom oozed from the monster's black wounds.
And so Time would not tarnish the fame of this deed
He founded sacred games for the crowds, called Pythian
From the name of the serpent he had overcome.
Here every youth who won with his fists or his feet,
Or his chariot, received a garland of oak leaves.
There was no laurel yet, and Apollo wreathed
His brow and the gorgeous locks of his hair
With a garland from whatever species of tree.

Apollo and Daphne

Apollo's first love was Daphne, Peneus' daughter,   470
Not by blind chance but because Cupid was angry.
Flush with his victory over Python, the Delian god
Saw him stringing and flexing his bow, and said:

"What do you think you're doing, you little imp,
With a man's weapons? That archery set

Belongs on my shoulders. I can take dead aim
Against wild beasts, I can wound my enemies,
And just now I laid low in a shower of arrows
Swollen Python and left his noxious belly
Spread out over acres. You should be satisfied   480
With using your torch to inflame people with love
And stop laying claim to glory that is mine."

The son of Venus replied:
                              "Phoebus, your arrows
May hit everything else, but mine will hit you.
And as much as animals are inferior to gods,
So is my glory superior to yours."
                                        He spoke
And, beating his wings with a vengeance, landed
On the shady peak of Parnassus. He stood there,
And drew from his quiver two quite different arrows,
One that dispels love and one that impels it.   490
The latter is golden with a sharp glistening point,
The former blunt with a shaft made of lead.
The god struck the nymph with arrow number two
And feathered the first deep into Apollo's marrow.

One now loved, the other fled love's very name,
Delighting in the deep woods, wearing the skins
Of animals she caught, modeling herself
On the virgin Diana, her tousled hair tied back.
She had many suitors but could not endure men,
So she turned them away, and roamed the pathless woods   500
Without a thought of Hymen, or Amor, or marriage.
Her father often said, "You owe me a son-in-law, girl."
Often observed, "You owe me grandchildren, my daughter."
But she hated the wedding torch like sin itself
And her beautiful face would blush with shame
As she hung from his neck with coaxing arms, saying,

"O Papa, please, won't you let me enjoy
My virginity forever? Diana's father let her."

Of course he agreed; but your very loveliness, Daphne,
Prevents your wish, your beauty opposes your prayer.   510

Apollo loves her at sight and desires to wed her.
What he desires he hopes for, but here his oracular
Powers desert him. As light stubble blazes
In a harvested field, or as a hedge catches fire
From embers a traveler has let get too close
Or has forgotten at daybreak, so too the god
Went up in flames, and all his heart burned
And fed his impossible passion with hope.
He sees the hair that flows all across her neck
And wonders, "What if it were combed?" Sees her eyes   520
Flash like stars; sees her mouth, which merely to see
Is hardly enough. He praises her fingers, her hands,
Her arms, which for the most part are bare,
And what is hidden he imagines is better.

Her flight is faster than if she were wind,
And she does not pause to hear him calling her back:

"Nymph of Peneus, I beg you, stop! I am not
Pursuing you as an enemy. Please, nymph, stop!
This is how a lamb runs away from a wolf,
A deer from a lion, a trembling dove from an eagle,   530
Each from her enemy, but Love makes me pursue you.
Ah, I am afraid you will fall, afraid that brambles
Will scratch your shins and that I, oh so wretched,
Will be the cause of your pain. This is rough terrain
You are running through. Run a little slower,
Please, and I'll slow down too. Or stop and ask
Who your lover is—no hillbilly or shepherd—
I don't mind the herds here, like some shaggy oaf.
You do not know, my rash one, you just don't know
Who you are running from, and that's why you run.   540
Delphi is mine; I am lord of Claros and Tenedos
And the realm of Patara. Jove is my father.
What shall be, what is now, and what has been

Are all revealed by me. It is through me that songs
Are played in tune on the lyre. My arrows are sure,
But one arrow more sure has wounded my heart
That once was carefree. I invented medicine,
I am called the Healer throughout the world,
The potency of herbs is my domain, but oh,
Love cannot be cured by herbs, and the arts   550
That benefit all are of no use to their lord."

He would have said more, but the Peneid nymph
Was running scared and left his words unfinished.
She was still a lovely sight. The wind bared her body
And as she cut through the air, her clothes fluttering
As her hair streamed out behind her in the breeze,
Her beauty augmented by flight. But the young god
Could not waste any more time on sweet talk,
Not with the Love God himself urging him on,
And he picked up the pace. A Gallic hound   560
Snuffs out and starts a hare in a field,
The hound running for prey, the hare for her life,
And now the hunter thinks he has her, thinks
Any moment now, his muzzle grazing her heels,
While she, unsure whether she is finally caught,
Writhes out of his jaws with a sudden spurt.
So too the virgin and the deity ran,
His speed spurred by hope and hers by fear,
But the pursuer closed in, boosted by Cupid's wings,
And he gave her no rest, staying right on her back,   570
His breath fanning the hair on the base of her neck.
She turned pale as her strength began to run out,
Beaten by the speed and the length of the race.
When she saw the waters of the Peneus, she cried,

"Help me, father! If your streams have divine power,
Destroy this too pleasing beauty of mine
By transforming me!"
                          She had just finished her prayer
When a heavy numbness invaded her body

And a sheathe of bark enclosed her soft breast.
Her hair turned into fluttering leaves, her arms   580
Into branches; her feet, once so swift,
Became mired in roots, and her face was lost
In the canopy. Only her beauty's sheen remained.

Apollo still loved her, and pressing his hand
Against her trunk he felt her heart quivering
Under the new bark. He embraced her limbs
With his own arms, and he kissed the wood,
But even the wood shrank from his kisses.
The god said to her:
                    "Since you can't be my bride
You will be my tree. My hair will be wreathed   590
With you, Laurel, and you will crown my quiver and lyre.
You will accompany the Roman generals
When joyful voices ring out their triumphs
And their long parades wind beneath the Capitol.
You will ornament Augustus' doorposts,
A faithful guardian standing watch over
The oak leaves between them. And just as my head
With its unshorn hair is forever young,
You will always wear beautiful, undying leaves."

Apollo was done. The laurel bowed her new branches   600
And seemed to nod her leafy crown in assent.

                    Io

There is a gorge in Thessaly with steep wooded slopes
That men call Tempe. The foam-flecked water
Of the Peneus River tumbles through this valley
From the foot of Mount Pindus, and its heavy descent
Forms clouds that drive along billowing mist,
Sprinkles the treetops with spray and, cascading down,
Fills even the distant hills with its roar.
Here is the house, the abode, the inner sanctum
Of the great River. Seated here, in a cavern   610

Carved from boulders, he lays down the law
To his streams, and the nymphs who live in his streams.
The neighboring rivers convened here first,
Unsure whether to console or congratulate
Daphne's father. Spercheios came sporting poplars,
Restless Enipeus, old Apidanos,
Gentle Amphrysos, Aeas too, and soon all the streams,
Whatever wandering courses their weary waters
Take down to the sea. Only Inachus is absent.
Hidden deep in a cave, his stream swelling with tears,   620
He laments in his misery his lost daughter, Io,
Not knowing if she lives or is lost among the shades.
Finding her nowhere, he imagines her nowhere,
And in his heart he fears even worse.

                    Jupiter
First laid eyes on her as she made her way
From her father's stream, and he said to her:

"Virgin worthy of Jove, clearly destined to make
Some man or other happy in your bed,
You should find some shade over there in the woods"
(Pointing) "while it is hot and the sun is high.   630
If you are afraid to go alone where the wild things live,
You can go with the safe protection of a god,
And no ordinary god either. I am the one who holds
The scepter of heaven and hurls the lightning bolts.
Do not run from me!"
                    She was already running
And had left Lerna's fields behind and the woods
Of Lyrcea, when the god covered the wide earth
In a blanket of mist and stole her chastity.

Juno, meanwhile, looked straight down at Argos
And wondered why this sudden fog had made night   640
Out of brilliant day. She knew there had not been
Any mist from a river or from any damp ground.
She looked around for her husband, suspecting

The intrigue of a spouse so often caught in the act.
When she could not find him anywhere in the skies,
She said, "Either I'm wrong or I'm being wronged."
And she glided down from the top of heaven,
Stood upon the earth and dissolved the clouds.
But Jove had a presentiment of his wife's approach
And had changed the daughter of Inachus   650
Into a glossy heifer. She was still stunning,
Even as a cow. Juno looked at her and couldn't help
But admire her looks. Then she asked whose she was,
Where from, of what stock, as if she didn't know.
Her husband, to forestall further inquiries, maintained
That she was born of the earth, but Juno countered
By demanding her as a gift. What should he do?
Cruel to surrender his love, but suspect not to.
Shame persuaded, Love dissuaded, and Shame
Would surely have yielded to Love, but to refuse   660
So slight a gift as a cow to his sister and wife
Might make the cow seem to be no cow at all.

So Juno received her bovine rival but was still
Suspicious of her husband and more escapades
Until she enlisted Argus, son of Arestor,
To watch over the heifer. Argus' head was ringed
With a hundred eyes that took turns sleeping
Two at a time while the others stood watch,
So whatever way he stood his eyes were on Io,
Even when she was behind his back. In the daytime   670
He let her graze, but when the sun went down
He locked her up with a collar—the indignity!—
Around her neck. Her diet was leaves from trees
And bitter herbs, and instead of a bed the poor creature
Lay on the ground, which was not always grassy,
And she drank from muddy streams. When she would stretch
Her suppliant arms to Argus, she had no arms to stretch,
And when she tried to complain she only mooed.
The sound startled her, and her own voice
Became a new source of fear. She came to the banks   680

Of the Inachus, where she had often played,
But when she saw those strange horns reflected
In the water, she shied away from herself in terror.
The Naiads did not know who she was; Inachus himself
Did not know. But she followed her father,
Followed her sisters, allowed herself to be petted,
Offered herself to be admired. Old Inachus
Held out to her some grass he had plucked. She licked
His hand, but as she kissed her father's palms
She could not hold back her tears. If only she could speak,   690
She would ask for help, tell her name, tell her sad story.
Words wouldn't come, but she managed to paw in the dust
Letters that spelled out her transfiguration.

"What misery," exclaimed her father, Inachus,
And draping himself on the lowing heifer's horns
And snow-white neck, he lamented again.

"What misery! Are you really my daughter
Whom I have searched for all over the earth?
Unfound you were a lesser grief than regained.
You are silent and do not respond to my words;   700
You only heave deep sighs from your chest, and—
All you can do—bellow and moo in reply!
Not knowing any better, I was preparing
Marriage rites for you, hoping for a son-in-law
And grandchildren later. But now your husband
Must come from the herd, from the herd a child.
And I cannot even end my sorrows with death.
It hurts to be a god, for death's door is shut,
And my grief extends into eternity."

As he mourned in this way, star-studded Argus   710
Pulled him away, and drove the daughter, torn
From her father's side, into a distant pasture,
Positioning himself on the top of a mountain
From which he could keep watch in all directions.

But heaven's ruler could no longer endure
Io's great suffering. He calls his son
Whom the shining Pleiad bore and orders him
To deliver Argus to death. It does not take long
For Mercury to lace up his winged sandals,
Grab his somniferous wand and put on his cap.   720
His gear in order, the son of Jupiter
Makes the jump from heaven to earth, where
He takes off his cap and sets aside his wings,
Keeping only his wand, which he used like a shepherd
To drive a flock of goats (rustled en route)
Through the back country, playing a pipe as he went.
Juno's guard was captivated by the strange music,
And called out,
               "You there, whoever you are, you
Might as well sit down here on this rock next to me,
There's no richer grass for grazing anywhere,   730
And you see there's shade here fit for a shepherd."

So Atlas' grandson sat down and passed the day
Talking about this and that and playing his reed pipe,
Trying to overcome those bright, vigilant eyes.
But Argus fought hard against the languors of sleep,
And though he allowed some of his eyes to slumber,
He kept some awake. And since the reed pipe, or syrinx,
Was a new invention, he asked where it came from.

Pan and Syrinx

So the god began:
               "In Arcadia's cold mountains
There was among the wood nymphs of Nonacris   740
An admired naiad. Her sister nymphs called her Syrinx.
She had eluded the pursuit of more than one satyr
And various other deities of the shadowy woods
And wild countryside. She cultivated the virginity
Of the Ortygian goddess, and in Diana's dress
She could pass for Leto's daughter, except that her bow
Was made of horn and Diana's was gold.

Even so she was often mistaken for the goddess.
Once, she was returning from Mount Lycaeum
When Pan saw her. Crowned with a circlet   750
Of sharp pine needles he called out to her . . ."

Here Mercury stopped with much still to tell—
How the nymph rejected Pan's advances
And fled through the trackless woods until
She came to the quiet, sandy stream of Ladon;
And how, with the water in her path, she prayed
To her aquatic sisters for transfiguration;
How just when Pan thought he had Syrinx in his hands,
Instead of the nymph's body he held marshy reeds,
And how his breath sighing over one reed   760
Made a thin, plaintive sound. The god was taken
With the strange sweetness of the tone, and he said,
"This communion with you I will always have, Syrinx."
And so graduated reeds joined together with wax
Became the instrument that still bears the girl's name.

Mercury was poised to tell the whole story
When he saw that all of the eyes had closed.
He stopped speaking and deepened Argus' slumber
By waving his wand over those languid orbs.
And then he brought his sickled sword down   770
On that nodding head where it joined the neck
And sent it spattering down the steep rocks.
Now you lie low, Argus, and all your lights are out,
Those hundred eyes mastered by one dark night.

Juno took the eyes and set them in the feathers
Of her own bird, filling the tail of the peacock
With starlike jewels. But her anger flared,
And the goddess lost no time in fulfilling it,
Setting a terrifying Fury before the eyes and mind
Of her Argive rival, and planting deep in her breast   780
A blind, compulsive fear that drove her in flight
Across the whole world. In the end it was you,

O Nile, who brought her immense ordeal to a close.
When she reached your waters she fell to her knees
On the riverbank, and turning back her long neck
She lifted her face, which was all she could lift,
To the stars. With groans and tears and pathetic lowing
She seemed to reproach Jupiter, to beg him for an end
To all her sorrows. And Jupiter threw his arms
Around his wife's neck and begged her to end   790
Her vendetta at last, saying, "Put aside your fear.
In the future this girl will never cause you grief."
And he called as witness the waters of Styx.

As the goddess calms down, Io regains
Her previous form and becomes what she was.
The bristles recede, the horns decrease, the great eyes
Grow smaller, the jaws contract, arms and hands
Return, and each solid hoof becomes five nails again.
Only the heifer's milk-white color remains.
Happy to have her two legs back, Io stands   800
Erect now, and fearing her speech will come out as moos,
She cautiously pronounces her neglected words.

Phaëthon and Clymene

Now she is worshipped as a goddess by throngs
Of linen-robed devotees. In due time she bore a child,
Epaphus, believed to be great Jupiter' son,
Coresident of his mother's civic temples.
He had a friend well-matched in age and spirit,
Phaëthon, a child of the Sun, who once began boasting
Of his solar parentage and would not back down
When Inachus' grandson rejected his claim: 810
"You're crazy to believe all that your mother says,
And you're swellheaded about your imagined father."
Phaëthon turned red. He repressed his anger out of shame
But brought Epaphus' slander to his mother, Clymene:

"And to make it worse, mother, I, the free, the fierce,
Said nothing. I am ashamed that such a reproach

Has gone unanswered. But if I really am born
Of divine stock, give me some kind of proof,
A claim to heaven."
                    With that he threw his arms
Around his mother's neck and begged her by his own life,   820
Her husband Merops' life, and his sister's marriages
To give him some sign of his true parentage.

Clymene, moved perhaps by her son's entreaties,
Or, more likely, by anger at the charge against her,
Stretched her arms to the sky and, looking up at the sun,
Said,
      "By the glittering radiance that you see here,
My son, and that hears and sees us, I swear
That you were born of this light that rules the world
And are a child of the Sun. If I am lying,
May he never let me look upon him again,   830
And may this be the last light that reaches my eyes!
It would not take long for you to find your father's house.
The country he rises from borders our own.
If you have a mind to do so, go ask the Sun himself!"

Phaëthon beamed happily at his mother's words
And, imagining the heavens in his mind,
He left Ethiopia in a flash, crossed India
Beneath its stars, and reached his father's Orient.

Book 2

Phaëthon and Phoebus

The palace of the Sun soared high on its columns,
Bright with the glint of gold and fiery bronze.
The gables were capped with gleaming ivory,
And the double doors were radiant with silver.
The workmanship surpassed the material,
For Vulcan had carved there the seas that surround
The central lands, the disk of earth, and the sky
That overarches all. The sea held dark blue gods,
Triton blowing his horn, shape-shifting Proteus,
And Aegaeon, each arm around a huge whale;　　　　　10
Doris and her daughters were there, some swimming,
Some sitting on a rock to dry their sea-green hair,
Some riding dolphins. While they were not identical,
They bore the resemblance that sisters should share.
The land has men and cities, woods and beasts,
Rivers, nymphs, and other rural deities.
Above these scenes was the shining sky, six signs
Of the zodiac on the right door, and six on the left.

When Clymene's son had climbed the steep path
And come under the roof of his putative father,　　　　20
He turned to move toward him, but stopped in his tracks,
Unable to bear the brightness at closer range.
Robed in purple, Phoebus sat on a throne
Brilliant with emeralds. To his right and left stood
Day and Month and Year and Century,
And the seasons stationed at equal intervals.
Young Spring was there wearing a crown of flowers;
Summer stood there nude, with a garland of grain;
Autumn was stained with the juice of trodden grapes;
And icy Winter bristled with hair white as snow.　　　　30

Seated in the middle, the Sun turned his eyes,
Eyes that see all, at the youth, who stood stunned
By this strange new world, and said to him:

"Why have you come to this high palace, Phaëthon,
A son whom no father should ever deny?"

And Phaëthon replied,
                    "O Universal Light of the World
Phoebus, my father, if I may call you father,
And if Clymene is not disguising her shame—
Give me a token by which all may know me
As your true son, and remove my mind's doubt."   40

He spoke, and his father took off his crown
Of glittering light and had the boy come close.
Embracing him, he said,
                    "You are worthy
To be called my own, and Clymene did tell you
Your true origin. And so you will doubt less,
Whatever you ask of me I will grant to you.
I take as my witness the Stygian marsh
By which the gods swear, though my eyes have not seen it."

His words were no sooner out than the boy asked
To drive his father's chariot for a day   50
And take control of all of that horsepower.
The father regretted his oath. Three times,
Four times, he shook his luminous head, saying,

"Your words show that my own were rash. I wish
That I could take back my promise. I confess,
This alone I would refuse you, my son, but now
All I can do is talk some sense into you.
What you want is not safe, quite beyond your strength
And your boyish years. Your lot is mortal;
What you ask for is not. Unaware,   60
You aspire to more than other gods can handle.
Though each of them may do as he pleases,
None, except myself, has the power to stand
On the running board of the chariot of fire.
Even the Olympian, for all his awesome thunderbolts,

Cannot drive these horses. And who is greater than Jove?
The first part of the road is steep, and my horses,
Though fresh in the morning, struggle to climb it.
In mid-heaven it is impossibly high. I often tremble
To look down from there on the sea and the land,   70
And my heart pounds with fear. The final stage
Is a precipitous drop that needs a firm hand.
Even Tethys, who receives me in waters below,
Fears I will plunge in headfirst. Then too, the sky's dome
Spins around in perpetual motion, drawing along
The high stars with dizzying speed. I make my way
Against this orbital motion, going in opposition
To all else in the universe. Imagine yourself
Driving my chariot. Do you think you could buck
That whirling axis and not be swept away?   80
And perhaps you suppose there are groves up there,
Cities of gods, temples rich with gifts. No,
The road runs through wild, threatening figures,
And even if you stay on course, you still must dodge
The horns of Taurus, the bow of Sagittarius,
Leo's ravenous maw, Scorpio's clutching claws,
And the pincers of Cancer. And the horses themselves,
Breathing fire through their nostrils and mouths,
Are not easy to control. They barely obey me
When their spirits are hot and their necks fight the reins.   90
But you, my son, don't let me give you a fatal gift,
And while there is still time, alter your request.
If you really want assurance that you are my son,
My anxiety should be all the assurance you need;
I am proved your father by a father's fear.
Just look at my face! If only you could look
Into my heart as well, and comprehend
What a father feels inside! Finally, look around
At everything the rich world holds, and choose
From all the boundless goods of earth, sea, and sky   100
Whatever you like. You will be denied nothing.
But this one thing I beg you not to ask, a thing which,
If called by its right name, is not a blessing

But a curse. You are asking for a curse, Phaëthon.
Why are your arms around my neck, foolish boy?
Don't worry, whatever you choose you will get—
I have sworn by the Styx—but choose more wisely!"

The admonition was over, but Phaëthon
Kept fighting back. He pressed on with his plan,
Burning with desire for that chariot.   110
His father delayed as long as he could,
And then led the boy to the sublime vehicle,
The work of Vulcan. Its axle was gold,
As was the chariot pole; the rims of the wheels
Were gold, and the spokes silver. Along the yoke
Chrysolites and gemstones set in a row
Reflected the brilliance of Phoebus' own light.

While the brave young soul gazed in wonder
At this work of art, Aurora awoke and threw open
The glowing doors to her rosy eastern courts.   120
The Morning Star ushered out all the others
And was last to leave his place in the sky.
When the Sun saw him go, saw the skies redden
And the horns of the waning crescent moon vanish,
He ordered the swift Hours to hitch up his horses.
The goddesses, quick to comply, led the stallions,
Breathing fire and sated with ambrosia,
Out from the high stables. Their bridles jingled
While the father anointed his dear son's face
With a sacred unguent to protect it from fire   130
And placed the rays on his head. Foreseeing grief,
And drawing up sighs from his troubled heart, he said:

"If you can take at least some of a parent's advice,
Spare the whip, boy, and pull hard on the reins.
They run fast on their own; your job is to hold back
A spirited team. And don't just go where you please
Driving straight across the five zones of heaven.
The course is laid out on an oblique curve, confined

To the three central zones, avoiding the south pole
And the starlit Bear with her frigid north winds.   140
That is your road—you will see the tracks of my wheels.
And so heaven and earth will receive equal heat,
Do not drive too low or stampede the horses
Up into the aether! Too high will scorch heaven's roof,
Too low the earth. The middle course is safest for you.
Don't veer right toward the writhing Serpent
Or steer left where the Altar lies on the horizon.
Stay between the two. I entrust the rest to Fortune.
I pray that she helps you and guides you better
Than you do yourself.
                              While I've been speaking,   150
Dewy Night has touched down on the western shore.
We are summoned, and may delay no longer.
Shining Aurora has put the shadows to flight.
Take the reins, or if your mind can still be changed,
Take my counsel instead of my chariot,
While you can, while you are still on solid ground
And have not yet taken your stand in the car
That you so foolishly want. Let me shed daylight
Over the world, light that you may see without risk."

But Phaëthon is already standing tall   160
In the sleek chariot, and, delirious with joy
To be holding the reins, thanks his father for the gift.

And now Pyrois, Eous, and Aethon,
The Sun's swift horses, and the fourth, Phlegon,
Fill the air with fire as they stamp and whinny
And punish the paddock bars with their hooves.
Tethys, ignorant of her grandson's fates, pushed back
The bars and opened the gates to the infinite skies,
And the horses were off, hooves pounding the air.
They parted the clouds in their path, and, lifted   170
On their wings, they outstripped the East Wind,
Which has its rising in this same quarter.
But the weight was too light for these solar horses,

And the yoke was without its accustomed drag.
As curved ships without the right ballast
Roll off kilter, prone to capsize in open water
Due to their lightness, so too the chariot
Without its usual burden was tossed around
And bounced in the air as if it had no one onboard.
As soon as they felt it, the team ran wild,   180
Leaving the well-worn track and going off course.
The driver panicked. He had no idea
How to handle the reins entrusted to him
Or where the road was. And even if he had known
He wouldn't have been able to master the horses.
Then for the first time the cold Bears grew hot
With the rays of the sun, and tried in vain to plunge
Into the forbidden sea. And Draco, the serpent
Coiled around the icy pole, until then always sluggish
With the arctic chill and formidable to none,   190
Began to seethe and rage with the feverish heat.
They say that you too, Boötes, ran in terror,
Slow though you were and held back by your cart.

When the very unhappy Phaëthon looked down
From heaven's summit and saw the lands
Spread out beneath him far, far below, the blood
Drained from his face, his knees shook in fear,
And his eyes swam with shadows, stunned by the glare.
He wishes now he'd never touched his father's horses
Or succeeded in his quest to know his origin.   200
He would much rather now be called Merops' son
As he is driven like a ship in a northern gale,
A ship whose pilot has dropped the rudder
And abandoned her to the will of the gods.
What should he do? Much of the sky was behind him,
But more was ahead. He measured both in his mind,
Looking toward the west he was not destined to reach,
And then back to the east. Dazed, he has no idea
Of what he should do, and can neither loosen the reins
Nor manage to hold them, nor call the horses by name.   210

And he saw in horror surreal images
Of astral predators strewn through the sky.
There is a place where Scorpio arcs its pincers
And with its hooked tail and curving arms sprawls
Over two constellations. When the boy saw it,
Oozing black venom and threatening to wound him
With its barbed stinger, his mind froze with fear
And he dropped the reins. When the horses felt them
Draped over their backs, they veered off course,
And with nothing to stop them they galloped across   220
Unknown regions of heaven. Rushing wherever
Their momentum took them, they made incursions
Into the fixed stars, hurtling the chariot
Along uncharted tracks, climbing at times
To the high stratosphere and then plunging down
To airspace not much above ground level.
The Moon was amazed to see her brother's horses
Lower than her own.
                        The heated clouds began to smoke,
And the earth burst into flames, the highest parts first,
As deep fissures open and its moisture dries up.   230
Meadows are drifted over with ash, leafy trees burn,
Scorched grain provides its own fuel for fire.
But I bewail lesser things. Walled cities perish,
Entire nations and whole populations
Are reduced to ashes. Woodlands burn with the hills.
Mount Athos is ablaze, Cilician Taurus,
Tmolus and Oeta, Ida, now arid though once
Crowded with springs, maiden Helicon,
And Haemus (not yet with its Oeagrian epithet).
Etna now burns with immense double flames,   240
The twin peaks of Parnassus, Eryx, Cynthus,
Othrys, Rhodope, at last losing its snow,
Mimas, Dindyma, Mycale, and Cithaeron,
Old in religion. Scythia's cold climate offers
Little refuge. The Caucasus is burning,
Ossa, Pindus, and, greater than both, Olympus,
The high Alps, and the cloud-capped Apennines.

Phaëthon sees the whole world on fire.
He cannot bear the terrible heat. The air he sucks in
Feels like it comes from the depths of a furnace,   250
And the chariot glows white-hot. The ashes
And sparks are unendurable; he is enveloped
In a dense pall of smoke, and in that pitchy blackness
He doesn't know where he is or where he is going,
Swept along by the will of the winged horses.

They think it was then that the Ethiopians,
As the heat drew the blood up close to the skin,
Became dark-complexioned. Robbed of their moisture,
Libya's hills then were bleached into desert.
Water nymphs tore their hair and wailed lamentations   260
For their pools and lakes. Boeotia searched
For the waters of Dirce, Argos for Amymone,
Ephyre for Pirene's rills. Nor were the rivers safe
Between their wide banks. The Don turned to steam,
As did old Peneos, Teuthrantean Caïcus,
The swift Ismenus, Arcadian Erymanthus,
The Xanthos (destined to burn yet again),
Tawny Lycormas, the Maeander as it played
In its meandering curves, Mygdonian Melas
And the Taenarian Eurotas. They all burned,   270
Along with the Babylonian Euphrates,
The Orontes, the Thermodon, the rushing Ganges.
The Alpheus boiled, Spercheios' banks burned,
The gold swept along in the Tagus' current
Liquefied in the heat, and the swans that carpeted
Maeonia with song were scorched in the Caÿster.
The Nile fled in terror to the end of the world
And hid its still hidden head, its seven mouths
Dry and empty, seven barren, waterless channels.
The rivers in Thrace, the Hebrus and Strymon,   280
Were likewise parched, as were those in the west,
The Rhine, Rhone, and Po, and the River Tiber,
Whose eddies held promise of universal power.

The ground cracks open, and light streams through the fissures
Down to Tartarus, alarming the underworld king and his queen.
The sea contracts, and what was once wide open water
Is now an ocean of sand; undersea mountains emerge,
Archipelagos added to the scattered Cyclades.
Fish dive deep, and dolphins no longer dare
To arc through the air. The lifeless bodies of seals   290
Float faceup on the sea, and Nereus himself,
The story goes, along with Doris and her daughters,
Hid in warm sea caverns. Three times Neptune tried
To lift his fierce face and arms above the sea's surface
And three times could not bear the incandescent heat.

Though surrounded as she was by a shrinking sea,
With her own streams withdrawn into the darkness
Of her own womb, Mother Earth still lifted up
Her parched and smothered face, and placing a hand
Before her fevered brow, heaved with mighty tremors   300
That shook the world. Then, sinking back a little lower
Than she was before, she spoke in solemn tones:

"If this is your pleasure and I have deserved it,
Why, lord of the gods, is your lightning idle?
If I must perish by fire at least let it be yours
And lighten my loss by having it come from you.
I can hardly open my mouth to speak these words."
The smoke was suffocating her. "See my scorched hair,
The ashes in my eyes and all over my face.
Is this how you reward my fertility, my service   310
In bearing the wounds of plow and mattock,
Worked and worked over year in and year out?
Is it for this that I provide fodder for flocks,
Grain for humankind, and incense for your altars?
But, supposing that I deserve destruction,
What does the sea, or your brother, deserve?
Why are the waters—which are his share by lot—
Reduced to shallows and so much farther from the sky?

But if you could care less about me or your brother,
Pity your own heavens! Look around:　　　　　　　　320
The entire vault of heaven is smoking. If the fire
Weakens its structure, your mansions will be ruins.
Even Atlas is struggling and can barely support
The white-hot dome on his shoulders. If the sea,
The land, and the celestial realms perish,
We will all be reduced to primordial chaos!
Save from the flames whatever still survives
And take counsel for the whole of the universe."

Earth stopped speaking, for she could no longer bear
The seething heat, and withdrew into herself　　　　330
And to caverns closer to the realm of shades.
But the Father Almighty called the gods to witness
(And especially the one who had given the chariot)
That unless he came to the rescue, the entire world
Was doomed. He then ascended to heaven's zenith,
His accustomed station when he covers earth with clouds,
Rolls out thunder, and hurls quivering lightning.
But now he has no clouds to cover the earth
Or rain to send down. He does have thunder, though,
And in his right hand balances a lightning bolt　　　340
Level with his ear, and hurls it at the charioteer,
Jolting him from the car and from his soul as well,
And quenching fire with caustic fire. The horses
Went mad and leapt in different directions,
Wrenching their necks from the yoke and breaking
Free of the bridles. The reins lie here, the axle
Over there, torn from the pole. The wheels
Are shattered, the spokes strewn all over the place
In the shower of debris from the chariot wreck.

But Phaëthon's red hair was a plume of flame　　　350
As he was propelled in a long arc through the air,
Leaving a trail the way a star sometimes does
When it seems to have fallen from a cloudless sky.
He was received in a distant part of the globe,

Far from his native land, by the greatest of rivers,
The Eridanus, who bathed his steaming face.
The Hesperian Naiads buried his body,
Still smoking from that jagged lightning bolt
And inscribed this epitaph upon the tomb:

HERE LIES PHAËTHON, WHO TOOK HIS FATHER'S REINS.   360
IF HE LOST HIS HOLD, HIS HIGH DARING REMAINS.

The father, sick with grief, hid his face,
And, if we are to believe it, an entire day passed
Without the sun. But since the wildfires gave light,
The catastrophe served some useful purpose.

Clymene said the words that must be said
In times so terrible, and then, out of her mind
With grief, clawing her breast, she wandered the world,
Looking first for his body, and then his bones,
And at last found his bones buried by the shore   370
Of a distant river. There she sank to her knees
And poured forth tears on the name carved in marble
And caressed it with her open bosom. Her daughters,
The Heliades lamented no less, giving tears
And other useless tribute to the dead, bruising
Their breasts with their palms, calling pitifully
Day and night on Phaëthon, who would never hear them,
And prostrating themselves on his sepulcher.

Four times the Moon had joined her crescent horns
To fill her orb, and, as had become their custom now,   380
The sisters were still mourning, when Phaëthousa,
The oldest, complained as she tried to prostrate herself
That her feet were growing stiff; and when Lampetië,
A radiant nymph, was coming to her aid,
She was rooted to the spot. A third sister, tearing
Her hair with her fingers, held a handful of leaves;
One grieved that her legs were now sheathed in wood,
Another that her arms forked into branches and twigs.

As they wondered at this, bark began to enclose
Their thighs, creep up over their waists, their breasts,   390
Their shoulders, their hands, until all that was left
Were their mouths, calling out for their mother.
But what could Mother do except flit from this one
To that one, kissing their lips as long as she could?
It won't do. She tries to pull the bark from their bodies,
Snapping their twigs in two, but blood trickles out
From each wounded branch. "Please, Mother, stop!"
Cries out whichever is hurt. "Please stop. It is my body
Inside the tree that you're tearing. And now, farewell."
And the bark sealed off her very last words.   400
Tears flow from those trees, and hardened by the sun,
Drip down from the virgin branches as amber,
And the bright river takes them and bears them along
To be worn one day by the brides of Rome.

Cygnus, son of Sthenelus, witnessed this wonder.
Though he was your kin, Phaëthon, on his mother's side,
He was even closer in spirit. Leaving his kingdom
(He ruled Liguria's great cities) he wandered in tears
Along the Eridanus. As he filled its green banks
And woods with grief, and the new stand of poplars   410
Weeping amber tears, his voice grew thin, and feathers
Of white down grew in place of his hair, his neck
Now stretched in an arc out from his chest, a web
Joined his reddening fingers, wings covered his sides
And a blunt beak his mouth. In this way Cygnus
Became a strange, new bird, but did not entrust himself
To the upper air or to Jove, ever mindful
Of the fire that unjustly came from on high.
He sought still pools and placid lakes, making his home
In water, the element opposed to hateful fire.   420

Meanwhile, Phaëthon's father mourns, bereft
Of his bright glory, as if he were in eclipse.
He hates the light, hates himself, hates the day.
He gives his soul over to grief, to grief adds rage,

And refuses his duty to the world.
                              "Enough," he says,
"From the beginning of time it has been my lot
Never to rest. I am weary of my endless toil,
My unhonored labor. Let someone else drive
The chariot of light. If there is no one else,
If all the gods admit it is beyond their power,   430
Let Jove himself do it, so that at least while he tries
To handle my reins he might put down the bolts
That deprive fathers of sons. Then he will know,
When he has felt the strength of those fire-shod horses,
That not to control them does not merit death."

As the Sun speaks, all the gods stand around him,
Pleading with him not to abandon the cosmos
To perpetual shade. Jupiter himself
Fashions excuses for the lightning discharge,
And adds to his prayers a few royal threats.   440
Phoebus finally yokes his horses again,
Trembling still and half-wild with fear, and in his grief
Savages them with goad and lash, savages them
And reproaches them with the death of his son.

Callisto

But the Father Almighty makes a circuit around
Heaven's monumental walls, inspecting them
For any structural faults caused by the fire.
When he sees that they are sound, just as strong
As they should be, he turns his attention
To the earth, and to human affairs.
                              Arcadia   450
Is of particular interest. He sets about restoring
Its springs and rivers, which had not yet
Dared to flow again; he gives the soil grass, leaves
To the trees, and bids the shattered woods grow green.
As he came and went, he would often stop short
At the sight of a girl from Nonacris, passion

Heating up in the marrow of his bones.
She was not the sort of girl to spin soft wool
Or worry about her hair. A simple clasp
Fastened her tunic, and a white headband   460
Held back her loose curls. She sometimes carried
A light javelin in her hand, sometimes a bow,
One of Diana's recruits, and no nymph on Maenalus
Was dearer to her; but no favor lasts forever.

The sun was high, just past the meridian,
When she entered a virgin grove. She slipped
Her quiver from her shoulder, unstrung her bow,
And lay down on the tufted grass, her head
Propped up on her painted quiver. When Jupiter
Saw her there, so worn out and all alone,   470
He said to himself, "My wife will never discover
This little deception, or if she does find out,
It will be well worth the quarrel!" Instantly
He adopted the face and dress of Diana
And said, "Chaste nymph, best of my companions,
What ridges did you hunt today?" She rose
From the turf and replied, "Hail, goddess, greater
Than Jove in my opinion, though he himself
Should hear me say it." He smiled to hear it,
Amused to be preferred to himself, and kissed her,   480
No modest kiss, nor one a virgin would give.
When she started to talk about which woods to hunt,
He stopped her with an embrace, betraying himself
With a less than innocent act. She did struggle,
As much as a woman can—had you seen it,
Juno, you would have been kinder—but what man
Can a girl overcome, and who can overcome Jove?
The god returned to the sky, flush with victory.
The girl loathed the woodlands that knew her secret.
As she retraced her steps she almost forgot   490
To retrieve the quiver and the bow she'd hung up.
But look—here comes Diana with a troop of nymphs
Along Maenalus' ridges, proud of her kills,

And catches sight of the girl and calls to her. At first
She runs, afraid that Jove lurks in Diana's skin,
But when she sees the other nymphs at her side,
She senses no tricks and joins their number. Ah,
How hard not to betray her guilt with her face!
She scarcely lifts her eyes from the ground, nor
Is she found at the goddess' side, at the front   500
Of the group as before. She walks in silence,
And her blushes betray her injured chastity.
If Diana herself were not a virgin,
She would recognize her guilt by a thousand signs.
They say the nymphs recognized it at once.

                                                Nine times
The moon had swollen from crescent to full,
When the goddess Diana, worn out with hunting
And the heat from Helius her brother, came upon
A cool grove through which a murmuring stream
Flowed gently over smooth sand. Voicing her delight,   510
She dipped her feet into the water, and delighting
In this too, she said, "There are no prying eyes here.
Let's bathe nude in the flowing water."
The Arcadian girl blushed. The rest disrobed;
One tried to stall, but as she hesitated
The tunic was removed and her shame revealed
Along with her body. Terrified, and trying to hide
Her belly with her hands, she heard Diana say,
"Begone from here, and do not pollute our sacred spring."
And the goddess expelled her from her company.   520

The Thunderer's wife had known all about this
For a while now, but held her vengeance in check
Until the time was right. There was no reason now
To wait any longer, for the boy Arcas had been born
To her rival, and this in itself infuriated Juno.
When she turned her enraged attention to this, she said,

"There was nothing else left, adulteress, than for you
To become pregnant and highlight your insult to me

By giving birth, publicizing my Jupiter's disgrace.
You won't get away with it. I'll take away that figure   530
You and my husband liked so much, you little slut."

She caught Callisto by her hair and threw her
Facedown in the dirt, and when the girl stretched out
Her arms in supplication, they began to bristle
With rough black hair, her hands curved into paws
With sharp claws, and her face, once praised by Jove,
Became a broad, ugly grin. And so that she could not
Pray to the god or move him with entreaties,
Her power of speech was taken away, and only
A low, menacing growl would come from her throat.   540
Her old mind remained, though now it remained
In the bear she'd become, and her constant moaning
Testified to her pain. She would lift to heaven's stars
What rough hands she had, and though she could not say it,
She still felt Jupiter's ingratitude. How often,
Afraid to sleep in the woods, she paced in front of
Her old home, trespassing in fields that once had been hers.
How often was she driven over rocky ground
By baying hounds, the huntress afraid of hunters!
Often she hid at the sight of wild animals, forgetting   550
What she herself had become, and though she was a bear
She shuddered when she saw other bears on the mountain,
And even feared wolves, although her father was one.

And now Lycaon's grandson, Arcas, who knew
Nothing of his parents, had just turned fifteen.
While he was out hunting, scouting the best spots,
And enmeshing Arcadia's woods with his nets,
He came upon his mother, who stopped in her tracks
At the sight of Arcas. She seemed to recognize him.
He shrank back from the gaze of those unmoving eyes,   560
Afraid without knowing why; and as the bear
Started to advance, panting and eager,
He raised his sharp spear to pierce her breast.
But the Omnipotent stopped him, removing at once

Both of the principals and the crime from the scene.
He whisked the pair up through the void in a whirlwind
And set them in the sky as conjoined constellations.

Juno was engorged with rage when she saw her rival
Twinkling among the stars, and went down into the depths
To see grey Tethys and old Ocean, to whom the gods   570
Often pay reverence, and when they asked her
Why she had come, she began:
                                    "You ask me
Why I, the queen of the celestial gods am here?
Another woman has replaced me in heaven.
I am a liar if you don't see, when the sky gets dark,
New constellations set on high to spite me,
In the smallest circle right next to the pole.
Why should anyone scruple to offend Juno now
In fear of my wrath, when my harm only helps?
Oh, how great am I, what vast power I have!   580
I make her an animal and now she's a goddess!
That's how I smite those who trespass against me,
That's how mighty I am! He might as well release her
From her animal form and give her back her old face,
Just as he did for Io of Argos! Why not,
With Juno out of the way, put her in my bed
And make himself Lycaon's son-in-law?
But you, if you are upset with this insult
To your foster child, debar those seven stars
From your blue waters, reject constellations   590
Whose path to heaven was paved by prostitution,
And don't let that whore bathe in your pure sea."

Apollo and Coronis

The sea gods assented, and Saturnia flew
Through the clear air in a chariot drawn
By her brightly trimmed peacocks, peacocks
Freshly ornamented with the eyes of slain Argus
At the same time that your feathers, garrulous raven,

Had suddenly changed from white to black.
He had been a silvery bird with snow-white plumage,
A match for immaculate doves, yielding nothing   600
To the Capitoline geese whose alert honking
Would save the city, or to the river-loving swan.
But his tongue undid him, and made the talkative bird
Who once was white the exact opposite color.

Coronis of Larissa was the most beautiful girl
In all Thessaly, and certainly pleased you,
O god of Delphi, as long as she was chaste,
Or at least undetected. But Apollo's raven
Discovered her adultery and the implacable tattle
Was on his way to his master to tell him her sin.   610
A gossiping crow flapped her wings beside him,
And when she learned the reason for the raven's trip,
She said,
          "This jaunt will cost you, mark my words.
Observe what I once was and what I am now
And then ask me why. You'll find that fidelity
Did me in.

The Crow and Minerva

          Once upon a time a child was created
Without any mother, Erichthonius by name.
Pallas put the baby in a basket woven
Of Actaean willows and gave it to the three daughters
Of Cecrops, the biform king, along with strict instructions   620
Not to pry into her secret. I hid in the fluttering leaves
Of a nearby elm to see what they would do.
Two of the girls, Pandrosos and Herse,
Watched the basket in good faith, but the third,
Aglauros, called her sisters sissies, and untied
The knots securing the lid. They saw a baby inside
With a snake stretched out beside it. I reported
All this to the goddess, and all the thanks I got
Was to be replaced as Minerva's attendant
By the night owl. My punishment serves   630

To remind all birds not to look for trouble
By talking too much. And to think that not only
I had not asked for her favor, but that she sought me out!
Ask Pallas yourself. She may be angry with me,
But she will not deny it.

The Princess and the Sea God

I was the daughter—
This is a well-known story—of Coroneus,
The famous king of Phocis, a regular princess
With rich suitors after me (please don't mock me),
But my beauty undid me. I was out one day
For my usual stroll on the beach, my toes in the foam,   640
When the sea god saw me and grew hot for me.
After wasting some time on pleas and flattery,
He resorted to force. I ran, but when I left the shore
And hit the soft sand beyond I lost all my strength.
I called on gods and men. My voice did not reach
Any mortal ear, but the virgin goddess
Was moved by a virgin and came to my rescue.
I stretched my arms to heaven; my arms began
To darken with feathers; I struggled to throw
My cloak from my shoulders, but it had become   650
Plumage, already sinking roots deep in my skin;
I tried to beat my bare breasts with my hands,
But I no longer had hands, and no breasts either;
I took off running, but the sand didn't slow my feet
As it had before; instead, I was lifted above it
And soon I was soaring high through the air,
And was made Minerva's unblemished companion.
But what good did it do me, if Nyctimene,
Who was made a bird for her hideous sins,
Has usurped my honor?

Nyctimene

Or have you not heard   660
What all Lesbos knows, how Nyctimene
Boldly desecrated her father's bed? And now,

Though she is a bird, she still feels guilty
And avoids being seen, shunning the light,
Hiding herself and her shame in evening shadows,
Hounded from the sky by all the other birds."

To which the raven replied, "I pray to god
This comes back to bite you. Enough empty omens!"
He went on to his master and told him he'd seen
Coronis lying with a young Thessalian.   670
When Apollo heard this, in love as he was,
The laurel slipped from his head, and the god's face,
His plectrum, and his color all fell.
Then, as his heart began to seethe with anger,
He seized his customary weapons, and bending
His bow from the horns at the tips, strung it and shot
An unswerving arrow straight through the breast
That had so many times been pressed to his own.
She groaned as it struck, and when the shaft was drawn out
Her perfect limbs were drenched with vermillion blood;   680
"I owe you this penalty, Phoebus," she said,
"But I should have birthed my child first. Now we two
Die as one." With these words she poured out her life
Along with her blood, and lay cold in death.

The lover regretted his vengeance, but all too late.
He hated himself for listening to the tale
And flaring up like that, and he hated the bird
By whom he felt compelled to know the offense
That caused him such grief. He loathed even his bow,
His hand, and the arrows that had the temerity   690
To be shot by that hand. He fondled the limp body
And struggled against fate to resuscitate her,
But he practiced his healing arts in vain.
When he saw his efforts fail, the pyre being built
And the funeral fires about to consume her limbs,
Then indeed the groans (for tears cannot moisten
The cheeks of the gods) issued deep from his heart,

Such groans as come from a heifer who watches
As the hammer poised high by the slaughterer's ear
Crashes down on the temples of her suckling calf.   700
Phoebus pours on her breast fragrant oils unfelt,
Gives the last embrace, unjustly performs just rites,
But cannot endure that his own son should perish
Into the same ashes. He snatched the unborn child
From his mother's womb and the funeral fires
And took him to the cave of the Centaur Chiron.
As for the raven's reward for telling the truth,
The god quarantined him from white-feathered birds.

Ocyrhoë

Meanwhile, the Centaur was delighted with his ward
Sprung from divine stock, happy in the honor   710
And the responsibility, when—look!—his daughter
Comes running, red-gold hair flowing and tumbling
Over her shoulders. The nymph Chariclo bore her
On the banks of a swiftly flowing river, and ever after
Called her Ocyrhoë. Not content to have mastered
Her father's arts, she also sang the Fates' secrets,
And now, her mind instinct with prophetic madness
And warming with the god deep in her breast,
She looks at the child and says:
                                    "Grow now, child,
Healer to the whole world. Mortal bodies will often   720
Be in your debt, and it will be your right to restore
Souls to the departed. But having dared this once
To the gods' disapproval, your grandsire's lightning
Will prevent you from ever giving life again.
From a god you will become a bloodless corpse,
And from a corpse a god, and renew your fates twice.
You also, dear Father, immortal now,
And created by law to last through the ages,
Will someday yearn for the power to die,
Infected and tortured by the blood of the Hydra.   730

Powers divine will at last make you mortal
And the Three Goddesses will unravel your thread."

There was more about the Fates, but she sighed deeply,
And with tears welling up and flowing down her cheeks,
She said:
             "The Fates forbid me to say any more,
And my power of speech is being choked off.
The prophetic arts were not worth the price
Of divine retribution. Better never to have known
What the future held. I feel my human face
Being withdrawn, feel a taste for grass, feel an urge   740
To gallop over broad fields. I'm becoming a filly,
My familial body. But why completely?
Surely my father is at least half human!"

Her sorrowful last words were hard to understand,
An incomprehensible jumble of sounds, and soon
The girl sounded neither human nor equine,
But like someone who imitates a horse's neigh.
But then she gave a clear whinny, her arms in the grass.
Her fingers fused, and the five nails of each hand
Became a solid hoof of light horn; her mouth enlarged,   750
Her neck extended, and her long trailing gown
Changed into a tail. The hair that spilled over her neck
Coursed to the right and became a mane. She was
Utterly transformed in voice and looks, and a new name
Came with the conversion: Ocyrhoë became Filly.

Mercury and Battus

The demigod Chiron, son of Philyra,
Wept and called upon you, Lord of Delphi,
But all in vain. You couldn't rescind the decree
Of the Almighty, and even if you could,
You were far away then, living in Elis   760
And the fields of Messene. In those days

You wore a shepherd's cloak, in your left hand a staff
And in your right a pipe of seven stepped reeds.
While you soothed your lovesick soul with your pipe,
The cattle you were watching strayed, they say,
Into the Pylian fields, where they caught Mercury's eye,
And Maia's crafty son drove them into the woods
And hid them there. No one witnessed the theft
Except a gabby old man the locals called Battus.
A hired hand of the wealthy Neleus, he watched over   770
Woods and pasture and a herd of purebred mares.
Mercury was wary of him and led him aside,
Saying,

       "I don't know who you are, mister, but if anyone
Asks about these cattle, say you haven't seen them.
And you can have a nice heifer as a little reward."

And he gave him the heifer. The old man took it and said,

"Happy trails, stranger. That stone will squeal on you
Before I will."
       And he pointed to a stone.
So Jupiter's son pretended to go away, but soon
Doubled back, changing his voice and appearance,   780
And saying,
       "Say, old-timer, if you've seen any cattle
Come this way, help me out. They're stolen. Tell me
And you can have this bull here, with a cow thrown in."

The old man, looking at the double reward, said,

"They're over there at the foot of that mountain."

Which is where they were. Mercury laughed and said,

"Are you snitching on me to my own face, betraying
Me to my very self?"
       And he turned that perjured heart

Into a piece of hard flint, even now called a snitch-stone,
And the innocent rock bears that ancient disgrace.   790

Mercury, Herse, and Aglauros

Caduceus in hand, the god rose on level wings
And looked down at the Munychian fields as he flew,
The land Minerva loves, the Lyceum's cultured groves.
That day happened to be a festival of Pallas
And virgin girls were bearing to the goddess' temple
Mystic flower-wreathed baskets balanced on their heads.
The winged god saw them on their way back
And glided over to them, not in a straight line
But in a long spiral, like a vulture that has spotted
Entrails on an altar, and, afraid of the priests   800
Still crowded around the victim, flies in circles
And hovers greedily over his hoped-for prey.
So too Mercury above the Acropolis,
Tracing circles in the same volume of air.
Below him, Herse outshone the other girls
As the morning star outshines its companions
And is itself outshone by the golden moon.
She was the jewel in that procession of virgins.
Hanging in midair, the son of Jupiter
Was astounded by her beauty, and burned with love   810
The way a lead bullet shot by a Balearic sling
Becomes incandescent as it flies through the air,
Picking up in the clouds heat it never had before.
He altered his course and headed from sky to earth
Without disguising himself, trusting his looks,
Although he did carefully touch them up,
Making sure his hair was smooth and his robe arranged
So it would hang with all the gold border showing.
He holds in his right hand the polished wand
He uses to induce sleep or to dispel it,   820
And on his trim feet the winged sandals gleam.

Deep inside the house were three bedrooms
Decorated with tortoiseshell and ivory. You, Pandrosos,
Had the room on the right, Aglauros on the left,
And Herse the one in between. The tenant
Of the room on the left was the first to see
Mercury coming, and was bold enough to ask
The god his name and his reason for coming.
The grandson of Atlas and Pleione replied:

"I am the winged bearer of my father's words,   830
And my father is Jupiter himself. I won't try to hide
Why I have come. Just be loyal to your sister
And consent to be called the aunt of my child.
I am here for Herse. Please help out a lover."

Aglauros glared at him with the same eyes
That had pried into golden Minerva's secret,
And demanded for her services a ton of gold.
Meanwhile she obliged him to leave the house.

The warrior goddess turned a fierce eye on her
And in her agitation drew such a deep breath   840
That her strong breast shuddered, as did the aegis
Strapped across that strong breast. She remembered
That this was the girl who had uncovered her secret
With sacrilegious hands when, contrary to orders,
She had seen Erichthonius, the son of Vulcan,
A child created without any mother.
And now this girl would be dear to a god
And to her sister, and rich with all the gold
Her greed had demanded. She set out at once
For the grimy and decaying house of Envy.   850

Her cave was hidden deep in a sunless valley,
Impervious to winds, gloomy, hideously cold,
Never a fire burning and eternally steeped in fog.
When the formidable virago Minerva arrived

She stood outside the cave (she had no right to enter)
And pounded the doors with the butt of her spear.
The doors flew open and revealed Envy
Dining on viper meat, which kept up her venom.
Minerva averted her eyes at the sight,
But the other rose slowly up from the ground,   860
Leaving the carcasses of the snakes half eaten,
And came sluggishly forward. When she saw
The beautiful goddess in her armored glory
She groaned and sighed, contracted her face,
Turned sickly pale and shriveled up all over.
Her eyes are askew, her teeth black and rotted,
Her breast green from bile, and her tongue drips venom.
She never smiles except at another's troubles;
Her sleep is fruitless, a fitful, anxious vigil.
She resents the sight of someone else's success,   870
Gnawing away at it and being gnawed in return,
And is herself her own punishment. Tritonia,
Though filled with loathing, spit out her message:
"Infect one of the daughters of Cecrops.
That's the job. Aglauros." Without another word
The goddess pushed off from the earth with her spear.

Envy squinted at the goddess as she sailed away
And muttered a while at her impending success.
Then she took her staff, wound with thorny briar,
Wrapped a mantle of dark mist around her   880
And was on her way. Wherever she goes
She tramples the flowers, withers the grass,
Blasts the treetops, and pollutes with her breath
Cities, homes, and whole populations. At last
Tritonia's city comes into view, Athens,
Verdant with genius, wealth, and peaceful joy;
It nearly pains her to tears because she sees
No cause for tears. When she entered the room
Of Cecrops' daughter she did as ordered,
First laying her hands across the girl's breast   890
And sowing her heart with thorns; then breathing

A viral poison into her, and distilling black venom
All through her bones and inside her lungs.
And to keep the cause of her malady present,
She fixed in her mind an image of her sister,
Happily married to the beautiful god,
And magnified it all. Tormented by this,
Aglauros was consumed with a secret grief.
Anxious night and day, she groans in misery
And wastes slowly away, like ice in weak sunlight.   900
She smolders with envy of Herse's happiness,
Burning no less quietly than a creeping fire
That consumes dry weeds with heat but no flame.
She would rather be dead than see something like this,
Felt impelled to tell her stern father about it
As if it were a crime. Finally she sat down
On her sister's threshold to block the god's entrance.
When he came he tossed at her beguiling words
And the gentlest entreaties, to which she responded,
"Stop! I will not budge until I have foiled you!"   910
"I can live with that," the swift Cyllenian said,
And opened the door with his celestial wand.
The girl tried to get up, but her legs were cramped
From all that sitting. As she struggled to stand
Her knees grew stiff, a chill crept through her body
Down to her nails, and blood drained from her flesh.
And as terminal cancer spreads through the body
Annexing more and more undiseased tissue,
So a lethal chill filled her chest by degrees
And sealed off the airways and vital channels.   920
She did not try to speak, and if she had tried,
Her voice had no passage. Her neck now was stone,
Her face had hardened. A bloodless statue sat there,
Nor was the stone white: Aglauros' soul had stained it.

Jupiter and Europa

When Mercury had exacted punishment
For impiety in thoughts and words, he left

The city named after Pallas and flew high
On outstretched wings. His father called him aside
And, without mentioning love as a motive,

"Son," he said, "loyal minister of my decrees,   930
Go quickly now in your usual way and glide
Down to that land that sees your mother's star
In the Pleiades from the eastern quadrant.
Sidon it's called. When you see a royal herd grazing
Off in the mountains, drive it down to the sea."

He had no sooner spoken than the cattle were headed
To the designated shore, where a great king's daughter
Used to play in the company of young Tyrian girls.
Majesty and Love do not go well together,
So setting his massive scepter aside,   940
The Gods' Father and Ruler, whose right hand wields
The forked lightning, who shakes the globe with a nod,
Assumed a bull's form and lowed with the cattle,
A beautiful beast shambling through tender grass.
He was as white as pristine, untrodden snow
Before it turns to slush in the South Wind's rain.
His neck rippled with muscles, dewlaps hung in front,
His horns were twisted, but you would have argued
They were made by hand, more lustrous than pearls.
He had no glowering brow or eye full of menace: 950
His expression was calm. Agenor's daughter
Admired him, so beautiful, so unthreatening.
Gentle as he was she feared at first to touch him,
But soon she drew near and held flowers out
To his shining mouth. The lover in him exulted
And while he waited for his expected pleasure,
He kissed her hands, scarcely able to distinguish
Now from soon. At one moment he cavorts
And leaps in the grass, at another he lies down,
Resting his snowy flanks on the yellow sand.   960
As her fear diminishes he offers, first, his chest
For her virgin hands to pat, and then his horns

To be twined with fresh flowers. The princess even
Dares to sit on the back of the bull, unaware
Of whose back it is, while the god moves insensibly
From dry land to shore, testing the shallows
With his deceitful hooves. Then he slips farther out
And soon bears his prize across the high sea.
In terror she watches the shoreline recede,
One hand gripping a horn, the other his back,   970
Her clothes fluttering in a stiffening breeze.

Book 3

Cadmus and the Earthborn People

The god shed his bull disguise, revealed to Europa
His true identity, and reached the island of Crete.
Meanwhile, the girl's father tells his son Cadmus
To go find his stolen sister, threatening him with exile
For failure, and so manages to be devoted
And execrable at once. After roaming the world
To no effect (who could ferret out Jove's loves?),
Agenor's son, now an exile, shuns his fatherland
And his father's wrath and consults the oracle
Of Phoebus Apollo to discover which land   10
He should settle in. This was Phoebus' response:

"A heifer will meet you in an empty field,
One who has never been yoked or drawn a plow.
Follow her wherever she goes, and when she
Lies down in the grass, build your city's walls.
And you shall call the land Boeotia."

Cadmus had no sooner left the Castalian cave,
When he saw a heifer moving slowly along,
Unguarded, and no mark of a yoke on her neck.
He followed her footsteps, and as he walked   20
Silently thanked Apollo for showing the way.
He had just crossed the Cephisus and Panope's fields
When the heifer halted, and lifting to heaven
Her beautiful head with its spiraling horns
She made the air pulse with her lowing. Then,
Looking back at the people following her,
She sank to her knees and lay in the soft grass.
Cadmus gave thanks, kissed this pilgrim land,
And greeted the unknown mountains and plains.

Meaning to sacrifice to Jove he sent out men   30
To find a source of fresh water for libation.
There was an ancient forest nearby, untouched
By any axe, and within it stood a cave

Set in thick shrubs, and with tight-fitting stones
Forming a low arch from which a rich spring flowed.
Hidden in that cave was a serpent, sacred to Mars
And with a magnificent golden crest; his eyes
Flashed fire; his body was swollen with venom;
His triple tongue flickered through three rows of teeth.
When the Tyrian scouting party reached this spring   40
With luckless steps, and their lowered vessel
Made a splashing sound, the dark blue serpent
Thrust his head from the cave with a horrible hiss.
The urns fell from the men's hands, their hearts stopped,
And they couldn't keep their limbs from trembling.
The serpent twists its scaly coils in slithering loops,
Springs himself into a huge arching bow,
And with more than half its length erect in the air
Peers down on the whole forest, his body as large,
If you could take it all in, as the Serpent that lies   50
Outstretched in the sky between the two Bears.
Whether the Phoenicians were preparing for fight
Or flight, or were simply frozen with fear,
We do not know. The serpent attacked instantly,
Killing some with its fangs, others in its coils,
And blasting some with its poisonous breath.

The zenith sun had contracted the shadows.
Cadmus wondered what was keeping his men
And went after them. He wore a lion's skin
And carried a spear with a gleaming iron tip   60
Along with a javelin, and better than any weapon,
He had a brave heart. When he entered the forest
And saw his men's bodies, saw their conqueror
Hulking hugely above them and licking
Their lamentable wounds with his bloody tongue,
"Loyal bodies," he said, "either I avenge your death
Or join you." And he lifted a massive stone
In one hand and put all his weight into the throw.
It would have been enough to make city walls
And their high towers quake, but the serpent escaped   70

Unscathed, protected from that mighty blow
By his armored scales and tough skin beneath.
But that dark, hard skin could not stop the javelin,
Which now stuck in a fold of the serpentine back,
The iron slicing down to the guts. Mad with pain,
He twisted his head toward the wound and bit the shaft
Until he finally worked it loose and tore it out,
But the iron head remained stuck in the spine.
Fresh motivation enhancing his usual rage,
The veins bulge in his throat, and white foam flecks   80
His deadly jaws. His scales rasp against the ground,
And a black breath, as if from the mouth of the Styx,
Fouls the tainted air. He coils in huge spirals,
Rears up straighter than a post, then rushes forward
Like a rain-swollen river, plowing down
All the trees in his path. The son of Agenor
Gives way a little, survives the serpent's attacks
By virtue of the lion's skin and keeps his jaws at bay
With the point of his spear. The serpent is furious,
Snaps uselessly at the iron and clamps it in his teeth.   90
Blood begins to flow from the venomous throat
And stains the green grass, but the wound is slight
Because the serpent keeps drawing back from the thrust,
Protecting his neck and preventing the spear point
From sinking in deeper and being driven home.
But the son of Agenor keeps pushing the iron
Into his throat until at last an oak tree
Blocks the serpent's retreat and his neck is pinned
Against the hardwood. Branches bend under his weight,
And the trunk groans as it is lashed by his tail.   100

As the conquering hero surveys the expanse
Of his conquered foe, a voice makes itself heard,
Impossible to say from where, but a real voice:

"Why, Cadmus, do you gaze at a slain serpent?
You will be gazed at as a serpent yourself."

He stood there a long time, trembling and drained,
The hair on his skin stiff with cold terror,
And then Pallas, helper of heroes, floating down
From the high air, was there, commanding him
To turn the earth and sow the dragon's teeth,   110
And so generate a new people. He obeyed,
And when he had opened a furrow with his plow
He started scattering in the teeth as human seed.
And then, beyond belief, the ground begins to move.
At first the points of spears appear from the furrows,
And then helmets nodding their colored crests;
Soon shoulders and chests come up, and arms
Loaded with weapons, a whole crop of warriors,
Just as when the curtain comes up in a theater
At the end of a festival and its pictures rise,   120
First revealing faces and then gradually the rest
With a steady motion, until whole figures appear
And place their feet on the curtain's lower edge.

Alarmed by this new enemy Cadmus began to arm,
When one of the earthborn people shouted,
"No! Do not get involved in our civil war!"
As his sword came down on one of his brothers
He himself went down with a spear in his back,
But the one who had thrown it lived no longer himself,
Breathing out the air that had just filled his lungs.   130
In the same way the entire mob raged, and they fell
In their war, brothers of a moment killing each other,
Youths with brief lives allotted beating the breast
Of Mother Earth, who grew warm with their blood.
Only five were left, one of whom, Echion,
Dropped his weapons at the command of Pallas
And pledged peace with his surviving brothers.
These men became the Sidonian's companions
When he founded the city foretold by Apollo.

And now Thebes stood, and you could seem, Cadmus,   140
Happy even in exile. The parents of your bride

Were Venus and Mars, and your children were worthy
Of so noble a mother, so many sons and daughters
To remind you of your love, and grandsons too,
Already young men. But a man's last day
Must always be awaited, and no one counted happy
Until he has died and received due burial.

Diana and Actaeon

Your first reason to grieve, Cadmus, amid
So much happiness, was your grandson Actaeon.
Strange horns grew on his forehead, and his hounds   150
Glutted themselves on the blood of their master.
But if you look well you will find the fault was Fortune's,
Not Actaeon's sin. What sin is there in error?

The mountain was stained with the slaughter of beasts,
Noon had already contracted the shadows,
And the sun was midway between both horizons,
When the imperturbable young Boeotian
Spoke to his hunting companions as they wandered
The trackless wild:
                    "Our nets and blades are wet with blood.
The day has brought us enough luck. When Aurora   160
Rolls in another dawn on her saffron wheels
We'll go at it again. But now Phoebus
Is in midcourse and splits the fields with heat.
Call it a day and bring in the nets!"
                                        The men
Did as he said and left off their work.

There was a valley there called Gargaphië,
Dense with pine and bristling cypress, and sacred
To Diana, the high-skirted huntress. Deep in the valley
Is a wooded cave, not artificial but natural,
But Nature in her genius has imitated art,   170
Making an arch out of native pumice and tufa.
On the right a spring of crystal-clear water

Murmured as it widened into a pool
Edged with soft grass. Here the woodland goddess,
Weary from the hunt, would bathe her virgin limbs.
When she arrives there she hands her spear and quiver
And unstrung bow to one of her nymphs. Another
Takes her cloak over her arm, two untie her sandals,
And Crocale, cleverer than these, gathers up
The goddess' hair from her neck and ties it in a knot   180
While her own is still loose. Nephele, Hyale,
Rhanis, Psecas, and Phiale draw water
And pour it from huge urns over their mistress.

While Diana was taking her accustomed bath there,
Cadmus' grandson, his work done for the day,
Came wandering through the unfamiliar woods
With uncertain steps and, as Fate would have it,
Into the grove. As soon as he entered the grotto,
The nymphs, naked as they were and dripping wet,
Beat their breasts at the sight of the man, filled the grove   190
With their sudden shrill cries, and crowded around
Their mistress Diana, trying to hide her body with theirs.
But the goddess stood head and shoulders above them.
Her face, as she stood there, seen without her robes,
Was the color of clouds lit by the setting sun,
Or of rosy dawn. Then, though her nymphs pressed close,
She turned away to one side and cast back her gaze,
And, as much as she wished she had her arrows at hand,
What she had, the water, she scooped up and flung
Into that male face, sprinkling his hair with vengeful drops   200
And adding these words that foretold his doom:
"Now you may tell how you saw me undressed,
If you are able to tell!" With that brief threat
She gave his dripping head the horns of a stag,
Stretched out his neck, elongated his ears,
Exchanged feet for hands, long shanks for arms,
Covered his body with a spotted hide,
And instilled fear in him. Autonoë's heroic son
Took off, marveling at how fast he was running.

But when he saw his face and horns in a pool,   210
He tried to say, "Oh, no," but no words came.
He groaned, the only sound he could make,
And tears ran down cheeks no longer his own.
Only his mind was unchanged. What should he do?
Return home to the palace, or hide in the woods?
Shame blocked one course, and fear the other.

While Actaeon hesitated his dogs spotted him.
First Blackfoot and keen-nosed Tracker bayed,
Tracker a Cretan, a Spartan breed Blackfoot.
Then others rushed at him swifter than wind,   220
Greedy, Gazelle, and Mountaineer, Arcadian all,
Powerful Deer Slayer, Hunter, and Whirlwind.
Then Wings, and Chaser the bloodhound, and Woody,
Lately gored by a boar, and wolf-bred Valley,
Trusty Shepherd and Snatcher with both her pups.
There was lean Catcher, a Sicyonian hound,
Runner and Grinder, Spot and Tigress,
Mighty and Whitey and black-haired Soot.
These were followed by Spart, known for his strength,
And by Stormy and Swift and the speedy Wolf   230
With her brother Cypriot. Next was Grasper,
A white spot in the middle of his jet-black forehead,
Blacky and Shaggy and Fury and Whitetooth,
With a Cretan sire and a Spartan dam,
Bell-toned Barker—and others we need not name.
The whole pack, lusting for prey, gave chase
Over cliffs and crags and inaccessible rocks,
Where the way was hard and where there was no way.
He fled through places where he had often chased,
And it was his own hounds he fled. He longed to shout: 240
"I am Actaeon! Know your master!"
But words wouldn't come, and the sky rang with barking.

Blackhair bit him in the back, then the bitch Killer,
Then Hill got hold of a shoulder and wouldn't let go.
These three had left late but got ahead of the others

By a shortcut over the mountain. While they held
Their master down, the rest of the pack converged
And sank their teeth into him. Soon there was no place
Left on his body to wound. He groans, making a sound
That is not human, but still not one any deer could make,   250
And fills the familiar ridges with his mournful cries.
On his knees now, he turns his silent eyes
From side to side, as if he were a suppliant
Stretching out his arms. And now the ravenous hounds
Are urged on by his friends, who know no better,
With their usual yells, looking around for Actaeon,
And outdoing each other with their shouts, "Actaeon!"
As if their friend were absent. He turns his head
At the sound of his name, but they go on complaining
That he is not there and through his sluggishness   260
Is missing the spectacle their prey presents.
He wishes he were absent, but he is there alright,
And would rather see than feel what his dogs are doing.
They are all over him, their jaws into his flesh,
Tearing apart their master in a deer's deceptive shape.
They say that Diana's anger was not appeased
Until he ended his life as a mass of wounds.

Jupiter and Semele

Opinion is divided: to some the goddess
Was unjustly vindictive for simply being seen;
Others praise her and call her violence worthy   270
Of her severe virginity. Both sides have a case.
Only Jupiter's wife neither praises nor blames
So much as she is glad that the house of Agenor
Has suffered catastrophe. By now the goddess
Had shifted her hatred of Europa to those
Connected to her Tyrian rival by birth.
Then another grievance ousted the old one,
The fact that Semele was pregnant by Jove.
As she warmed up her tongue for her usual reproaches,

It hit her:

            "What have I ever gained from reproaches? 280
It's her I have to get if I am rightly to be called
Juno most great, if I am to hold the jeweled scepter,
If I am the queen, the wife and sister of Jove—
Well, the sister at least. . . . But then I think she is content
With her little secret, a minor dent in my marriage,
Which would be fine if she were not pregnant!
That is what really damages me—the swollen belly
That makes her crime visible. And that she wants
What I have barely achieved, to be the mother
Of Jupiter's child. She trusts her beauty that much. 290
I'll make that trust betray her. I am not Saturn's daughter
If her precious Jove doesn't plunge her into the Styx."

She rose from her throne and, wrapping herself
In an ochre cloud, she came to Semele's door
And stayed in the cloud until she disguised herself
As an old woman grey in the temples, plowing
Wrinkles into her skin and walking bent over
With faltering steps. Assuming also the voice
Of an old woman, she became Beroë,
Semele's Epidaurian nurse. Gossiping on, 300
Jupiter's name came up, and the disguised goddess sighed,

"I hope he really is Jupiter. I mistrust things like that.
Many men have gone into chaste girls' bedrooms
Under the name of a god. And it's not enough
For him to be Jove. He has to give proof of his love
If it really is him. Ask him to embrace you
In the same form, the same size, as Juno herself
Receives him—and with all the marks of his power."

This is how Juno set up the guileless Semele,
Who asked Jove for a gift yet to be named, 310
To which request the god responded,

"Choose,
And you shall not be refused. Believe me:
I swear by the powers of the churning Styx,
Whose divinity all the gods hold in awe."

And Semele, happy to have prevailed
In what would be her destruction, and doomed
By her lover's compliance, said to him,

"Give yourself to me in just the same form
As you have when you and Juno make love."

The god wanted to stop her in midsentence,   320
But the words were already out. He groaned.
She cannot retract her wish, nor he his oath,
And so in utter gloom he ascends the steep sky.
Lifting an eyebrow he draws in mists and clouds
And brews up a storm with wind and lightning,
Taking up last the inevitable thunderbolts.
As best he could, he reduced his potency,
Choosing not, for instance, the bolts that blasted
Typhoeus from heaven, bolts far too lethal,
But a lighter bolt the Cyclopes had forged,   330
One with less firepower and containing less ire;
Ordnance Number Two the gods all call it.
Taking one of these he entered the palace
Of the son of Agenor. Semele's mortal body,
Unable to endure the celestial explosion,
Was incinerated in the conjugal embrace.
The tender babe, still unformed, was snatched
From his mother's womb, and, if it can be believed,
Sewn into his father's thigh, where he was brought to term.
His mother's sister, Ino, secretly cradled him,   340
And then he was given to the nymphs of Nysa,
Who hid him in their cave and nursed him with milk.

Tiresias

While Fate worked itself out on earth in this way,
And the cradle of twice-born Bacchus was safe,
They say that Jupiter, soused with nectar,
Put aside his grave concerns and joking around
With an idle Juno said to her, "Your sex's pleasure
Is clearly greater than any felt by males."
She said no, and so they agreed to ask Tiresias
His opinion, familiar as he was with either sex.   350
For he had once struck with his staff two great serpents
As they were mating in the greenwood,
And, transformed amazingly from man to woman,
Spent seven autumns in that state. In the eighth
He saw the same two snakes again and said,

"If hitting you has power sufficient
To change the sex of the author of the blow,
I'll strike you again now."
                              The vipers being struck,
His former form returned and he was himself again.
Chosen as arbiter of this lighthearted spat,   360
He confirmed Jove's opinion. Saturnian Juno,
Taking it harder than the case warranted,
Condemned the umpire to everlasting blindness.
The Almighty Father could not render null and void
Another god's decree, but in recompense
For his loss of sight, gave Tiresias the power
To see the future, lightening the penalty
With this honor. He went on to be celebrated
Throughout the cities and towns of Boeotia
For the faultless responses he gave to petitioners.   370

Echo and Narcissus

The first to test the truth of his utterances
Was Liriope, a water-blue nymph
Caught by Cephisus in a bend of his river

And prevailed upon by force. When this beauty
Gave birth, it was to a child with whom even then
One could fall in love. She called him Narcissus.
When Tiresias was asked if this boy would live
To a ripe old age, the soothsayer replied,
"If he never knows himself." The seer's words
Long seemed empty, but the outcome—the way he died,   380
The strangeness of his passion—proved them to be true.

Narcissus had just reached his sixteenth birthday
And could be thought of as either a boy or a man.
Many a youth and many a girl desired him,
But in that tender body was a pride so hard
That not a youth, not a girl ever touched him.
Once, when he was driving spooked deer into nets,
He was seen by a nymph who could not stay quiet
When another was speaking, or begin to speak
Until someone else had—resounding Echo.   390

Up until then Echo had a body, not just a voice,
But talkative as she was she could only speak
As she does now, repeating the last words said.
Juno had made her like this because many times
When she might have caught Jove on top of some nymph
Up in the hills, Echo would cleverly detain the goddess
In long conversation until the nymph had fled.
When Saturn's daughter realized this, she said,
"This tongue that has tricked me is hereby restricted
To only the briefest use of speech."
                              The outcome   400
Confirmed her threat, and Echo can only repeat
The final words of whatever she hears. Now,
When she saw Narcissus wandering the countryside
She flushed with love and followed him secretly.
The more she followed him, the hotter she burned
From his proximity, the way sulphur smeared
On the top of a torch ignites when a lit torch

Is brought close to it. Ah, how often she wishes
She could go up to him with seductive words
And whisper prayers in his ear, but her nature   410
Won't let her, or even allow her to initiate talk.
But what it will allow she is prepared for:
To wait for words she might return as her own.
So when the boy, separated by chance
From his loyal companions, cried out, "Anyone here?"
"Here," Echo responded. Narcissus was puzzled.
He looked around in every direction and shouted
"Come!" and "Come!" Echo calls to the caller.
He looks behind, sees no one coming, calls again,
"Why run from me?" and gets his own words back.   420
He stands still, beguiled by the answering voice,
And cries, "Meet me here; I'm here!" And Echo,
Never again to answer a sound more gladly, cries,
"I'm here!" and follows up her words by coming
Out of the woods to throw her arms around
The neck she longed for. He runs, and says on the run,
"Take your hands off! I'll die before I let you have me!"
And Echo comes back with nothing but "Have me!"
Rejected, she lurks in the woods, hiding her shamed face
In the leaves, and lives from then on in lonely caves.   430
Still, love clings to the spurned girl and grows on grief.
Sleepless and anxious, she begins to waste away;
Her skin shrivels and her body dries up, until
Only her voice and bones are left, and then
Only her voice. They say her bones turned into stone.
She hides in the woods, and is seen no more in the hills
But can be heard by all, and lives on as sound.

So Narcissus mocked this girl, as he had mocked
Others before, nymphs of water and mountain,
And the company of men. One of these scorned youths   440
Lifted his hands to the heavens and prayed,
"So may he himself love, and not get what he loves!"
A just prayer, to which Nemesis assented.

There was an unsullied pool with silvery water
That no shepherds used, no pasturing goats
Or any other cattle, and that no bird or beast
Or even falling twig ever caused to ripple.
It was surrounded with grass fed by its moisture
And shaded by trees that kept it from getting too warm.
Narcissus, worn out and hot from hunting,   450
Lies down here, drawn by the setting and the pool,
And, seeking to quench his thirst, finds another thirst,
For while he drinks he sees a beautiful face
And falls in love with a bodiless fantasy
And takes for a body what is no more than a shadow.
Gaping at himself, suspended motionless
In the same expression, he is like a statue
Carved from Parian marble. Prone on the ground
He looks at the double stars that are his eyes,
His hair, worthy of Bacchus, worthy of Apollo,   460
His impubescent cheeks, his ivory neck, the glory
That is his face, the blush mixed with snowy white,
And admires all for which he is himself admired.
He desires himself without knowing it is himself,
Praises himself, and is himself what is praised,
Is sought while he seeks, kindles and burns with love.
How often did he offer ineffective kisses
To the elusive pool? How often plunge his arms
Into the water to clasp the neck he saw there
And fail to take hold of himself? He does not know   470
What he sees, but what he sees he burns for,
And the same illusion lures and lies to his eyes.
Gullible boy, grasping at passing images!
What you seek is nowhere. If you look away
You lose what you love. What you see is a shadow,
A reflected image, and has nothing of its own.
It comes with you and it stays with you,
And it will go with you, if you are able to go.

No thought of food, no thought of rest can draw him
Away from that spot. Sprawled on the shaded grass   480

He gazes at the mendacious vision with eyes
That cannot get enough and through which he perishes.
Lifting himself up a little and stretching his arms
To the surrounding trees, he cries,
                    "Is there anyone,
O trees, who has ever been more cruelly in love?
You know, for you've been convenient cover
For many couples. Do you remember
In ages past (for your life spans centuries)
Anyone who has ever pined away like this?
I'm in love and I see him, but what I see and love   490
I cannot find. What a deluded lover!
And to make it worse for me, no great ocean
Separates us, no road, no mountain, no shut city gates.
A little water keeps us apart!
                    He wants to be held.
Whenever my lips approach the limpid water,
He tries to come to me with his face upturned.
You'd think he could be touched, so small a thing
Stands in the way of our love.
                  Whoever you are,
Come out! My looks and my age can't be the sort
You would shun. Even nymphs have been in love with me.   500
You give me some cause for hope with your friendly smile,
And when I stretch out my arms, you stretch yours, too.
When I smile, you smile back, and I have often seen
Tears in your eyes when I am in tears. When I nod
You do too, and from the way your lovely lips move
I suspect you answer my words as well, though yours
Never reach my ears.
           Oh—that's me! I just felt it,
No longer fooled by my image. I'm burning with love
For my very own self, burning with the fire I lit.
What should I do? Beg or be begged? Why beg at all?   510
What I desire I have. Abundance makes me a beggar.
Oh, if only I could withdraw from my body, and—
Strange prayer for a lover—be apart from my beloved.
And now I'm growing weak with grief; not much time

Is left for me, and I will die in the prime of my life.
Death is not heavy for me, but the end of my sorrows.
I wish that my beloved could live longer, but now
We two die with one heart, and in the same breath."

He spoke and, beside himself with grief, turned
To the same face again, but his tears disturbed the pool,　　520
And the reflection was lost in the troubled water.
When he saw the image disappearing, he cried,

"Where are you going? Stay! It would be cruel
To desert your lover. Let me at least look at
What I cannot touch, and feed my obsession."

As he grieved, he opened the top of his tunic
And beat his bare breast with his ashen hands.
His chest took on a roseate glow, just as apples
Can be pale in one part and flush red in another,
Or as grapes in a cluster begin to turn purple　　530
As they are just getting ripe. When he saw this
In the water, after it had again become clear,
He could bear no more, and as yellow wax melts
Over a gentle flame, or frost in the morning sun,
So too Narcissus, thin and meager with love,
Melts and is consumed by a slow, hidden fire.
No longer is his color a blushing white,
He no longer has his old vigor and power
And all that made him so beautiful to see—
Not at all the same body that Echo once loved.　　540
When she saw him now, though she was still angry,
She grieved for him, and whenever the poor boy said,
"Alas," her responsive voice repeated, "Alas."
And when his hands beat on his shoulders and arms,
She gave back the sound of his lamentation.
His last words were, as he gazed into the pool,
"Ah, loved in vain, beloved boy," and the place
Rang with these words. And when he said good-bye,

Echo said good-bye too. His weary head drooped
To the green grass, and death closed the eyes   550
That had gazed in wonder at their master's beauty;
And even after he had gone to the world below,
He kept gazing at himself in the waters of Styx.
His naiad sisters beat their breasts, cut their hair
For their brother, and the dryads, too, lamented,
And all the sounds of woe were repeated by Echo.
And now they were preparing the funeral pyre,
Shaking the torches and readying the bier,
But Narcissus' body was nowhere to be found.
In place of his body they found a flower   560
With white leaves surrounding a saffron center.

Pentheus and Bacchus

News of this spread the seer's reputation
Throughout Greece's cities and exalted his name.
Echion's blasphemous son, Pentheus,
Was the only man who held him in contempt.
He mocked the old man's prophetic words, even
Taunted him with his blindness. But Tiresias
Just shook his greying head and told him,

"Better for you if you were deprived of this light
So you would never see the rituals of Bacchus,   570
For the day will come, and I foresee it is near,
When the new god will come here, Semele's son,
Liber. If you do not honor him with worship,
You will be torn into a thousand pieces
And scattered all over, and your blood will defile
The woods, your mother, and your mother's sisters.
It will happen! For you shall deny the god honor
And complain I have seen too well in this darkness."

Echion threw him out while he was still speaking,
But his words came true; the prophecy was fulfilled.   580

Now the god Liber is here, and the fields resound
With the noise of festivities. Crowds of people
Rush out, men and women of all ages, nobles
And plebeians all milling together
To the strange new rites. Pentheus cries to them all,

"What madness has stricken you, Sons of the Serpent,
Children of Mars? Do you think clashing cymbals,
Curved hornpipes, magic tricks, women's shrieks,
Drunken lunacy, obscene mobs, and booming drums
Can overcome men who do not flinch in war   590
When trumpets blare and swords are drawn in battle?
I am surprised that you elders, who made the long
Sea voyage and founded Tyre here, established here
Your city's exiled Penates, now permit them
To be taken without a fight! And you young men,
More of my generation, who once thought it fit
To bear arms and not wands tipped with pinecones,
To wear helmets on your heads instead of grape leaves,
Remember, I beg you, from what stock you come,
And show a little of the spirit of the Serpent,   600
Who by himself killed many. He died fighting
For his spring and his pool, but you will prevail
Fighting for your glory! He killed brave men.
All you have to do is rout men who are women
And save your ancestral honor. If the Fates forbid
Thebes to stand for long, I would rather that men
Destroy her walls with roaring fire and iron.
We would be wretched then, but without dishonor,
Have a fate to bewail but not to conceal,
And our tears would not have the taint of shame.   610
But now Thebes will be taken by an unarmed boy
Without weapons of war or cavalry. No,
His weapons are pomaded hair, delicate garlands,
Robes embroidered with purple and gold!
But I will soon force him—just you stand aside—
To admit that his father's name is assumed
And his sacred rites a sham. If Acrisius

Was spirited enough to despise his false godhood
When he came to Argos, and keep the gates closed,
Should Pentheus and all Thebes tremble at him?   620
Go quickly," he ordered his guards, "bring him here,
Bring him back bound—and don't dawdle at it!"

His grandfather, and Athamas, and all his men
Worked hard to dissuade him and hold him back,
But he became more fanatical when he was warned.
His madness grows rabid when it's restrained
And attempts to curb it only make it worse,
Like a stream I saw once that flowed smoothly along
When nothing obstructed it, but when dammed
With timber and stone became a seething torrent.   630

Now the guards are back, covered with blood
And explaining that they never saw Bacchus,
But, "We got one of his devotees," they said,
And handed him over, hands bound behind him,
An Etruscan and follower of the god's sacred rites.
Pentheus looked at him with eyes full of anger,
And though it meant delaying his punishment, said,

"You're about to die and serve as an example,
But first tell me your name, your parents' name
And country, and why you follow this strange new cult."   640

Acoetes

"My name is Acoetes," he said, "and my country
Is Maeonia. My parents were simple people.
My father left me no fields or bulls to plow them,
No flocks of wooly sheep, no cattle at all.
He was poor himself and used to catch fish
With hook, line, and rod, and draw them in leaping.
His craft was all he had, and when he passed it on
He said to me, 'Take what I have, use it,
And be my successor and heir.' When he died

He left me nothing but water, my only inheritance.   650
Not wanting to be stuck on the same rocks forever,
I learned how to steer ships, studying the stars,
Capella, the Pleiades, the Hyades, the Bears.
I learned the winds' directions, the best harbors.
En route to Delos once, I was driven off course
To the shore of Chios and made land with oars,
Leaping onto a wet beach where we spent the night.
When dawn began to redden I rose and told the crew
To haul in fresh water, pointing out a path to the spring.
Myself, I observed the wind from a hilltop   670
Then called the men and started back to the ship.
'Here we are,' called Opheltes, the ship's first mate,
Leading along the shore a prize, as he thought of it,
That he had found in a deserted field, a little boy
As beautiful as a girl. He staggered along
As if he were sleepy, or drunk. I gazed at him,
His face, clothes, his gait, and everything I saw
Seemed more than mortal, and I said as much:
'I don't know what divinity is in this body,
But there is a divinity! Whoever you are,   680
Be gracious to us all, and pardon these men.'
'Don't pray for us!' This was said by Dictys,
Who could climb to the topmost yard and slide
Down the ropes faster than anyone. Libys
Seconded this, as did Melanthus, the blond lookout,
And both Alcimedon and Epopeus, who marked time
For the rowers and called out encouragement.
The others all chimed in, all out of blind greed.
'Still, I won't allow this ship to be profaned,'
I said. 'And I have the most authority here.'   690
So I'm blocking their boarding, when Lycabas,
The most reckless of them, a murderer
Exiled from Tuscany for an appalling crime,
Starts working his knuckles into my throat
And would have thrown me overboard, but I
Somehow kept my grip on a rope. The godless crew
Was cheering on Lycabas, when Bacchus—

That's who it was—as if wakened by all the noise
Or coming out of a drunken stupor, said,

'What are you doing? What's all this shouting?   700
And you sailors, how did I get here, and where
Are you planning to take me?'
                        Proreus answered,
'Don't be afraid. Just tell us what port you want,
And you can disembark wherever you like.'
'Sail for Naxos,' Liber said. 'That's where I'm from,
And you'll find it to be hospitable too.'
And the treacherous crew swore by the sea
And all its gods that it would be done, and ordered me
To get our painted ship out to sea. Naxos
Lay off to the right, and as I was trimming the sails   710
To head off that way, Opheltes said to me,
'What are you dong? Are you crazy?' Everyone
Said the same thing, 'Head left,' most of them
Signaling me with nods, some whispering in my ear.
I was stunned, and said to them, 'Someone else
Will have to captain.' And I removed myself
From playing any part in their wicked scheme.
The whole crew jeered me, muttering curses,
And Aethalion said, 'As if our whole safety
Depended on you alone!' And he came up   720
And took over my job, leaving Naxos at our stern.
Then the god, toying with them, as if he had just now
Discovered their treachery, looked out to sea
From the curved prow and, pretending to cry, said,

'These are not the shores you promised me, sailors,
And this is not the land I asked for. What have I done
To deserve this? And what glory will you get
If grown men cheat a boy, many against one?'

I had long since been weeping, but the godless crew
Mocked our tears as they beat the sea with their oars.   730
Now I swear by that god—and no god is closer—

That what I am saying is true, however beyond belief.
The ship stands still in the water, just as if
She were in dry dock. The astounded crew
Keep pushing the oars and spread sail as well
Hoping to get running again under double power.
But ivy twines around the oars and, looping around,
Creeps up the mast and festoons the sails
With heavy clusters of grapes. The god himself,
Brow circled with clustering berries, waves a wand   740
Wreathed with ivy. Around him lie tigers, lynxes
And (all just phantoms) fierce spotted panthers.
The men, driven mad, panicking, jump overboard.
Medon's body was the first to turn black
And his back to be bent into an arching curve.
Lycabas started to say, 'What kind of monster
Are you turning into?' but as he was speaking
His own jaws widened, his nose flattened out,
And his skin became hard and covered with scales.
Lybis was still trying to row the recalcitrant oars   750
When he saw his hands suddenly shrink in size
To what had now to be called not hands, but fins.
Another one, trying to catch hold of a rope,
Finds he has no arms, and his truncated body
Goes sailing backward into the sea, his tail
Curved at the end like a crescent moon's horns.
They leap up around the ship, scattering spray
When they break the surface, then dive down again,
Flipping their bodies like a troupe of dancers
And spouting seawater from their broad nostrils.   760
The ship had held a crew of twenty men
And I alone was left. As I stood there trembling,
Hardly myself, the god gave me courage, saying,
'Shake off your fear and set a course for Naxos!'
When we got there I joined the devotees of Bacchus."

Then Pentheus said,
                    "We have lent our ears
To these long ramblings knowing our anger

Might lose strength from delay. Off with him,
Torture him mercilessly, and send him down
To Stygian night."
         And so Acoetes   770
The Tyrrhenian was dragged out and locked
In a strong dungeon. But while fire and iron,
The instruments of torture, were being prepared,
All on their own the prison doors flew open,
And the chains dropped from the prisoner's arms.

This did not stop Pentheus. He no longer
Sent envoys but went himself to where Cithaeron,
The chosen site for the rituals, resounded
With the shrill ululations of the Bacchic women.
As a spirited horse snorts and lusts for combat   780
When a brass trumpet signals the start of battle,
So too the cries pulsing in the air stir up Pentheus,
Whose wrath glows white-hot when he hears the noise.

Halfway up the mountain was an open plain
Bordered with woods and in full view from all sides.
It was here that Pentheus, spying on the rites
With profane eyes, was first spotted by his mother,
Who was also the first to rush madly at him,
First to throw her thyrsus at her son, crying,

"Come, my sisters! See that enormous boar   790
Roaming our field? He's going to get it from me!"

The whole mad throng bear down on the terrified man,
Terrified, and speaking less hostilely now,
Cursing himself and confessing his sins.
Wounded, he manages to say, "Please help me,
Aunt Autonoë! Remember poor Actaeon!"
She has no idea who Actaeon is, and tears off
The suppliant's right arm. Ino in her rapture
Tears off the left. The poor man has no arms now
To stretch out to his mother, but he shows her   800

The gaping wounds where his arms used to be,
Crying, "Mother, look!" Agave howls at the sight
And whips her hair around in the wind. Then,
Tearing off his head, she holds it in her bloody fingers
And shouts, "Sisters, see what I've done, see what I've won!"
Leaves touched by frost are not more quickly whirled
From the high branches to which they barely cling
Than the man is dismembered by their impious hands.
The Thebans, thus put on notice, flock to the new rites,
Offer incense, and worship the god at sacred altars.   810

Book 4

The Daughters of Minyas

But not Alcithoë, one of Minyas' daughters.
She rejected the god's orgiastic rites,
Even denied that Bacchus was Jupiter's son,
And her sisters shared her impiety.
The priest had ordered a Bacchic festival,
With female servants to be released from work,
And their mistresses to wear animal skins,
Loosen their hair and weave it with flowers
And have in hand a vine-wreathed thyrsus.
And he prophesied that the wrath of the god   10
Would be severe if he were slighted.
Matrons and young wives all obeyed, setting aside
Their looms and baskets and unfinished wool
To burn incense and summon Bacchus, calling him
Bromius, Lyaeus, son of heaven's fire, twice-born
Son of two mothers, Nyseus, unshorn Thyoneus,
Lenaeus, genial vine planter, Nyctelius,
Father Eleleus, Iacchus, Euhan,
And all the names you have throughout Greece,
O Liber. For yours is youth without end,   20
You are the child eternal, most lovely in heaven,
Your head most pure when you appear without horns,
Conqueror of the East even unto the bounds
Where brown India is bathed by the Ganges.
You killed Pentheus, O Lord, and axe-wielding Lycurgus,
Blasphemers both, hurled the Tuscan sailors
Into the sea. You drive a chariot drawn
By lynxes harnessed in bright-colored reins.
Maenads and satyrs follow behind, and that old man,
Drunk with wine, staggers along with a staff,   30
Clinging weakly to a rickety jackass.
Wherever you go you are cheered by the young,
And women's voices blend with the sounds
Of tambourines, of drums and long reed flutes.

"O, be with us, most merciful and mild,"
The Theban women pray as they perform the rites.
Minyas' daughters alone remain inside,
Unsettling the festival with the untimely work
Of the goddess Minerva, spinning wool,
Thumbing the thread as it turns, staying close   40
To the loom, and keeping the women on task.
One of the sisters, deftly drawing out thread,
Says to the others,
                        "While other women
Are neglecting their work and running in droves
To those so-called rituals, why don't we,
Devotees of Pallas, a truer divinity,
Lighten the useful work of our hands
And make the time go by telling stories?
We could all take turns."
                        Her sisters agree
And ask her to start. She thought for a while   50
Of which story to tell, for she knew quite a few.
Perhaps she should tell the tale about you,
Decretis of Babylon, who the Palestinians say
Changed into a fish all covered with scales
And swam in a pool; or how her daughter spent
The last years of her life perched on towers,
Clad in white feathers; or how a certain naiad
Used incantations and powerful herbs
To turn boyish bodies into mute fish
And finally became one herself; or how a tree   60
That once bore white fruit now yields fruit darkened
With the stain of blood. She liked this last one
Because it was not yet well known, and so she began,
Telling her yarn while her wool spun into thread:

Pyramus and Thisbe

"Pyramus and Thisbe, he the loveliest of boys,
She the most beautiful girl in the Orient,
Lived next door to each other in the steep city

They say Semiramis encircled with walls of brick.
Proximity led to their early acquaintance;
Love grew with time; and they would have married,   70
But their parents forbade it. What they could not forbid
Was the mutual passion they felt for each other.
There was no go-between; their talk was nods and gestures,
And the more the fire was covered, the hotter it burned.
There was a slender chink in the common wall
Between the two houses, from when they were built.
No one had noticed this crack in all these years—
But what does love not see? You lovers discovered it
And made it a channel for speech. Your loving words
Would slip safely through it in the softest whispers.   80
Often, when they had moved into place, Thisbe here,
Pyramus there, and each had felt the other's breath,
They would say,
                    'Jealous wall, why do you stand
Between lovers? Would it be asking too much
For you to let us embrace, or at least open enough
To allow us to kiss? Not that we are ungrateful.
We owe it to you, we admit, that our words
Have passage to the ears that long to hear them.'

So they would talk in frustrated separation,
And when night came on they said 'Good-bye,'   90
Each pressing their lips on one side of the wall,
Kisses that did not go through to the other side.
The next dawn had banished the stars of night,
The sun's rays had dried the frosty grass,
And the lovers came to their accustomed place.
After many whispered complaints the pair decided
That they would try to slip past their guardians
In the still of night, and when they were outdoors
They would leave the city as well. And they agreed,
So as not to be wandering around in the fields,   100
To meet at Ninus' tomb and hide under its tree.
The tree there was full of snow-white berries,

A tall mulberry tree next to a cool spring.
They liked the plan. The light seemed to last forever,
Then sank into the waters from which night arose.

Stealthily cracking open the door Thisbe sneaks out
Through the shadows with veiled head, comes to the tomb
And sits beneath the appointed tree. Love made her bold.
But now here comes a lioness, her jaws smeared
With the blood of cattle she's just killed, on her way   110
To slake her thirst at the spring. Babylonian Thisbe
Sees her far off by the light of the moon
And runs on trembling feet into a dark cave,
And as she runs her cloak slips off her back.
When the savage lioness has drunk her fill
She turns back to the woods and happens upon
The cloak (without the girl in it) and shreds it
In her bloody jaws. Coming out a little later,
Pyramus sees the tracks the lioness left
In the deep dust. The color drains from his face,   120
And when he finds the cloak too, smeared with blood,

'One night,' he cries, 'will be the death of two lovers,
But of the two she was more deserving of life,
And mine has done all the harm. I have destroyed you,
Poor girl, telling you to come by night to this place
Full of terror, and not coming first myself!
Come and tear my body apart, devour my flesh,
Gulp down my guilty heart with your savage jaws,
O all of you lions who have lairs in this cliff!
But it is cowardly just to pray for death.'   130

He picked up Thisbe's cloak and carried it
To the shade of the trysting-tree. And while
He kissed and shed tears upon the garment
He knew so well, he cried, 'Drink my blood too!'
Drawing the sword that hung by his waist,
He drove it down deep into his flank, then, dying,
Withdrew it from the hot wound. As he lay

Stretched out on the earth his blood spurted high,
Just as when a lead pipe has sprung a leak
At a weak spot, and through the hissing fissure   140
Long jets of water shoot far in the air.
The fruit on the tree, sprinkled with Pyramus' blood,
Turned dark; and the tree's roots, soaked with his gore,
Dyed the mulberries the same purple color.

And now Thisbe, still afraid, but anxious too
That her lover will miss her, comes back from the cave,
Seeking Pyramus with her eyes and her soul
And excited to tell him about her brush with death.
She recognizes the place and the shape of the tree,
But the color of the fruit makes her wonder   150
If this is really it. While she hesitates, she sees
A body writhing on the blood-soaked ground.
She stepped back, her face paler than boxwood,
Shivering like the sea when a light breeze
Grazes its surface, but when, a moment later,
She recognized her lover, she slapped her guiltless arms
In loud lamentation and tore her hair out,
And holding his beloved body she filled his wounds
With her tears, mingling them with his blood,
And as she kissed his cold lips, she wailed,   160

'Pyramus, what happened, what took you from me?
Answer me, Pyramus. It's your dearest Thisbe
Calling you. Please listen, please lift up your head.'

At Thisbe's name, Pyramus lifted his eyes,
Heavy with death, saw her, and closed them again.
Then she noticed her cloak, and saw his ivory scabbard
Without his sword in it, and said,
                                        'Your own hand,
And your love, killed you, poor boy. I, too, have a hand
Brave for this one deed; I too have love, and it will give me
The strength to face wounds. I will follow you in death,   170
And I will be called the most wretched cause

And companion of your death. Death alone
Could tear you from me, but not even death will.
And I pray to my wretched parents and to his
On behalf of both of us: do not begrudge
A common tomb to those whom faithful love
And death's final hour have joined. And you, O tree,
Whose branches now cover one pitiful body
And soon will cover two, keep our death's tokens
And always have fruit that is dark and mournful   180
As a memorial to the blood that we both shed.'

She spoke, and placing the point beneath her breast
She fell onto the blade, still warm with her lover's blood.
Her prayers touched the gods and touched their parents,
For mulberries turn dark red when they ripen,
And the lovers' ashes rest in a single urn."

The story ended, and after a short intermission
Leuconoë began while her sisters listened:

Mars and Venus

"Even the Sun, who rules heaven with his light,
Has fallen in love, and his loves are my tale.   190
The Sun, they say, was the first immortal to see
Mars and Venus in bed. He sees everything first.
Disturbed by this, he told Vulcan that Venus
Was cheating on him, and showed him where. Vulcan
Was stunned. Dropping whatever he was working on,
He crafted a net of fine bronze mesh, so subtle
It could not even be seen, more tenuous
Than the finest woolen weave, wispier
Than the web a spider drops from the rafters,
And he fashioned the net so that it would conform   200
To the slightest touch, the least little movement.
Then he spread it adroitly over the bed,
And when the married goddess got in with her lover
They became enmeshed in each other's arms
And her cunning husband's ineluctable trap.

Vulcan abruptly threw the ivory doors open
And let the other gods in. There the two lay
In shameful bondage, and one of the gods,
Who were in a good mood, said he wouldn't mind
Suffering such shame. The other gods laughed,   210
And the story became a classic in heaven.

Leucothoë and the Sun

The Cytherean certainly did not forget
Who told on her, and got back at him
For ruining her love affair by ruining his.
Son of Hyperion, what good is your brightness,
Your radiant beauty? You inflame all lands
But are yourself inflamed by an unfamiliar fire,
And your eyes, which should be watching the world,
Are fixed on a single girl, Leucothoë.
You rise too early in the eastern sky   220
And sink too late in the western waves, prolonging
The short winter hours by gazing at her.
Sometimes you fade out, when your fretful mood
Blots your eyes, a darkness terrifying to human hearts.
It is not the moon passing between you and earth
That dims your face: it is that love of yours.
She alone is your chosen one. Clymene
No longer appeals, nor that girl from Rhodes,
Nor Circe's mother, beautiful as she is,
Nor Clytië, who, though rejected by you,   230
Is still smitten and wants to lie in your bed.
Leucothoë makes you forget them all.
Most beautiful Eurynome gave birth to the girl
In the land of sweet scents, and when she grew up,
The daughter eclipsed her mother in beauty
As much as her mother surpassed all the rest.
Her father, Orchamus, ruled over Persia,
Seventh in succession from ancient Belus.

Under the western sky there lies a pasture
For the horses of the Sun. There they browse   240

Not on grass but ambrosia to restore their strength
After a long day's work. While his horses were here
Munching celestial fodder, and Night began her shift,
The god entered the chambers of the girl he loved,
Assuming the form of her mother, Eurynome.
There was Leucothoë sitting in the lamplight
Among twelve handmaidens, spinning fine woolen yarn.
He kissed her as a mother would a dear daughter
And said,

> 'I would like a private word, and so you
Won't intrude on a mother's right to tell secrets   250
You servants may retire.'

> They promptly obeyed
And with no witnesses left in the room,

'I am he,' said the god, 'who measures the year,
Who sees all things, and by whom the earth sees all—
The eye of the world. And you please me well.'

She was trembling with fear. Distaff and spindle
Dropped from her fingers. But fear became her,
And he waited no longer to resume his true form
And usual radiance. This sudden apparition
Terrified the girl, but the god's splendor won out,   260
And she endured his advances without any complaint.

Clytië and the Sun

Clytië was jealous, for her passion for the Sun
Had not diminished, and now she was furious
That she had a rival. She told everyone,
And especially Leucothoë's father,
About her shameful affair. He flew into a rage
And did not relent when she prayed, or stretched
Her hands to the Sun, or pleaded, 'He forced me,'
And brutally buried her deep in the earth,
Heaping a mound of heavy sand on top.   270
The son of Hyperion bored through with his rays
And made a passage through which you could push

Your buried head, but it was too late, O nymph,
For you to lift your head, and there you lay,
A bloodless corpse. They say the driver
Of the soaring chariot had seen nothing more pitiful
Since Phaëthon's fiery death. He tried indeed
To revive her cold limbs, using his warmth
To coax her back to life, but since Fate opposed him,
He sprinkled her body with aromatic nectar   280
And after reciting a litany of grief,
He said, 'At least you will still reach the upper air.'
As soon as it absorbed the celestial nectar
The body melted away, scenting the ground
With its fragrance, and a shrub of frankincense,
Deeply rooted, slowly rose through the soil
And pushed its head through the top of the mound.

But Clytië, though love could excuse her pain
And pain her snitching, was no longer an object
Of the Sun's affection. And so she pined away,   290
And her love drove her mad. Enduring the clouds
And exposed to the rain, she sat under the open sky
Day and night on the ground, head bare and unkempt.
For nine days, without food or drink, living on dew
And her own tears, she did not move from the ground,
Only gazed on the face of the circling god,
Bending her own face around. They say that her limbs
Became rooted in the soil, and they say her ghostly pallor
Changed in part to a bloodless plant, but in part turned red,
And a flower much like a violet covered her face.   300
Still, though firmly rooted, she turns toward the Sun,
And though changed herself, she preserves her love."

The marvelous tale had enchanted the sisters.
Some said such things could never happen, others
That true gods can do anything, but that Bacchus
Is not one of them. After they grew quiet,
Alcithoë went next. Running her shuttle
Through the threads of her loom, she began:

"As to the well-known love life of Daphnis,
The shepherd from Ida whom a jealous nymph   310
Turned into a stone, I have little to say.
Such grief does inflame lovers. Nor will I tell you
How Sithon, in a stunning reversal of natural law,
Was sometimes a woman, sometimes a man;
Nor how you, Celmis, now adamantine,
Were once the best friend of a very young Jove;
Nor how the Curetes were born from a cloudburst;
And I will also pass over how Crocus and Smilax
Were changed to tiny flowers. I will instead
Hold your attention with a sweet novelty.   320

Salmacis and Hermaphroditus

Learn now why the infamous spring of Salmacis
Enervates men who bathe in its waters. The cause
Is hidden, but the font's power well-known.
Mercury and Venus had a little boy
Whom naiads nursed in the caverns of Ida.
You could tell from his face who his parents were,
And he was named after both his mother and father.
When he turned fifteen he left his native mountains
And nourishing Ida. Exploring new places
And seeing unknown rivers was all his joy,   330
His enthusiasm making light of the toil.
He even reached Lycia and neighboring Caria,
And there he saw a pool of crystal water,
Clear to the bottom. There were no marsh reeds,
Barren sedge or rushes, only translucent water
Edged with fresh turf and grass verdant year-round.
A nymph lived in that pool, a nymph not inclined
To hunt or shoot arrows or go racing along,
The only naiad unknown to Diana.
Her sisters were always saying to her,   340
'Salmacis, pick up a javelin or a painted quiver
And vary your leisure with a little hard hunting.'
But she did not pick up a javelin or painted quiver
Or vary her leisure with any hard hunting.

She only bathes her beautiful limbs in her pool;
Often arranges her hair with a boxwood comb;
Looks into the water to see what becomes her;
Wraps her body in a transparent robe
And reclines in the leaves or on the soft grass.
She also picked flowers, and was picking flowers   350
When she saw the boy and wanted to have what she saw.

But, eager as she was, she didn't go up to him
Until she composed herself, looked at her robes
From all angles, touched up her face, and did
Everything she could to look beautiful.
Then she said:
                    'Boy or god? If you are a god
You must be Cupid. But if you are a mortal
Blessed be your parents, your brother, your sister,
If you have one, and the woman who nursed you.
But happier than any of these is your bride to be,   360
If there is any girl you think worthy. If there is one,
Let me steal my pleasure. If there is no one yet,
Let me be the one, and let's get married right now.'

The naiad fell silent. A blush crossed the boy's cheeks,
For he knew nothing of love, but it was a becoming blush,
The color of apples ripening in a sunny orchard,
Of dyed ivory, or the moon's scarlet glow
When bronze cymbals clash to end an eclipse.
When the nymph kept begging for a sister's kiss
At least, and was twining her arms around   370
His ivory neck, he cried out, 'Just stop!
Or I'll leave this spot, and leave you with it.'
Salmacis trembled and said, 'It's all yours,'
And turning away, pretended to leave.
But she kept looking back, and hid in a thicket,
Crouching on one knee. He, as a boy will
Who thinks he's alone, explored the green bank
And dipped first his toes in the ripples, and then
His feet up to the ankles. Finding the water

Enticing, and just the right temperature,   380
He slipped the clothes from his supple body.
The nymph was spellbound, burning with passion,
And her eyes now were as bright as sunlight
Reflected in a mirror. She could barely endure
Any more delay, any further deferral of joy,
And was out of her mind with desire to hold him.
The boy, clapping his body with cupped palms,
Dove in quickly and began swimming the crawl,
His body gleaming in the translucent water
As if it were an ivory figurine, or a lily   390
Encased in glass.
                         'I've got him now!' cried the nymph,
As she threw off her clothes and dove into the pool.
He tries to hold her off as she steals contested kisses,
Runs her hands down his body, fondles a reluctant breast,
Enfolds him on one side and then on the other.
Finally, as he struggled to release himself,
She twisted around him as if she were a snake
Snatched by an eagle up into the sky:
Hanging from his claws the snake slithers around
The raptor's head and feet and entangles his wings;   400
Or as if she were ivy entwining a tree trunk;
Or an octopus holding its prey undersea
With its tentacles wrapped completely around it.
The boy hung in there and denied the nymph
The pleasure she hoped for, and yet she held on tight,
As if her whole body were welded on to his,
'You may fight me, you little rascal,' she said,
'But you'll never escape. Gods, may the day not dawn
That will separate him from me or me from him!'
Her prayer was answered. Their bodies were blended   410
Into one face and form. Just as when a twig
Is grafted onto a tree, you can see two branches
Mature into one, so too these bodies fused
In tenacious embrace, not two, not double,
Neither woman nor man, and yet somehow both.

When he saw that the waters he entered as a male
Had left him half a man and softened his limbs,
Hermaphroditus stretched out his hands and cried
In a voice no longer manly,
    'Father and Mother,
Grant to the son who bears both of your names   420
That whoever enters this pool as a man
Comes out as a half man, weakened by the water.'

His parents blessed the words of their biform son
And drugged the pool to engender confusion."

The Daughters of Minyas Become Bats

The story was over, but the daughters of Minyas
Worked on, spurning the god and his festal rites.
Suddenly, unseen timbrels assaulted their ears
With raucous sound, along with curved cornel flutes
And tinkling bronze. Saffron and myrrh
Scented the air, and, straining belief,   430
The warp on the loom turned green; the hanging cloth
Changed into ivy, part into grapevines; threads
Became tendrils; the weft sprouted grape leaves,
And clusters of grapes empurpled the fabric.
The day was already at an end, a time
That you could not say was either bright or dark,
Night's borderland perhaps, but still with some light.
Suddenly the house's rafters seem to tremble,
The oil lamps flare up, the whole building
Blazes with ruddy flames, and ghost animals   440
Fill the rooms with their howls. The sisters
Scatter to hide in the smoke-filled house,
Scurrying to different rooms to escape
The glaring flames, and while they seek cover,
A membrane spreads over their slender limbs,
Sheathing their arms with papery wings. The darkness
Prevents them from knowing how they have changed.

They have no feathers, yet they are borne aloft,
Sustaining themselves on translucent pinions.
They try to speak, but their tiny voices match   450
Their shrunken bodies, and they squeak with anguish.
They inhabit houses, not forests, and hating
The light of the sun they flit about in the evening,
Twilight creatures that are called vesper bats.

Athamas and Ino

No Theban now doubted Bacchus' divinity,
And Ino, his aunt, was always telling stories
About the new god's power. Of all her sisters
She alone escaped grief, except for the grief
Her sisters caused her. Proud of her children,
Of her marriage to Athamas, and proud above all   460
Of her divine foster child, she was seen by Juno
As intolerable. The goddess said to herself:

"That whore's son has the power to transform
Maeonian sailors and throw them into the sea;
To have a son ripped to shreds by his own mother;
To enfold Minyas' three daughters with batwings,
And all Juno can do is bemoan her grievances
Still unavenged? Is that enough for me?
Is that all the power I have? But he himself
Teaches me what to do. Learn from your enemy.   470
He has demonstrated the power of madness
More than sufficiently. Why should not Ino, too,
Be driven mad, and go where her sisters have led?"

There is a downhill path shrouded with yew trees
That leads through dead silence to the realms below.
The sluggish Styx exhales its vapor there,
And the newly dead, their funeral rites done,
Go down that way to an immense wasteland,
Dim and cold and full of decay. The new shades
Struggle to find the road to the Stygian city   480

And the grim palace of the Dark Lord, Dis.
This city has a thousand wide entrances
And the gates are always open. As the sea
Receives rivers from all over the earth,
This place receives all the souls of the dead,
Never too small for its rising population,
A place that never feels crowded. Bloodless shades
Without body or bones wander around. Some
Mill about in the forum, some in the palace;
Some busily imitate whatever they did   490
In their old lives, and some are being punished.

Saturnian Juno, leaving her place in heaven,
Had the fortitude to go there—hatred and wrath
Meant that much to her. When she made her entrance
And the threshold groaned under her sacred body,
Cerberus' three throats bayed thrice in unison.
The goddess summoned the daughters of Night,
The implacable Furies, grim in their godhead.
They were seated before the closed, adamantine gates
Of Hell's prison, combing black snakes from their hair.   500
When they recognized Juno coming through the gloom,
The goddesses rose.
                          This place is called Damned,
Where Tityos, stretched out over nine acres,
Has his liver lacerated; where your lips,
Tantalus, can never touch the water, and the tree
Above you is always just out of reach. Here Sisyphus
Shoves his stone uphill and goes back to retrieve it;
Ixion wheels around in self-pursuit and self-flight;
And Belus' granddaughters, who dared to murder
The cousins they had wed, fetch water forever.   510
Saturnia frowned at all of these, but especially
At Ixion, and then looking back at Sisyphus, said,
"Why does this one, of all his brothers, suffer
Eternal torment, while Athamas struts
In a royal palace? Athamas, who with his wife
Holds me in scorn?" And she goes on to explain

The reasons for her hatred, why she has come,
And what she wants. She wants the house of Cadmus
To fall, and for the Furies to make Athamas
Criminally insane, and she solicits their aid,   520
Blending high command with promises and pleas.
When Juno was done speaking, Tisiphone,
Just as she was, shook her disheveled grey hair,
And tossing back a straggling viper or two, said,

"There is no need to ramble on. Consider it done,
Whatever you want. Now leave this hellhole
And go back to the lovelier air of the sky."

Juno went back happy, and as she entered heaven
Iris sprinkled her with water as pure as dew.

Tisiphone wasted no time. She grabbed a torch   530
That had been drenched in gore, put on a robe
Dripping red blood, cinched it with a writhing snake,
And sallied forth. She was accompanied by Grief,
By Terror and Dread, and by quivering Madness.
When she stood on the threshold of Athamas' house,
They say the very doorposts cowered before her,
The maple doors lost their luster, and the sun went out.
Ino was terrified, as was her husband, Athamas.
They tried to run from the house, but the Fury opposed,
Blocked their way, extending her serpent-twined arms   540
And shaking out her hair. All the snakes there,
And those draping her shoulders and coiled in her bosom,
Hissed, spewed out gore, and flicked their tongues.
Her putrid hand tore two from her hair and threw them,
One each, onto Ino and Athamas. The serpents slithered
Over their breasts and breathed evil vapors
Into their very souls. Their bodies were unwounded;
It was their minds that felt an insidious blow.
The Fury's accoutrement included horrible poisons,
Spittle from Cerberus' jaws, venom from Echidna,   550

Along with hallucinations, spells of oblivion,
Crying jags, crime, rabies, and bloodlust,
All brewed together in a brazen cauldron
And laced with fresh blood and green hemlock juice.
As Ino and Athamas stood there quivering,
Tisiphone poured this maddening concoction
Over their chests and made it sink down
Deep into their hearts. Then she whirled her torch
Around and around to make a moving wheel of fire,
And, her mission accomplished, the Fury returned   560
To great Pluto's kingdom of shadows
And unbound the snake she had used as a sash.

Athamas immediately began to rave
In his great hall, "Spread the nets in these woods!
I just saw a lioness here with two cubs!"
And insanely followed the tracks of his wife
As if she were a beast. His son Learchus
Laughing and stretching out his little arms,
Athamas snatched from his mother's bosom
And spun him through the air two or three times   570
Just as if he were whirling a sling, then madly dashed
The baby's head against a hard rock. Ino herself
Now went over the edge, whether grief
Had driven her mad, or the drenching poison.
She began to howl and in her demented state
Ran off bearing you, little Melicertes,
In her naked arms, hair streaming in the wind
And shouting, "Io, Bacchus!" Juno smiled
At the name of Bacchus and said scornfully,
"May your foster son ever serve you like this!"   580
There was a cliff overhanging the sea,
Its base hollowed by the waves, and its flinty top
Jutting far out over the open water.
Ino climbed up here (madness gave her the strength)
And, slowed by no fear, leapt with her burden
Out over the deep. The impact made a little white splash.

But Venus, pitying her granddaughter's
Undeserved suffering, entreated her uncle:

"O god of the sea, Neptune, whose power
Is closest to heaven's, the favor I ask for   590
Is great, to be sure, but please be merciful
To these, my loved ones, whom you see plunged
In the vast Ionian Sea, and add them to your gods.
The sea owes me something, if it is true
I was born in the foam of your divine depths,
And my name in Greek comes from that conception."

Neptune nodded, and subtracted what was mortal
From mother and son, making them beings
Worthy of worship, and as he changed their forms
He changed their names too, calling the new god   600
Palaemon, and his mother Leucothoë.

Juno and the Theban Women

The Theban women followed Ino's footprints
As best they could, and saw from the cliff's edge
Her final act. Believing her dead, they beat their breasts
In mourning for the house of Cadmus, tore their hair
And their garments, and rebuked Juno, calling her
Unjust and too cruel to her rival in love.
Juno found their reproaches unwelcome, saying,
"I will make you my cruelty's greatest memorial."
No sooner said than done. The most devoted   610
Of Ino's women cried, "I will follow my queen
Into the sea!" and as she was about to leap
She could hardly move at all, rooted to the rock.
Another, lifting her arms to beat her breasts,
Felt her lifted arms grow stiff. One had happened
To stretch her hands out to the waters below
And now held them outstretched as a figure of stone.
And one over here, tearing hair from her head,
You could see with stiff fingers still in her hair.

Whatever gesture these women were caught in,   620
There they remained. Others were changed into birds
And skim those waters with their wings to this day.

Cadmus and Harmonia

Agenor's son Cadmus did not know that his daughter
And little grandson were now sea gods. Overwhelmed
By the string of disasters, the suffering he had seen,
He now left the city he had founded, as if
The place itself and not his own misfortunes
Were weighing upon him. His long wandering
Took him and his wife to Illyria's borders,
Where, sad and old, they thought of their family's   630
Original destiny and rehearsed their sorrows.
Cadmus said,
              "That serpent I pierced with my spear
Must have been sacred. There I was, fresh from Sidon,
And I scattered its teeth, a strange seed, on the earth.
If that is what the gods have been avenging
In their terrible anger, may I lay out my length
As a long-bellied snake."
                        And as he spoke, he did
Lay out his length as a long-bellied snake
And felt his skin turn into hard black scales
Checkered with blue. As he lay on his stomach   640
His legs fused together and tapered to a point.
What was left of his arms he stretched out to his wife,
And with tears running down his still human cheeks,

"Come here," he said, "my poor, ill-starred wife,
While there is still something left of me. Come here
And touch me, hold my hand while it is still a hand,
While the serpent has not yet usurped me completely."

He wanted to say much more, but suddenly
His tongue was forked and words wouldn't come,
And even plaintive sounds came out as a hiss,   650

The only voice that his nature allowed him.
Then, striking her naked breast with her hands,
Harmonia cried out,
                    "My poor Cadmus, wait!
Shake this off, this monstrosity! Cadmus,
What is it? Where are your feet, your hands,
Your shoulders, your face, your color—everything
Changing as I speak? Change me as well, you gods,
Into this same serpentine form!"
                                She spoke,
And his tongue flickered over the face of his wife,
And he slid down between the breasts that he loved,   660
And his embrace sought the neck he knew so well.
Their companions were horrified, but Harmonia stroked
The glistening neck of the crested serpent,
And suddenly not one but two snakes were there,
Their coils intertwined, until they sought the shelter
Of the neighboring woods. And even now as serpents
They neither avoid people nor try to harm them,
Quietly remembering what they once were.

Perseus and Andromeda

A great consolation to them in their altered form
Was their grandson, worshipped now in conquered India,   670
And adored as well in Achaean temples.
Only Acrisius, son of Abas, born
Of the same stock as the god, still banned him
From his city, Argos, campaigning against him
And refusing to admit he was Jupiter's son.
Nor would he admit that Perseus, whom Danaë
Had conceived in golden rain, was Jupiter's son.
But truth has its own power, and Acrisius
Soon regretted that he had repulsed the god
And not acknowledged his grandson. The one   680
Had now been installed in heaven; the other
Was soaring through thin air on whistling wings,
Bearing the snake-haired monster's memorable spoils.

As the victor hovered over the Libyan desert
Bloody drops from the Gorgon's head fell down
And were received by Earth, who reanimated them
As various species of snakes, and this is why
The land there swarms with poisonous vipers.

From there he was driven by conflicting winds
Like a raincloud through vast regions of air.   690
He flew over the whole world, looking down
From dizzying heights on distant lands. Three times
He saw the cold stars of the Bears, and thrice
The Crab's claws. He was blown more than once
Beyond the western horizon, and into the east,
And now as the day faded, wary of the night
He put down in the farthest reaches of the west,
In Atlas' kingdom, hoping to catch a few hours sleep
Before the Morning Star summoned Aurora
And Aurora in turn the chariot of Day.
                              Here Atlas,   700
Son of Iapetus, who for sheer bulk
Exceeded all men, ruled the edge of the world
And the sea that welcomes the Sun's panting horses
And his weary chariot. He had a thousand flocks,
And as many herds of cattle, wandering
Grassy plains that stretched on without borders.
And there was a tree whose golden leaves
Concealed golden branches and apples of gold.

"My lord," Perseus said to him, "if high birth
Carries any weight with you, mine is from Jupiter;   710
Or if you admire great deeds, you'll admire mine.
I ask for hospitality and a place to rest."

But Atlas remembered an ancient prophecy
Given to him by Themis on Mount Parnassus:
"Atlas, a day will come when your tree will be stripped
Of all its gold, and a son of Jupiter will take the credit."
Fearing this, Atlas had enclosed his orchard

With massive walls, and set a huge dragon to guard it,
And he kept all strangers away from his borders.
Now he said to Perseus,
                              "Get out of here,   720
Or your supposed glory and that Jupiter of yours
Will be long gone."
                              His heavy hands backed up
The threat with force. Perseus interspersed
Gentle words into his heroic resistance,
But finding himself outmanned (who could outman
Atlas himself?) he said to him,
                              "Well, now,
Since you are able to show me so little kindness,
Here's a little kindness for you!"
                              And turning away,
He held out on his left the horrible head
Of the Gorgon Medusa. As big as he was,   730
Atlas immediately turned into a mountain
Of just the same size. His hair and beard
Were changed into trees, and into ridges
His shoulders and hands. What had been his head
Was now a summit, and his bones became stones.
Then every part grew to an enormous size—
For you gods wished it so—and the entire sky
With all its many stars now rested upon him.

Aeolus, son of Hippotas, had confined the winds
Under Mount Etna, and the Morning Star,   740
Who rouses us to work, shone brightest of all
In the eastern sky. Perseus strapped on
His feathered sandals, slung on his scimitar,
And cut through the pure air in a blur of winged feet.
Leaving in his wake innumerable nations,
He now had a clear view of Ethiopia
And the lands of Cepheus. There Jupiter Ammon
Had unjustly ordered that innocent Andromeda
Pay the penalty for the arrogant tongue

Of her mother, Cassiopeia.
        When Perseus,   750
Abas' great-grandson, first saw her chained to the rock,
He might have thought she was a marble statue,
Except that a light breeze was rippling her hair,
And warm tears flowed down from her eyes. Perseus
Was stunned. Entranced by the vision
Of the beauty before him, he almost forgot
To keep beating his wings. As soon as he had landed,
He said,
     "Surely you do not deserve these bonds,
But those that tie true lovers together. Please,
Tell me your name, and the name of your country, 760
And tell me why you are wearing these chains."

At first she was silent, a virgin not daring
To address a man, and out of modesty
She would have hidden her face with her hands
If they had not been fastened behind her.
All she could do was let her eyes fill with tears.
Only when he had asked again and again,
And only because she did not wish to create
The impression of concealing a fault of her own,
Did she tell him her name, the name of her country, 770
And how overconfident her mother was
In her own beauty. The girl was still speaking,
When the sea roared, and a monster rose from the deep,
Breasting the waves as it came toward the shore.
The girl screamed; her grieving father and mother
Stood at her side, both wretched, the mother perhaps
With more justification. They bring no aid,
Only tears and laments to suit the occasion
As they clasp her fettered body. Then the stranger speaks:

"There will be plenty of time for tears later,   780
But only a brief hour to come to the rescue.
If I asked for this girl's hand as Perseus,

Son of Jupiter and that imprisoned Danaë
Whom the god impregnated with his golden rain;
The Perseus who conquered the snake-haired Gorgon;
Who braved the stratosphere on soaring wings—
Surely I would be preferred to all other suitors
As your son-in-law. Now, if the gods favor me,
I will try to add meritorious service
To what else I bring, my bargain being   790
That the girl, saved by my valor, will be mine."

Her parents accept the proposal (who would refuse it?)
And promise a kingdom, as well, for a dowry.

Behold now the monster cutting through the waves
Like a warship driven to ramming speed
By the sweat-covered arms of a crew of rowers.
When it was as far from the cliff as a Balearic sling
Can fire a lead bullet through the air, the young hero
Pushed off hard and ascended high among the clouds.
When the shadow of a man appeared on the water,   800
The sea monster savaged the apparition;
And, as Jupiter's eagle, when it sees a snake
Sunning its mottled back in an open field,
Seizes it from behind, eagerly sinking its talons
Into its scaly neck lest it twist its fangs back,
So the descendant of Inachus, swooping down
Through empty space, attacked the bellowing monster's back,
Poised at its right shoulder, and buried his curved blade
Up to the hilt in its neck. Gravely wounded,
It reared high in the air, then dove underwater,   810
And then turned like a boar when a pack of hounds
Is baying around it. Perseus evaded
The snapping jaws on flashing wings, his scimitar
Slashing the monster wherever it was exposed—
Its barnacled back, its ribcage, and where its spine
Tapered into the tail of a fish. The beast belches
Seawater mixed with purple blood, and Perseus' wings

Are becoming so soggy with all the spume
That he can no longer trust them. He spots
A ledge exposed when the sea is calm, but hidden   820
Whenever the waves run high. He steadies himself here,
Taking hold of the rock face with his left hand,
And plunges his sword three times and once more
Into the monster's gut.
                    The shore is filled
With wild applause that reaches the heavens.
Cassiopeia and Cepheus rejoice
And hail Perseus as their son-in-law,
The pillar of their household and its savior.
Forth from her chains steps Andromeda unbound,
The motive for Perseus' feat and the prize.   830
The victor washes his hands in a basin of water,
And so the hard sand won't hurt that viperous face,
He makes a bed of leaves, strews seaweed on top,
And rests upon this the head of Medusa,
Daughter of Phorcys. The seaweed's porous tendrils
Absorb the monster's power and congeal,
Taking on a new stiffness in their stems and leaves.
The sea nymphs test this wonder on more tendrils
And, delighted to find the result confirmed,
Scatter these tendrils as seeds in the sea.   840
Even now coral has retained this property,
So that its stems, pliant under water,
Turn to stone once exposed to the air.

Perseus now builds three turf altars, one for each
Of three gods: the left for Mercury, the right
For you, virgin warrior, the center for Jove.
He sacrifices a heifer to Minerva,
A calf to the winged god, and to you,
O greatest of gods, a bull. Then he claims
Andromeda, without a dowry, as the reward   850
For his heroic act. Hymen and Amor
Shake the marriage torches; the fires are fed
With rich incense; flowers hang from the roofs;

Lyre, flute, and chorales permeate the air,
Giving sweet testimony of joyful hearts.
The massive double doors swing open to reveal
The golden central court with tables already set,
And noble Ethiopians stream in to the banquet.

When they had finished the feast and their spirits
Were swimming in wine, Bacchus' generous gift,   860
Perseus inquired about the local customs,
Who the people were and what they were like.
The guest who answered said to him in turn,

"Now tell us, Perseus, by what prowess, what arts,
You made off with that head and its curls of snakes?"

And so the hero in the line of Agenor
Told them about a cave hidden in the rock
Under the frozen slopes of Atlas. At its entrance
The Graiae lived, twin daughters of Phorcys,
Who shared the use of a single eye, which the hero   870
Cleverly stole as they passed it back and forth.
Then he made his way through trackless lands,
A barren landscape of blasted trees and rocks,
To where the Gorgons lived. In the fields there
And along the paths he saw the shapes of men
And of animals who had been changed to stone
By Medusa's gaze. But he managed to glimpse
Her dread form reflected in the polished bronze
Of a circular shield strapped to his left arm.
And while the snakes and Medusa herself   880
Were sound asleep, he severed her head from her neck,
And the winged horse Pegasus and his brother,
The warrior Chrysaor, were born from her blood.

He went on to tell of his long journeys
And the dangers he faced—all of this true—
The seas and the lands he had seen far below,
And the stars he had brushed with his beating wings.

When he finished his tale they still wanted more,
And one of them asked why Medusa alone
Among her sisters had snakes in her hair.   890
The guest replied:
             "Here's the reason, a tale in itself.
She was once very beautiful and sought by many,
And was admired most for her beautiful hair.
I met someone who recalled having seen her.
They say that Neptune, lord of the sea,
Violated her in a temple of Minerva.
The goddess hid her chaste eyes behind her aegis,
But so that the crime would not go unpunished,
She changed the Gorgon's hair to loathsome snakes,
Which the goddess now, to terrify her enemies   900
With numbing fear, wears on her breastplate."

Book 5

Perseus and Phineus

While Danaë's heroic son was speaking
Among the Ethiopians, the royal halls
Were filled with an uproar, not the kind of sound
That goes with marriage songs, but that announces
Armed strife. The feast was in sudden tumult,
Not unlike the sea when raging winds
Roughen its quiet water to churning waves.
Front and center was Phineus, the king's brother
And a born troublemaker, brandishing an ash spear
Tipped with bronze.

         "Take a good look," he said,   10
"At the man who will avenge the theft of his bride.
Your wings won't get you out of this, nor will
Jupiter, changed to fool's gold!"

         He was on the verge
Of hurling his spear when Cepheus cried out:

"What are you doing, brother? What madness
Is driving you to crime? Is this how you repay
Extraordinary service? Is this the dowry
For saving the girl's life? If you want the truth,
It was not Perseus who took her away from you,
But horned Ammon, the Nereids' dread deity,   20
And the sea monster who came to glut himself
On my own flesh and blood. It was when she was
Doomed to death that you lost her, unless perhaps
It is her death now that you cruelly demand,
To ease your grief with mine. It was not enough
For you to look on without lifting a finger
While she was being chained, uncle though you were
And promised husband. No, you'll take it hard
That someone did save her, and rob him of his prize.
If the prize seemed so great, you should have taken it   30
From the rocks where it was chained. Now let the man
Who did take it—and saved me from a childless old age—

Keep what he has earned and has been promised him,
A man preferred not to you but to my daughter's death."

Phineus said nothing, but kept shifting his gaze
Between Cepheus and Perseus, undecided
Where to aim his spear. After a short delay
He hurled it at Perseus with all the strength
Wrath could give it, but the throw came to nothing,
And the spear stuck in the bench. Perseus then   40
Furiously returned the throw and would have hit Phineus
Right in the heart, but the wretch had sought refuge
Behind the altar and unworthily found it there.
But the weapon still had some effect, hitting Rhoetus
Full in the face. Rhoetus went down, and when the spear
Was yanked from the bone, he thrashed about
And his blood spattered the banquet tables.
The mob got into it now, tempers flaring,
Spears flying around, and some saying that Cepheus
Should go down with his son-in-law. But the king   50
Had already withdrawn from the palace,
Calling to witness Justice and Faith, and all the gods
Who protect strangers and guests, that this was done
Under his protest. And then Pallas was there,
The warrior goddess, shielding her brother
Behind her aegis and giving him courage.

There, too, was an Indian boy, whom Limnaeë,
A nymph of the Ganges, is said to have borne
Under her glassy stream. His outstanding beauty—
He was a well-knit sixteen—was enhanced   60
By his rich attire: a gold-fringed purple mantle,
A golden necklace, and a circlet of gold
Clasping his hair, which was perfumed with myrrh.
He could hit quite distant targets with a javelin
But was even better with his bow, which he was now
In the act of bending, when Perseus snatched up
A torch smoldering on the altar and used it
To crush the boy's face into splintered bones.

When his companion Lycabas, an Assyrian
Close to the boy and his avowed true lover,   70
Saw him gasping out his life through that bitter wound,
His exquisite features now a mass of blood,
He wept aloud for his beloved Atthis,
And then picked up the bow that the boy had bent
And cried,
              "It's between you and me now,
And you won't have long to celebrate a death
That brings you contempt rather than glory."

His words weren't out before the piercing arrow
Flashed from the string, but it only hung up
In a fold of Perseus' robe. Acrisius' grandson   80
Turned upon Lycabas the sickled sword
That had seen Medusa off and drove it home
Into his chest. But even as he was dying,
His eyes swimming in the dark, he looked around
For Atthis, and let his body fall down beside him,
Taking to the shadows the consolation
That they had been together even in death.

Then Phorbas of Syenes, Metion's son,
And Libyan Amphimedon, eager to fight,
Slipped on the blood that covered the floor   90
And went down hard. As they tried to get up
The sword came down, through the ribs of the latter
And through Phorbas' throat.
                          When Perseus encountered
Actor's son, Eurytus, who swung a broad battle-axe,
He sheathed his scimitar and lifted high with both hands
A huge mixing bowl, embossed and massive,
And flung it at the man. He spewed up red blood
As he lay on his back, and in his death throes
He beat the floor with his head.
                          Then Perseus killed
Polydaemon, a descendant of Semiramis,   100
Abaris from the Caucasus, Lycetus,

Whose home was near the Spercheios River,
Unshorn Helices, Phlegyas, and Clytus,
As he slogged his way through heaps of the dying.

Phineus did not dare to close with his enemy
But threw another javelin, which hit Idas
By accident. Favoring neither side,
Idas had kept out of the fight, but now,
Glaring at the unsympathetic Phineus,
He said,
   "Since I'm forced into this, Phineus,   110
You have a new enemy. It's wound for wound now."

And just as he was about to hurl back the spear
He had pulled from his own body, he collapsed,
All of the blood having drained from his limbs.

Then Hodites, the foremost Ethiopian
After the king, fell to Clymenus' sword;
Hypseus hit Prothoënor; and Lyncides,
Hypseus.
   There was one old man there,
Emathion, who loved justice and feared the gods.
Too old for battle, he fought with his tongue now,   120
And strode forward cursing their iniquitous arms.
As he clung to the altar with trembling hands
Chromis' sword lopped off his head, which fell
Down on the altar, and kept uttering curses
With its half-alive tongue until it exhaled
The last of its life amid the sacred fires.

Two brothers next fell by Phineus' hand,
Broteas and Ammon, invincible boxers,
If only they could outbox swords. Ampycus
Fell also, Ceres' priest, temples bound in white;   130
And you fell also, Lampetides, a musician
Invited to grace the feast with your lyre

And sing the festal song.
                        As he stood to one side
Holding a peaceable quill, Petalus mocked him:
"Sing the rest of your song to the Stygian shades!"
And he drove his spear through Lampetides' temple.
His dying fingers touched the strings of his lyre
And as he fell there arose a few plaintive notes.

Enraged at the sight, Lycormas would not let
His death go unavenged. Prying a heavy bar   140
From the right doorpost he broke Petalus' neck;
The man sank to the earth like a slaughtered bull.
Cinyphian Pelates, trying to pry
Another bar from the doorpost's left side,
Had his good right hand pinned to the wood
By the spear of Corythus of Marmarida.
Stuck like that, Abas drilled him; he did not fall
When he died, but hung from the post by his hand.
Melanius, one of Perseus' men, went down,
As did
           Dorylas, the richest man in Nasamonia—   150
An extensive estate, huge stores of spices—
With a spear in his groin entering from the side,
A fatal spot. The spear had been cast
By Halcyoneus of Bactria, who said
As he watched Dorylas rolling his eyes
And coughing up his life,
                              "Of all your lands,
The land you lie on is all you have now."

And he left the bleeding body. Perseus
Lost no time avenging him, pulling the spear
From the still warm wound and driving it into   160
Halcyoneus' nose, down through his neck
And out the other side. While he had a lucky hand
He dispatched Clytius and Clanis,
Born of one mother, with two different wounds,

Stitching Clytius' thighs with a mammoth spear thrust,
And shoving another down Clanis' throat.
Other casualties were Mendesian Celadon;
Astraeus, born of a Syrian mother,
Father unknown; Aethion, formerly a seer,
Who did not see this coming; Thoactes,   170
The king's armor-bearer; and Agyrtes,
Whose fame was that he had killed his father.

There were many more left for the exhausted hero,
United in their will to obliterate him
In a cause that rejected fidelity and honor.
On his side stood his loyal but helpless
Father-in-law, his new wife and her mother,
Filling the hall with their quavering shrieks,
Which were drowned out by the sound of clashing arms
And the groans of men dying, while Bellona   180
Drenched with blood the polluted household gods
And did all she could to keep the battle going.

Perseus, surrounded by a thousand men
With Phineus at their head—spears flying
Thicker than winter hail past flanks, eyes, ears—
Stands with his back against a great stone column
And, protected in this way from the rear, faces
The oncoming onslaught. Chaonian Molpeus
Leads the attack on the left, and on the right
Ethemon of Arabia. Just as a hungry tigress   190
Hears bulls bellowing in two separate valleys
And cannot decide which one to rush upon
But burns to rush upon both, so too Perseus
Did not know whether to strike right or left.
He went with Molpeus, wounding him in the leg,
And then let him go because Ethemon was on him,
Going for his neck with a swing of his sword,
Strong but poorly aimed, and hitting instead
The edge of a column. The blade broke off

And stuck in the man's throat, not deeply enough   200
To kill him outright but leaving him standing there
Trembling and stretching out his empty hands
As Perseus gutted him with Mercury's sword.

But when the hero saw strength yielding to numbers,
"Since you force me to," he cried, "I will enlist the aid
Of my enemy. Hide your face if you are a friend."
And he lifted high the head of the Gorgon.
Theseclus shouted at him,
                           "Go work your miracles
On somebody else,"
                        and raising his lethal javelin
Adhered to this pose as a marble statue.   210
Ampyx was next, thrusting his sword at Perseus' heart,
But in midthrust his right hand stiffened and froze.
Then Nileus, who lied that he was born of the Nile,
And who had its seven mouths engraved on his shield
In silver and gold, cried,
                           "See, O Perseus,
The great source from which I have sprung.
It will be a consolation to you among the shades
That you died at the hand of so mighty a man."

The words died on his lips, which looked like
They were still trying to speak, but through which   220
No speech emerged. Eryx rebuked these two, saying,
"You're stiff because you're scared, not because of
Some Gorgon. Run up with me and let's lay low
This wizard warrior." He had begun to run,
But the floor held his feet, and there he stayed,
A motionless rock and an armored image.

These at least deserved their punishment,
But there was one, a soldier on Perseus' side
Named Aconteus, who in the course of the fight
Happened to look on the Gorgon's face   230

And hardened into stone. Astyages,
Mistaking him for a still living man,
Brought his sword down on him, and the blade
Rang shrilly. While Astyages stared dumbly,
The same force acted on him, and he stood
With an astonished look on his marble face.
It would take too long for the whole roll call.
Two hundred warm bodies survived the battle;
The Gorgon's gaze turned two hundred to stone.

Phineus now repents. The battle was unjust.   240
But what can he do? He sees figures
In various postures and recognizes his men.
He calls them by name, asks for their help,
And not trusting his eyes he touches those
Closest to him. They were marble. He turns away
And stretching out sideways suppliant hands
That admit defeat, he says,
                              "Perseus,
You win. Just remove that petrifying thing,
Whatever it is, that Medusa, just take it away,
I beg you. It wasn't hatred or lust for the throne   250
That drove me to war. I fought for my wife.
Your claim was better, mine just earlier.
It's all right; I yield. I only ask for my life,
O bravest of men, and all the rest is yours."

As he spoke he did not dare to look
At the man he was supplicating, who said,

"Phineus, most cowardly of men,
What I can give you—and it is a great good thing
For a slug like you—I will certainly give.
You will not die by my sword. Instead you will be   260
A monument that will last through the ages
And always on view in my wife's father's house,
A statue to remind her of her plighted lord."

He spoke, and brought the Gorgon's head around
Where Phineus had turned his terror-stricken face,
And even as he tried to avert his eyes, his neck
Stiffened, the tears on his cheeks hardened to stone,
And the cowardly face, the suppliant expression,
The pleading hands, and the guilty look
Are all permanent in the marble statue.   270

Victorious Perseus now enters with his bride
His ancestral city, and to avenge his grandfather,
Who did not deserve vengeance, he wages war
Against his uncle, Proetus, who had driven out
His brother Acrisius and seized the citadel.
But neither Proetus' armed might nor his possession
Of the citadel, which he had unjustly seized,
Could resist the dread gaze of the snake-crowned monster.

And you, Polydectes, ruler of tiny Seriphos,
Were mollified neither by the proven valor   280
Of the young hero, nor by his suffering,
But remained hard in your inexorable hatred,
Nor was there an end to your iniquitous wrath.
You withheld praise, denied honor, and even claimed
That the death of Medusa was only a lie.
"We will give you certain proof," Perseus said
To the king; and then to his friends, "Shield your eyes!"
And with the face of the Gorgon Medusa
He changed the king's face into bloodless stone.

Minerva and the Muses

All this time Athena had been with her brother   290
Born of the golden shower. Now, pulling a cloud
Around her, she left the island of Seriphos,
Passing Cythnos and Gyaros on the right
As she took the most direct route over the sea
To Thebes and Helicon, home of the Muses.

Pegasus and the Spring of the Muses

Gaining the mountain she came down and addressed
The cultivated sisters,
               "Rumor of a new spring
Has reached my ears, a spring that burst forth
Under the hoof of Medusa's winged horse.
I would like to see this marvel. The horse himself   300
I saw when he was born from his mother's blood."

Urania replied,
              "Whatever cause brings you
To visit our home, goddess, you are most welcome.
But the story is true; Pegasus is indeed
The source of our spring."
                   And she led Pallas
To the sacred waters. The goddess looked long,
Wondering at the spring created by the stroke
Of the horse's hoof, and at the ancient woods,
The grottoes, the flowering meadows,
And she declared the daughters of Memory   310
As blest in their locale as in their pursuits.
And one of the nine sisters answered her:

Pyreneus and the Muses

"O Tritonia, if you did not have
A higher calling, you might well be one of us.
Yes, we are blest in our vocations and home,
And our life is happy—if only it were safe.
But anything can happen now, and it frightens
Our virgin souls. The appalling thought
Of Pyreneus keeps running through our minds,
And I have not yet recovered. This villain   320
Had invaded Daulis and the Phocian fields
And exercised there unjust dominion.
One day he saw us as we were on our way
To the temple on Parnassus, and feigning reverence

For our divinity, he said,
                              'Daughters of Memory,'
(He knew who we were), 'please do not hesitate
To take shelter from this heavy weather
Under my roof,'—it was raining—'for gods
Have often deigned to enter humbler homes.'

Persuaded by his words and the weather   330
We agreed and went in. When the rain stopped,
And the south wind had been routed by the north,
And the sky had cleared, we wanted to go,
But Pyreneus shut his doors and got violent.
We escaped by putting on our wings.
He stood, as if he would follow us, high
On a parapet, and shouted, 'Whatever way
You go, I will go too,' and leapt insanely
From the pinnacle of the tower. He fell
Headlong to his death, crushing his bones   340
And staining the ground with his accursed blood."

The Contest of the Muses
and the Daughters of Pierus

The Muse was still speaking when wings whirred in the air
And words of greeting came down from the high branches.
Jupiter's daughter looked up and tried to make out
Where the sound, which was clearly speech, came from.
She thought it was a human being talking,
But it was a bird. Nine birds, in fact, had perched
In the branches, lamenting their fate—magpies,
Which can imitate anything. The Muse, one goddess
To another, explained to the wondering Minerva: 350

"It is only recently that these creatures,
After being bested in a contest, have joined
The tribes of birds. Their father was Pierus,
Who owned most of Pella, and their mother
Was Euippe of Paeonia. Nine times in labor,

Nine times she called on mighty Lucina.
This clump of dull-witted sisters, swollen with pride
Because of their numbers, traipsed through all the towns
Of Haemonia and Achaea and came here
To challenge us to a contest, saying things like,   360

'Stop gulling the ignorant with your empty charm,
Thespian goddesses, and if you dare, compete with us.
We are invincible in the vocal arts, and there are
As many of us as there are of you. If you lose,
You give us Medusa's spring and Boeotian Aganippe,
Or we cede to you the Emathian plains
Up to snowy Paeonia. And let nymphs be the judges.'

It was shameful to compete with them, but it seemed
More shameful not to. So some nymphs were chosen
As judges, and they swore by their rivers   370
And sat down on benches carved from the rock.
Then, without drawing lots, the sister who had
Issued the challenge began.

Song of Typhoeus

                    She sang of the battle
Between the gods and the Giants, making up things
To honor the Giants and slight the great gods,
How Typhoeus rose from the depths of the earth
And inspired fear in the heavenly gods,
Who turned and ran until, weary, they found refuge
In the land of Egypt and the seven-mouthed Nile,
And how Typhoeus, son of the earth, pursued them   380
And the gods hid themselves in deceptive forms.

'Jupiter became a ram,' she said, 'the lord of flocks,
And Ammon is still pictured with curving horns;
Apollo hid in the shape of a crow, Bacchus as a goat,
Diana a cat, Juno a heifer as white as snow,
Venus as a fish, and Mercury as an ibis.'

Hymn to Ceres

That was her song, accompanied by her lyre,
And then we, the Aonian sisters, were on—
But perhaps you have neither time nor inclination
To hear our song?" "Have no doubt; sing it straight through,"   390
Pallas replied, and took a seat in the shade.
The Muse continued, "We decided on a solo,
And Calliope stood up, her flowing hair
Bound in ivy. She strummed a few plaintive chords,
And then laid a song beneath the notes of her lyre:

'Ceres was the first to turn the soil with a plow,
First to give grain and kindly nourish the world,
The first to make laws. All things come from Ceres,
And Ceres I must sing. If only my song were
Worthy of the goddess: the goddess is worthy of song.   400

The huge island of Sicily, with all its weight,
Has been heaped upon the gigantic body
Of Typhoeus, who dared aspire to heaven.
He struggles, yes, and often tries to get back up,
But his right hand is under Ausonian Pelorus,
And his left under Pachynus. Mount Libaeum
Presses on his legs, and Aetna weighs down his head.
Flat on his back beneath this mountain, Typhoeus
Spouts up ashes and vomits flame from his mouth.
Sometimes he struggles with all his might   410
To push the weight of the earth, and roll the cities
And all the great mountains, off of his body.
Then there are earthquakes, and even the lord
Of the silent realms is afraid the earth's crust
Will split wide open and let in the daylight
To terrify the shades. Fearing this catastrophe,
He left the undergloom, and in his chariot
Drawn by black horses toured all of Sicily
To inspect its foundations. After he was sure
That nothing was slipping, he put aside his fears.   420

From her mountain seat Venus Erycina
Saw him wandering, and embracing her winged boy
The goddess exclaimed,
                              "My weapons, my hands,
My power—my son! Go get those arrows, Cupid,
That conquer everyone, and shoot them into the heart
Of the god who came in last in the lottery
And got the third realm. You rule the gods,
Including Jove himself; you control the deities
Of the sea, and the god who rules those deities.
Why should Tartarus be an exception? Why not   430
Extend your mother's empire and your own?
We're talking about a third of the world. Yet,
Up in heaven no one respects me—the patience
I've shown in this!—and with my own power
Love's power is declining too. You must have seen
That Pallas and the huntress Diana
Have turned away from me. And Ceres' daughter
Will be a virgin forever if we allow her to,
For she wants to be like them. As my ally,
In sovereignty, if that means anything to you,   440
Unite the goddess with her uncle."

                              Thus Venus,
And at his mother's request, Cupid opened his quiver
And of the thousand arrows it held he selected
The sharpest, the surest, the one most attuned
To his bow, and bracing the bow on his knee
He sent the barbed shaft through the Dark Lord's heart.

Not far from Henna's walls is a wide pool,
Pergus by name. Not even the Caÿster
Hears the songs of more swans on its gliding waters
Than this pool does. A wood surmounts the slopes   450
All around its shore and keeps off the sun's rays
As if its foliage were an awning. It is cool
Amid the branches, and the moist ground bears
Deep purple flowers. It is always spring there.

Proserpina was playing in this grove, gathering
Violets and bright lilies with girlish enthusiasm,
Filling her basket and the folds of her dress
And trying to outdo her friends, when Pluto
Saw her and wanted her and carried her off
All in the same moment, so precipitous his love.   460
The divine girl cried out plaintively to her mother
And to her friends, but mostly her mother.
Since she had torn her dress at the upper edge
All the flowers came tumbling out, and so young
And innocent was she that the loss of the flowers
Aroused her virginal grief. Her abductor
Drove his chariot and urged on his horses,
Calling each one by name and shaking the dark reins
On their manes and necks. He passed through deep lakes
And the pools of the Palici, reeking with sulphur   470
And boiling up through a crack in the earth
And where the Bacchiadae, a Corinthian people,
Had built a city with two different ports.

Between Cyane and Pisaean Arethusa
There is an inlet of the sea. Here the most famous
Of Sicily's nymphs lived, in the spring of Cyane
For which she was named. She was standing
In the waist-high water, and, recognizing
Proserpina, she called to Pluto:

                              "Hold it right there!
Do you think you can be the son-in-law of Ceres   480
Without her permission? The girl should be asked,
Not raped! If you don't mind the comparison,
Anapis loved me, and I finally married him,
But after I was wooed, not scared out of my wits
Like this poor girl!"

                     And she stretched out her arms
To block his way. The son of Saturn
Could no longer restrain his wrath. Urging on

His terrifying horses, he whirled his royal scepter
With his strong right arm and brought it down hard
To the bottom of the pool. Under this blow   490
Earth opened up a road to Tartarus and received
The plunging chariot into her yawning abyss.

But Cyane, grieving for the rape of the goddess
And the trampled rights of her spring, bore
The unendurable wound in her silent heart
And was consumed by her tears, dissolving
Into the very waters whose great divinity
She had been until now. You might have seen
Her limbs softening, her bones becoming pliant,
Her nails losing stiffness. The slenderest parts   500
Melted away first: her dark blue hair, her fingers,
Her legs and her feet. It is a brief passage
From willowy limbs to chilly water.
Next her shoulders, back, and breasts
Vanish into rivulets, and in her veins
Clear water flows instead of blood,
And nothing is left that you could grasp.

Meanwhile the frightened mother looks in vain
For her daughter, searching every land and sea.
Aurora, rising with her dewy hair,   510
Does not see her pause, nor does the Evening Star.
She has a pine torch in each hand, kindled in Aetna,
And bears them without rest through the frosty night;
And when the warm day has dimmed the stars
She still seeks her daughter, sunrise to sunset.
Weak and thirsty, her face unbathed in any spring,
She happened to see a straw-thatched hut. She knocked
At the small door, and out came an old woman,
Who saw the goddess, and when she asked for a drink.
Gave her sweet water with roasted grains of barley   520
Floating on top. While the goddess was drinking,
A sassy boy with a crude face was watching
And started to mock her and call her greedy.

Offended, she threw what she had not yet drunk
Into his face, barley grains and all. In an instant
His face became spotted, his arms changed into legs,
And a tail was appended to his mutated limbs.
He shrank down in size so he couldn't do harm,
And he looked like a lizard, but even smaller.
The old woman wondered and wept, but when she tried   530
To touch the little monster it ran off and hid.
His name suits his shame, since we call the newt
Stellio, and it has stars all over its body.

It would take too long to list the lands and seas
The goddess wandered through. She finally
Ran out of world to search and returned to Sicily,
And in her extensive travels came to Cyane.
If the nymph had not already been transformed
She would have told her all, but though she wanted to,
She had no lips or tongue or any way to speak.   540
She did, however, give clear evidence, showing
On her pool's surface a thing the mother knew well,
Proserpina's sash, that had happened to fall
Into the sacred water. As soon as she saw it,
As if she had just learned her daughter was stolen,
The goddess tore her hair, and beat her breast
Again and again. She did not yet know
Where her daughter was, but she reproached all lands—
Calling them ingrates, unworthy recipients
Of the gift of grain—but most of all Sicily,   550
Where she had found traces of what she had lost.
And so in her rage she broke all the plows there,
Destroyed farmers and cattle, forbad the fields
To produce promised yields, and blighted the seeds.
The island's fertility, famed the world over,
Betrayed its reputation. Crops died as seedlings,
Now too much sun, now too much rain. Stars and winds
Were adverse, greedy birds ate the newly sown seeds,
And stubborn weeds and darnel choked out the wheat.

Then Arethusa, who had mingled with Alpheus,   560
Lifted her head from the Elean waters
And, brushing her dripping hair from her brow
And back to her ears, addressed the goddess:

"Mother of the maiden sought through the world
And mother of crops, cease now your vast labors,
And do not be so hard on a land true to you.
The land does not deserve this; it opened unwillingly
To the abduction. Nor am I pleading
For my own country, for I am not from here.
Pisa is my native land, and I came here from Elis.   570
I live in Sicily as a foreigner, but I love this country
More than any other. This is my home now,
My true dwelling place. And I beg you to save it,
O most merciful goddess. Why I moved from my home
And crossed such a stretch of sea to come to Ortygia
(As Sicily is also called) I will tell you
At a better time, when you are free from care
And your face is more cheerful. But Earth did
Open a path for me, and having passed below
Through her cavernous depths I lifted my head here   580
And saw the forgotten stars. So, while I glided along
In my Stygian stream, I saw Proserpina there
With my own eyes. She did seem very sad,
And her face still looked frightened, but she was a queen,
She was the great queen of all that dark world,
And the powerful consort of the lord of the dead."

The mother heard these words as if she were stone,
And was in shock for a long time. When her numbness
Was displaced by searing pain, she left in her chariot
For the shores of heaven, and there, face clouded,   590
Hair disheveled, and full of indignation,
She stood before Jove, and,
                              "I have come," she said,
"As a suppliant, Jupiter, on behalf of my own child
And yours. If the mother does not find favor with you,

Let the daughter touch her father's heart, and, I pray,
Do not care less for her because it is I who bore her.
My daughter, long sought for, has at last been found,
If you call finding her being more sure to lose her,
Or if you call it finding just to know where she is.
That she was stolen, I will bear, if he will only   600
Return her. Your daughter does not deserve
A robber for a husband, if she is mine no more."

Jove answered her,
                    "Yours and mine, our common pledge
And common concern. But if we agree to call things
By their right names, this has not been a hostile act,
But an act of love. Nor will he shame us
As a son-in-law, if only you give your consent,
Goddess. Even if he had nothing else to offer,
It is a great thing to be the brother of Jove.
But he does have more to offer, and he is   610
No less than I am except by chance of the lot.
But if your desire to separate them is so great,
Proserpina will return to heaven, provided that
She has tasted no food in the world below,
For this is an iron-clad decree of the Fates."

Thus Jove. Ceres was resolved to get her daughter back,
But the Fates would not allow it, for the girl
Had already broken her fast. The innocent child,
Wandering through the formal gardens, had plucked
A pomegranate from a bending bough,   620
And peeling off the pale yellow rind, had eaten
Seven of the seeds. The only person to see this
Was Ascalaphus, who was a son of Orphne,
Not the least renowned of the Avernal nymphs,
Who bore him to Acheron in the darkling woods.
The cruel little boy saw, and his tattling annulled
Proserpina's return. The Queen of Erebus moaned
And changed the informer into a profane bird.
Sprinkling his head with water from Phlegethon

She gave him beak and feathers and enormous eyes.   630
No more himself, he is cloaked in tawny wings,
Grows into his head and curves down in long claws,
Hardly moving the feathers that now envelop
His sluggish arms. He been transformed
Into an odious bird and harbinger of grief,
The slothful screech owl, an evil omen to men.

He at least seemed to have earned his punishment
With his tattling tongue, but daughters of Acheloüs,
Why do you have feathers and birds' feet, though your faces
Are still young women's? Is it because   640
When Proserpina was gathering springtime flowers
You, now the Sirens, were among her companions?
After you had searched every land for her
You wanted the sea to feel your care, and so prayed
That you could skim over the waves on plying wings.
You found the gods compliant and suddenly saw
Golden plumage covering your arms, but that you not lose
Your rich repertory of beguiling songs,
Your faces and human voices remained.
Caught between his brother and grieving sister.   650
Jove now divided the revolving year in two.
Half of the months the goddess, who belonged
To two separate realms, spends with her mother
And half with her husband. In no time at all
The look on her face and her state of mind changed.
She had seemed sad even to Pluto, but now
The goddess' brow is joyful, like the sun
When it emerges from a bank of dark clouds.

Arethusa and Alpheus

And now kindly Ceres, with her daughter back,
Asks you, Arethusa, why you fled, why you are now   660
A sacred spring. The waters fall silent
As the goddess lifts her head from the depths of her pool

And dries her green hair with her hands. Then she tells
Of the ancient loves of the Elean river.

"I used to be one of the nymphs in Achaea,"
She said, "and no other was as eager as I
In roaming the glades and setting out nets.
But although I never tried to be known for beauty,
And although I was brave, I had a name for beauty.
I didn't enjoy all the praise my face got.   670
Other girls love that sort of thing, but I would blush
Just like a farm girl at my well-endowed body,
And I thought it wrong to be pleasing. One day,
Weary from hunting, I was coming back
(I remember it well) from the Stymphalian wood.
It was hot, and all my work made it hotter.
I came upon a stream without an eddy or ripple,
Flowing without a sound and crystal clear
Down to bottom. You could count every pebble,
And you would think the water hardly was moving.   680
Pale-white willows and poplars fed by the water
Gave natural shade to the sloping banks.
I came down to the water and first dipped my feet in,
Then up to my knees, and not content with that,
I took off my clothes and hung them on a willow
And dove in naked. While I was moving my arms
In all sorts of strokes and just gliding along,
I thought I heard a murmur deep in the pool.
Terrified, I got out on the closer bank.
'Where, Arethusa, are you hurrying off to?'   690
It was Alpheus, calling from his own waters.
'Where are you hurrying off to?' Again he called me
In his hoarse voice. Just as I was, without any clothes,
Which were on the other bank, I was off and running.
He was all the more hot for me because I was naked
And seemed readier to him. And so the race was on,
Me running like a dove fluttering away from a hawk
And he like a hawk after the terrified dove.

All the way past Orchomeus, past Psophis and Cyllene,
Past the valleys of Maenalus, chill Erymanthus and Elis   700
I kept up the pace. He was not any faster,
But he had more endurance, and I could not hold my speed
As long as he could. And yet I ran, through level plains
And over mountains covered with trees, over rocks and cliffs
Where there were no paths I ran and I ran.
The sun was at my back, and I saw the long shadow
Of my pursuer stretching out ahead of me—
Unless it was fear that saw it—but I certainly heard
The awful sound of feet, and his colossal panting
Fluttered the ribbons tying back my hair.   710
I was bone-tired from running and cried aloud,

'Help me or I'm caught, help your armor-bearer,
Goddess Dictynna, to whom you have often given
Your bow to carry and your quiver of arrows!'

Moved by my prayer, the goddess threw a cloud
Of thick mist around me. The river god
Circled around the darkness that enveloped me,
Wondering where I was. He circuited twice
The hiding place the goddess had made for me,
Unknowing where I was, and twice he called out,   720
'Arethusa, O Arethusa!' How did I feel then?
As wretched as a lamb when it hears the wolves
Howling around the high sheep pen; or a hare
Hiding in the brambles, watching the dog's muzzles,
That does not dare even to twitch its nose.
Alpheus did not go far, for he saw that my footprints
Went no farther. He just watched my misty hiding place.
Cold sweat poured down my overstressed limbs,
Dark drops of it dripping from my whole body.
Wherever I placed a foot, a pool collected,   730
My hair rained dew, and sooner than I can tell it
I was changed to a stream. And, sure enough,
He recognized the waters as what he loved,
And dropping the human form he had assumed,

He resumed his own proper watery shape
To mingle with me. The Delian goddess
Split the earth open, and after plunging down
Into the dark depths, I made the passage to here,
Ortygia, another name for my beloved goddess,
Where I was first welcomed back into the upper air."   740

Arethusa was done. The goddess of fertility
Then yoked her two dragons to her chariot,
Cinched back the reins, and drove off through the air
Midway between heaven and earth, until she came
To Pallas' city. There she gave her chariot
To Triptolemus and ordered him to scatter seeds,
Partly on untilled ground and partly in fields
That had long lain fallow. And now the youth had gone
High over Europe and the land of Asia
And came to Scythia, where Lyncus was king.   750
He entered the palace and Lyncus asked him
How and why he had come, what his name was
And where he was from. Triptolemus answered:

"My country is illustrious Athens. My name
Is Triptolemus, and I came neither by sea
On a ship, nor on foot overland. The open air
Was my path. I bring the gifts of Ceres.
Scattered on your fields they will give a return
Of fruitful harvests and mild sustenance."

The barbaric king was envious, and so that   760
He himself could be the great benefactor
He welcomed his guest, and when he was asleep
Attacked him with steel. As he was about to pierce
Triptolemus' chest, Ceres transformed him
Into a lynx, and told the Athenian youth
To drive her sacred team back through the air.'

Our eldest sister here ended the song
Which I have recited. The nymphs acting as judges

Agreed that the Muses of Helicon had won.
When the defeated sisters started to hurl   770
Insults at us, I responded by saying,

'Since it was not enough that your challenge earned you
A penalty, and you must add abuse to your offense,
And since our patience is not unlimited,
We will proceed directly to punishment
And let our anger be our guide.'

                              The Pierides laughed
At her threatening words, but when they tried to speak
And were making rude gestures with their hands
They saw feathers growing from their fingernails
And plumage covering their arms. Each of them watched   780
A sister's face contract into a rigid beak
And become a strange new bird to range the woods.
When they tried to beat their breasts, their flapping arms
Lifted them into the air, and there they hovered,
Magpies, the woodland's scolds. Even as birds
They still have their old gift of gab, their raucous
Garrulity, and their enormous passion for talk."

Book 6

The Contest of Arachne and Minerva

Tritonia had lent her ears to these stories
And approved both the song of the Muses
And their righteous indignation. But then she thought,
"It's not enough to praise; let me be praised,
And not allow my godhead to be scorned
Without reprisal." And she turned her mind
To the fate of Arachne of Maeonia,
Who she heard would not yield to her the glory
In the art of working wool. The girl was not famed
For where she was from or who her family was,   10
Only for her art. Her father, Idmon of Colophon,
Used to dye the wool for her with Phocaean purple.
Her mother was dead. She was a commoner herself,
As was her husband. Nevertheless, Arachne
Had made a name for herself throughout Lydia
Although she came from a small, humble house
And lived in a small town called Hypaepa.
The nymphs would often leave their vineyards
On Mount Tmolus to see her wondrous work,
And the naiads of Pactolus would leave their waters,   20
And it was a joy to see not just her finished fabrics,
But to see them being made, to see such grace and skill.
Whether she was winding up a ball of rough yarn,
Or pressing it with her fingers, or teasing out
Clouds of wool to spin into a long, soft thread,
Or twirling the spindle with a light touch of her thumb,
Or embroidering with her needle—you would know
She had been taught by Pallas. Yet she denied it,
Offended by the notion that she had a teacher,
Even one so great. "Let's have a contest," she said.   30
"There is nothing I wouldn't forfeit if I lose."

So Pallas showed up looking like an old woman,
Grey at the temples, limping in on a staff,
And started to talk.
                    "Old age does have some things

We shouldn't shun; experience comes with long years.
Don't spurn my advice. Seek all the fame you want
In mortal society for working with wool,
But yield to the goddess, and humbly beg her pardon
For what you said. She will pardon you if you ask."

Arachne glowered at her. Dropping the thread   40
She had been spinning, she could barely hold back
From slapping the old woman, and with undisguised
Anger in her face, answered the disguised goddess,

"You doddering old fool, coming in here like this.
You've lived too long, is your problem. Go talk
To your daughter-in-law, your daughter, whatever.
I've got enough good sense, and just so you'll know
You didn't do any good with all your advice,
I haven't changed my mind. Why does your goddess avoid
A contest with me? Why doesn't she come herself?"   50

"She has!" said the goddess, shedding her disguise
To reveal Pallas Athena. The nymphs
Worshipped her divinity, as did the Mygdonian women.
Arachne alone was unafraid, although she did jump up,
And a sudden blush marked her unwilling cheeks
And then faded away, as the sky turns dark pink
When dawn first appears, and after a little while pales
When the sun comes up. But she persists in her folly,
Eager to win the prize. The daughter of Jupiter
Does not decline, issue any more warnings,   60
Or delay the contest a bit. They set up identical looms
In separate places and stretch out the fine warp.
The web is bound to the beam, a reed separates
The threads of the warp, and the weft is threaded through
By the sharp shuttles worked by their fingers.
Once drawn through the warp, the threads of the weft
Are beaten down into place by the comb's notched teeth.
They each worked quickly, with their clothes tucked in
And tied under their breasts, moving their trained hands

With so much enthusiasm it didn't seem like work.   70
Threads dyed purple in bronze Tyrian vats
Are woven in, and lighter colors shade gradually off.
Just as after a rainstorm, when the sun strikes through,
A long curving bow will tint the vast sky,
And though a thousand colors are shining there,
The eye cannot see the transitions between them,
So too the adjacent threads seem the same color,
But those far apart look different. They worked in
Threads of gold too, telling ancient tales in the weaving.

Pallas depicts the hill of Mars in Athens   80
And that old dispute over naming the city.
Twelve celestials, with Jove in the middle,
Sit on high thrones in august majesty.
Each god has his own distinctive appearance.
Jupiter is royal. The sea god stands with his trident
Striking a cliff, and seawater pours from the broken rock,
His claim to the city. To herself the goddess gives
A shield, a spear, a helmet for her head,
And the aegis protects her breast. And she pictures
A pale-green olive tree laden with fruit   90
Sprouting from the earth where her spear has struck.
The gods look on in awe; Victory crowns her work.

Then, to teach her rival by choice examples
What prize to expect for her outrageous daring,
She weaves four contests in the web's four corners,
Miniature designs each with its own colors.

One corner shows Rhodope and Haemus,
Icy peaks in Thrace that were once mortal beings
Who assumed the names of the gods on high.
Another corner shows the miserable fate   100
Of the queen of the pygmies, defeated by Juno
And transformed by her into a crane
And ordered to fight against her own people.
And she pictures Antigone, whom Juno changed

Into a bird for having the gall to compete
With great Jupiter's consort. Neither Ilium,
Her city, nor her father Laomedon
Could help her now, a stork with white feathers
Applauding herself with her clattering beak.
The last corner shows Cinyras, bereft.   110
Clasping the temple steps that were once the limbs
Of his own daughters, he lies on the stone and weeps.

She bordered it all with peaceful olive wreaths
And with her own tree brought the work to an end.

Arachne depicts Europa deceived by the false bull,
But you would think the bull real, and the water too.
She looks back at the shore and calls to her friends,
And, afraid of the waves, tucks up her dainty feet.
She made Asterië struggling in the eagle's claws,
And Leda lying beneath the swan's wings.   120
She showed how Jove, imaged as a satyr,
Filled lovely Antiope with twin offspring,
And how as Amphitryon he cheated you, Alcmena;
Tricked Danaë as gold, Aegina as fire,
Mnemosyne as a shepherd, and Deo's daughter
As a mottled snake.
                    She showed you also, Neptune,
As a snorting bull with an Aeolian girl,
As Enipeus begetting the Aloidae,
And deceiving Bisaltis in the shape of a ram.
The golden-haired mother of the grain, Ceres,   130
Knew you as a horse; the snake-haired mother
Of the winged horse had you as a winged bird;
And Melantho as a dolphin.
                          Arachne gave each
A local setting and a face. Here is Phoebus
As a farmer; here he is in hawk feathers,
Here in a skin of a lion; here he's a shepherd
Deceiving Macareus' daughter, Isse.
Here we have Bacchus tricking Erigone

With a false bunch of grapes, and here Saturn
As a horse engendering Chiron, the centaur.   140
The narrow border running around the edge
Has flowers intertwined with clinging ivy.

Neither Pallas, nor Envy personified,
Could carp at that work. The golden virago,
Incensed at Arachne's spectacular success,
Ripped the fabric apart with all its embroidery
Of celestial crimes. And, as she had in her hand
A shuttle made of Cytorian boxwood,
She used it to box Arachne's ears. The poor girl
Could not endure this, and she slipped a noose   150
Around her neck. As she was hanging,
Pallas lifted her in pity and said,
                              "Live on,
Wicked girl, but keep hanging, your legacy
(So you will always be wary) to your offspring
For all posterity."
                              And as the goddess left
She sprinkled her with extracts of Hecate's herb.
Touched by this potion, the girl's hair fell off
Along with her nose and ears. Her head became
Her smallest part, and her body small, too,
With her slender fingers clinging to it as legs.   160
The rest was belly, from which she still spins thread
And plies as a spider her old art of weaving.

Niobe and Latona

All of Lydia buzzed with the story, which spread
Through Phrygia, too, and filled the world with talk.
Niobe, before her marriage, had known Arachne
When she lived as a girl near Mount Sipylus.
Yet she did not learn from her countrywoman's fate
To yield to the gods and not to talk big. Her pride
Had many sources, but it was not her husband's music,
Or the high birth of both, or their royal power   170

That pleased her as much, although all this did please her,
As her children did. And Niobe would have been called
The happiest of mothers, had she not thought so herself.
What happened was that Manto, Tiresias' daughter,
Who could see the future, had gone through the streets
Prophesying to all with divine inspiration:

"Women of Thebes, go in great numbers
And offer to Latona and her two children
Pious prayer and incense, with laurel in your hair.
Latona speaks through my mouth."

                            They obey;   180
All the Theban women wreathe their hair with laurel,
Burn incense at the altar and murmur their prayers.

But now here comes Niobe with a large retinue,
A striking figure in her Phrygian robes
Filigreed with gold, and beautiful, as far as
Her anger would allow, her shapely head tossing
Her long hair from one shoulder to the other
As she walked into the temple. Then she stopped,
And sweeping the crowd with disdainful eyes,

"What madness is this," she cried, "preferring gods   190
You have only heard of to those you have seen?
And why is Latona worshipped at altars,
While my divinity is still without incense?
My father is Tantalus, the only mortal
Ever allowed at the table of the gods;
My mother is a sister of the Pleiades.
One grandfather is Atlas, who supports
The sky's wheel on his shoulders, and the other
Is Jupiter himself, in whom I also glory
As my father-in-law. The Phrygian nations   200
Hold me in awe. The royal house of Cadmus
Is under my dominion, and the walls of Thebes,
Which owe their existence to my husband's lyre,

Along with the people of Thebes, are under our rule.
Wherever I look in the palace I see vast wealth.
And, of course, my beauty is worthy of a goddess.
To top it off, I have seven sons and seven daughters
And soon will have sons- and daughters-in-law.
First ask if I have any cause for pride,
And then have the courage to put me before   210
The Titaness Latona, daughter of Coeus
(Whoever that is), Latona whom the great earth
Refused a tiny spot for her to birth her children.
Neither heaven, nor earth nor sea would welcome
Your beloved goddess, until Delos pitied the vagrant.
'You wander the land and I the sea,' she said,
And gave her an unstable place to stand on,
Where she bore two children, one-seventh of mine.
Yes, I am blessed—who would deny it?—
And I will remain blessed—who would doubt it?   220
Sheer abundance has made me safe. I am too great
To be harmed by Fortune. Even if she took much
From me, she would leave me with much more.
My blessings have driven out fear. Suppose
That some part of my population of children
Were taken from me. Even so despoiled
I would not be reduced to the number of two—
Latona's whole brood—and just how far
From childlessness does that leave the goddess?
Enough with the sacrifices! Get out of here!   230
And take that laurel out of your hair."

They took off their wreaths and left the sacrifice
Unfinished. But they could still pray in their hearts.

The goddess was enraged, and from Cynthus' high peak
She addressed the twins, Diana and Apollo:

"So, I, your mother, proud of my children
And second to no other goddess but Juno,
Have my divinity doubted and will be forever denied

Worship at altars, unless you come to my aid.
Nor is this my only grievance. This Tantalid   240
Has added insult to injury, daring to favor
Her children over you and to call me childless—
May that come back to bite her!—displaying
The same iniquitous tongue her father had."

She was about to add pleas to her presentation
When Phoebus broke in, saying,
                                        "Enough!
Vengeance belabored is vengeance delayed."
Phoebe agreed, and they glided through the air
Down onto Cadmus' citadel, wrapped in clouds.

Near the walls was a broad, level plain   250
Where chariot wheels and the hooves of horses
Had softened and leveled the clods beneath them.
There some of Amphion's seven sons
Were mounting strong stallions. They sat tall
In the saddles, bright with Tyrian purple,
And the horses' bridles were heavy with gold.
One of them, Ismenus, his mother's firstborn son,
Was guiding his horse around a turn, pulling back
On the foaming bit, when suddenly he cried,
"Ah me!" and with an arrow fixed in his chest   260
He dropped the reins from his dying hands
And sank slowly down the horse's right shoulder.
The next moment, Sipylus heard the quiver
Rattling the empty air, and he gave full rein,
Like a ship captain who senses an approaching storm
When he sees a cloud and raises sail to the breeze.
But even as he gave full rein, the inevitable arrow
Caught up with him. The shaft quivered where it stuck
In his neck, and the point punched through his throat.
He was already leaning forward and now pitched   270
Over the horse's mane and into his forelegs
And stained the ground red with his warm blood.

Meanwhile, ill-fated Phaedimus and Tantalus,
Named after his grandfather, had finished their chores
And come over now to practice some wrestling.
Their bodies gleamed as they pressed together,
Straining chest to chest, when an arrow sped
From the taut string and pierced both together.
They groaned in unison and, doubled over in pain,
In unison slumped to the ground, and lying there   280
Saw their last light and breathed their last together.
Alphenor saw them die. Clawing and beating his breast
He ran up to lift their cold bodies in his arms
And died in this devoted act, pierced through the gut
With fatal steel shot by the Delian archer.
When the arrow was extracted, part of the lung
Was stuck to the barb, and his blood poured out,
Along with his life, into the open air.
But one wound was not all for young Damasichthon.
Hit in the belly of the thigh just above his knee,   290
He was trying to pull the shaft out with his hand
When a second arrow punched into his throat
All the way to the feathers. The blood drove it out,
And spurted in a thin stream high into the air.
Ilioneus was the last, stretching out arms
That would accomplish nothing in prayer, and saying,
"Gods, O all gods together," not knowing
He did not have to pray to all, "spare me."
Apollo was moved by this, but a little too late
To recall the arrow. Still, it was only a slight wound   300
That killed the boy, the point just touching his heart.

Rumor, the people's grief, and the tears of her friends
Informed the mother of this sudden disaster.
She was amazed that it could happen, and incensed
That the gods would dare this, that they had the right
And the power to do this. As for the boys' father,
Amphion had ended his grief with his life, dying
With a dagger stabbed through his heart. How different

Was this Niobe from the Niobe who had just now
Driven the people from Latona's altar   310
And walked with her head high through the city streets,
The envy of her friends. Now she was someone
For even her enemies to pity. She threw herself
Upon her sons' cold bodies, giving each of them
A final kiss. Then, lifting her bruised arms
To heaven, she cried,

           "Feed now, cruel Latona,
Upon my grief, and glut your bloodthirsty heart
On my sorrow! I have died seven deaths.
Exult, my enemy! Triumph in your victory!
But why your victory? In all my misery   320
I still have more than you in your happiness.
After so many deaths, I am still victorious!"

She spoke, and the bowstring twanged, terrifying
Everyone except Niobe, whom tribulation
Had made bold. The sisters were standing
Around their brothers' biers, robed in black
And with their hair unbound. One of them,
Drawing an arrow out of her brother's body
Collapsed and died with her face upon him.
Another, trying to console her mother, stopped,   330
Doubled over in pain with an unseen wound
And kept her lips closed until her last breath.
One fell vainly trying to flee; another died
Upon her sister, one hidden by the other,
Whom you could see trembling. Six had now died
By various wounds, and only one remained.
Her mother shielded her with her whole body
And all her robes.

         "Leave me one, the smallest,"
She cried. "Of my many children, spare the smallest,
Just one."

        The girl that she prayed for died   340
While she prayed. The childless mother sat down
With the lifeless bodies of her sons, her daughters,

And her husband, and she stiffened in grief.
No wind stirs her hair, her face is bloodless,
Her eyes stand motionless in her sad face.
There is nothing alive at all to be seen.
The tongue in her mouth cleaves to her palate,
Her veins no longer pulse, her neck won't bend,
Her arms cannot move, her feet cannot go.
All of the organs inside her are stone.   350
But she still weeps. And a great whirlwind
Takes her away to her own native land,
Where still she weeps, set on top of a mountain,
And even today tears flow down the marble.

Thebes Responds to Niobe's Calamity

After this public display of divine wrath,
Men and women alike feared and worshipped
The dread power of the goddess who bore
A pair of divinities. And, as usually happens,
The latest story brings up earlier ones
That people retell. So someone told this one: 360

The Altar in the Pond

"In Lycia's fertile fields, too, some old-time peasants
Scorned the goddess—and without impunity.
The story is little known (for the men involved
Were not nobles) but amazing all the same.
I myself saw the pond and the place made famous
By the phenomenon. My father, getting old then
And too weak to go far, had told me to go drive
Some prime cattle grazing in that country,
And he gave me a local man to act as a guide.
Well, I was going through the grasslands with him,   370
And there, in the middle of this pond stood
An ancient altar, black with ashes from sacrifices
And surrounded with a stand of quivering reeds.
My guide stopped, and said in an awestruck whisper,
'Bless me.' And so I whispered 'Bless me,' too.

Then I asked him if this was an altar
To the naiads, or Faunus, or some local god,
And he answered me like this:

Latona and the Lycians

'No, young man,
There's no mountain deity in this altar.
The goddess who calls this altar hers was shut out   380
From all the world by heaven's royal lady.
Even Delos just barely welcomed her
When it was an island bobbing on the sea.
Leaning against a palm tree there, and an olive,
She birthed twin babes in spite of their stepmother.
But she still had to keep running away from Juno,
New mother that she was, carrying in her bosom
Her infant children, both of them divine.
Finally she reached the borders of Lycia,
Where the Chimaera lives. The sun beat down,   390
And the goddess, all worn out, was faint with the heat
And parched with thirst, and her hungry babes
Had drained her breasts of milk. Then she saw a lake,
Not very big, down in a valley. Some peasants there
Were gathering reeds, rushes, and nice swamp grass.
Latona came down to the shore of the lake
And kneeled on the ground for a drink of cool water,
But the rabble wouldn't let her. So she told them,

"Why do you deny me water? Everyone
Has a right to water. Nature hasn't made the sun   400
Private, or the air, or water either. I'm here
For a common right, but I'll still beg you
To give it to me. I wasn't going to bathe
My weary body here in your pool, only
Quench my thirst. Even just talking to you
My mouth is dry, and my throat is so parched
I barely have any voice left. A drink of water

Will be like nectar to me, and I'll tell anyone
I got my life back with it. You'll be saving my life
If you let me drink. And don't these children move you,   410
Stretching their little arms out from my bosom?"

And by luck the children did stretch out their arms.
Who wouldn't have been touched by the goddess' soft words?
But they kept denying her no matter how much she prayed,
Threatening her if she didn't go away, even insulting her.
And as if that wasn't enough, they stomped in the water
And muddied it up with slime from the bottom,
Just to be mean. Well, anger postponed thirst now.
Coeus' daughter wasn't about to keep humbling herself
Before this worthless crowd and could no longer bear   420
To speak as less than a goddess, so she stretched her arms
Up to the sky and cried, "Live in that pond forever!"
And it happened just as the goddess wanted.
They like it in the water, plunging on down
And then sticking their heads up to swim on the surface.
Sometimes they sit on the swampy bank, only
To leap back into the cool water. But even now
They're foulmouthed and quarrelsome, no sense of shame.
They curse a blue streak, even under the water,
And they still have hoarse voices. Their throats bulge out,   430
And all their quarreling only widens their jaws.
They stretch out their heads too, and hardly have necks.
Their backs are green, and their big bellies are white.
These splashers through the muck are new creatures: frogs.'"

Marsyas and Apollo

When whoever it was had finished telling
About the ruin of these Lycians, someone else
Remembered Marsyas, the flautist satyr
Whom Apollo had defeated in a music contest
And then punished.
                    "Why are you tearing me

Out of myself?" Marsyas cried. "I'm sorry!   440
No flute is worth this."
                            As the satyr screamed
His skin was peeled from his body's surface
And he was one massive wound. Blood flowed
All over the place; his muscles were laid bare;
His veins throbbed and quivered without any skin;
You could count the pulsing entrails; the fibers
Of his lungs showed clearly through his chest.
The country people, the woodland gods, fauns
And his brother satyrs all wept. Olympus wept,
His friend dear to him still, and all the nymphs,   450
And everyone who pastured his wooly flocks,
Or horned cattle, in those hills. The fruitful Earth
Was soaked through and drank all of those tears
Deep into her veins, and changing them to water
She sent them into the open air, a stream that runs
Swiftly through its sloping banks down to the sea.
Marsyas is its name, the clearest stream in Phrygia."

Pelops

The conversation turns from tales like this
To present matters, and they mourn for Amphion,
Dead with his children. Everyone blames the mother,   460
But one man, her brother Pelops, is said
To have wept for her, and, drawing back his mantle,
He revealed the ivory in his left shoulder.
When he was born this shoulder was the same color
As his right one, and made of flesh. But they say
That after his father had cut him into pieces
And the gods were putting him back together
They found everything else except the part
Where the neck joins the arm, so some ivory
Was substituted for the missing part,   470
And this is how Pelops was made whole again.

Procne and Philomela

Now all the neighboring cities sent their rulers
To offer sympathy, and princes assembled
From Argos, from Sparta, and from Mycenae,
From Calydon, not yet on Diana's bad side,
Fertile Orchomenos, Corinth famed for its bronzes,
Martial Messene, Patrae, lowly Cleonae,
Nelean Pylos, and (not yet Pitthean) Troezen,
And all of the cities below the Isthmus
And those cities above the Isthmus as well.   480
Only you, Athens—who could believe it?—were missing,
The courtesy prevented by war. Barbarians
From overseas had besieged the city. Tereus,
Bringing relief from Thrace, routed them
And by this victory made a name for himself.
He was also strong in wealth and men
And traced his descent from Mars. So Pandion,
Athens' king, formed an alliance with him
By wedding him to his daughter Procne.
But neither Juno, the bridal goddess,   490
Nor Hymen attended. The Furies lit the way
With torches stolen from a funeral, and
The Furies made their bed. An eerie screech owl
Brooded and sat on the roof of their chamber.
Under this omen Procne and Tereus
Were married, and they conceived their child
Under this omen. Thrace, to be sure, rejoiced,
And the couple thanked the gods, both on the day
When Pandion's daughter married the king
And on the day Itys was born. We never know   500
Where our true advantage lies.
                                        Now the Titan Sun
Had led the year through five autumnal seasons,
When Procne, using all her charm, said to Tereus,

"If I am pleasing to you, either send me
To visit my sister, or have my sister come here.

You can tell my father that he will have her back
After a brief stay. It will mean a lot to me
If you give me a chance to see my sister."

Tereus had his ship hauled to the water,
And entered Athens' harbor under sail and oar,   510
Putting in at the Piraeus. As soon as he came
Into his father-in-law's court, they clasped hands,
Exchanged greetings and began to converse.
He was about to present his wife's request,
Which was why he had come, and to promise
A speedy return of the visiting daughter,
When in walked Philomela, richly dressed,
But richer in beauty. She was like the naiads
We hear about, or dryads walking in the woods,
If only they had elegant clothing like hers.   520
Tereus was inflamed the moment he saw her,
As if one were to set fire to a field of grain,
Or a pile of leaves, or to hay in a loft.
Her beauty was reason enough, but with Tereus
His own libido and the passionate nature
Of men from his region were also factors.
Nature and race both caused him to burn.
His first impulse was to corrupt her attendants,
Or her nurse, and then to tempt the girl herself
With lavish gifts, even if it cost his kingdom,   530
Or perhaps just to carry her off and rape her
And then defend his rape with a bloody war.
Mad with passion, he would dare anything,
And his heart could not contain the fires within.
Impatient now, he repeated Procne's request,
Using her as a pretext to plead his own case.
Love made him eloquent, and as often as
He sounded too urgent, he would say that Procne
Wanted it so. He even threw in some tears,
As if she had ordered that too. Gods above,   540
Men's minds are pitch-black! In the very act
Of constructing his crime, Tereus is credited

With a kind heart and gets praised for his sin.
And what about this? Philomela herself
Has the same wish. She drapes her arms
Upon her father's shoulders and coaxes him
To let her go and visit her sister,
Pleading for (and against) her own well-being.
Tereus gazes at her and paws her by looking;
As he sees her kisses, and sees her arms   550
Around her father's neck, he takes it all in
As fuel for the fire, food for his passion;
And whenever she embraces her father
He wishes he were her father, nor would he be
Any less impious. Pandion is won over
By the pleas of both. Philomela is happy
And thanks her father, poor girl. She thinks
It is a great success for her and her sister,
But it will be sheer agony for both of them.

Now Phoebus had only a little work left,   560
His horses treading the sky's downward slopes.
A royal feast was spread, wine in golden cups,
And then they retired for a good night's sleep.
But although the Thracian king was in bed,
He could not stop thinking about her, recalling
Her looks, the way she moved, her hands,
And what he had not seen he readily imagined,
Feeding his own fires, and he could not sleep.
Dawn came. Pandion, wringing his son-in-law's hand
As he was leaving, committed his daughter   570
To Tereus' care and, with tears welling up, said,

"My dear son, since it is for a good reason,
And both my daughters want it, and you do too,
I give her to you, Tereus, and by your honor
And the ties between us, and by the gods above,
I beg you to watch over her with a father's love,
And to send back as soon as possible
(It will seem forever to me) the sweet solace

Of my anxious old age. And, Philomela,
If you care for me, return as soon as you can.   580
It is enough that your sister is so far away."

He kissed his child good-bye as he said these things,
Gentle tears falling from his eyes the while.
He asked for their right hands as a pledge
And joined them together. And he begged them
To greet his daughter and grandson for him.
Sobbing, choked with tears, he could barely say
His last farewell, and was filled with foreboding.

As soon as Philomela was on his painted ship,
And the oars churned sea, and land drifted away,   590
"I've won!" Tereus shouted. "My answered prayers
Are freight onboard!" The barbarian lout exults,
He can barely defer his pleasures, and he never
Twists his eyes away from her, just like an eagle,
Jove's bird, who has dropped a hare from his talons
Into its high aerie. The captive has no chance
To escape, and the raptor sits eyeing his prey.

The voyage was done; they got off the battered ship,
And Tereus dragged the daughter of Pandion
To a hut in the gloom of an ancient forest   600
Where he shut her in, pale, trembling, afraid
Of everything, and begging with tears to know
Where her sister was. He told her the outrage
He was about to commit and then overpowered her,
One girl, all alone, calling often for her father,
Often for her sister, but above all the great gods.
She trembled like a quivering lamb, who,
After it has been wounded and then spat out
By a grey wolf, cannot yet believe it is safe;
Or like a dove whose feathers are smeared   610
With its own blood and who still shudders with fear
Of those greedy talons that pierced her skin.

When her senses returned she clawed at her hair,
And beat and scratched her arms like a mourner,
And then stretched out her hands as she cried:

"Oh, you horrible monster, what have you done?
Don't you care anything about my father's charges,
His tears, my sister's love, my own virginity
Or the bonds of marriage? You've jumbled it all up!
I've become my sister's whorish rival, and you   620
A husband to us both! Procne now must be
My enemy. Why don't you just kill me,
So there's no crime left for you to commit,
You traitor? I wish you had killed me before
That unspeakable bedding! Then my shade
Would have been innocent. If the gods above
See these things, if there are any gods at all,
If all things have not perished with me, then,
Sooner or later, you will pay for this!
I will shrug off shame and tell everyone   630
What you have done. I'll go to the marketplace
If I can, and if I'm shut up in these woods,
I'll fill the woods with my story and move
Even the rocks to pity. Heaven's air will hear it,
And if there's any god there he'll hear it too."

Tereus' savage, tyrannical wrath
Was aroused by her words, and his fear no less.
He drew his sword from its sheath, caught her by the hair
And tied her hands behind her back. When she saw the sword
Philomela offered her throat, hoping for death.   640
But he gripped her protesting tongue with pincers
As it kept calling her father's name and cut it off,
Still struggling to speak, with his pitiless blade.
The root writhed in her throat; the tongue itself
Lay quivering on the dark earth, murmuring low;
And, as the tail of a snake twitches when severed,
So too her tongue, and with its last dying spasm

It sought its mistress' feet. Even after this atrocity
He is said to have gone back—it strains belief—
Again and again to her torn body in lust. 650

And then he had the nerve to go back to Procne,
Who, as soon as she saw her husband, asked
Where her sister was. He forced a groan
And made up a story about how she had died.
His tears made it plausible. Then Procne
Tore from her shoulders the robe that shone
With a broad gold border, and, dressed now in black,
Built an empty tomb and made pious offerings
To shades that were not, and mourned her sister's fate
In a way that her fate should not have been mourned. 660

And now the sun god has passed through twelve
Zodiacal signs again. What can Philomela do?
A guard precludes flight, the hut's walls are stone,
Mute lips cannot tell. But grief has its own genius,
And with trouble comes cunning. She sets up
A Thracian web on a loom, and weaves purple signs
Onto a white background, revealing the crime.
When it is done she gives the woven fabric
To her sole attendant and asks her with gestures
To take it to the queen. She takes it to Procne 670
Without knowing the inner message it bears.
The tyrant's wife unrolls the cloth and reads
The strands of her sister's song of lament,
And (a wonder that she could) says nothing.
Grief seals her mouth, and her tongue cannot find
Words indignant enough. There is no room for tears,
But she rushes ahead to confound right and wrong,
And all she can do is imagine her vengeance.

It was the time when the Thracian women
Celebrate the twice-yearly festival of Bacchus. 680
Night witnesses the rituals. Mount Rhodope
Rings at night with loud, tingling bronze.

So it is by night that the queen goes forth
Equipped for the god's rites and arrayed for frenzy,
Her head wreathed with vines, a deerskin hanging
From her left side, a light spear on her shoulder.
She streaks through the woods with an attendant throng,
Procne in her rage, driven on by grief's fury,
And mimicking yours, Bacchus. She comes at last
To the hut deep in the woods, and shrieks "Euhoë!"   690
She breaks down the doors, seizes her sister,
Dresses her as a Bacchant, and hiding her face
In ivy leaves, leads the stunned girl into her house.

When Philomela saw that she had been brought
To that accursed house, the poor girl trembled
And the color drained from her face. Procne
Found a good place, took off all the ritual garb,
And, unveiling her sister's embarrassed face,
She took her in her arms. But Philomela
Could not lift her eyes to her, seeing herself   700
As having betrayed her sister. Looking down
And wanting to swear, to call the gods as witness
That her shame was forced upon her, she used her hands
In place of her voice. But Procne is burning,
Unable to control her rage, and scolds her sister
For her weeping.
                    "This is no time for tears," she said,
"But for steel, or, if you have it, something stronger
Than steel. I am ready for any crime, sister,
Either to burn this palace down and throw Tereus,
Whose fault all this is, into the flames,   710
Or to cut out his tongue and eyes and the parts
That stole your chastity and squeeze his guilty soul
Out through a thousand wounds. I am prepared
For some great deed; I just don't know what."

While Procne was saying these things, Itys
Came in to his mother. She now realized
What she could do, and looking at the boy

With pitiless eyes, said,
                    "Ah, how much
You look like your father."
                            And saying no more,
She planned a grim deed in her seething rage.   720
But when the child came up to greet his mother
And he put his small arms around her neck,
Kissing and charming her as little boys do,
The mother in her was moved, her anger dissolved,
And she began to shed tears in spite of herself.
But when she felt herself wavering through excess
Of maternal love, she turned toward her sister's face
And then back and forth between both of them.

"One coos, the other has no tongue with which to speak.
He calls me mother; why can't she call me sister?   730
Look at whose wife you are, daughter of Pandion!
Will you disgrace your husband? But fidelity
To a husband like Tereus is criminal."

And she dragged Itys off as if she were a tigress
Dragging a suckling fawn through the Ganges' dark woods.
When they reached a remote part of the great house
And the boy saw his fate, he stretched out his hands,
Screaming, "Mother! Mother!" and tried to put his arms
Around her neck. Procne struck him in the side
With a sword, and did not change her expression.   740
This one wound was fatal, but Philomela
Slit his throat also, and they sliced up the body
Still warm with life. Some pieces boil in bronze kettles,
Some hiss on spits, and the room drips with gore.

To this feast Procne invites Tereus,
All unknowing. She pretends that the meal
Is a sacred Athenian custom,
And that only the husband may partake,
And she removes all the attendants and slaves.
So Tereus sits on his high, ancestral throne   750

And stuffs his belly with his own flesh and blood.
So great is his mind's blindness that he cries,
"Get Itys here!" Procne cannot conceal
Her cruel joy, and eager to be the herald
Of her butchery, "You have him inside,"
She says. He looks around, asks where he is,
And as he asks again and calls, Philomela,
Just as she was, her hair stained with blood,
Leaps forward and throws the gory head of Itys
Into his father's face, nor was there ever a time   760
When she longed more to be able to speak
And proclaim her joy in words that matched it.
The Thracian overturns the table with a roar
And calls upon the viperish Furies of Styx.
If only now he could lay open his chest
And draw out the feast, vomit his son's flesh.
But all he can do is weep, and call himself
His son's wretched tomb. Then he draws his sword
And pursues the two daughters of Pandion.
You would think that the two Athenians' bodies   770
Were poised on wings, and poised on wings they were,
Philomela flying off to the woods
As a nightingale, and Procne as a swallow
Rising up to the eaves. And even now their breasts
Retain the marks of the slaughter, and their feathers
Are stained with blood. Tereus' desire for vengeance,
And his grief, made him swift, and he himself
Was changed into a bird, with a crest on his head
And an outsized beak instead of a sword.
He is the hoopoe, a bird that seems to be armed.   780

Boreas and Orithyia

This tragedy sent Pandion down to the shades
Of Tartarus before he had reached extreme old age.
His scepter passed to Erechtheus, in whom
Justice was as strong as or stronger than might.
He had four sons and four daughters as well,

Of whom two were equally beautiful. One of them,
Procris, made Aeolus' grandson Cephalus
Happy in marriage. Boreas loved the other,
Orithyia, but being from the north,
Tereus and the Thracians counted against him,   790
And the god was long without his beloved—
While he relied on courtship instead of force.
When being nice was getting him nowhere,
His all too characteristic anger swelled,
And he said to himself:
                              "I deserve it!
Why have I given up my own weapons—
Violence and rage and threatening moods—
And resorted to prayers, which just don't fit me?
Force is what suits me. I use force to drive
The gloomy clouds, force to smash the sea,   800
To uproot gnarly oaks, to pack the snow hard
And pelt the land with hail. And it's the same
When I meet my brothers in the open sky
(Which is my battlefield). We struggle so hard then
That the midair thunders when we collide
And fires flash out from the hollow clouds.
And when I go down into the vaulted caverns
Beneath the earth, and make a ferocious stand,
I frighten the ghosts and the whole world too.
I shouldn't have begged Erechtheus to be   810
My father-in-law; I should have made him be."

With these words, or words not much less forceful,
Boreas shook out the wings that blast the whole world,
And the wide sea bristled. Trailing a cloak of dust
Over the mountain tops, he swept the land
And, shrouded in dark mist, he embraced Orithyia
With his dusky wings as she shivered with fear.
As he flew he fanned the flames of his passion,
Nor did the raptor halt his flight through the air
Until he reached the walls of the Cicones.   820
There the Athenian girl married the chill tyrant

And, becoming a mother, gave birth to twins
Who took after her in everything else
But had their father's wings. These were not present
On their bodies at birth, and while they were beardless
They were wingless too. But when they sprouted
Wings on their shoulders their cheeks too grew tawny.
And when their boyhood ended the young men sailed
With the Minyans as Argonauts, on that first ship,
Seeking the shining wool of the Golden Fleece.   830

Book 7

Jason and Medea

The Argo now was cutting through the sea,
And the Minyans aboard had already seen
Phineus, dragging out his hopeless life
In perpetual night, and the sons of Boreas
Had chased the Harpies from the old man's head;
And brilliant Jason had led his Argonauts
Through many other adventures, when the ship
Pulled into the strong current of the muddy Phasis.
Negotiations with king Aeëtes were under way
For the Golden Fleece that Phrixus had given him,   10
And harsh conditions, hair-raising tasks,
Were being imposed upon Jason. Meanwhile,
The king's daughter had developed a heavy crush
On the Argonauts' leader. She struggled with her feelings
For a long time, and when reason failed,

"Why fight it, Medea?" she said to herself.
"Some god is behind this. I wonder if this
Is what they call love, or something a lot like it.
Else, why should my father's conditions seem too harsh?
They certainly are too harsh. And why do I fear   20
That this man—whom I have just now laid eyes on—
Will perish? What is all this trepidation?
Shake it off, girl! If only I could, I might be
Unhappy, but far more sane. But some strange power
Has me in its grip. Desire pulls me one way.
Reason another. I see what is better,
And approve it, but go after what's worse.
Why should I, a princess, fall for a stranger,
Want to marry a foreigner from across the world?
This land too can give me something to love.   30
Whether he lives or dies is up to the gods.
May he live all the same! And I can pray for this
Even without loving him. What has Jason done?
Who, except a monster, would not be moved
By his youth, his high birth, his manhood?

Or by his beauty alone? He's certainly moved me.
But unless I help him, he will be blasted
By the bulls' fiery breath, and fight an army
Sprung up from the earth he has plowed, and be fed
To the greedy dragon. If I let this happen   40
Call me the child of a tigress, say that I have
Cold stone and iron for a heart. But why can't I
Look on as he dies, why is that anathema?
Why don't I cheer on the bulls against him.
And the earthborn warriors, the sleepless dragon?
Oh, God, no! But that is not a matter
Of my prayers but of what I do. Well then,
Do I betray my father's throne? Do I save
An unknown stranger so that when he is safe
He sails off without me and marries another   50
While I, Medea, am left behind to be punished?
If he can do that, prefer another woman to me,
Let the ungrateful fool die! But no,
Look at his face, his noble soul, his grace—
I don't have to fear deceit or ingratitude.
And he will pledge his faith beforehand, with the gods
As witness to our compact. Why do you fear
What is perfectly safe? Let's get this going!
Jason will be yours forever in holy matrimony
And Greek women everywhere will celebrate you   60
As his deliverer. So will I sail away
And leave my sister behind, my brother,
Father, gods, and native land? Well, my father
Is a mean man, my land is simply barbarous,
My brother is still a baby, my sister
Is with me all the way, and the greatest god of all
Is inside me! I won't be leaving great things,
I'll be going to great things: being called
The girl who saved Jason, getting to know
A better land, cities famous even over here,   70
Culture, art—and the man for whom I would trade
Everything in the world, the son of Aeson.
With him as my husband I will be called

The gods' darling, and my head will touch the stars.
But what about those mountains that they say
Clash in the sea? And Charybdis, that sinks ships
By sucking the saltwater in and then spewing it out?
And marauding Scylla, with all those wild dogs
Howling around her waist in the Sicilian seas?
Oh but if I just hold what I love and nestle   80
In Jason's arms, I can make any sea voyage
Without fear, or if I do fear it will be
Only for my husband. But, Medea,
Are you calling it marriage just to gloss your fault?
You'd better take a good look at how big a sin
You're about to commit, and avoid it while you can."

As she spoke, Propriety stood before her eyes,
Along with Filial Piety and Modesty,
And Love was prepared to turn tail in defeat.

She went to an ancient altar of Hecate   90
Hidden deep in a dark forest. She was strong now,
And her passion had cooled. Then Jason appeared,
And the flames that had died down flared up again,
Her cheeks flushed, then her whole face turned pale.
Just as a tiny spark hidden beneath ashes
Is fanned by the wind and coaxed into new life
Until it glows warmly and regains its old strength,
So too her dormant love, which you would have thought
As good as dead, blazed up again when she saw
The young hero before her in all his glory.   100
Jason happened to be even more handsome
Than usual that day; you could easily forgive her
For loving him. She kept her eyes fixed on the hero
As if she had never seen him before,
Convinced in her infatuation that she gazed upon
A face more than mortal. She could not turn away,
And when her guest began to speak, took her hand
In his and in a low voice requested her help,
Promising marriage in return, she cried out

With tears in her eyes,
                    "I see what I am doing,   110
And I will be undone not by ignorance
But by love. I will save you. But when you are saved,
Keep your promise!"
                    He swore by the holy rites
Of Hecate, by whatever divinity inhabited that grove,
By the all-seeing Sun, father of his future father-in-law,
By his own triumphs and by the great perils he faced.
She believed him, and he received from her at once
The charmed herbs and learned how to use them.
He was a happy man when he returned to his room.

Dawn had blotted out the last twinkling stars   120
When the crowds began to gather on the field of Mars,
With standing room only on the ridge above, the king
Took his seat in the middle, resplendent in purple
And wielding an ivory scepter. And now, look—
The bronze-hooved bulls trot in, breathing fire
From their adamantine nostrils. The grass touched
By those vapors burns to a crisp. The bulls' chests
Roar like furnaces, their scorched throats hiss
Like limestone doused with water in a hot kiln.
Jason nonetheless went forward to meet them,   130
And as he approached the animals swiveled
Their fierce faces toward him, and their iron-tipped horns,
Pawing the dusty earth with their cloven hooves
And filling the place with their fiery bellowing.
The Minyans were frozen with fear, but Jason,
Close now, did not feel the bulls' breath at all—
That's what drugs can do. He patted their dewlaps
With a fearless hand, put the yoke on their necks,
And made them pull the heavy plowshare,
Cutting through the field that had never felt steel.   140
The Colchians didn't know what to say, but the Minyans
Cheered their hero on. Next he took from a bronze helmet
The dragon's teeth and sowed them in the field he had plowed.
The teeth and been steeped in venom, and softened now

By the earth, they grew into new bodies.
And just as an infant in its mother's womb
Gradually assumes a complete human form
Before emerging into the common air,
So too when these human forms were complete
In the womb of pregnant earth, up they rose   150
Through the teeming soil and—even more wonderful—
They were born with weapons, which they now clashed.
When the Argonauts saw them poised to hurl
Their finely honed spears at the Minyan hero
Their faces fell with fear, and their hearts sank.
Even Medea, who had safeguarded him thus far,
Trembled now; and when she saw her Jason
Out there alone, attacked by so many,
The blood drained from her face, and she sat there
Pale and cold. Afraid that the magic herbs   160
She had given him would not be strong enough,
She reached deep into her occult arts and chanted
An auxiliary spell. Jason's next move was to throw
A heavy stone into his enemies' midst,
Diverting their fury away from him
And onto themselves. And so these brothers
Born of the earth killed each other in civil strife.
The Greeks were all over the victorious hero,
Slapping him on the back and hugging him.
You would have gladly embraced your victor, too,   170
Colchian girl, but modesty prevented you.
Still, you would have held him, but for all the talk.
But you could, and did, rejoice in secret love,
Thanking your spells and the gods who gave them.

There was still the dragon to drug to sleep,
With his crest, his curved fangs, and a tri-forked tongue,
The ever-wakeful guardian of the golden tree.
But Jason had sprinkled him with the narcotic juice
Of a Lethaean herb and recited three times
A spell of slumber that could calm the sea   180
And stop a raging river. Sleep came to those eyes

That had never slept before, and Aeson's heroic son
Had the Golden Fleece.
                              Riding high with this prize
And taking with him the one who bestowed it,
Herself another prize, the victor at last arrived
At the harbor of Iolchos with his new wife.

Thessalian mothers and aging fathers
Brought gifts in honor of their sons' return,
Burned heaps of incense and sacrificed
The victim they had promised with gilded horns.   190
Aeson, though, was absent from these celebrations,
An old man now and close to death. Turning to Medea
His son now said,
                        "My wife, I owe you everything.
My very life, and the sum of your services
Has exceeded all my hopes. Still if it can be done—
And what can your spells not do?—take some years
From my own life and add them to my father's."

He could not hold back his tears. Medea was moved
By his filial piety, and she thought of Aeëtes,
Deserted. Supressing her feelings of guilt,   200
She replied,
              "What a thing to say, my husband!
Do you think I can transfer a part of your life
To someone else? Hecate would never permit this,
And your request is not just. But I will try to give you
More than what you ask for, Jason, to renew
Your father's life span not with years from yours
But through my witchcraft, if only Hecate
Will help me undertake this daring deed."

There were three nights still before the moon
Filled her globe with light. When she did shine   210
At her fullest and looked down at the earth
With her round and perfect face, Medea
Stole out of her house barefoot, robes unsashed,

Hair fanning out on her shoulders, and wandered
All alone through the silence of midnight.
Men, birds, and beasts were lost in slumber.
The hedgerow was quiet, the leaves motionless
And hushed, and the dewy air still. Only
The stars twinkled. Stretching up her arms to these
She twirled thrice around, thrice sprinkled water   220
Scooped up from a stream on her hair, and thrice
Parted her lips in a quavering wail.
Then, kneeling on the hard earth,
                                    "O Night,"
She prayed, "truest to the mysteries; golden stars,
Who with the moon succeed to the fires of day;
Triform Hecate, who knows our undertakings
And come to the aid of magic arts and spells;
Earth, who provides us with your potent herbs;
And all the breezes, winds, mountains, streams, and pools;
Gods of the groves and gods of the night, all gods,   230
Be with me now. With your help I have willed
Rivers to run backward through their astonished banks;
My spells calm the raging and enrage the calm seas,
Dispel the clouds and conjure them up, lay the winds
And make them blow; with chanted words I crush
Dragons' throats, uproot rocks and oaks, put forests
In motion. Mountains tremble at my incantations;
The earth bellows, and ghosts crawl from their tombs.
I draw you, Luna, down from the sky, though all the bronze
Of Temesa clangs to relieve your pain. The chariot   240
Of my grandfather, the Sun, dims when I chant.
Aurora pales at my poisons. You dulled for me
The bulls' fiery breath, made their necks submit
To the weight of a yoke, turned the serpent-born men
Against themselves, lulled to sleep the guardian dragon,
And sent the golden prize to the cities of Greece.
My need now is elixirs to return old age
To the bloom of youth, to regain life's early days—
And you will give them! For the stars did not
Flash in vain just now, and here is my chariot   250

Drawn by winged dragons."
                              And there the chariot was,
Sent down from heaven. Medea mounted,
Stroked the dragons' bridled necks, shook the reins,
And was up and away. She looked down below
On Thessalian Tempe and steered the dragons
To certain regions she knew, surveying all the herbs
That Mount Ossa bore, and Pelion, Othrys
And Pindus, and Olympus greater than Pindus.
Those that she liked she either pulled up by the root
Or cut off with a bronze-bladed pruning hook,   260
And then chose many more from the banks of rivers,
From the Apidanus and from the Amphrysus,
And you, Eripeus contributed some, Peneus too,
Spercheios, and Boëbe with its reedy banks.
She also plucked, from the Euboean Anthedon,
A life-giving plant, one not yet famous
For the way it transformed the body of Glaucus.

Nine days had seen her cruising all the lands,
And nine nights, drawn by her flying dragons.
On her return the dragons, at the mere touch   270
Of odor of those magic herbs, sloughed off
Their layers of old, wrinkled skin. Medea stood
Beyond the threshold of her house, covered
By the sky alone, avoiding any contact
With the opposite sex. She built two turf altars,
One on the right to Hecate, and one to Youth on the left,
And wreathed them with greenery from the wild forest.
Close by she dug two trenches in the earth
And performed her ritual, sinking a knife
Into the throat of a black sheep and letting the blood   280
Drain into the open pits. Then she topped it off
With bowls of pure honey and bowls of warm milk.
Muttering incantations the whole time,
She summoned the gods from beneath the earth,
Praying to the lord of the shades and his stolen bride
Not to steal too quickly the old man's last breath.

When her long, murmured prayers had appeased
These divinities, she had Aeson's worn-out body
Brought into the open air. Putting him into a deep sleep
With her spells, she stretched him out on a bed of herbs   290
As if he were dead. Then she ordered Jason
And all the servants to remove themselves, warning them
Not to peer at her mysteries with profane eyes.
They all withdrew. Medea, hair streaming
Like a Bacchant's, circled the blazing altars,
And dipping torches in the dark, gory trenches
She lit them in the sacred flames. Thrice she blessed
The old man with fire, thrice with water, with sulfur thrice.
All the while a strong potion is boiling
In a bronze pot, bubbling up with frothy white foam.   300
She adds ingredients one by one: roots culled
In a Thessalian valley, seeds, flowers
And pungent juices, gemstones from the farthest Orient,
Sand washed by the Ocean's ebbing tide,
Frost scraped up under the full moon's light,
The wings of a screech owl with flesh intact,
And a werewolf's entrails. She did not leave out
The scaly skin of a Cinyphian water snake,
The liver of a long-lived stag, the beak and head
Of a crow nine generations old, not to mention   310
A thousand other things that don't even have names.
When the barbarian woman had concocted
This more than mortal brew, she stirred it up
With a withered branch of olive, mixing it well
In the steaming pot. The desiccated old stick
Was tinged with green, soon sprouted leaves, and suddenly
Flourished with teeming ripe olives. Wherever the kettle
Bubbled over and warm froth splashed the ground
The earth grew green with soft grass, and flowers bloomed.
When she saw this, Medea unsheathed her knife   320
And cut the old man's jugular. Letting all the old blood
Run out, she filled his veins with the potion. When Aeson
Drank it in, partly through his mouth, partly
Through the open wound, his beard and his hair

Suddenly turned from grey to black. No more
Was he gaunt and haggard; his wrinkles filled in,
His body rippled with muscles, and Aeson
Remembered in amazement that this was he,
This was his body forty years ago.

Bacchus, watching from the sky, saw this miracle,   330
And surmising that his old nurses could be restored
To their youth, the god got Medea to do just that.

And now, treachery. Medea feigned a quarrel
With Jason and took refuge in the house of Pelias,
Whose daughters received her hospitably,
For old age weighed heavy upon their father.
The crafty Colchian quickly won them over
With a false show of friendship, telling them
All about the amazing things she'd done
And especially about rejuvenating Aeson.   340
This gave the girls the idea that their father
Could likewise be made young again by magic.
They begged Medea to do it, and to name her price.
She hesitated, silent, pretending to be in doubt,
Keeping them in suspense with her phony pondering.
Finally she promised, saying,
                              "So that you can trust
What I am going to do for you, through my drugs
The oldest ram in your flocks will become a lamb."

An old, wooly ram was promptly brought out,
His horns curling around his hollow temples.   350
His throat was so scrawny that when she slit it
The blood barely stained the Thessalian blade.
Then the witch threw his carcass, along with potions
Of surpassing potency, into a bronze cauldron.
The ram's body shrank, his horns were burnt away,
And with his horns his years evaporated. To their wonder
A soft "baa" was heard from the pot, and out jumped
A frisky lamb, who ran off to find an udder to suck.

Pelias' daughters were dumbstruck, and after seeing
This show of good faith they were even more insistent.   360
Phoebus had unyoked his horses three times
After their plunge into the Iberian Ocean,
And on the fourth night the stars were twinkling
When Aeëtes' guileful daughter put a bronze vat
Filled with pure water over a roaring fire
And stirred in a few herbs of no potency at all.
By now the king, along with his guards,
Were in a deep sleep, a slumber induced
By strong incantations. The king's daughters,
Who had their instructions, entered his room   370
And encircled his bed.
                    "What are you waiting for?"
Medea said, "Draw your swords and drain his old blood,
So I can fill his veins with a fresh transfusion.
Your father's life and youth rest in your own hands.
If you love him, and if you trust what you're about,
Do your duty by your father, use your weapons
To expel his old age, let out his clotted gore
By slipping in steel."
                    Urged on like this,
The most filial daughter was most promptly unfilial,
And so as not to be sinful, each committed a sin.   380
Still, none of them could bear to see her own blows.
They turned away their eyes and blindly struck
With cruel hands. The old man was a bloody mess,
But managed to raise himself up on one elbow
And mangled as he was, tried to get out of bed,
Stretching out his pale arms in that welter of swords
And crying,
                    "What are you doing, my daughters?
What has made you draw steel to kill your father?"

The girls wilted, and before the old man could say
Anything else, the Colchian witch cut his throat,   390
And plunged his torn body into the boiling water.

She never would have escaped without her
Winged dragons, drawing her now across the sky
High over shady Pelion, home of Chiron,
Over Othrys and the lands famous for the adventures
Of old Cerambus, who, aided by certain nymphs,
Flew off on wings when the earth was deluged
And so escaped being drowned in Deucalion's flood.
She passed Aeolian Pitane on the left
With its huge stone statue of a sinuous dragon;   400
Soared over Ida's grove, where Bacchus made an ox
Look like a deer to conceal his son's theft;
Over Corythus' father entombed in sand; the fields
Maera terrorized with her strange barking;
Eurypylus' city, where the Coan women wore horns
When Hercules and his men at last withdrew;
Over Rhodes, Apollo's favorite city,
And the Telchines of Ialysus,
Plunged by Jupiter beneath his brother's waves
Because their odious eyes blighted all they saw.   410
And she passed also ancient Carthaea
On the island of Cea, where Alcidamas would marvel
That a dove could rise from his daughter's body.

Then she saw Hyrië's pool, and Tempe,
Famous for the sudden transformation of Cygnus
Into a swan. Phyllius used to bring him,
At the boy's command, birds he had tamed
And even a lion. When Cygnus asked him
To tame a bull, Phyllius tamed one.
But, tired of being rejected by the boy,   420
He withheld this last gift. Furious,
Cygnus said, "You'll wish you had given it,"
And jumped off a cliff. They all thought he had fallen,
But, turned into a swan, he hung in the air
On snow-white wings. His mother, Hyrië,
Had no idea her son was safe, and she melted away
Into tears, becoming a pool that is named after her.

Close by lies Pleuron, where on trembling wings
Ophius' daughter, Combe, eluded her murderous sons.
Next over she sees Calaurea, Latona's island,   430
Where the king and his wife were changed into birds.
On her right is Cyllene, where Menephron
Would sleep with his mother, like any wild beast.
In the distance she spots the Cephisus River
Mourning his grandson, who was changed by Apollo
Into a plump seal; and she makes out the home
Of Eumelus, lamenting his airborne son.

The dragons finally set her down in Corinth,
Where the elders say men originally were born
From mushrooms soaked with rain.
                                        However,   440
After Jason's new bride was melted by the heat
Of the Colchian's poisons, and the two seas
On either side of the Isthmus had seen
The king's palace in flames, she drenched her sword
In the blood of her sons (some mother!)
And, thus avenged, escaped Jason's own vengeance.
On her Titanic dragons she rode to the Acropolis
In Athens, which had seen you, Phene most just,
And you, old Periphas, flying side by side,
And Alcyone aloft on her newfound wings.   450
Aegeus took her in, which was enough to doom him,
And not content with that, married her as well.

Theseus now arrived in town, a son unknown
To his father Aegeus and whose heroic acts
Had brought peace to the Isthmus. Medea
Wanted him dead and brewed up some aconite
She had culled long ago from Scythia's shores.
They say that this poison came from the fangs
Of Cerberus, born from Echidna. There is a cave
With a dark, gaping mouth and a sloping path   460
Up which Hercules, the hero of Tiryns,

Dragged Cerberus bound with adamantine chains.
The dog struggled hard, twisting his eyes
From the bright light of day and, rabid with rage,
Filled the air with howls from all three of his throats,
Flecking the green fields with white, foaming slobber.
Country folk maintain that the slobber congealed
And, drawing sustenance from the fecund earth,
Developed noxious powers; and because it grows
And thrives on hard stone, they call it aconite.   470
This was the poison that Medea in her cunning
Had Aegeus serve to his son as if to a stranger.
Theseus had lifted the cup all unaware
When his father recognized on his ivory sword hilt
The family's emblems and dashed that cupful of sin
From the lips of his son. Medea escaped again,
This time in an enchanted capsule of mist.

Aegeus was overjoyed that his son was safe
But horrified that such a monstrous crime
Had been so closely skirted. He kindled fires   480
On altars and made offerings to the gods;
Axes struck the muscled necks of ribboned bulls.
No day ever dawned for the Athenians
More festive than that. Patricians and commoners
Partied together, wine making them witty
As they sang their songs:

Hymn to Theseus

"Theseus the Great,
Marathon loves that you killed the Bull of Crete;
You made farmers safe from the Crommyonian Sow;
Epidaurus saw you lay Periphetes low,
Though he was Vulcan's son, with a massive club;   490
Though his cast-iron bed reduced guests to a stub,
The Cephisus saw you take Procrustes out;
And Eleusis is glad that Cercyon's not about.
You cut down Sinis who would bend down trees
And catapult people through the morning breeze.

The Isthmus is safe now that Sciron's no more;
His bones won't rest on the land or on shore.
The waves will rattle those bones like skiffs
Until finally they form Sciron's cliffs.
If we cheered for each of your honors and years   500
You'd find that your honors would have more cheers.
We praise and thank you, hero divine,
And for you we drain our cups of wine."

Minos' Embassy to Aegina

The palace resounded with fervent applause,
And there was not a sad face in the whole city.
But pleasure is never unalloyed, and care
Accompanies joy. Minos was planning war.
He was strong in ships and men, but his greatest strength
Was his anger as a father, and he meant to avenge
The death of Androgeos with a righteous war.   510
His first step was to enlist allies, and his fleet,
A tactical advantage, scoured the sea.
He recruited Anaphe and Astypalaea
(The first with promises, the second with threats),
Low-lying Myconos and chalky Cimolos,
Syros flowering with thyme, flat Seriphos,
Paros with all its marble, and Siphnos
Betrayed by impious Arne. She took the gold
Her greed had demanded and then was changed
Into a bird that still likes gold, the jackdaw,   520
With its black feet and all feathered in black.
Nor did Oliaros and Didymae, Tenos and Andros,
Gyaros and Peparethos with its rich olive crop
Fail to give aid to the Cretan fleet. Veering left,
Minos made for Oenopia, the ancient name
Of the Aeacid realm, but Aeacus himself
Renamed it Aegina after his mother.
As Minos pulled in, a crowd came out to greet
The great man. Telamon came, and Peleus,
Somewhat his junior, and Phocus, still younger.   530

Aeacus himself emerged, slowed down by his years,
And asked Minos why he had come. Reminded
Of his grief, the ruler of a hundred cities
Sighed and answered,

      "I ask you to assist me
In a just war. I seek solace for my buried son."

And Aeacus responded,

       "What you ask for
My city cannot give, for none is allied
So closely to Athens as is Aegina."

Minos scowled and said as he left,

        "You will pay
For your treaty."

     He thought it a better strategy   540
To threaten war rather than to waste his resources
By waging it then.

Cephalus' Embassy to Aegina

    The Cretan fleet could still be seen
From the city walls when an Attic ship
Under full sail pulled into the friendly port
Bringing Cephalus and a message from Athens.
It had been a long time since they laid eyes on Cephalus,
But Aeacus' sons recognized him, clasped his hand,
And brought him into their father's house.
The hero was something to look at, and you could tell
He had been even more beautiful once. He carried   550
A branch of his country's olive as he entered
And was flanked by two younger men,
Clytos and Butes, sons of Pallas.

        Greetings exchanged,
Cephalus got down to business, asking Aeacus
For military aid. He referenced the terms
Of the treaty struck by their ancestors
And added that Minos had designs on all Greece.

When his eloquence had supported his mission,
Aeacus, his left hand resting on his scepter's hilt,
Said in response,
        "Ask not for our aid, Athens,   560
But take it! All of the forces this island has,
And all that I control, are at your command.
I have enough soldiers for our defense (thanks to the gods!)
And for your enemy."
        "May it be so,"
Said Cephalus, "and may your city flourish.
On my way here I was delighted to meet
Such fine young men—and all of the same age!
But I missed seeing many that I came to know
On my last visit here."
        Aeacus sighed
And in a sad voice said,

The Plague at Aegina

        "It was pitiful   570
When it started, but better times followed.
I wish I could tell you the last part
Without the first, but, not to keep you in suspense,
The ones you remember and inquire about
Are dust and bones. Much of my kingdom
Died with them. A terrible plague hit my people,
Brought on by Juno, who hated our island
Because it is named after her rival in love.
As long as it seemed to have a natural cause
We combated the plague with medicine,   580
But its devastation drained our resources dry.
First, the sky pressed thick and black on the earth
And held the oppressive heat in the clouds,
And while the moon waxed four times to full
And four times waned, hot winds from the south
Breathed disease upon us. At the same time
The infection reached our springs and pools,
And a thousand snakes infested our deserted fields
And poisoned our rivers. At first the swift plague

Destroyed only dogs and birds, sheep and cattle,   590
And beasts in the wild. The poor plowman
Couldn't believe his strong bulls collapsed
And lay down into the furrow. The wooly flocks
Bleated feebly while their tufts fell off
And they wasted away. Thoroughbred horses
Renowned on the race course forgot their victories
And groaned in their stalls facing inglorious deaths.
Boars forgot their rage, deer were no longer fleet,
And bears no longer attacked the great herds.
Lethargy reigned. Decaying carcasses littered   600
Woods, fields, and roads. The stench fouled the air,
And neither dogs, scavenging birds, nor grey wolves
Would touch them. The bodies rotted where they lay,
And their noxious odor spread the contagion.

The plague gained strength; it attacked country folk,
And its power was felt within the city walls.
The first symptoms are a deep burning inside,
A scarlet rash, and labored breath. The tongue is rough
And swollen, the mouth hangs open, dry from panting
And gulping the heavy air. Patients cannot bear   610
To be in bed or to be covered at all, but lie
Face down on the ground, which itself becomes warm
Rather than cooling their bodies. No one
Can control the disease; physicians themselves
Come down with bad cases, and the closer one is
To the sick, the more faithfully he treats them,
The more quickly he gets sick himself and dies.
As they lose hope, seeing that their sickness
Will only end in death, they indulge their desires
And do not care about what helps. Nothing helps.   620
They lie shamelessly about everywhere, in springs,
Streams and the basins of wells, but succumb
Before drinking ever quenches their thirst. Too weak
To stand, many die in the water. Yet others drink
That very water. For many of those suffering
Their beds are so wearisome that they jump out,

Or if they're too weak, roll out onto the ground
And leave their homes, which seem like death itself.
Since the cause of the disease is unknown,
Their poor homes are blamed. You could see them out there,   630
Wandering the roads half dead, while they could still stand.
Others would be lying on the ground, weeping.
They would lift up their eyes with one final effort,
Stretch their arms to the stars above, and here, there,
Wherever death caught them, breathe their last.

What was it like for me then? Should I have not
Hated my life and wanted to be with my friends?
Wherever my eyes turned, corpses lay in heaps,
Like rotten apples fallen from a shaken tree,
Or acorns from a storm-beaten oak. Do you see   640
That temple over there, with the long stairs?
It is sacred to Jupiter. Who did not bring
Useless offerings of incense to its altars?
How often did a husband, praying for his wife,
A father for his son, die at those altars
While still saying his prayer, the unused incense
Still clutched in his hand? How often has a bull,
The priest still praying and pouring pure wine
Between his horns, collapsed before the axe's stroke?
While I myself was sacrificing to Jove   650
For myself, my country, and for my three sons,
The victim bellowed awfully and fell untouched,
Then barely stained the knife with its paltry blood.
Its disease-ridden entrails could not be read,
For the infection infiltrates all the vital parts.
I saw corpses dumped before the temple doors,
Even before the altars, making their deaths
All the more odious. Some hung themselves,
Escaping their fear of death with death, inviting in
Their approaching fate. The dead were not buried   660
In the usual way, for the city could not handle
So many funerals. They either lay on the ground
Unburied, or were piled on pyres without ceremony.

Soon there was no reverence for the dead at all.
Men fought for funeral pyres and were burned
With stolen flames. No one was left to mourn the dead,
As unwept they wandered, the souls of sons
And of husbands, souls of young men and old.
There was no space for graves, no wood for fire.

The Origin of the Myrmidons

Overwhelmed by this flood of misery,   670
I cried out,
              'O Jupiter, if it is true
That you loved Aegina, daughter of Asopus,
And if you, Great Father, are not ashamed
To be our father, either restore my people
Or bury me in my tomb.'
                        He gave me a sign,
Lightning seconded by a peal of thunder.
'I accept the sign,' I said, 'and I pray
That these omens signal your generous intent.'

It happened that there was an oak nearby
With spreading branches, a magnificent tree   680
Of Dodona's stock, and on it we saw
A long column of ants gathering grain,
Each insect bearing a heavy load in its mouth
And holding its line on the wrinkled bark.
Marveling at the bustling swarm, I said,
'Fill my empty kingdom, Father Almighty,
With that many citizens.'
                        And the great oak
Trembled, its leaves rustling in the windless air.
I bristled with fear, and my hair stood on end.
Yet I kissed the earth and the tree, and although   690
I would not admit it, I was filled with hope.
Night came and blanketed our careworn bodies.
As I slept, that same oak tree seemed to stand
Before my eyes, with just as many branches
And just as many ants upon it, and it shook

In just the same way, but now it scattered
All of the insects onto the ground below.
They seemed suddenly to grow larger and larger
And to raise themselves up and stand erect,
Losing their leanness and their multiple feet   700
And their black color, and assuming human form.
Then I awoke. Dismissing my dream, I complained
There was no help from the gods. But the palace
Was thrumming, and there came to my ears
The now unfamiliar sound of human voices.
I thought I was still dreaming, but Telamon
Came running up, threw open the doors, and said,
'Father, come see more than you ever hoped for!'
I went outside and saw exactly the same men
As in my dream. They came up to me now   710
And greeted me as their king. I gave thanks
To Jupiter, and to my new subjects
I parceled out my city and the fields
Left empty by their former occupants.
And I called my new people Myrmidons,
Honoring their origin as ants. You have seen
Their bodies. They retain their former habits,
A thrifty people who know how to work,
To go after something and keep what they get.
They will follow you to war well matched in age   720
And temper, as soon as the propitious East Wind
That brought you here" (for it was the East Wind
That brought Cephalus there) "shifts to the south."

They filled the day with such talk and more. As the light
Faded they feasted, and when darkness fell they slept.
When the golden sun lifted his crest of light,
The East Wind still blew, keeping the ships
From sailing back home. The two sons of Pallas
Came to Cephalus, who was older, and together
They went to see the king, but he was still fast asleep.   730
Aeacus' son Phocus met them at the door,
For Telamon and his brother Peleus

Were marshaling the troops. Phocus led the Athenians
Into a beautiful inner courtyard
And there the four of them sat down together.
Phocus noticed that Cephalus had in his hand
A javelin made out of an unusual wood
And tipped in gold. After saying a few words,
He interrupted himself:

                    "I love the woods
And am a hunter myself, but I've been wondering   740
What kind of wood that javelin is made of.
If it were ash, it would have a tawny color,
And if it were cornel it would be knotty.
I don't recognize the wood, but I've never seen
A javelin more beautiful than the one you have."

One of the Athenian brothers replied,

"You'll like its use more than its looks. It goes
Straight to the target, no luck involved,
And comes back bloodied all on its own."

Young Phocus wanted to know all about it then,   750
Where it came from, and who gave Cephalus
Such a wonderful gift. Cephalus told him
What he wanted to know, but was ashamed to say
What that javelin cost him. He fell silent,
Then, thinking of his lost wife, burst into tears.

Procris and Cephalus

"Who could believe that it is this weapon
That makes me weep? And it will make me weep
All the rest of my life. This javelin destroyed me
Along with my dear wife. I wish I'd never had it.
My wife was Procris. You may have heard of   760
Orithyia, the beauty ravaged by the North Wind;
She was her sister, and if you were to compare
The two sisters in character and beauty,
Procris would be more worthy to be stolen away.

Erechtheus gave her to me in marriage,
But Love tied the knot. I was called happy,
And I was. I might have still been happy now,
But the gods saw it differently.

                      In the second month
After our wedding, while I was spreading my nets
To catch antlered deer, Aurora, golden in her dawn,   770
Had just dispelled the shadows when she saw me
From the top of flowering Hymettus
And took me against my will. May the goddess
Not be offended if I speak the truth,
But as sure as her face is lovely as a rose,
As sure as she holds the border of day and night
And drinks nectar, it was Procris I loved,
Procris in my heart, Procris ever on my lips.
I kept talking about our wedding and the first time
We made love in our now desolate bed.   780
The goddess was upset and said,

                         'Quit complaining,
You little ingrate. Keep your Procris! But if I can
Prophesy at all, you'll wish you never had her.'

And mad as can be, she sent me back to her.
As I made my way home the goddess' warning
Kept going through my mind, and I began to fear
That my wife had not kept her marriage vows.
Her youth and beauty made adultery credible,
But her morals made it unthinkable.
Still, I'd been gone a long time, and the goddess I'd left   790
Was a shining example of infidelity herself, and,
Well, we lovers fear everything. I decided
To create a grievance for myself by tempting
Her fidelity with gifts. Aurora helped me
With my jealous fear by changing my form
(I felt it happen), and so I entered Athens
Incognito. When I went into my house
There was no sign of guilt anywhere; everyone
Was anxious for the return of their absent lord.

It took all my ingenuity to gain an audience   800
With Erechtheus' daughter. When I looked at her
My heart skipped a beat and I almost abandoned
The test of her fidelity that I had planned.
It was all I could do to keep from coming clean
And kissing her as she deserved. She was sad,
But no woman could be more beautiful
Than she was in her sadness, and all of her grief
Was longing for the husband that she had lost.
Imagine, Phocus, how beautiful she was,
How her grief itself made her more beautiful.   810
I don't have to tell you how often her chastity
Defeated my attempts, how often she said,

'I keep myself for one man alone; wherever he is,
All my joy is for him.'
                        What man in his right mind
Would need more proof than that? But no,
I wasn't satisfied, and wound up hurting myself.
By promising fortunes for one night with her
And then promising more, I made her hesitate,
And then, gloating in my false victory, I exclaimed,

'Ha! There's no adulterer here, but your real husband,   820
And I've caught you betraying me.'
                                  She said nothing.
In total silence, overcome with shame, she fled
Her pathetic husband, left his treacherous house.
Loathing me and hating the entire male race
She took to the mountains and followed Diana.
Alone, I felt love burning deep in my bones.
I begged forgiveness, confessed that I had sinned,
Admitted that I too might have succumbed
If someone had offered me gifts like that.
When I said these things and she had avenged   830
Her outraged sense of self-respect, she came back,
And spent sweet years with me, two hearts as one.
Then, as if she herself were too slight a gift,

She gave me a hound that she had received
From her own Cynthia, and said that this dog
Would outrun any other. And she gave me also
A javelin, the one you see in my hands.
Would like to hear the story of both gifts?
It is a strange tale, and you will be moved.

After Oedipus had solved the riddle of the Sphinx   840
She plunged to her death, and the dark prophetess lay
Forgetful of her mysterious sayings.
But Themis does not allow such things
To go unpunished, and a second monster
Was promptly dispatched to Aonian Thebes.
The whole countryside lived in constant terror
Of this beast, fearing for themselves and their herds,
And so all of us neighboring young heroes
Surrounded the wide fields with our hunting nets.
Well, she just sailed right over the top of the nets   850
With one light leap and then kept on going.
We unleashed the hounds, but she made fools
Out of the entire pack, leaving them all behind
As if she had wings. Then all of the hunters,
Myself included, called for Whirlwind (my dog's name).
He was already straining to slip free of his chain,
And as soon as he was released we couldn't tell
Where he might be. You could see his prints in the dust,
But that dog was gone. No spear is faster,
No bullet whirled from a sling, no reed arrow   860
Shot from a Gortynian bow. I climbed up
To the top of a hill that overlooked the plain
To get a better view of that amazing chase.
The wild thing looked like it was almost caught
And then would slip right out of the dog's open jaws,
And she was cunning, wouldn't run in a straight line,
But would feint and then wheel sharply around
To make her enemy lose his momentum.
Lailaps pressed her hard, matching her speed,
But just when you thought he had her,   870

His jaws would snap on empty air. I went
To my javelin, and just as I had it balanced
And was twisting my fingers into the loop,
I glanced away, and when I turned my eyes back,
I saw two marble statues out on the plain.
Incredible. One of them you'd swear was running away
And the other was about to catch its prey.
If there was any god with them in that race,
That god must have wanted neither to lose."

Cephalus fell silent. Phocus asked,
                              "What then   880
Do you have against the javelin?"
                              So Cephalus
Told him what he had against the javelin.

"My sorrow began in joy, son of Aeacus,
And it is a joy now to recall that blessed time,
Those years when I was happy with my wife,
As is only right, and she with her husband.
Mutual cares and shared love bound us together.
She would not have preferred Jupiter's love
To mine, and no woman could have taken me
Away from her, not even Venus herself.   890
We were passionately in love with each other.

When the rising sun struck the mountains' peaks
I used to go hunting in the woods. I was young,
And I went out alone, no attendants with me,
No horses, no dogs on the scent, no knotted nets.
I was safe with my javelin. And when I had my fill
Of bringing down game, I would look for shade
And the breeze gently stirring in the cool valleys.
I looked for that soft breeze in the summer heat,
Waited for the breeze, relief from my labors.   900
'Come, Aura,' I remember I used to croon,
'Help me out, blow on my chest, you know
I love you, cool down my heat as only you can.'

And I might, since my fates were drawing me on,
Add some sweet nothings, saying things like.
'You're my greatest pleasure,' and 'You make me feel
So good. I'm crazy about the woods because of you.
I just love to feel your breath on my face.'
Someone overhearing this mistook its meaning,
And thought that by 'Aura' I meant not the breeze   910
But some nymph, that I was in love with a nymph.
This tattletale went to Procris with a story
That I had been unfaithful and whispered to her
The words he had heard. Love is a credulous thing.
She was overwhelmed and, I heard, fainted
And only came to after a long time, weeping
And cursing her fate, complaining about
My supposed infidelity. Deeply troubled
By an imaginary crime, she feared what was nothing,
A name with nothing behind it, the poor woman,   920
Grieving as if 'Aura' were an actual rival.
Yet she often thought, in her misery,
That she might be wrong and said she would not
Believe it, would not condemn her husband,
Until she saw it herself.
                              The next morning,
As soon as Aurora had dispelled the dark,
I went out into the woods, and after a good hunt
I lay in the grass, and as I was calling, 'Aura,
Come relieve my suffering,' I thought I heard
Someone moaning. Still, I went on, 'Come, dearest.'   930
The fallen leaves rustled in reply. Thinking
It was a wild animal, I threw my javelin.
It was Procris, clasping her wounded breast
And crying out, 'Ah, me.' Recognizing
My wife's voice, I ran frantically toward the sound.
I found her half alive, her clothes spattered with blood
And trying to pull the spear, this spear that she gave me,
Out from the wound. What misery. I lifted
Her body, dearer to me than my own,
As gently as I could, tore the clothes from her breast   940

And tried to stop the bleeding, begging her
Not to leave me guilty of her death. Dying,
And with little strength left, she still forced herself
To speak a few words, saying,
                             'By the bed
We swore to share, by the gods I pray to above
And by my own gods, by any good I deserve of you,
And by the love that even in death remains
And is the cause of my death, do not allow
This Aura to replace me.'
                             It was then I realized,
Too late, the error the name caused, and told her.   950
But what good did it do to tell her? She sank back,
Her last bit of strength ebbing away with her blood.
While her eyes could still focus on something,
She looked at me, and breathed out on my lips
Her unfortunate spirit, but as she died
Her face at last seemed to be free from care."

The hero had finished his story in tears
When Aeacus came in with his other two sons
And an army of newly enlisted men
That he presented to Cephalus, all heavily armed.   960

Book 8

Nisus and Scylla

When the Morning Star had chased away the night
And let the shining day peek through, the East Wind fell
And moist clouds rolled in. The soft South Wind
Offered easy sailing to Cephalus and Aeacus' troops
And blew them into harbor sooner than they had hoped.
Minos meanwhile was pillaging the coast of Megara
And was flexing his muscles against the city itself,
Where Nisus was king. This Nisus had a head
Of distinguished grey hair, but one of the locks
Was bright purple, and on this one lock of hair   10
The security of his kingdom depended.

The horns of the moon had been retipped six times
And the outcome of the war still hung in the balance,
Victory hovering on uncertain wings.
There was a royal tower topping the tuneful walls
Where Apollo had set down the golden lyre
Whose music still clung to the stones. The daughter
Of King Nisus used to climb this tower
And throw pebbles to clatter on the rocks below
In the days when there was still peace. When the war came   20
She would often look out at the hard fighting.
And now, as the war dragged on, she came to know
The enemies' names, their armor, their horses,
And their Cretan quivers. Above all she knew the face
Of their commander, Europa's son, knew it
Better than she should. If Minos' head were encased
In a crested helmet, he was in her eyes
Just lovely helmeted. If he carried a shining bronze shield,
He looked good with a shield. When he threw a spear
The girl raved about his strength and skill.   30
When he pulled his bow into a great arc
With an arrow on the string, she swore that Phoebus
Was standing there with his arrows. But when
He showed his face, bareheaded, wearing purple
Astride his white horse, pulling on the embroidered reins

As he managed the foaming bit—then Nisus' daughter
Could hardly be said to be in her right mind.
She thought the javelin he touched was felicity itself,
And the reins in his hands had gone to heaven.
She would, if she could, run on her virginal feet   40
Into the enemy's lines. She wanted to leap
From the tower into the Cretan camp, fling open
The city's bronze-bound gates and let the enemy in,
And to do any other thing that Minos might want.
And as she sat gazing at the Cretan's white tents,

"Should I rejoice," she said, "at this horrible war,
Or should I grieve? I can't make up my mind.
I grieve because Minos is the enemy
Of the girl who loves him. But without this war
I would never had known him. If I were his hostage   50
He could give up the war. He would have me with him
As a pledge of peace. If the mother who bore you,
The most beautiful thing in all the world,
Was anything like you, the god's passion for her
Was justified. Oh I would be happy, happy, happy
If I could fly through the air and stand in the camp
Of the Cretan king, confess my own passion,
And ask him what dowry he would like for me—
Anything except my fatherland's citadel.
I would rather give up all hope of wedding him   60
Than to do so by treachery! And yet,
The clemency of an appeased victor
Has made life better for many conquered cities.
Surely the war he wages is justified
By the murder of his son, and he is strong
Both in his cause and the arms that back it.
I'm sure we will be conquered, and if that is the doom
That awaits my city, why should his war
Unbar my city's gates, and not my love? Better
For him to conquer without prolonged massacre   70
And the cost of his own blood. And that way

I wouldn't have to fear that someone might
Unwittingly wound you, Minos. No one is so hard
That he would knowingly throw a spear at you."

She liked her plan. She would give herself to him
With her country as a dowry, and so end the war.
But to decide is not enough.
                                    "The entry is guarded,
And my father holds the keys to the gates.
He's the only one I fear, and the only one
Who blocks my heart's desire. Would that the gods   80
Make me fatherless! But we are all our own gods,
And Fortune resists a cowardly prayer.
Any other girl burning with passion this great
Would have long since merrily destroyed
Whatever stood in the way of her love.
And why should any girl be braver than I?
I would dare to go through fire and sword,
But there is no need here for any fire or sword.
All I need is one strand of my father's hair.
That is more precious to me than gold.   90
That purple strand of hair will make me blessed
And will give me all that my heart desires."

Night, that great nurse of our worries, fell as she spoke,
And as the darkness came on her boldness grew.
The first rest had come, when sleep enfolds the heart
Weary with the cares of day, when Nisus' daughter
Silently entered her father's bedroom
And (ah!) despoiled him of the fatal strand of hair.
With this nefarious prize in her possession
She went through the enemy camp—so sure she was   100
Of being welcomed there for what she had done—
And straight to Minos, whom she startled, and said,

"Love made me do this. I, Scylla, daughter of Nisus,
Deliver to you the gods of my country and my house.

I ask for no reward but you. As a pledge of my love
Take this purple strand of hair, and know that I give you
Not only a strand of hair but my father's life."

And she held out her gift in her sinful right hand.
Minos recoiled from her offering, horrified
At the sight of such an unprecedented act,   110
And answered her,
                        "May the gods banish you,
The infamy of our age, from their world,
And may neither land nor sea receive you.
You can be sure I will never allow such a monster
To set foot on Crete, which is both my world
And the cradle of Jove in his infancy."

Thus Minos, and when this most just lawgiver
Had imposed terms upon the conquered Athenians
He ordered his bronze-bound ships to cast off
Under full rowing power. When Scylla saw   120
That the ships had been launched, and that the king
Was not forthcoming with the reward for her sin
Despite her full complement of prayers, she shifted
Into a mode of extreme rage. Stretching out her arms,
Hair spreading out into fiery points, she screamed,

"Where are you going, abandoning the one
Who handed you your success, putting you before
My fatherland, before my father himself?
Where are you going, you inhuman man
Whose victory is my sin but to my credit too?   130
Does neither my gift nor my love for you
Move you, nor all of the hopes I placed in you
And in you alone? Where will I go now, deserted?
Back to my country? It has been overthrown.
But even if it weren't it is closed to me
Because of my treachery. Back to my father?
Whom I betrayed to you? My countrymen
All hate me, as well they should, and I am feared

By the neighboring cities for what I have done.
I've had myself banished from the rest of the world   140
So that Crete might be open to me. Close that
And leave me here, show me no gratitude,
And Europa could never have been your mother,
But the quicksands of Syrtis, an Armenian tigress,
The whirlpool of Charybdis! You're no son of Jove,
The semblance of a bull didn't beguile your mother—
That story of your birth is a lie—no, it was
A real bull, a savage beast who loved no heifer,
Who fathered you! Punish me, O Nisus, my father!
Rejoice in my suffering, city that I betrayed!   150
I deserve your hatred, and I deserve to die,
But at the hands of those whom I have injured
In my impiety. Why should I let you,
Who have triumphed through my sins, be the one
Who punishes my sins? You should see this act
That was a crime against my father and country
As a service to you. But you have your true mate
In the adulteress whose unnatural passion
Was satisfied by deceiving a savage bull
With a wooden contrivance, and who then bore   160
A hybrid offspring in her womb. Do my words
Reach your ears, or do the winds that fill your sails
Blow them away into the void, you ingrate?
No wonder Pasiphaë preferred the bull
To a monster like you! O God, he's ordering
Full speed ahead, the oars are smacking the waves,
And I and my land are falling behind him!
But it won't do you any good, forgetting
Everything I've done for you. I'll follow you
Against your will, clinging to your ship's stern   170
And dragged through the long sea."

                            With these words
She dove into the sea, swam up to the ship
With strength born of passion, and clung to the stern
Of the Cretan vessel, despised and unwelcome.

When her father—who had just been turned
Into an osprey with golden wings and was hovering
In the air—saw her clinging there, he swooped down
To attack her with his hooked beak. Terrified,
She let go of the stern, and as she fell
The light air seemed to hold her up and keep her   180
From touching the water, as if she were a feather.
Changed into a feathered bird, she is called Ciris,
The "Shearer," from the shorn lock of hair.

Minos and the Minotaur

Minos paid his vows to Jove, a hundred bulls,
As soon as he set foot on the beach in Crete
And adorned his palace with the spoils of war.
But now the family disgrace had grown up
And its mother's sordid adultery was revealed
In the strange hybrid monster. Minos intended
To remove this shame from his chambers and enclose it   190
In a dark, winding labyrinth. Daedalus,
A renowned master architect, did the work,
Confounding the usual lines of sight
With a maze of conflicting passageways.
Just as the Maeander plays in Phrygian fields,
Flowing back and forth and winding around
In its ambiguous course so that sometimes it sees
Its own waters flowing toward it, and flows itself
Now back toward its source, now toward the sea—
So Daedalus made all those passageways wander,   200
And he himself had a hard time finding his way
Back to the entrance of the deceptive building.

After Minos had shut up the Minotaur there
He fed him twice on Athenian blood,
Once every nine years. But the third tribute
Of Athenian youths was the creature's undoing,
And when Theseus, with Ariadne's help,
Found his way back to the difficult entrance—

Which no previous hero had ever done—
By winding up the thread, he took Minos' daughter   210
And sailed for Dia, and then abandoned her
On that island's shore. Marooned and reciting
A litany of complaints, she received the aid
And love of Bacchus, and so that she might shine
Among the eternal stars, he took the tiara
That circled her brow and sent it off to the sky.
It flew through the thin air, and as it flew
Its gemstones were changed into gleaming fires
That found their place, still in the shape of a Crown,
Between Ophiouchus' and Hercules' stars.   220

Daedalus and Icarus

Daedalus, meanwhile, hating his long exile
In Crete, and longing for the place of his birth,
Was locked in by the sea.
                              "He may block
Land and sea," he said, "but the sky is open;
We will go that way. Minos may own everything,
But he does not own the air."
                              And turning his mind
Toward unknown arts, he transformed nature.

Spreading out feathers, he arranged them in order
From shortest to longest, as if climbing a slope,
The way reeds once rose into a panpipe's shape.   230
Then he bound the midline of the quills with thread
And the ends with wax, and bent the formation
Into a slight curve, imitating a real bird's wing.
His son Icarus stood at his side, and, unaware
That he was touching his peril, the beaming boy
Would try to catch feathers blown by the breeze,
Or would knead the yellow wax with his thumb
And as he played generally get in the way
Of his genius father at work. When he had put
The finishing touches on his craft, the artisan   240

Suspended himself between two identical wings,
And his body hovered in the moving air.
Then he equipped his son, saying,
                              "Stay in the middle,
Icarus. I warn you, if you go lower
The water will weigh down the feathers; higher,
The sun's heat will scorch them. Fly in between,
And don't gawk at Boötes, the Dipper,
Or the sword of Orion! Pick out your path
By following me."
                    He gave him flying instructions
While fitting the unfamiliar wings to his shoulders,   250
And what with the work and the admonitions
His old cheeks grew moist, and his father's hands trembled.
He kissed his dear son, a kiss never to be repeated,
And rising on wings he flies ahead in fear
For his companion—like a bird who leads
Its tender young into the air from its aerial nest—
Urging him to follow, teaching him ruinous arts,
And beating his own wings as he looks back at his son.
A fisherman with a trembling rod sees them—
Or a shepherd leaning on his staff, or a plowman—   260
They gape at these beings negotiating the air
And take them for gods. Juno's isle Samos
Is now on the left (Delos and Paros are long gone)
And on the right are Lebinthos and honeyed Calymne,
When the boy begins to enjoy this daring flight
And veers off from his leader. He is drawn to the sky
And goes higher. Proximity to the blazing sun
Softens the scented wax that bound the feathers,
And the wax melts. He beats his naked arms
But lacking plumage cannot purchase air,   270
And his mouth was shouting his father's name
When the blue water, which takes its name from his,
Closed over the boy. His bereft father,
A father no more, cried "Icarus, where are you,
Icarus, where should I look for you?" and kept calling,
"Icarus." Then he saw the feathers in the waves.

He swore off his arts and buried the body,
And the land is known by the name on the tomb.

Daedalus and His Nephew

While Daedalus was burying his poor son,
A chattering partridge peeked out from a muddy ditch,   280
Flapped its wings, and burst into joyful song.
The bird was one of a kind, never seen before,
And only lately made a bird, a lasting reproach
To Daedalus, whose sister, ignorant of the fates,
Had sent her son to him to be an apprentice.
The boy was twelve years old and had a clever mind.
Using the backbone of a fish as a model,
He notched a row of teeth into a strip of iron
And so invented the saw. He was also the first
To bind two arms of iron together at a joint,   290
So that by fixing one arm in place and keeping
The span the same, the other arm could draw a circle.
Daedalus was envious and pushed the boy
From Minerva's sacred citadel, and then lied
That he had fallen. But Pallas, who is partial
To the quick-witted, caught him and made him
Into a bird, giving him feathers in midair.
The vigor of his mind passed into his wings and legs,
But he kept the name he had before being transfigured.
This bird does not fly high, or build her nest   300
In trees or on high peaks. She flutters on the ground
And lays her eggs in hedgerows. Remembering
That old fall, she remains afraid of high places.

Meleager and the Calydonian Boar

Now Sicily received the weary Daedalus,
Where Cocalus defended the suppliant
And was thought of as kind. And now, too, Athens
Stopped paying the grim tribute, thanks to Theseus.
They wreathe the temple, call on Minerva,

The warrior goddess, and upon Jupiter,
And worship all gods with blood sacrifices,   310
Bestowing gifts upon them and burning incense.
Theseus' fame spread through all the Greek cities,
And all Achaea sought his help in times of peril.
Calydon too, although she had her own Meleager,
Anxiously begged for his help.

                   The cause of the trouble
Was a boar, servant and avenger of an outraged Diana.
They say that Oeneus, king of Calydon,
Giving thanks for a bounteous harvest,
Offered the firstfruits to Ceres, wine to Bacchus,
And poured to blond Pallas libations of oil.   320
From the rural deities to the gods of high heaven,
Each received due honor. Only Diana's altar
Was left without incense. Gods can get really angry.

"This will not go unpunished," she said to herself.
Although we may be unhonored, it will not be said
We are unavenged."

                  And the scorned goddess sent
An avenging boar through Oeneus' fields,
A boar as big as the bulls that graze in Epirus,
Bigger than Sicilian bulls. His eyes blazed
With blood and fire; he had a long, thick neck;   330
His bristles were like a forest of spear shafts;
His hoarse grunts came out with steaming foam
That lathered his shoulders; his tusks were as long
As an Indian elephant's; lightning issued
From his mouth, and his breath burned vegetation.
He tramples the green shoots of the growing grain,
And now he destroys the mature crop of a farmer
Doomed to mourn, cutting off the ripe ears.
Entire vineyards heavy with grapes are leveled
And branches with their olives are ripped from trees.   340
He savages cattle too. Neither shepherds nor dogs
Can protect their flocks, nor bulls their herds.
The people run off everywhere and don't feel safe

Except behind city walls.
                                Finally Meleager
And a picked band of young heroes assembled,
Bound for glory:
                        The twin sons of Leda,
The boxer Pollux and Castor the horseman;
Jason, who built the first ship; the best friends
Theseus and Pirithoüs; the two sons of Thestius;
Lynceus and swift Idas, sons of Aphareus;   350
Caeneus, no longer a woman; fierce Leucippus
And Acastus the spearman; Hippothoös
And Dryas; Amyntor's son Phoenix;
Actor's two sons and Elean Phyleus.
Telamon was there too, and great Achilles' father;
Admetus, son of Pheres, and Boeotian Iolaus,
Impulsive Eurytion, Echion the great runner;
Locrian Lelex, Panopeus, Hyleus
And ferocious Hippasus; Nestor, who was then
In the prime of his life; those whom Hippocoön   360
Sent from ancient Amyclae; Laertes,
Penelope's father-in-law; Arcadian Ancaeus;
Ampycus' son, the prophet Mopsus; Amphiaraus,
Oecleus' son, not yet undone by his wife;
And Atalanta, pride of the Arcadian woods.
A polished pin fastened her robe at the neck,
Her hair was pulled back in a simple knot.
Her arrows rattled in an ivory quiver
Hanging from her left shoulder, and her left hand
Held her bow. That was how she was dressed.   370
Her face was one that you could truly say
Was girlish for a boy and for a girl boyish.
For Meleager it was love at first sight
(Denied by a deity), and he felt the heat,
Saying to himself, "What a lucky guy
If that girl ever says yes." It was not the time—
And he was embarrassed—for him to say more.
The great contest was about to begin.

There was a virgin forest, dense and primeval,
Running from the plain to the slope of a valley.   380
When the heroes reached it, some stretched the nets,
Others slipped the dogs from their leashes, and some
Followed the boar's well-marked trail, eager to meet
Their mortal peril. At the bottom of the valley
The rainwater drained into a marshy spot
Overgrown with willows, swamp grass, and rushes
And with an undergrowth of reeds. It was from here
The boar was flushed out and came at his tormentors
Like lightning from a cloud. The grove was laid low
By his charge, and the battered trees crashed   390
As the heroes yelled and clenched their spears
With their broad iron heads pointed toward the boar.
He kept coming, scattering the baying dogs
With sidelong thrusts of his tusks as one by one
They tried to impede his furious onrush.
Echion cast first, but his throw was wasted.
The spear sticking lightly in a maple tree.
The next, thrown by Jason, would have pierced
The boar's back, but had too much force and went long.
Then Mopsus prayed,

                "Apollo, if I have ever and still do   400
Worship you, let my spear hit its mark."

                          The god did his best
To answer his prayer. The boar was hit but uninjured.
Diana had snapped the iron off from the spear in flight
And the shaft arrived without any point.
The beast's anger now burned no less gently than lightning.
Fire gleamed from his eye and breathed from his throat,
And as a huge rock launched by a catapult
Heads toward soldiers stationed on walls and towers,
So too, with that kind of irresistible power, the boar
Rushed on the heroes, flattening Eupalamus   410
And Pelagon, who manned the right wing. Their comrades
Carried them off. But Enaesimus, son of Hippocoön,
Did not escape the boar's fatal stroke. As he turned to run
In terror, he was hamstrung and his muscles failed.

Pylian Nestor would have never made it to Troy,
But with a supreme effort he planted his spear
And vaulted into a tree, from whose branches
He looked down in safety at his enemy below.
He was whetting his tusks on the trunk of an oak,
An ominous sign, and with renewed confidence   420
In his sharpened weapons he sliced through the thigh
Of great Hippasus with a hooking stroke.
And now Castor and Pollux, not yet stars in the sky
But still conspicuous among the rest, came riding up
On horses whiter than snow, pumped their spears
And sent them humming through the air. Both would have
Hit the boar, too, except that that the beast took cover
In a thicket, where neither horse nor spear could follow.
Telamon did try to follow, but got careless and tripped
Over a root, and while Peleus was helping him up   430
Atalanta notched an arrow on the string and let fly.
It grazed the boar's back and stuck beneath his ear,
Staining the bristles red with a trickle of blood.
She was not happier over her shot's success
Than Meleager was. He saw the blood first
And was the first to point it out to his comrades.
"You will be honored," he said, "for this bold achievement!"
The men's faces turned red, and they spurred each other on,
Their spirits rising as they shouted and hurled spears
But in no good order, their very volume preventing   440
Any from hitting the target. Then Ancaeus,
Himself an Arcadian, armed with a battle-axe
And determined to meet his destiny, cried out,

"All right, boys, let's find out how much a man's weapons
Outweigh a girl's. Leave this to me. I don't care
If Diana herself protects this boar with her arrows.
I'm taking this animal down, Diana or not!"

That was his boast, all swollen with pride,
And he lifted the axe overhead with both hands,
Standing on tiptoe and ready to strike. The boar   450

Went for his adversary's most vulnerable spot,
Both tusks slashing fiercely at the top of the groin.
Ancaeus went down, his entrails flowing out
Along with his blood; the ground was soaked with gore.
When Ixion's son, Pirithoüs, advanced on the enemy
Balancing a hunting spear in his strong right hand,
Theseus called to him,
                    "Back away, O dearer to me
Than I am to myself, half of my soul, stop!
It's all right for the brave to fight from a distance.
Ancaeus' rash valor has done him no good."   460

As he spoke he hurled his heavy hardwood spear
Tipped with bronze, but although it was well thrown
And looked like an answer to all their prayers,
A leafy branch of an oak tree turned it aside.
Then Jason hurled his javelin, which, as it happened,
Swerved off and killed a perfectly good hound,
Passing through his flanks and pinning him down.
But Meleager showed a different hand. He threw
Two spears; one of these punched into the earth,
But the other one stuck in the spine of the beast.   470
While the boar spins around and around in his rage,
Spewing foam and fresh blood, Jason presses on,
Jabbing at him and driving him mad until at last
He buries his hunting spear deep in the shoulder.
The others go wild, shouting applause and crowding around
To clasp hands with the victor. They gaze in wonder
At the huge carcass covering so much ground
And still are not sure it is safe to touch it,
But each of them wets his own spear in its blood.

Then Meleager, standing with his foot   480
Upon that lethal head, spoke to Atalanta:

"Take the spoils, Arcadian, that are mine by right,
And let my glory come in part to you."

And he gave her the spoils, the bristling hide
And the magnificent head with its enormous tusks.
Both the gift and the giver made Atalanta glad,
But an envious murmur rose through the company,
And Thestius' two sons stretched out their arms
And cried in a loud voice,
                              "Back off, girl,
And don't take our honors. And don't be a fool   490
Trusting your beauty, or this lovesick giver
Might not be around for you."
                              And they took
The gift from her and from him the right to give.
This was too much for the son of Mars.
                                        "Learn,"
He said, "You two who plunder another's right,
The difference between a threat and a deed."

And he drained Plexippus' unsuspecting heart
With sinful steel. His brother Toxeus
Stood there hesitating, wanting to avenge
His brother but fearing to share his brother's fate,   500
But Meleager cut short his deliberations.
While the spear was still warm from its prior victim
He warmed it again in his brother's blood.

Althea was bringing gifts to the temple
In thanksgiving for the victory of her son
When she saw her brothers' corpses carried in.
She filled the city with her loud lamentation
And changed her robes from golden to black.
But when she learned who the murderer was
All of her grief became a lust for vengeance.   510

There was a log of wood which, when Althea
Was in labor, the three Fates threw into the fire
As they spun the thread of Meleager's life.

"We give to you," they said, "and to this log
The same span of time."
                              When the three sisters
Had chanted this prophecy and disappeared,
The mother snatched the burning log from the fire
And doused it with water. It had long been hidden
In the depths of the house, and, kept safe there,
Safeguarded your life for years, young hero.   520
Now Meleager's mother brought out this log,
And had her servants pile up pine and kindling.
She lit the unfriendly fire. Four times
She was about to throw the log in the flames,
And four times she stopped. Mother fought sister,
Two names tugging at the one heart she had.
Her cheeks would pale at what she was about to do,
Then her burning anger would glow in her eyes.
At times she was an ominous, threatening figure,
And then you would think her some pitiful thing.   530
And although her anger had dried up her tears,
Tears would still come. It was like a ship
Driven both by the wind and an opposing tide,
Feeling the two forces at work and yielding
Uneasily to both. So too Thestius' daughter
Wavered between her uncertain emotions,
Extinguishing her wrath and fanning it again.
But the sister in her begins to prevail
Over the mother, and to appease with blood
Her blood-relatives' shades, Althea becomes   540
Pious in her impiety. When the pestilential flames
Reached full strength, she said,
                              "Let that pyre
Turn my own flesh to ashes."
                              And holding
The fateful log in her dire hand, she stood
In her misery before the sepulchral altars
And said:
          "Triple goddesses, vengeful Furies,
Eumenides, turn your faces toward these rites.

I avenge, and I do evil. Death must be atoned by death,
Crime added to crime, funeral to funeral.
May mounded grief destroy this accursed house.   550
Shall Oeneus enjoy his victorious son
And Thestius be childless? Better that both grieve.
But may you, new ghosts of my brothers,
Feel my devotion and accept the sacrifice
I offer to the dead at so great a cost,
The doomed tribute of my own womb. Ah,
Where is this taking me? Brothers, forgive
A mother's heart! My hands cannot finish this.
I confess that he deserves to die, but I cannot bear
To cause his death. But, then, shall he go unscathed,   560
Live victorious, all puffed up with success,
The great lord of Calydon, while the two of you
Are scanty ashes and pale, shivering ghosts?
I will not allow it. Let him die in his malice
And drag to perdition his father's hopes,
His father's kingdom and his fatherland's ruins.
Ah, where is my mother's mind? A parent's care?
The misery I endured for ten long months?
Oh, you should have burned to death as an infant
In that first fire—if only I could have borne it!   570
You lived by my gift; now you will die
For what you have done. Pay the price for it,
And give back the life I gave to you twice,
Once at your birth, once by saving the log—
Or put me on my brothers' pyre too. Oh,
I want to and I can't. What shall I do?
My brothers' wounds are before my eyes now,
All that blood; and now the name of mother
And a mother's love are breaking my heart.
God, I am wretched! It isn't right that you win,   580
Brothers, but go ahead, win! Just let me have
The solace I give you, and let me follow you."

Althea spoke, and as she turned her face away
Her trembling hand dropped the mortal log

Into the flames. It groaned, or seemed to groan,
As it flared up and burned in the unwilling fire.

Far away and knowing nothing of this,
Meleager burns in those flames. Feeling
A scorching fire deep inside his body,
It takes all his courage to master the pain.   590
Yet he grieves that he will die a bloodless
And ignoble death, and he calls Ancaeus
Happy for his wounds. With his last breath
He calls upon his aged father, his brothers,
His devoted sisters, his wife and, with a groan,
Perhaps his mother. The fire intensifies,
And with it the pain. Then both die down,
And fire and pain go out together.
As his spirit slips away into gentle air,
Grey ash slowly veils the glowing coals.   600

All of Calydon was devastated. Young and old
Lamented, noble and common both groaned.
The women of Calydon by Evenus' waters
Tore their hair and beat their breasts. The father
Lies on the ground and defiles his white hair
And aged head with dust, bitterly complaining
That he has lived too long; for the mother,
Seeing what she had done, has punished herself
With a dagger through her heart. Not if some god
Gave me a hundred speaking mouths, sheer genius,   610
And all Helicon has, could I ever capture
The lamentation of his wretched sisters.
Without a thought for decency they beat their breasts
Black and blue; caressed their brother's corpse,
While there was a corpse, and caressed it again;
Kissed the body and the bier where it stood;
Scooped up the ashes and pressed them to their breasts;
Threw themselves on his tomb, and clasping the stone
On which his name had been carved, drenched it with tears.
In the end Diana, satisfied with the destruction   620

Of the house of Parthaon, feathered their bodies—
All of them except Gorge and Deianeira—
Stretched out wings over the length of their arms
And gave them horny beaks, sending them forth
As Meleagrides, guinea hens, into the air.

Tales from Acheloüs' Feast

Theseus, meanwhile, having played his part
In the heroic hunt, was returning to Athens,
But the Acheloüs River, swollen with rain,
Blocked his way.
           "Come into my house,"
Said the river god, "illustrious Athenian,   630
And do not trust my rapacious waters.
The current sweeps away solid tree trunks
And tumbles boulders along with a crashing roar.
I have seen great stables that stood on the banks
Hauled off with their flocks, and in that torrent
Neither a bull's strength nor a horse's speed
Does any good at all. Many strong young bodies
Have drowned in the whirlpools when the snowmelt
Pours down from the mountain. Safer to rest
Until the stream flows between its usual banks."   640

Theseus replied,
           "I will use your house,
Acheloüs, and your advice."
               And he did use both,
Entering the great hall built of porous pumice
And rough tufa. The floor was damp with soft moss,
And purple shells and conches paneled the ceiling.
Hyperion the Sun had measured half the sky
When Theseus and his companions from the hunt
Stretched out on the couches. Ixion's son,
Pirithoüs, was there, and Lelex too,
The old hero from Troezen, his hair flecked with grey,   650
And others whom the Acarnanian river god

Had thought worthy to invite. He was delighted
To have such a noble guest. Barefoot nymphs
Wasted no time in setting the tables,
And when the feast was done they poured wine
Into jeweled cups.

Acheloüs and the Echinades

       Then the noblest of heroes,
Looking out on the level expanse of water,
Pointed with his finger and asked,

                "What is the name
Of that island out there—or is it only one island?"

The river god answered,

             "No, what you see   660
Is not one island, but five close together.
The distance blurs their divisions. What Diana did
When she was slighted may seems less odd to you
When you learn the story behind them. Those islands
Once were nymphs. They had slaughtered ten bulls
And invited all of the gods of the countryside
To the sacrifice, but they forgot me
When they led out their festal dances.
I swelled with rage, as full as I ever get,
An angry flash flood tearing forests apart,   670
Filleting fields. I swept away the nymphs,
Who remembered me then, with the ground they stood on,
Into the sea, and the sea's waves working with mine
Divided that continuous stretch of land
Into as many parts as the Echinades have
Out there in the water.

Acheloüs and Perimele

           But beyond the others—
Look and you can see—is the one island I love.
Sailors call it Perimele. She was my beloved,
And I took her virginity. Hippodamas,

Her father, was furious and threw his daughter   680
Off a high cliff into the deep. She would have perished,
But I caught her, and holding her up as she floated
I prayed,
       "Lord of the Trident, whose lot
Is the realm of water next to the world,
Help a girl drowned by her father's cruelty.
Give her a place, Neptune, or let her become
A place herself."
          While I was speaking,
New earth embraced the girl's floating body,
And her transformed limbs grew into an island."

Then the river was silent. Everyone was moved   690
By this miracle story, except for one,
A man who laughed at believers and scoffed at the gods,
Ferocious in spirit, Ixion's son Pirithoüs.

"You're making all this up, Acheloüs," he said,
"And you're giving too much power to the gods
If you think they can give and take away forms."

Philemon and Baucis

They were all shocked, and disapproved of such words,
Especially Lelex, mature in judgment and years,
Who said,
      "Immense is the power of heaven
And knows no end. Whatever the gods want   700
Is done, and, to boost your faltering faith,
There is an oak tree right next to a linden
Up in the Phrygian hills, ringed by a low wall.
I saw the spot myself when Pittheus
Sent me to the country his father once ruled.
There's a marsh close by, once habitable land
But now coots and other waterfowl live there.
Jupiter once went there disguised as a mortal,
And his son Mercury tagged along with him
But without his caduceus or winged sandals.   710

Looking for a place to rest, they knocked on
A thousand doors; a thousand doors stayed shut,
But one house did let them in, a little one
Thatched with straw and reeds from the marsh.
Pious old Baucis lived there with Philemon,
Who was the same age as his wife. The couple
Married in that cottage when they were young
And grew old there together. They made light
Of their poverty and so bore it easily.
There were no masters or servants. These two   720
Were the whole household, and the same people
Gave orders and obeyed. So, when the gods arrived
At this humble hearth and stooped to enter,
The old man set out a bench and told them
To sit down and relax, and Baucis bustled up
And threw on a rough coverlet. She scraped
The ashes from the fireplace and fanned
Yesterday's embers, feeding them with leaves
And dry bark and blowing them into flames
With her old woman's breath. Then she took down   730
Some split wood and dry twigs from the rafters,
Broke them up and put them under the bronze kettle.

Her husband had picked a cabbage from the garden,
And she chopped the leaves off from the stalk.
The old man had a forked stick and was fetching
A chine of smoked bacon that was hanging
From a blackened beam. Cutting off a little piece
Of this long-seasoned pork he put it in the pot
To boil with the cabbage. They passed the time talking,
And then put a long cushion stuffed with soft sedge   740
Onto a couch with a willow frame and legs.
They draped this with a cloth that they only used
On festal occasions, but even this was cheap
And worn with age. It went well with the couch.
The gods reclined. The old woman, skirts tucked up,
Put the table in place with trembling hands.

One of its legs was too short, so she propped it up
With a broken piece of tile. When she had it level
She wiped down the table with fresh mint
And set out some olives, both green and black,   750
Autumn cornel cherries pickled in wine lees,
Endive and radishes, cream cheese, and eggs
Lightly roasted in warm embers, all served
In earthenware dishes. After these appetizers
An embossed mixing bowl, no less silver
Than the rest of the ware, was put on the table
Along with beech-wood cups coated inside
With yellow wax. The steaming main course
Soon arrived from the hearth, and wine of no great age
Was served all around. Then a little space was made   760
For the dessert: nuts, wrinkled dried dates, plums,
And fragrant apples served in wide baskets
Along with purple grapes just picked from the vine.
A clear white honeycomb was set in the middle.
Besides all this, they brought to the table
Cheerful faces, high spirits, and abundant good will.

Meanwhile wine kept welling up in the mixing bowl
All by itself, so that as often as it was drained
It was never empty. Baucis and Philemon saw this
And didn't know what to think. They lifted   770
Their upturned hands and prayed, asking pardon
For the food they served and the poor accoutrements.
They had one goose, who guarded their little estate,
And were going to kill it for their divine guests.
But the goose was swift on the wing and wore out
The slow old people trying to catch it, dodging them
For a long time and finally taking refuge
With the gods themselves, who told them to let it live.

'We are gods,' they said. 'This wicked neighborhood
Will get its just deserts, but you will be spared.   780
Leave your house now and come along with us

Up the high mountainside.'
                    The couple obeyed
And leaning on their staffs they struggled step by step
Up the long slope. When they were within a bowshot
Of the summit, they looked back and saw
Everything covered with water, except their house.
While they wondered at this, and wept for their friends,
The old house, which had been too small for two,
Turned into a temple. Forked poles became columns,
The thatch grew yellow and became a golden roof,   790
Figured gates appeared, and marble pavement
Covered the ground. Then Jupiter said calmly,

'And now, just old man, and woman worthy
Of your just husband, ask whatever you want.'

After he and Baucis had talked a little,
Philemon told the gods their joint decision:

'We ask to be your priests and your temple's caretakers,
And, since we've spent our lives together in harmony,
We ask to be taken the very same hour, so that I
May never see my wife's tomb, nor she bury me.'   800

Their prayer was answered. They took care of the temple
For the rest of their lives, until one day,
Old and worn out, they happened to be standing
In front of the sacred steps, talking about the place
And all that had happened there, when Philemon
Saw Baucis, and Baucis saw Philemon
Sprouting leaves. As the canopy grew
Over their faces, they cried out while they could
The same words together, 'Good-bye, my love,'
Just as the bark closed over their lips.   810
To this day the Bithynians who live there
Point out two trees growing close together
From a double trunk. These things were told to me
By sober old men with no reason to lie.

I certainly saw wreaths hanging from the branches
And when I put a fresh one there myself, I said,

'Whom the gods love are gods. Adore and be adored.'"

Erysichthon

Lelex ended here; both the tale and the teller
Moved them all, and especially Theseus.
He wanted to hear more about the gods' miracles,   820
And so the Calydonian river god,
Leaning on one elbow, said this to him:

"There are some, great hero, whose form never varies
Once it has been changed; others have the power
Of assuming many forms, such as you, Proteus,
Who live in the encircling sea. Sometimes you are seen
As a young man, sometimes a lion or a raging boar;
A snake no one would want to touch; or horns
Might make you into a bull; you could be a stone,
Or take the form of running water, a river,   830
Or you could be the enemy of water, fire.

Erysichthon's daughter, who married Autolycus,
Had this kind of power. This Erysichthon
Scorned the gods and burnt no sacrifices
On their altars. He even violated,
The story goes, the sacred grove of Ceres,
Chopping down those ancient trees with an axe.
Among them stood an enormous oak, its wood
Strong with years, a grove in itself. On it hung
Wool fillets, votive tablets, and wreaths of flowers,   840
Memorials of earnest prayers answered.
The wood nymphs often held their festival dances
Under this tree, circling with their hands joined
The mighty trunk that was fifteen ells around,
And the rest of the trees were as far below it
As the grass was below them. Yet Erysichthon,
For all that the tree was, did not hold back his axe.

He had ordered his slaves to cut it down,
But when he saw them cringing from his commands,
He snatched an axe from one of them and said,   850

'Whether this be the goddess' tree, or even
The goddess herself, it's coming to the ground.'

He spoke, and while he held his axe poised
For a slanting stroke, the oak of Deo groaned,
Its leaves and acorns grew pale, and the pallor
Began to spread throughout its long branches.
When the sacrilegious stroke cut into the trunk,
Blood poured out from the crushed, shattered bark,
As it does from the cloven neck of a bull
When it falls at the altar as a sacrifice.   860
The men were all astonished, and one of them,
Bolder than the rest, tried to stop this atrocity
And stay the cruel axe. But Erysichthon
Just looked at the man and said,
                                        'Take that
For your pious thoughts,'
                              as he turned the axe
From the tree to the man and lopped off his head.
Then, as he cut into the oak again and again,
A voice came out from the middle of the tree:

'I am a nymph most dear to Ceres, alive
In this timber, and I foretell as I die   870
Punishment for your crime, solace for my death.'

Still, he saw his crime through, and finally the tree,
Tottering from innumerable blows and pulled by ropes,
Crashed down, its bulk crushing much of the grove.

The dryad sisterhood were stunned at their own
And their forest's loss. Wearing black for mourning
They went to Ceres and prayed, asking her
To punish Erysichthon. The beautiful goddess

Nodded in assent, and with that motion
Shook the heavy fields of ripening grain.   880
Then she devised a method of punishment, pitiable
Were there anything pitiable in what he had done.
She would torture the man with dreadful Famine.
But she couldn't go herself, since Fate had decreed
That Famine and Ceres never come together,
So she summoned an oread down from the mountains
And addressed the rustic deity like this:

'There is a place on the far edge of Scythia,
A glacial land, gloomy, without anything growing,
No crops, not a tree. Lethargic Cold lives there,   890
Pallor and Tremor—and emaciated Famine.
She is to ensconce herself in the sinful stomach
Of that sacrilegious man. No abundance
Is to satisfy her, and she is to overcome
Even my power to feed. And so you won't dread
The rather long journey, take my chariot
And drive my dragons across the steep sky!'

The nymph, airborne in her borrowed chariot,
Touched down in Scythia on a mountain peak
(They call it Caucasus) and unyoked the dragons.   900
She found Famine in a stony field, scrounging
Scrawny weeds with her nails and teeth. Her hair
Was all matted, her eyes sunken, her face pale;
Her lips were a dirty grey, her throat scaly,
Her skin so taut you could see her guts through it;
Her hips were bony knots under hollow loins,
Her belly just a place for a belly; her breast
Seemed to hang suspended from her scrawny spine;
Her gauntness made all her joints seem large;
Her kneecaps were swollen, her ankles lumps.   910

When the nymph saw her from afar—she didn't dare
Get close—she delivered the goddess' orders.
Though she hadn't stayed long and kept her distance,

She still seemed very hungry as she drove
The aerial dragons back to Thessaly.

Famine did what Ceres said, even though their roles
Are forever opposed. She flew on the wind
And got off at Erysichthon's mansion,
Entering promptly the impious ruler's room.
It was night, and he was lost in slumber.   920
Wrapping her arms around him she injected herself
Into his body by breathing on his mouth,
His throat and his chest, sowing hunger
Deep in his veins. Having discharged her duty,
She left the fertile world and made her way back
To the barren realms and her familiar caves.

Gentle Sleep still soothed Erysichthon
On peaceful wings. He dreamed about a feast,
Gnawing on fantasies, and cheating
His gullet with imagined food, devouring   930
Instead of a banquet only empty air.
But when he awoke, a furious appetite
Raged in his jaws and in his burning stomach.
Without a moment's delay he calls for everything
That sea and land and air can produce,
And with tables of food complains of hunger,
Looking for feasts in the middle of feasts.
What would be enough for a city, enough
For a whole nation, is not enough for one.
The more he crams down his maw the more he wants,   940
And as the ocean receives all the rivers on earth
Yet does not have enough but drinks in the streams;
And as voracious fire never refuses fuel
But burns countless logs, and the more it is fed
The more it wants, quantity increasing its greed:
So too the mouth of irreligious Erysichthon
Devouring banquets and always asking for more.
Food for him only occasions more food,
And by always eating he is forever empty.

And now hunger and the maelstrom of his belly   950
Have exhausted all of his ancestral stores,
But ravenous Famine still raged unabated
In his burning gullet. When his entire fortune
Had gone into his belly, only his daughter,
Worthy of a better father, was left. Destitute,
He sold her too. But the spirited girl
Refused to have a master. Stretching her hands
Over the sea, she prayed,
                              'Save me from slavery,
You who have stolen my virginity from me!'

That would be Neptune, who now granted her prayer,   960
And although her master, who had followed her,
Had just now seen her, the god transformed her
Into a fisherman, with all the clothing and gear.
Looking at her, her master said,
                              'You with the rod,
Baiting your hook, I wish you calm seas, trusting fish,
And bona fide strikes, if you'll only tell me
Where she is, the girl with cheap clothes and straggly hair
Who was just now standing on the shore here.
I saw her myself, right here, and her footprints
Don't lead any farther.'
                              She saw that the god's gift   970
Was working well, and delighted to be asked herself
About herself, she responded like this:

'I beg your pardon, whoever you are,
But I have not taken my eyes from this pool
To look anywhere else. I've been concentrating
On my fishing. But, so help me Neptune,
No one has been here for quite some time now,
No man and no woman, except for me.'

He believed her and walked away on the sand,
Completely taken in. Then her former shape   980
Was restored to her. But when her father learned

That she had the ability to change her form
He sold her again and again, to many new owners,
Sometimes as a mare, a bird, a cow, or a deer,
And off she would go, keeping her father in food,
Albeit unjustly. When his terrible malady
Exhausted these provisions too, only adding
To his fatal disease, he began to take bites
Out of his own limbs, and in his misery
Fed himself by consuming his body.   990

But why spend my time talking about others?
I myself, young heroes, have often changed forms,
Although my power is limited to only a few,
Sometimes I am seen as you see me now,
Sometimes I switch to a serpent, and sometimes
I put my strength into horns as leader of the herd,
Into horns, that is, when I still could. But now,
As you see, part of my forehead's weaponry
Is quite missing."
                    He ended his speech with a groan.

Book 9

Acheloüs and Hercules

Theseus asked the river god why he groaned
And what happened to his horn. And Acheloüs,
Binding up his hair with a reed, replied,

"It's not very pleasant to talk about defeat,
But I'll tell you just what happened, and really,
It wasn't so much a disgrace to lose
As it was an honor to compete at all,
And the exalted status of my conqueror
Is some consolation to me.
                              Deianeira
(I'm sure you've heard her name) was at one time   10
Exceedingly beautiful and the envied hope
Of many suitors. I was one of them,
And when along with the others I entered
Her father's house,
                      'Take me for your son-in-law,
O son of Parthaon.' I said.
                              Hercules said the same,
And all the others backed off. The hero
Put himself forward as the son of Jupiter
Renowned for his labors and the trials overcome
At his stepmother's command. I rejoined, saying,

'It is shameful for a god to yield to a mortal'   20
(Hercules was not yet a god). 'You see in me
The lord of all the waters that wind through your realm.
Wedding your daughter, I will not be a stranger
From a foreign shore, but one of your people,
A part of your kingdom. Do not count it against me
That Juno does not hate me, and so I have no labors
Imposed as a punishment. Son of Alcmena,
The Jupiter you boast of is either not your real father,
Or is so only through your mother's adultery.
Would you rather say that this Jove is made up,   30
Or that you are a bastard conceived in disgrace?'

Hercules scowled at me as I was speaking
And, unable to control his burning rage, said,

'My right hook is better than my tongue. As long as I
Win in a fight, you can be the prize speaker.'

And he came at me ferociously. I was ashamed
To retreat, after what I had said. Taking off
My green robes I shook out my arms, put up
My fists, took a few practice jabs, and got set.
He scooped up some dust and threw it on me   40
And then coated himself with the yellow dirt.
Then we began. He caught me by the neck,
Or you might have thought that he caught me.
Then he went for my legs, looked for any opening,
But my sheer weight protected me, and all his moves
Were useless. I was like a massive pile
That the roaring sea assaults but stays put,
Secure in its bulk. We backed off a little
And then started in again, not giving an inch,
Foot against foot, leaning into each other   50
With fingers interlocked, chests out, head to head.
I have seen two strong bulls go at it like that
With the sleekest heifer in the herd as the prize
And the herd watching fearfully to see which one
Would come out on top. Three times Hercules tried
To push my glistening chest from his, and the fourth time
He did it, broke my grip, got out of my arm hold,
And with a smack of his hand—oh yes, he did it—
Spun me around and glued his weight to my back.
I'm not trying to get credit by exaggerating,   60
But it seemed like I had a mountain on my back.
I was just able to get my sweaty arms up
In between his and break the hold he had on me,
But he pressed hard, giving me no chance
To catch my breath, and got a good grip on my neck.
This finally brought me down, and I bit the dust.
Seeing that I was no match for him in strength

I switched to my arts and slipped out of his grasp
In the form of a long snake, but when I coiled up
And hissed at him, darting out my forked tongue,   70
The hero from Tiryns just laughed at me and said,

'I was strangling snakes when I was in my cradle.
And even if you're the baddest snake there is, do you think
One snake can come close to the Lernaean Hydra?
Wounding it just made it stronger. Every time I cut off
One of its hundred heads, that neck spouted two more,
Serpent heads everywhere, feeding on death,
But I beat the monster down and then cut it to bits.
So what do you think will happen to you,
A fake serpent fighting under false pretenses?'   80

And he got his iron hands around my neck. I felt like
My throat was being squeezed by tongs, struggled
To tear myself from those fingers' viselike grip.
It was no good being a snake. My last resort was
To turn into a wild bull and fight him like that.
He got his arms around my neck on the left
And stayed with me, dragging me down, until
He rammed my horns into the earth and forced me
Down in the sand. But this was not enough.
Holding one of my horns in his right hand   90
He broke it off, tearing it right out of my forehead.
The naiads took it and filled it with fruit
And fragrant flowers, and now it enriches
The Goddess of Abundance, a cornucopia."

Nessus and Deianeira

Acheloüs finished, and then one of the attendants,
A nymph with flowing hair and dressed like Diana,
Served them all from her plentiful horn, full
Of autumn's harvest, with apples for dessert.
Dawn came, and when the rising sun's first rays
Struck the mountain peaks, the young heroes left,   100

Not waiting for the floodwaters to subside
And the rivers to flow within their banks again.
Then Acheloüs hid his rustic face, and the scar
Where his horn once was, beneath his waters.
Still he had only the loss of his beautiful horn
To be sorry about. Otherwise he was fine,
And he could hide his loss with willow and reeds.
But you, Nessus, took an arrow through the back
Because of your passion for the same girl
And were utterly destroyed. It happened   110
When Hercules was going home with his bride
And had come to the swiftly flowing Evenus.
The water was higher than usual, swollen
With winter rains and swirling with eddies,
An impassable stream. As the hero stood there,
Afraid not for himself but for his bride,
Nessus came up, a strong Centaur who knew the fords.

"I'll get her to that other bank," he said. "With your strength
You can just swim across, Hercules."
                              And so,
Hercules entrusted Deianeira to Nessus.   120
She was trembling, afraid of the water
And of the Centaur. The hero, just as he was,
Still wearing his lion's skin and bearing his quiver
(He had tossed his club and bow to the opposite bank)
Jumped in, saying,
                    "All right, I'm in,
So much for this river."
                        And without bothering
To feel his way where the current ran smoothly
He made it across. He was just picking up his bow
When he heard his wife's voice. And he shouted
To Nessus, who was about to betray him,   130

"Where do you think you're going, you rapist?
I'm talking to you, Nessus, you half-breed! Don't even
Think about coming between me and mine!

If you're not afraid of me, remembering
Your father spinning on a wheel in Hell
Ought to be enough to stop you in your tracks.
I don't care how fast the horse half of you is;
If I can't run you down, I'll get you with my bow."

He made his last words come true, shooting an arrow
Straight into the back of the fleeing Centaur.   140
The barbed point stuck out from his chest. He tore it free,
And blood from both wounds came spurting out
Mixed with the venom of the Lernaean Hydra.
Saying to himself, "I will not die unavenged,"
Nessus gave Deianeira his tunic, still warm and wet
With poisoned blood, claiming it was a love charm.

The Death of Hercules

Time passed, and the deeds of great Hercules
Had filled the earth and appeased Juno's hate.
Fresh from a victory at Oechalia
He was preparing to fulfill his vows to Jove   150
At Cenaeum, when Rumor came ahead
Gossiping in your ears, Deianeira, Rumor,
Who loves to add the false to the true.
Small at first, she grows huge through lying,
And now she spread the tale that Hercules
Was enthralled with Iole. His loving wife
Believed the story and, devastated
With this report of her husband's new love,
She indulged her grief with a flood of tears.
But soon she said,
                    "Why am I weeping?   160
My tears would make my rival glad. But since
She is on her way here, I need to make a plan
While I can, before another woman
Takes over my bed. Should I complain
Or grieve in silence? Go back to Calydon
Or, if I can't do more, stay here and oppose her?

O Meleager, what if I remember
That I am your sister and steel myself
To show what great evil a woman scorned
Is capable of—by slitting my rival's throat?"   170

She considered various courses of action
But in the end preferred to send her husband
The tunic soaked in Nessus' blood, hoping
That it would reinvigorate his failing love.
It was to Lichas that she brought the tunic
With no idea of the grief it would bring her.
With soft words the unhappy woman asked him
To take this present to her husband. The hero
Received the gift without knowing what it was
And clothed himself with the Hydra's poison.   180

He had just lit incense and was pouring wine
From a shallow bowl onto the marble altar.
The poison, released from the fabric by the heat,
Spread through Hercules' limbs. Hero that he was,
At first he held back his groans, but when the pain
Became unendurable, he pushed over the altar
And filled the woods of Oeta with his cries.
He tried to tear off the lethal tunic,
But it either stuck to his flesh, or, more horrible,
His skin came off with it, laying bare   190
His torn muscles and enormous bones. His blood
Seethed and hissed with the burning poison,
Like glowing hot metal plunged into water.
The insatiable heat dissolved his innards,
Black sweat flowed down his body, his sinews
Crackled and burned, and as his marrow melted
He stretched his hands to heaven and cried,

"Feast on my destruction, Saturnian Juno,
Feast! Look down from above on my affliction,
Cruel goddess, and glut your savage heart!   200
Or, even if I am your enemy, pity me,

Take away this hateful life, my tortured soul,
Born to suffer. Death will be a kindness
Fitting for a stepmother to bestow.
Was it for this that I overcame Busiris
Who defiled his temple with the blood of strangers?
That I hefted Antaeus the giant off the earth
Away from the strengthening touch of his mother?
That I did not fear Geryon's triple strength,
Or yours, Cerberus? That these hands of mine   210
Broke the strong bull's horn? That Elis knows
What these hands did, or the river Stymphalus,
The Parthenian woods, hands that brought back
The Amazon's belt chased with Scythian gold,
The golden apples guarded by the sleepless dragon?
For this that the centaurs could not withstand me,
Nor the boar that wasted Arcadia? That the Hydra
Couldn't win despite redoubling its heads?
What about when I saw the man-eating mares,
Their mangers full of mangled corpses, and killed   220
Both the horses and Diomedes, their master?
These arms strangled the Nemean lion; this neck
Held up the sky! Jupiter's savage wife
May be tired of imposing labors, but I
Am not tired of performing them. But now
A strange enemy is here, one that I cannot defeat
By courage or arms—a fire that eats my lungs
And all my body. But Eurystheus thrives!
How can anyone still believe in the gods?"

He spoke, and wounded to his heart's core,   230
Ranged along the steeps of Oeta, like a bull
Trailing a spear in its side, though the hunter
Has long since fled. You could see the great hero there,
Groaning, roaring in agony, trying again and again
To tear off his clothes, crashing down trees,
Filling the mountains with fury, stretching out his arms
To his father's sky.
          Then he saw Lichas,

Cowering in fear on an overhanging cliff,
And all of his suffering came out as rage.

"You, Lichas," he cried, "didn't you bring me this gift?   240
Aren't you the cause of my death?"
                                    Pale and trembling,
Lichas offered his timid excuses,
But while he was still speaking, still trying
To clasp the hero's knees, Hercules
Picked him up, and whirling him again and again
Over his head, flung him farther than a catapult could
Into the Euboean Sea. The man grew stiff and hard
As he hung in the air, and just as raindrops
Congeal in cold air and turn into snow
And then the snowflakes become solid hail,   250
So too Lichas, hurled from Hercules' hands
Through empty air, became bloodless with fear
And dried up into stone, the old story says.
And even today there is off the coast of Euboea
A low rock that preserves its old human form,
And, as if it could feel, sailors are afraid
To set foot on it, and they call this rock Lichas.

But you, Jupiter's illustrious son,
Cut down the trees on Oeta's steep slopes
And built a massive pyre. You told Philoctetes   260
To light the fire and take your bow, great quiver
And arrows, destined to see action in Troy again.
And as the flames began to lick the pyre's wood,
You spread the skin of the Nemean lion
On top, and with your club for a pillow, lay down
With a smile on your face, as if at a banquet
With wine flowing and a wreath on your head.
The crackling flames had enveloped the pyre
And reached the peaceful limbs of the hero,
Who scorned their strength. The gods were anxious   270
For the world's protector. Then Saturnian Jove,
Pleased with their sentiments, addressed them all:

"Your fear gladdens me, divine ones, and I rejoice
With all my heart that I am called lord and father
Of a grateful race of gods, and that my offspring
Enjoys the safety of your protective care,
And although he earned it by his prodigious deeds,
Still, I am obliged. But do not let your faithful hearts
Be filled with needless fear. Forget Oeta's flames!
He has conquered all and will conquer them too,   280
Feeling Vulcan's power only in the mortal half
His mother gave him. What he took from me
Is immortal, immune from fire and death,
And when it is done with earth I will receive him
On the shores of heaven. I trust that this
Will please all the gods, but if there is anyone
Who is sorry that Hercules will be a god,
Let him begrudge the prize, but he will also know
That it was deserved, and be obliged to approve."

The gods all assented; even Juno seemed pleased,   290
Although not perhaps with the last words of Jove,
Which annoyed her because they singled her out.
Meanwhile Mulciber had consumed what fire could,
And naught that could be recognized as Hercules
Now remained. Of his mother's contribution
Nothing was left, only traces of Jupiter.
And as a snake sloughs off age along with his skin
And luxuriates in new life, resplendent
In its fresh scales, so too when the Tiyrnthian
Sloughed off his mortal coils, his better part   300
Began to seem grander and more august,
And the Father Almighty drove his chariot
Down through the clouds to take him to heaven
And set him transfigured among the glittering stars.

The Grief of Alcmena and Iole

Atlas felt the weight of the new constellation.
But even now Eurystheus was not satisfied

And kept up his bitter hatred for Hercules
By persecuting his children. Alcmena,
Hercules' mother, worn down by sorrows,
Now had Iole to whom she could confide   310
An old woman's troubles and relate the labors
Of her world-renowned son. For Hercules
Had told his son Hyllus to take Iole
Into his bed and his heart, and she was now
Pregnant with a child of that noble race.
Alcmena now said to her,

Alcmena and Galanthis

                    "May the gods
Be merciful to you at least, and grant you
A quick delivery when your time comes
And you call on Ilithyia, goddess of childbirth
And frightened women in labor. Thanks to Juno,   320
She was hard on me. When Hercules' time
For birth was near, and the sun was passing
Through the zodiac's tenth sign, my burden
Was so heavy, my belly so huge, you could tell
That Jove was the father of that hidden bundle.
I get all clammy just talking about it
And can feel those pangs again. For seven nights
And seven days it was just torture for me.
When I couldn't take it any more I stretched out
My arms to heaven and called on Lucina   330
And her helpers, the Nixi. Lucina came,
But Juno had gotten to her, and she was ready
To deliver my life to that harsh goddess. She sat
Right there, on that altar by the door, just listening
To my groans, with her right leg crossed
Over her left and her fingers interlocked,
Which held up the birth. She also muttered charms
And chanted spells to stop the baby as he crowned.
I was mad with pain, struggling and shrieking
Useless curses against ungrateful Jupiter.   340

I wanted to die, and the things that I said
Would have softened stone. The Theban women
Stood all around me, praying to heaven
To get me through the pain. One of my servants
Was a plain red-haired girl whose name was Galanthis.
She was lower-born, but I really loved her
Because she worked hard and always did what I said.
She was sure that Juno had put a hex on me,
And as she was going out she saw Lucina
Sitting on the altar with her hands clenched in a knot   350
Around her knees and said to her,
                            'Whoever you are,
Congratulate our mistress. Alcmena's delivered
And has the child she prayed for.'
                           Lucina,
That powerful goddess of wombs, leaped up in dismay
And unclenched her hands. The bonds were broken
And I delivered my child. They say that Galanthis
Laughed at the goddess, who caught her by the hair
And dragged her on the ground, holding her there
As she tried to get up until her arms changed
Into a weasel's forelegs. Galanthis remained   360
Active as ever, and had the same color hair,
But her shape changed. And because she had helped
Her mistress in labor with her deceitful mouth,
It is through her mouth that she must give birth.
She still frequents my house as she always did."

Dryope

She finished speaking and sighed, thinking about
Her former servant. While she was grieving,
Her son's wife, Iole, said to her,
                        "This change at least
Affected someone not of our own blood.
What if I told you about my sister's strange fate?   370
It's hard for me to talk about it. Dryope
Was her mother's only child—I was born

From my father's other wife—and she was known
As the most beautiful girl in Oechalia.
She lost her virginity to Apollo, lord of Delos
And Delphi, but Andraemon married her
And was thought lucky to have her as his wife.

There is a pool whose steep, shelving banks
Are crowned with myrtle. Dryope went there
In all innocence, and—what is more upsetting—   380
With a notion to gather garlands for the nymphs.
At her breast she held her sweet baby boy,
Less than a year old, and was nursing him. Close by,
A lotus tree was growing in the water's edge,
Its red and purple blooms holding the promise of fruit.
Dryope picked one of these blossoms
For her little boy, and I (who was with her)
Was about to do the same, when I saw the blossoms
Dripping with blood, and saw the branches recoil
And shiver with fear. It turns out, as we heard   390
Too late from the locals, that the nymph Lotis
Took this form to escape from Priapus'
Obscene pursuit, and so became a tree
While keeping her name. My sister, though,
Knew nothing of this. Startled, she stepped back
With a prayer to the nymphs, and tried to leave,
But her feet were rooted to the ground. She struggled
To tear herself away, but only her upper body
Could move, as the bark crept slowly up from below
Until it had covered her groin. When she saw this   400
She tried to tear her hair out, but only got
Fistfuls of the leaves that now covered her head.
The little boy, Amphissos, a name his grandfather
Eurytus had given him, felt his mother's breast
Turn hard, and could no longer suck milk. And I,
I stood there and saw your cruel fate, my sister,
But could not help you, could only delay the change
By embracing your growing trunk and branches,
And, yes, I wanted to hide myself under that bark.

And now her husband, Andraemon, and her father,   410
Wretched as could be, were there looking for Dryope.
All I could do was point to the lotus tree.
They kissed the warm wood, and lay on the ground
Clinging to the roots of their tree. Now my dear sister
Had only her face left; the rest was all tree.
Your tears sprinkled the leaves your poor body made,
And, while they could, your lips let your voice
Pour these sad notes out into the air:

'If the oaths of those who suffer are trusted,
I swear by the gods I do not deserve this.   420
I endure punishment without a crime; my life
Has been innocent. If this is not the truth,
May I be parched by a drought and lose my leaves,
Cut down with an axe and burned in a fire.
But take this baby from his mother's limbs
And find him a nurse, and let him come often
To nurse beneath my tree, let him play
Beneath my tree, beneath my tree let him
Tumble and play. And when he learns to talk
Have him greet his mother and sadly say,   430
"My mother is hidden in the trunk of this tree."
But make sure he fears the pool, and plucks no blooms
From the tree, and thinks all shrubs are goddesses.
Good-bye, dear husband, and you, my sister,
And good-bye, father. If I am dear to you,
Protect my branches from sharp knives, my leaves
From browsing sheep. And since I may not
Bend down to you, reach up here so that I may
Kiss you while I can. And lift my little son.
I can speak no more. The bark is creeping softly   440
Up my white neck, and I am being buried
In its outer sheath. You need not close my eyes.
Let the bark creep up and close them as I die.'

In the same moment she ceased to speak and to be,

But the new branches long kept her body's warmth."

Iolaus and the Bickering of the Gods

While Iole was relating this wonder
And Alcmena, weeping herself, dried the tears
Of Eurytus' daughter with a sympathetic hand.
A startling event muffled all their grief.
For there, framed in the doorway, stood a youth   450
With a hint of down covering his cheeks.
It was Iolaus, Hercules' nephew,
Alive again and restored to his early years.
Persuaded by Hercules, her newly divine husband,
Juno's daughter Hebe had done this for him,
But as she began to swear that she would never give
A gift like this to anyone else, Themis intervened.

"No," she said, "For Thebes is now embroiled
In civil war. Only Jove himself will defeat Capaneus.
Eteocles and Polynices will achieve fraternal harmony   460
By killing each other. The seer Amphiaraus,
Swallowed alive by the earth, will see the shades
Of his own dead, and his son Alcmaeon
Will avenge him with the death of his mother,
Filial and sinful in the selfsame act. Maddened
By his own evil, exiled from his house and his sanity,
Haunted by the Furies and his mother's ghost
Until his wife, Callirhoë, demands the necklace,
Golden and fatal, and Phegeus' sword
Has drained his kinsman's blood. Then at last   470
Callirhoë, daughter of Acheloüs,
Will prevail upon Jove to make her infant sons
Instant adults, so that they may avenge the death
Of their vengeful father. Jupiter therefore
Reserves the right to grant the gift that you,
His stepdaughter and daughter-in-law, have granted,
And change beardless boys into full-grown men."

When Themis had uttered these prophecies
The gods began talking all at once, asking why

They weren't allowed to grant the same gift 480
To other mortals. Aurora complained about
The doddering years of her husband Tithonus,
Mild Ceres that Iasion's hair was greying.
Vulcan wanted new life for Erichthonius;
And Venus, looking to the future, bargained
For restoration of old Anchises' years.
All of the gods had their own favorites,
And the bickering was reaching the point
Of sedition, when Jupiter opened his mouth
And spoke.
        "What is this coming to?" he said. 490
"Do you have no respect for me? Does anyone think
He can alter Fate's decrees? It was Fate's will
That Iolaus be restored to his former years.
Callirhoë's sons will age prematurely
By Fate, not through ambition or war.
Fate also controls (and I say this in order
To improve your attitude) both you and me.
If I could change Fate, old age would not bend
My Aeacus low, and my Rhadamanthus
Would forever be young, as would Minos, 500
Who because of the galling weight of his years
Is despised, and no longer the king he once was."

This won the gods over. They couldn't complain
When they saw Minos, Rhadamanthus, and Aeacus
Worn down with age.
                The very name of Minos,
When in his prime, had held nations in awe;
But now he was old and weak, and he feared
Miletus, son of Deione and Apollo,
A man proud of his parentage and youthful strength.
Minos believed he was planning a rebellion 510
But did not dare banish him. In the end, Miletus,
You left on your own, sailed across the Aegean
To Asia's shores, and founded a city there
That still bears your name. And there you met

The nymph Cyaneë, daughter of Maeander,
As she wandered the meandering loops and coils
Of her father's stream, and from your union she bore
Twins of terrible beauty, Caunus and Byblis.

Byblis and Her Brother

The example of Byblis warns girls to avoid
Illicit love, Byblis who burned with passion   520
For her brother Caunus, Apollo's grandson,
And not as a sister should love a brother.
She did not at first recognize the fires of love
And thought nothing of kissing him often
Or throwing her arms around her brother's neck,
Long deceived by the semblance of sisterly love.
But things went downhill. She would come
Carefully made up to see her brother,
Too anxious to look beautiful for him,
And she was jealous of anyone else who might   530
Seem more attractive. But her own emotions
Were not yet clear to herself. She had no
Conscious desire, but the fire smoldered inside.
She would call him her lord instead of brother,
Irritated by the mention of family ties,
And wanted him to call her not sister but Byblis.
While awake she would not allow herself
Fantasies of her obscene love, but in her dreams
Her desire was often explicit. She saw herself wrapped
In her brother's arms and blushed in her sleep.   540
She awoke and lay silent, recalling her dream,
And with doubts in her mind she said to herself,

"Oh, I am miserable! What is this silent dream
Trying to express? I don't want it to come true.
Why do I have these dreams? There is no doubt
He is beautiful, even to unfriendly eyes,
And I do like him. I could even love him
If he were not my brother, and he would be

Worthy of me, but it is my bad luck
That I am his sister. As long as I don't do   550
Anything like that when I am awake,
Dreams like that can come any time they want.
Dreams lack witnesses, but one thing they don't lack
Is the semblance of pleasure. O, Venus and Cupid,
Sweet mother and boy, how happy I was,
How real it all felt! I just melted lying there.
How sweet to remember! But the joy was brief,
And night, envious at once, rushed on.

Oh, Caunus, if only I could change my name
And marry you! What a good daughter-in-law   560
I would be to your father, what a good son-in-law
You would be to mine. We would share everything,
The gods willing, except our grandparents.
I would want you to be better born than I.
Gorgeous as you are, you will make someone a mother,
But not me. Having the same parents that I do
You will never be anything except my brother.
That very obstacle is all we have in common.
So then what do my dreams mean for me?
What weight do they have, or do dreams have weight?   570
The gods forbid this! But gods have loved their sisters.
Saturn married Ops, though they were joined by blood,
Oceanus married Tethys, and Olympus' lord married
His sister Juno. But the gods have their own laws.
Why try to compare human to celestial unions?
Either my passion will pass from my heart
If I forbid it, or, if I cannot, I pray I may die
Before I give in, and be laid out on my couch,
And as I lie there, may my brother kiss me.
But that would require the consent of two!   580
It might please me, but he will think it a sin.
Yet the sons of Aeolus did not shy away
From their sisters' bedrooms. Where did I learn that,
I wonder? Why cite these examples? Where am I headed?
Go away, obscene love, and let my brother

Be loved only as a sister should love him.
But if he loved me first, I might well be able
To indulge his passion. So, if I would not
Reject his advances, I should make them myself!
But will I be able to speak, able to come out with it?   590
Love will force me to be able. If shame seals my lips,
I will confess my secret love in a letter."

She liked this idea and settled upon it.
Propped now on her left elbow she said to herself,

"Let him see. Let me confess my insane desires.
Ah, me, how far will I fall? What passion
Has taken hold of my mind?"
                                        And with trembling hand
She starts to set down the words she has thought of,
Stylus in her right hand, in her left the wax tablet.
She begins, hesitates; writes and censors   600
What she has written; writes more and erases;
Edits, finds fault, approves, sets down the tablet,
Takes it up again. She doesn't know what she wants
And doesn't like whatever she is about to do.
Boldness and shame are blended on her face.
She had written "sister," then rubbed "sister" out,
And scratched these words on the amended wax:

"Health and long life, which she will never have
Unless you give it to her, your own true lover
Wishes for you. She is ashamed, too ashamed   610
To tell you her name. If you want to know
What I desire, I would rather be nameless
As I plead my case, and not be known as Byblis
Until my hopes were sure.
                                        You might have guessed
My heart was wounded from my pale, thin face,
My eyes moist with tears, my sighs for no reason,
My frequent embraces and all my kisses, which,

You might have noticed, were more than sisterly.
Yet, though my very soul has been stricken
And I burn within, I have done everything   620
(The gods are my witnesses) to come to my senses.
I have fought long and hard to escape Love's onslaught,
And borne more than you would think a girl ever could.
But I have lost this war, and now with shy prayers
I beg your help. For you alone can save
Your own true lover, and only you can destroy her.
Choose what you will do. You are beseeched
Not by an enemy, but by someone who,
Though most closely joined to you, seeks to be
Bound to you by an even more intimate tie.   630

Let old men be sure of what's right, of what is allowed
And what is forbidden, of fine points of law.
Impetuous Love is what suits people our age.
We don't yet know the rules, and so we think
All is allowed, following the example
Of the great gods. You and I are not impeded
By a harsh father or fear for our reputations,
And even if there were anything to fear,
We can conceal our sweet joys under the name
Of brother and sister. I am free to speak to you   640
In private, and we may embrace and kiss
In front of others. How much is missing?
Pity the one who confesses her love to you
But would not unless utmost passion compelled,
And let my grave not say that you caused my death."

Her hand filled the wax with these futile words,
The last line clinging to the tablet's edge.
She promptly stamped the incriminating letter
With her seal, moistening it with her tears
Because her tongue was so dry. Then,   650
Blushing with shame, she called one of her servants
And said to him in her shy and charming way,

"Take this tablet, my most faithful servant,
To my . . ." There was a long silence; then she added
"Brother."
           While she held out the tablet
It slipped from her hands, and although
This omen disturbed her, she sent it just the same.
The servant found a good time to deliver
The tablet with its message. Maeander's son
Had read it only halfway, when he threw the tablet down   660
In a fit of rage, barely able to hold back his hands
From the trembling servant's throat, crying,

"Get out of here while you can, you pimp!
If your fate did not involve our disgrace
You would pay with your life."
             He fled in terror
And reported to his mistress Caunus' savage response.
Byblis, when you heard that you had been rejected
You turned pale, your body cold as glacial ice.
Then when you came to, all your passion returned
And you were hardly able to gasp out these words: 670

"I deserve it. Why did I have to tell him
How wounded I was? Why was I in such a hurry
To commit to writing what should have stayed hidden?
I should have felt him out first with subtle hints,
Tested the wind with my sails reefed up
And seen how it was blowing. Now my heart
Is like a ship caught in mid-ocean, under full sail
And hit by a storm, driven onto the rocks
And without any way to reverse course for home.
As far as that goes, clear omens told me   680
Not to give in to my love. When the letter fell
As I was passing it on, it meant that my hopes
Were doomed to fall too. Shouldn't I have switched
To another day, or another plan perhaps?
Another day, for sure. God himself warned me

And gave me clear signs, clear that is
If I had been in my right mind. Anyway,
I should have told him in person and not
Committed myself to tablets of wax.
He would have seen my tears, seen his lover's face;   690
I could have said more than any tablet could hold.
I would have put my arms around his unwilling neck,
And if I were rejected, I could have seemed
About to die, could have embraced his feet
And, lying there, could have begged for my life.
I could have done all sorts of things, none of which
All on its own would have won his hard heart,
But acting together would have changed his mind.
Perhaps the servant I sent was somehow at fault,
Did not approach him right, or picked a bad time,   700
When he was really busy. I'll bet that was it.

This has all worked against me. For he himself
Is no tigress' son, doesn't have a heart
Of stone or iron, wasn't nursed by a lioness.
He's going to be conquered! I'm going back,
I'll keep asking him until I have no breath left.
If it is too late now to undo what I've done,
It would have been best never to have started.
But now that I have begun, the second best thing
Is to fight through to the end. If I were to quit,   710
He could not help but remember how much I've dared,
And that being the case, if I did give up now,
I would seem to be fickle, or else just a temptress
Out to catch him. And he will never believe
That I have been overcome by the great god
Who burns in our hearts, but conquered simply by lust.
So I cannot undo the terrible wrong I have done.
I have wooed him in writing, my desire is unveiled.
Though I do nothing else, I cannot be called guiltless.
At this point, then, there is much to hope for   720
And little more that I could be accused of now."

Thus Byblis, her mind so much at odds with itself
That she regrets her attempt but wants to try again.
The unhappy girl tried everything, and was rejected
Again and again. When the young man could see
No end in sight, he left his country, left this shame,
And founded a new city abroad in Caria.

They say that Miletus' wretched daughter
Went out of her mind then. She tore her clothes
From her breast and beat her arms black and blue   730
In a frenzy of grief. Her madness now
Played out in public, as she proclaimed her hope
For this illicit love by leaving her country
And her hated home and following after
Her fleeing brother. And just as the women
Of Ismaria, crazed by your thyrsus
O Dionysus, throng to your orgies
Every three years, so the women of Caria
Saw Byblis go shrieking through their wide fields.
She went farther, through the armor-clad Leleges,   740
Through Lycian country, past Cragus and Limrye,
Past the Xanthus River and past the mountain ridge
Where the Chimaera lived, that fiery monster
With a lion's head and chest and a serpent's tail,
Beyond the woods there until at last, O Byblis,
Exhausted from pursuit, you fell down and lay
With your hair fanning out upon the hard ground
And your face pressed down in the fallen leaves.
The Lelegian nymphs kept trying to lift her
In their tender arms, kept trying to tell her   750
How her love could be healed, offering comfort
To her numb soul. Byblis lay without a word,
Clutching the green grass, and watering it
With a river of tears. They say that the naiads
Gave her a vein of tears that could never run dry.
What greater gift could they give? And soon,
As pitch seeps from the gashed bark of a pine,
Or as coal tar oozes from the heavy black earth,

Or as ice melts under the warm West Wind,
Water trickling in the sun after a freezing winter—   760
So too Byblis, consumed by her own tears,
Turned into a spring, which to this day
Is known in those valleys by her mistress' name
And flows out from under a dark ilex tree.

Iphis and Ianthe

Ordinarily the strange story of Byblis
Would have been the talk of Crete
And its hundred towns, but the Cretans
Had their own marvel to discuss, the transformation
Of a child named Iphis.
      There lived near Phaestus,
And not far from the royal city of Cnossus,   770
A man named Ligdus, a freeborn citizen
Of humble birth and property to match,
Obscure otherwise, but blameless and true.
When the time was near for his wife to give birth,
He whispered in her ear these words of counsel:

"I pray for two things: that your delivery
Have the least possible pain, and that you give birth
To a baby boy. Girls are a much greater burden,
And it is their misfortune to be weak.
I hate to say it, but if you have a girl—   780
Heaven forgive me—it will have to be killed."

He said this, and their cheeks flowed with tears,
Both his wife's and his own. Telethusa
Kept begging her husband to change his mind
And not leave her with such little hope left,
But he would not relent. The hour had come
For the child to be born, and at midnight
Telethusa saw, or thought she saw in her dreams,
The goddess Isis standing before her bed
With a retinue of sacred beings. She wore   790

The horns of a crescent moon on her forehead
And was crowned with a golden garland of wheat.
The dog Anubis was with her, sacred Bubastis
With the head of a cat, the dappled bull Apis,
And the silent god with a finger on his lips.
The sacred rattles were there, and Osiris,
Forever sought for by Isis, and the serpent
Whose venom puts even the gods to sleep.
She seemed to be awake and see all this clearly
As Isis said to her,
                              "O Telethusa,   800
My devotee, you can stop worrying now
And forget about your husband's commands.
When Lucina has brought the child to light
Do not hesitate to raise it, be it girl or boy.
I am the goddess who helps my suppliants,
And you will never be able to complain
That you have worshipped an ungrateful goddess."

With these words, the deity left her room,
And the Cretan woman rose with joy from her bed,
Raising pure hands to the stars in earnest prayer   810
That the vision she had would prove to be true.

The pangs increased and at last she pushed her burden
Into the air and light. It was a girl,
But the father didn't know that, and the mother
Told the nurse, who was in on the lie,
To feed the boy. The father fulfilled his vows
And named the child after his grandfather,
Whose name had been Iphis. Telethusa thought
That this name was perfect. Its common gender
Meant it could be used without any deceit,   820
And so what began as a pious fraud
Remained undetected. The child wore boys' clothes,
And its face was beautiful whether it belonged
To a boy or a girl. Thirteen years went by,
And then, O my Iphis, your father arranged

A marriage for you with a girl named Ianthe,
Daughter of Cretan Telestes. She had golden hair
And all the women of Phaestus thought
She was the city's most beautiful girl. The two
Were matched in age and equally lovely.   830
They had gone to school together, and love
Touched their innocent hearts with equal longing
But not equal hope. Ianthe looked forward
To her wedding day, believing that Iphis,
Whom she thought was a man, would be her man.
But Iphis loved someone she never hoped to have,
And this in itself increased her passion,
A girl in love with a girl. She could barely
Hold back her tears.
                    "What will become of me,"
She said, "possessed by a strange and monstrous love   840
That no one has heard of? If the gods wanted
To spare me, they should really have spared me. If not,
And they really wanted to ruin me, at least
They should have given me some natural malady.
Heifers do not burn with love for heifers, nor mares
For mares. No, rams go for sheep, and does follow stags.
Birds mate like this too, and so do all animals:
No female desires another female.
I wish I'd never been born! Sure, Crete has produced
Every monstrosity, and Pasiphaë did make love   850
To a bull, but that was male and female. My passion
Is clearly even more insane. She had her bull
By being disguised as a heifer, and the male lover
Was the one taken in. But no ingenuity,
Not even if Daedalus himself flew back here
On his waxen wings, could change me from a girl
Into a boy. Or could he change you, Ianthe?

No, pull yourself together, Iphis, be strong,
And shrug off this useless and foolish love.
Look at what you were born, unless you want   860
To deceive yourself, and love what a woman should.

It is hope that begets love, and hope that feeds it.
And the facts of the matter deny you all hope.
No guardian keeps you from her dear embrace,
No jealous husband, no strict father, and she herself
Would not say no. But you still can't have her,
Can't be happy, even with all in your favor,
With men and all of the gods on your side.
None of my prayers have ever been denied;
The gods have given me all that they could.   870
She wants what I want, and both fathers approve,
But Nature won't allow it. Nature, more powerful
Than all of the gods, is working against me.
And now my long-awaited wedding has come,
And soon Ianthe will be mine—and not mine.
We'll be thirsty with water everywhere around.
Why would you, Juno, or you, Hymen, come
To a wedding with no groom but only two brides?"

She said no more. The other bride was burning
With equal passion, and prayed that you, Hymen,   880
Would come quickly.
            Telethusa, meanwhile,
Fearing what Ianthe desired, put off the wedding
With a variety of excuses: pretended sickness,
Ominous visions. With no excuses left
And the postponed wedding only one day off,
She removed the sacred bands from her head
And from her daughter's, so that their hair hung loose,
And clinging to the altar, she prayed,
                    "O Isis,
Goddess of Paraetonium and the Mareotic fields,
Of Pharos and the seven mouths of the Nile,   890
Help us, I pray, and relieve our distress.
I saw you once, Goddess, you and your symbols
And knew them as I heard the bronze sistrum sound
And inscribed your commands on my mindful heart.
That my daughter here still looks on the light
And I have not been punished—this is your gift

And your counsel, Goddess. Pity us both
And lend us your aid."
                              Tears followed her words.
The goddess seemed to move, did move, her altar;
The temple doors shook, and the horns of the goddess   900
Shone like the moon as the bronze sistrum rattled.
Not yet carefree, but gladdened by this omen
Telethusa left the temple, followed by Iphis,
Whose stride was longer than before. Her complexion
Was now more tan than white, her features more chiseled,
Her hair now shorter and unadorned. There was more strength
In that frame than a girl would have, and in fact you were
No longer a girl, but a boy.
                              Go make offerings
At the temple, rejoice and be glad!
                              The two of them
Made offerings together, and in the temple   910
Set up a votive plaque with this inscription:

HIS VOWS AS A GIRL IPHIS FULFILLED AS A BOY.

The morning sun had unveiled the world,
When Venus appeared with Juno and Hymen,
And Iphis had his Ianthe at last.

Book 10

Orpheus and Eurydice

Trailing his saffron robes through the immense aether
Hymen flew down to the shores of the Cicones,
Heeding the vain summons of Orpheus' voice.
He was present, yes, but brought no solemn words,
No joyous expressions, no happy omen.
Even the torch that he held just hissed with teary smoke
And no matter how much he shook it, it would not catch fire.
The outcome was worse than the portent: the bride,
Walking through the grass with her naiad friends,
Was bitten in the heel by a snake and died.   10

When the Thracian bard had filled the upper air
With his laments, he made a bold descent
To the Taenarian Styx to try the spirits below,
And wading through the insubstantial images
Of the buried dead he came before Proserpina
And the lord of the unlovely realms of shades.
Touching the strings of his lyre, he sang,

"Rulers of the world beneath the earth,
To which all of us mortal creatures recede,
If you will permit me to speak the simple truth   20
Without a hint of lies, I have not come down here
To see lightless Tartarus, or to chain
The Medusan monster's three viperous throats.
I have come for my wife, bitten in the heel
By an adder whose poison has stolen her youth.
I wanted to be able to bear this, and I did try.
Love prevailed, a god known well in the world above
And perhaps, I think, even here below:
If the story of that old abduction is true,
Love joined you two as well.
                              By this place full of fear,   30
By immense Chaos and the silence of this vast realm,
Reweave, I beg you, Eurydice's hurried fates.
We are all owed to you, and after a brief delay

Sooner or later we all rush down to this place.
This is our destination, our last home, and you
Hold the longest reign over the human race.
She too, after she has lived a normal span of years,
Will be yours by right. We are asking for a loan.
But if the fates deny pardon for my wife,
I will not go back. Delight in the death of two."   40

As he said these things, plucking the strings
To his words, the bloodless shades wept. Tantalus
Stopped trying to scoop up the receding water,
And Ixion's wheel was stunned. The vultures
Left off from Tityus' liver, Belus' granddaughters
Put down their urns, and even you, Sisyphus,
Sat on your stone. Then for the first time, they say,
The Furies, charmed by his song, wet their cheeks,
Nor could the royal consort or her dark lord
Refuse his request. They called Eurydice,   50
Who was still among the recent shades,
Walking slowly with a limp from her wound.

Orpheus received her along with this condition:
He must not look back until he had left
The Valley of Avernus, or the gift would be void.
The path wound up through deafening silence
Along a steep, dark slope shrouded in fog.
They were approaching the upper rim when the lover,
Fearing for his partner and eager to see her,
Turned his eyes. She fell back at once,   60
Stretching out her arms, trying to catch and be caught,
And sorry to take hold of nothing but air.
Dying again, she did not blame her husband—
What could she complain of except she was loved?
She said her last good-bye, which he could barely hear,
And whirled back again to where she had been.

His wife had died twice now. Orpheus was as stunned
As that nameless man who saw Cerberus chained

And whose fear left him only when his nature did,
Cold granite numbing his entire body;   70
Or as Olenus, who willingly took on
The guilt of Lethaea, too proud of her beauty,
As the loving pair turned into a pair of stones
On watershed Ida. Orpheus yearned and prayed
To recross the Styx, but the ferryman refused.
For seven days he sat on the banks of the river,
Filthy and unfed, his only sustenance tears
And anguish of soul. Complaining that the gods
Of Erebus were cruel, he withdrew to the high,
Windswept steppes of Rhodope and Haemus.   80

The circling sun had three times returned
To watery Pisces, and Orpheus had rejected
All love of woman, whether because his love
Had turned out so badly, or he had pledged his faith.
Still, many women fell in love with the poet,
And many grieved when rebuffed. It was Orpheus
Who began the custom among Thracian men
Of giving their love to tender boys, and enjoying
That brief springtime of blossoming youth.

There was a hill, and on the hill a wide plain,   90
An area green with grass but without any shade.
When the poet born of the gods sat down there
And touched the resonant strings of his lyre,
Shade came to the place. Not a tree stayed away,
Not the Chaonian oak or the Heliades' poplars,
The high-crested chestnut, soft lindens and beech,
The virgin laurel, the brittle hazel, the tough ash
Used for spear shafts, many smooth-grained firs,
The ilex drooping with acorns, pleasant plane trees,
Colored maples, riverbank willows, watery lotus,   100
Evergreen boxwood and slender tamarisks,
Bicolor myrtles, and viburnum dark with berries.
You also came, tendriled ivies and grapes,
And elms cloaked in vines, mountain ash and pines,

Arbute trees loaded with ruby-red fruit,
The pliant palm, victory's prize, and the girded pine
With high crown, pleasing to the Mother of the Gods
Ever since Cybele's beloved Attis
Shed his human form and stiffened into its trunk.

Cyparissus and the Stag

Among this crowd came the cone-shaped cypress,   110
Now a tree, but once a boy beloved by that god
Who tensions both the bow and lyre with strings.
For there was once, sacred to the nymphs who haunt
The Carthaean plains, an enormous stag
Whose spreading antlers steeped his head in shade.
The antlers gleamed with gold, and a jeweled collar
Hung down from his shoulders on his rounded neck.
A silver boss, which he'd worn all his life,
Dangled before his forehead from small leather straps,
And pearls gleamed from his ears and hollow temples.   120
He was quite tame, with none of his natural fear;
He often visited people's houses, and even allowed
His neck to be stroked by the hands of strangers.
But he was dearer to you than to all the rest,
O Cyparissus, loveliest of the Ceans.
It was you who led the stag to pastures new
And brought him to clear springs. And you would weave
Colored garlands through his antlers, and riding
Like an equestrian upon his back would smile
As you guided his soft mouth with purple reins.   130

It was high noon in summer, when Cancer's claws
Are burning in the sun's heat. The weary stag
Had lain down in the grass and was enjoying
The cool forest shade when the boy Cyparissus
Carelessly pierced him with a sharp javelin,
And when he saw him dying of the cruel wound
Resolved to die himself. What did Phoebus

Not say to comfort him, admonishing him to grieve
Moderately and in proportion to the event?
The boy only groaned and begged as the gods' last gift   140
That he mourn for all time. And now, as his life
Ebbed away in endless weeping, his limbs began
To grow green, and his hair, which just now had hung
Over his snow-white brow, became a bristling crest,
And he stiffened into a tree with a slender top
That looks up to heaven's stars. The god groaned,
"You shall be mourned by me, you shall mourn others,
And you shall always be where others grieve."

The Songs of Orpheus

Such was the grove the bard had attracted,
And he sat in the middle of an assemblage   150
Of wild beasts and birds. When he had tuned his lyre,
Touching the strings with his thumb, and was satisfied
That all the different notes were in harmony,
He sang:

"Muse, my mother, let my song begin
With Jupiter, for all things yield to Jupiter's rule,
And often have I sung of his power before,
Sung of the Giants in a heavier strain
And the lightning victorious on the Phlegraean plain.
But I need a lighter lyre now, for I sing of boys
Beloved by gods, and girls dazed by unnatural desire   160
And who paid the penalty for their lust.

Jupiter and Ganymede

The lord of heaven once burned with love
For Phrygian Ganymede, and found something
He preferred to be rather than what he was.
But not just any bird would do, only the eagle,
Who bore his thunderbolts. And so off he went

Through the world's air on lying wings and stole
The Trojan boy, who, against Juno's will,
Still serves cups of nectar to his Jupiter.

Apollo and Hyacinthus

And you, Hyacinthus, Phoebus would have placed   170
You in the sky, if grim Fate had given him time.
Still, you are eternal in your own way.
Every time spring pushes winter out
And Aries comes in after watery Pisces,
You come up and bloom in the emerald grass.
My father loved you above all others,
And Delphi, which is the navel of the earth,
Missed its master while the god was haunting
The banks of the Eurotas and unwalled Sparta.
He no longer honored the bow or the lyre   180
And, forgetful even of himself, was willing
To bear hunting nets, hold the dogs on leash,
Accompany you on the rough mountain ridges,
And with long intimacy feed his love's flame.

And now the Titan Sun was midway between
Night that was done and the still coming dusk,
When the two stripped down and, their skin gleaming
With rich olive oil, competed with the discus.
Phoebus swung it back, paused, and sent it flying
Off through the air to part the clouds with its weight.   190
It stayed aloft a long time before it fell to the ground,
A throw that exhibited both strength and skill.
The Spartan boy, incautious and caught up in the game,
Ran out to get the discus, but the hard earth
Kicked it back up and full into your face,
O Hyacinthus. The god turned as pale as the boy.
He picked up his limp form, tried to give him warmth,
Staunch his terrible wound, sustain his life with herbs.
But his arts were useless, the wound past curing.
Just as in a garden, if someone breaks the stems   200
Of violets or poppies or lilies, bristling

With their yellow stamens, they suddenly go limp
And droop, no longer able to stand upright,
Their heads bowed low, looking to the ground—
So too lies Hyacinthus' dying face. His neck,
Unable to sustain its own weight, falls back
On a shoulder. And Apollo said to him,

'You are fallen, cheated of the prime of youth,
And I see my guilt in your wound, O my sorrow
And my most grievous fault. My hand must be charged   210
With your destruction; I am the author of your death.
And yet what is my fault, unless playing with you
Can be called a fault, unless loving you
Can be called a fault? If only I could die with you
And give up my life! But since we are barred from this
By Fate's laws, you will always be with me,
And your name will ever be on my lips.
You will be the sound of my lyre, my songs
Will all be of you. And you will as a new flower
Imitate my groans with your petals' design.   220
And the time will come when a very great hero
Will be known by the name inscribed on this flower.'

Apollo spoke the truth. The blood that spilled
On the ground, staining the grass, was no longer blood,
But a flower more brilliant than Tyrian dye,
Rising up like a lily except that its color
Was deep purple instead of silvery white.
Apollo was not done with this miraculous tribute
Until he inscribed the petals with his own groans—
AI AI—and the flower still bears these letters of grief.   230
Sparta, too, was proud that Hyacinthus was hers,
And his honor lasts to this day, a yearly celebration,
The ancestral festival of the boy Hyacinthus.

The Cerastae

But if you were to go to Cyprus and ask Amathus,
Rich in ore, if she is proud to have produced

The daughters of Propoetus, she would reject
Both these women and the race of men as well
Known from the horns that roughened their foreheads
As the Cerastae. Before their gates once stood
An altar to Jove, god of hospitality.   240
If any visitor, ignorant of the atrocity,
Had seen this altar all smeared with blood,
He would have thought that suckling calves
Or young Amathian sheep had been sacrificed there.
It was actually the blood of slaughtered guests.
Offended by these impious rites, Venus,
A nourishing goddess, was making ready
To desert her cities and her Ophusian plains.

'But,' she said, 'what has this pleasant place,
What have my cities done wrong? Where is their crime?   250
This impious race should pay the penalty,
By exile or death, or by something in between.
And what is midway between exile and death
If not the penalty of a change of form?'

While she considered how she should change them,
She turned her eyes to their horns, and realizing
That these could remain, she metamorphosed
Their oversized bodies into savage bulls.

The Daughters of Propoetus

But the obscene daughters of Propoetus dared
To deny Venus' divinity. The goddess' wrath   260
Is said to have caused these women to be the first
To prostitute their bodies and tarnish their names,
And as their shame left they could no longer blush,
For the blood in their faces grew stiff and hard,
And it was a small change to turn them to flint.

Pygmalion

Pygmalion had seen these women living in shame,
And, offended by the faults that nature had lavished

On the female psyche, lived as a bachelor
Without any bedmate. Meanwhile he sculpted
With marvelous skill a figure in ivory,   270
Giving it a beauty no woman could be born with,
And he fell in love with what he had made.
It had the face of real girl, a girl you would think
Who wanted to be aroused, if modesty permitted—
To such a degree does his art conceal art.
Pygmalion gazes in admiration, inhaling
Passion for a facsimile body.
He often touches the statue to find out whether
It is ivory or flesh, and is unwilling to admit
That it is ivory. He kisses it and thinks   280
His kisses are returned. He speaks to it,
And when he holds it he seems to feel
His fingers sinking into its limbs, and then fears
He might leave bruises where he has pressed.
He makes sweet talk to it, and brings it gifts,
The kind that girls like, shells and smooth pebbles,
Little birds and colorful flowers, and the Heliades'
Amber tears that drip down from trees. He drapes
Robes around it, puts jeweled rings on its fingers
And long necklaces around its décolletage.   290
All these things are beautiful, but the statue
Is no less beautiful nude. He lays it on a bed
Spread with coverlets dyed Tyrian blue and calls
The statue his bedmate, resting its reclining head
On downy pillows, as if it could feel them.

And now it was the festal day of Venus,
And all of Cyprus turned out to celebrate.
Heifers with gilded horns had fallen when the axe
Came down on their snowy necks, and incense
Smoked on the altars. Pygmalion offered   300
His sacrifice, and standing at the altar
Timidly prayed,
    'O gods, if you can grant all things,
My prayer is that I may have as a wife,'

He didn't dare say, 'my ivory girl,'
But said instead, 'someone like my ivory girl.'

But golden Venus, who of course was present
At her own festival, knew what his prayer meant,
And as an omen of her divinity's favor
The flame on the altar flared up three times.
Back home, he went to his simulacrum   310
And bending over the couch gave it a kiss.
She seemed to be warm. He kissed her again
And touched her breast with his hand. The ivory
Was growing soft to the touch, and as it lost
Its stiff hardness it yielded to his fingers,
As Hymettian wax softens under the sun
And can be kneaded and molded by the thumb
Into many forms, its use growing through use.
The lover is astounded. Cautiously rejoicing
And fearing he is mistaken, he tests his hopes   320
Again and again with his hand. It's a real body!
The veins were throbbing under his thumb.
Our Paphian hero poured out thanksgiving
To the goddess Venus, and pressed his lips
Onto real lips at last. The girl felt the kisses,
Blushed, and lifting her shy eyes up to the light
Took in the sky and her lover together.
The goddess attended the marriage she'd made,
And when nine moons had filled their crescent horns
A daughter was born to them, Paphos,   330
For whom the island of Paphos is named.

Myrrha and Cinyras

Her son was Cinyras; if he had been childless
He might have been counted among the fortunate.
My song is dire. Daughters, stay away; and fathers, too.
Or if my songs charm you, do not believe this story;
Believe instead that it never happened,
But if you do believe it, believe the punishment too.
And if nature allows a thing like this to be seen,

I congratulate this land on being far removed
From the regions that beget such iniquity.   340
Let the land of Panchaia be rich in balsam,
Let it bear cinnamon, costmary, and frankincense
Dripping from the trees, let it bear flowers galore,
Provided that it bears the myrrh tree too.
A new tree was not worth such a price as this.

Cupid swears that his weapons did not harm you
And absolves his torches of your crime, Myrrha.
One of the three Stygian sisters with a firebrand
And swollen vipers must have breathed on you.
It is a great offense to hate your father,   350
But love like this is a greater crime than hate.
You have your pick of the Orient's princes,
All of them vying to bed you in marriage.
Out of them all choose one man, Myrrha,
So long as a certain one is not among them.

She is aware of her despicable passion
And tries to resist it, saying to herself,

'What is my mind doing? What am I scheming?
O Gods, I pray, and Piety, and the sanctity
Of a parent, keep this sin from me and help me   360
To resist this crime—if indeed it is a crime.
But Piety refuses to condemn love like this.
Other animals mate without restriction,
And it is not shameful for a heifer to have
Her sire cover her, nor for a horse's offspring
To be his mate. A goat will go in among
Flocks he has fathered, and birds conceive
From birds who conceived them. Lucky them!
But humans have made malevolent laws,
And what Nature allows, their spiteful laws forbid.   370
Yet they say there are tribes where daughter and father,
Mother and son are joined, doubling natural affection.
It's just my bad luck not to have been born there.

Why do I keep thinking about things like that?
Forbidden hopes, begone! He's worthy to be loved,
But as a father. So, if I were not the daughter
Of great Cinyras, I could sleep with Cinyras,
But because now he is mine, he is not mine,
And my nearness is my loss. I'd be better off
As a stranger. I would leave my fatherland   380
To avoid this sin, but love keeps me from leaving,
Keeps me here so that I can be in Cinyras' presence,
See him, touch him, speak with him, kiss him,
If that's all I can do. But how could you hope for more,
You perverse creature? Do you have any idea
Of the names and relationships you are confusing?
Do you want to be your mother's rival
And your father's mistress? Your son's sister
And your brother's mother? And do you not fear
The sisters whose hair is bound with black snakes   390
And who shake their torches before the eyes
Of guilty souls? But since you have not yet sinned
With your body, don't conceive it in your heart
And pollute natural law with taboo fantasies.
Suppose you do want it; reality forbids it.
He's upright and moral, even old-fashioned—
And, oh, how I wish he had a passion like mine!'

Thus Myrrha. Cinyras, meanwhile, could not choose
Among the swarm of noble suitors his daughter had
And so went to her with their names and asked her   400
Whom she wanted as a husband. The girl was silent.
She stared into her father's face, and her eyes
Filled with warm tears. Cinyras took this to be
A virgin's shyness. He told her not to cry,
Wiped the tears from her cheeks and kissed her lips.
Myrrha was overjoyed, and when she was asked
What kind of husband she might want, she answered,
'Someone like you.' Cinyras did not understand
What his daughter meant and praised her, saying,

'Stay this devoted.' At the word 'devoted,'   410
The girl looked down, conscious of her sin.

Midnight, and sleep had calmed human cares,
But Cinyras' daughter was awake all night,
Consumed by uncontrollable passion
And obsessed with her lust. Filled with despair
And then with resolve, flushing with shame
And then with desire, she does not know what to do.
As a tall tree that is being cut down,
All but the axe's last blow having fallen,
Wavers this way and that, threatening every side,   420
So too Myrrha, her mind and will weakened
By many blows, tottered this way and that
And tries to go in two directions at once.
She can find no rest from her passion but death,
And she decides on death. She rises, determined
To hang herself, and ties her sash from a rafter.
'Good-bye, dear Cinyras,' she says, 'and know
The reason for my death,' as she fits the rope
Around her pale neck.
                            They say her blurred words
Reached the ears of her nurse just outside her door.   430
The old woman went in and when she saw
The attempted suicide, she—all in the same moment—
Screamed, beat her breasts, tore her nightgown,
And unwound the rope from her darling's neck.
Then she had time to weep, hold her, and ask
The reason for the noose. The girl is mum
And keeps her eyes on the floor, regretting
That her halfhearted attempt to die was detected.
The old woman insists, bares her white hair
And depleted breasts, and begs by the girl's cradle   440
And first nourishment that she trust her nurse
With her grief's cause. The girl turns away groaning.
The nurse is determined to find out and promises
More than confidence.

'Tell me,' she says,
'And let me help you. I may be old
But I'm not a dolt. If it's some kind of madness
I have charms and herbs that will heal you.
If someone has put a spell on you, magic rites
Will dispel it. If the gods are angry with you,
They can be appeased with a sacrifice.   450
What else could it be? Your domestic affairs
Are safe and sound. Your mother and your father
Are alive and well.'
                          At the word 'father'
Myrrha sighed from the bottom of her heart.
Even then the nurse had no idea
Of the girl's sinful thoughts, but she guessed
It was some love affair, and she kept pleading
For Myrrha to tell her, whatever it was.
The old woman held the weeping girl close
In her feeble arms and said to her,
                                    'I know,   460
You are in love. Now don't worry. In this affair
I will be completely devoted to you,
And your father will never know.'
                                    The girl
Leapt madly from the old woman's bosom
And pressed her face into her bed, saying,

'Please, go away, or at least stop asking
Why I am so upset. It's horrible, sinful,
What you are trying so hard to know.'

The old woman was shaken. Stretching out hands
That trembled with age and fear, she fell   470
At the feet of the girl she had nursed
And pleaded with her, now softly coaxing,
Now frightening her if she does not tell her secret.
She threatens to report her attempted suicide,
And she promises support if her love is confided.
The girl lifts her head and fills her nurse's bosom

With welling tears. She keeps trying to confess
But swallows her words and covers her shamed face
With her robes. Then she says,
                          'O my mother,
Blessed in your husband.'
                          Just that, and she moans.   480
The nurse understood. Cold fear sank into her bones,
And the white hair stood stiffly on her head.
She said all that she could to drive this mad passion
Out of the girl, who understood how true
Her nurse's warnings were. Still, she was resolved
To die if she could not obtain her desire.
'Live then,' said the nurse. 'You will have your—'
She did not dare say 'father.' She said no more,
Except to confirm her promise with an oath.

Ceres' yearly festival was being celebrated   490
By pious married women. Clothed in pure white,
They brought garlands of wheat as first offerings,
And for nine nights abstained from love, or even
The touch of a man. Cenchreis, the king's wife,
Was among them, observing the secret rites.
The king's bed being void of a legitimate wife,
The nurse, attentive but with bad intentions,
Told Cinyras, whom she found had drunk too much,
Of a spectacular beauty (she gave a false name)
Who was in love with him. When he asked the girl's age,   500
She said, 'The same as Myrrha.' Told to go get her,
She cried out as soon as she got home,
                                      'Rejoice,
My child. We've won!'
                          The unhappy girl
Did not feel joy with all her heart, but felt
Sad presentiments. Still, she was glad too,
So discordant were the feelings she had.

It was the hour when all is hushed,
And between the Bears Boötes has turned

The pole of his wagon down to the horizon.
Myrrha came to her evil deed. The golden moon   510
Fled from the sky; the stars hid behind black clouds
And deprived the night of its fiery sparks.
You were the first, Icarius, to cover your face;
And you, Erigone, his daughter, translated
To the stars for your pious love of your father.
Three times Myrrha stumbled, an omen
Calling her back. Three times the eerie cry
Of the funereal owl served as a portent,
But still she went on, her shame diminished
By the shadows of night. With her left hand   520
She clutches her nurse, and with the other
She gropes her dark way. Now she has reached
The chamber's threshold and is opening the door,
Now she is led within, but her knees buckle,
She is pale and bloodless, and there is no life
In her limbs as she moves. The nearer she gets
To her abomination, the more she shudders at it,
Regrets her boldness, and wishes she could go back
Unrecognized. The nurse leads her by the hand
Up to the high bed and delivers her,   530
Saying, 'Take her, Cinyras, she is yours,'
As she joins them together in unholy love.
The father receives his own flesh in his bed
And tries to calm down the frightened girl,
Encouraging her and calling her 'Baby,'
Just as at some point she calls him 'Daddy,'
So that names would play a part in their sin.

She went from the chamber full of her father,
Carrying in her womb desecrated seed
And a maculate conception. The next night   540
Doubled their sin, nor was it the last.
Finally, after so many beddings, Cinyras,
Eager to know what his mistress looked like,
Brought in a lamp and saw his crime and his daughter.
Speechless with grief, he unsheathed his bright sword,

And Myrrha escaped death only by fleeing
Into the shadows of night. She made her way
Through the back country, leaving Arabia's palms
And the fields of Panchaia. Utterly weary
After nine months of wandering, she finally rested   550
In the Sabaean land, now hardly able to bear
The burden of her womb. Perplexed,
Caught between fear of death and weariness of life,
She embraced this prayer:
                                    'If there is any god
Open to my prayers, I do not refuse
The punishment I deserve. But to avoid
Offending the living by my life or the dead
By my death, exclude me from both realms.
Transform me, and deny me both life and death.'

Some god answered her final prayer. The earth   560
Closed over her legs as she spoke, and roots
Popped out of her toes to support the high trunk.
Her bones became sturdier, and while the marrow
Remained much the same, her blood became sap,
Her arms became branches, her fingers became twigs,
And her skin hardened to bark. The growing tree
Had now bound her heavy womb, buried her breast,
And almost covered her neck; but she could not wait,
And sank her face down into the rising wood,
Plunging it into bark. And although she has lost   570
Her old senses and feelings along with her body,
She still weeps, and the warm drops flow down the tree.
Even her tears are honored, and the myrrh
That drips from the bark preserves its mistress' name,
Which will be spoken through all the ages.

Meanwhile, the misbegotten baby had grown
Inside the tree and was now trying to find a way
To leave its mother and come into the world.
The pregnant tree swells in its midsection
And the pressure strains the mother. The pangs   580

Cannot be voiced, nor can Lucina be called
In the voice of a woman in labor. But like one,
The tree bends, groans, and is wet with falling tears,
And gentle Lucina stood near the moaning branches,
Laid on her hands, and chanted childbearing spells.
The tree cracked open and through its split bark
Delivered a baby boy. The naiads nestled
The wailing infant in leaves and anointed him
With his mother's tears. Even Envy would praise
The boy's beauty, for he looked like one   590
Of the naked Cupids you see in paintings.
Either give him a light quiver or take theirs away
And you wouldn't be able to tell them apart.

Venus and Adonis

Time glides by and slips away from us
Before we know it; nothing is swifter than years.
The son of both his sister and grandfather,
Lately concealed in a tree and lately born,
Then a most beautiful baby boy, then a youth,
Now a young man and even more beautiful.
He arouses Venus herself, and so avenges   600
His mother's passion. It happened this way.
While the goddess' son, quiver on his shoulder,
Was kissing his mother he accidentally
Grazed her breast with a protruding arrow.
The wounded goddess pushed her son away,
But the scratch was deeper than it looked.
Before she knew it she was deeply in love
With a beautiful man. She cared no more
For the shores of Cythera, forgot about Paphos
Ringed by the deep sea, and about Cnidos   610
With all its fish, and Amathus with its copper mines.
She even stayed away from heaven. Adonis
Is more appealing than heaven. She has him
And holds him, is his companion, and although
She is used to her beauty rest in the shade,
Now she tucks up her robes just like Diana

And ranges over the mountain ridges,
Over rocks and thorns, urging on the hounds
In pursuit of animals that are safe to hunt,
Headlong hares or stags with branching antlers   620
Or timid does, avoiding ravenous wolves
And things with claws, like bears, and lions
All bloody with the slaughter of cattle.
And she warns you too, Adonis, for what it's worth,
To fear these beasts.
                              'Be brave,' she said,
'With prey that runs away; boldness isn't safe
With bold animals. Do not be rash, dearest boy,
At my expense; and don't challenge those beasts
That nature has armed, or your glory may come
At great cost to me. Neither youth nor beauty,   630
Nor anything that has moved the goddess Venus,
Moves bristling boars and lions, or touches the minds
Of things in the wild. A boar's curving tusks
Strike like lightning, and a lion's angry charge
Is just as bad. I hate animals like that.'

When he asks her why, she says,
                                        'I'll tell you why,
And you will be amazed at an ancient monstrosity.
But I'm tired from all this unaccustomed effort,
And, look, there's a poplar with inviting shade,
And turf for a couch. I'd love to lie here with you'   640
(And down she lay), 'on the ground.'
                                        She rested
Both on the grass and on him, cushioning her head
On his chest, and interspersing words and kisses,
Told him the tale of Atalanta and Hippomenes.

Atalanta and Hippomenes

'You may have heard of a girl who used to beat men,
Fast men, in a footrace. That wasn't just a story:
She really did beat them. And you couldn't say
Whether her speed or beauty deserved more praise.

Now when she asked the oracle about a husband
The god responded,
                "You don't need a husband,   650
Atalanta. Run away from all husbands. And yet,
You will not run away, and will lose yourself living."

The god's oracle terrified the girl, and she lived
In the shady woods unwedded, and repelled
Her insistent suitors with a harsh condition.

"I am not to be won," she said, "until I lose a race.
Line up and run against me. A wife in bed
Will go to the swift; the slow pay with their death.
Those are the rules."
               She was pitiless alright,
But her beauty was so overwhelming that even   660
On this condition, a crowd of rash men lined up.
Hippomenes had taken a seat to watch
This travesty of a race and had asked,
"Who would take a risk like this just to get a wife?"
And he condemned the young men's undue love.
Then he saw her face and unclothed body,
Beauty such as mine, or yours, if you were a woman.
He was amazed, and stretching out his hands,

"Forgive me," he said, "for blaming you just now.
I had no idea of the prize in this contest!"   670

As he praises her he conceives a passion,
And, jealous and fearful, hopes that none of the youths
Will win the race.
             "But why don't I take a chance
And give it a try?" he asks. "God helps the bold."

While Hippomenes was thinking it over,
The girl flew by with wings on her feet.
Though she seemed as fast as a Scythian arrow,
It was her beauty that he admired more,

And her running itself creates its own beauty.
Her sandals' feathers swoosh in the breeze,   680
Her hair floats back from her ivory shoulders,
Embroidered ribbons flutter at her knees,
And her girlish body flushes with pink
The way a marble courtyard is stained with light
That is filtered through a purple awning.
While the stranger observed all this, the finish line
Was crossed. Atalanta took the winner's wreath,
And the losers groaned and paid the penalty.

Hippomenes, undeterred by what happened to them,
Stepped forward and looked the girl in the eye   690
As he said,
            "Why are you going for easy victories
Over slugs like this? Come on and race against me.
If I happen to win, there's no shame in you losing
To someone like me. Megaerus of Onchestus
Is my father and his grandfather is Neptune,
So I am the great-grandson of the Lord of Sea.
And my own prowess matches my pedigree.
Then again, if I lose, you will have the glory
Of having defeated Hippomenes."

As he said these things, the daughter of Schoenus   700
Had a soft look on her face and couldn't decide
Which she wanted, to be conquered or conquer.
She said to herself,
                    "Some god must not like
Beautiful boys and wants to destroy this one
By making him risk his life so he can marry me.
In my opinion, I am not worth the price.
It's not just his good looks, although I like his looks,
But the fact that he really is still just a boy.
It's not he himself, but his youth that moves me.
And then there's his courage, his fearlessness   710
In the face of death. And let's not forget
That he's four generations removed from Neptune.

And that he loves me, and thinks marrying me
Is worth so much that he's willing to die
If cruel Fortune denies me to him.
Leave while you can, stranger! Run far away
From this bloody wedlock. Trying to marry me
Is a deadly affair. No girl would refuse you;
You could easily be wed to a girl with good sense.
But why do I care about you so much   720
When so many others have already died?
He can take care of himself! And he can die, too,
Since he didn't take the warning of the others' deaths
And doesn't value his life. But will he be killed
Because he wanted to live with me? Undergo
Undeserved death as the penalty for love?
My victory will mean unbearable hatred for me.
But it's not my fault. Oh, please, just withdraw!
Or since you're so crazy, I hope you run faster.
Oh, look how young and girlish he looks. Ah,   730
Poor Hippomenes, I wish you'd never looked on me.
You were so worthy of life. If I were happier,
If the cruel Fates did not deny me marriage,
You were the only one I would have in my bed."

Now her father and the crowd were calling out
For the usual race, when Hippomenes
Called upon me:
              "Cytherea, help my daring,
And encourage the fire of love that you've lit!"

A kindly breeze brought me this very nice prayer,
And it touched my heart, but there wasn't much time.   740
There's a field called Tamasus, the richest soil
In all of Cyprus, and from ancient times
Dedicated as one of my sacred precincts.
In the middle of the field is a gleaming tree
With rustling gold leaves and golden branches.
I had just been there and happened to have
Three golden apples I had picked in my hands.

I approached Hippomenes, showing myself
Only to him, and told him how to use them.

The trumpets blared and the runners were off,   750
Skimming the sand with flying feet. You would think
They could run on waves without wetting their soles
Or graze ears of ripe grain standing high in a field.
The boy's spirits were buoyed by encouraging shouts,

"Go, Hippomenes, turn on your sprint!
Give it all you've got. You've got her now!"

But who knows whether Megaerus' heroic son
Or Schoenus' daughter was more pleased with these words?
There were many times she could have passed him
But lingered a while to look at his face   760
Before reluctantly leaving him behind.
He was panting hard, and the finish line
Was still far off when he lobbed the first apple.
She was astonished and veered off course
To pick up the spinning gold. Hippomenes
Was pulling ahead and the spectators cheered,
But she made up the ground and passed him again.
She delayed to go after the second apple,
Then surged once more. They were coming down the stretch
When he prayed, "Be with me now, Goddess,   770
Who gave me this gift," and threw the shining apple
Hard and sideways into the field. It would take longer
For her to get it back, and the girl hesitated.
But I made her go get it and made the fruit heavier,
Slowing her down with both the detour and weight.
But my story is getting longer than the race itself.
The virgin was passed; the winner led away his prize.

Now, Adonis, did I deserve to be thanked,
Have incense offered? He didn't think to thank me
Or offer me incense. I was hurt by his contempt   780

And flew into a rage. To forestall future slights
I decided to make an example of them both.

They were passing a temple deep in the woods,
A temple of Cybele, the Mother of the Gods.
Great Echion had built it in days gone by,
Fulfilling a vow. They had journeyed far
And wanted to rest. My divine power
Instilled in Hippomenes an untimely desire
To make love. There was a dim, shallow cave
Close to the temple, roofed with natural pumice,   790
A sanctuary of the old religion, where priests
Had installed wooden figures of the ancient gods.
They went in and desecrated that holy place
With forbidden intercourse. The sacred images
Averted their gaze, and the Great Mother,
With her turreted crown, was about to plunge
The guilty couple into the waters of Styx,
But the punishment did not seem severe enough.
Instead, tawny manes covered their once smooth necks,
Their fingers curved into claws, their arms changed to legs,   800
Their weight shifted to their chests, and they swept
The sandy ground with tails. Their faces were angry,
Their words were growls. Instead of bedrooms
They now haunt the wilds. Terrifying to others,
Their teeth champ the bit of Cybele as lions.
These and all other wild beasts like them
That don't run away but attack head on,
Please, my dearest, for my sake, avoid,
Or your manly courage might undo us both.'

With that warning the goddess made her way   810
Through the air, drawn by her swans. But the boy
Felt himself too much a man to take such advice.
His hounds were soon on the trail of a boar
And rousted it from its hiding place. As it charged
Out of the woods Cinyras' young grandson
Got his spear into him with an angled thrust,

But the enraged animal used his curved snout
To root out the spear, drenched with his blood,
And went after the boy, who was panicking now
And running for his life. The boar sank his tusks   820
Deep into his groin and left Adonis to die
On the yellow sand. The Cytherean,
Her light car pulled through the air by flying swans,
Had not yet reached Cyprus when she heard the groans
Of the dying boy far off in the distance
And turned her white swans. When she saw him from the air,
His life ebbing away with his blood, she leaped down,
Tore her garments and hair, and beat her breast
With hands not suited to such lamentation.
And remonstrating with the Fates,
                                   'But not all,'   830
She said, 'will be yours to decide. My grief,
Adonis, shall be memorialized, and every year
Your death and my grief will be reenacted
In ritual. But your blood will be transmuted
Into a flower. If Proserpina once
Could change the nymph Menthe into fragrant mint,
Shall I be begrudged the transformation
Of Cinyras' heroic grandson, Adonis?'

And she sprinkled the blood with aromatic nectar.
Imbued with this essence, the blood swelled up   840
Like a clear bubble that rises from yellow mud,
And within an hour up sprang a flower
The color of blood, like a pomegranate bloom.
But its enjoyment is brief, for it does not cling
To its stem but easily falls when shaken
By the winds for which the anemone is named."

Book 11

The Death of Orpheus

While the poet from Thrace was enthralling trees,
Wild beasts and even stones that followed him,
The Ciconian women, animal skins draping
Their raving breasts, saw Orpheus from a hilltop
Arranging a song to the chords of his lyre,
And one of them, hair floating in the breeze, said,
"There he is, the man who scorns us!" and hurled
Her spear at the Apollonian singer's mouth,
But the shaft sprouted leaves and only grazed him.
The next missile was a stone. Stopped in midair   10
By the sound of voice and lyre, it fell at his feet
As if begging forgiveness for its audacity.
But the assault escalated without restraint,
And mad Fury ruled. Everything they threw
Would have been mollified by his music,
But the enormous clamor of Berycyntian flutes,
Of drums and breast-beating and Bacchic ululation,
Drowned out the lyre's sound. The stones finally grew red
With the blood of the poet, unheard in the end.

The Maenads first tore apart the innumerable birds,   20
The snakes, the animals still entranced by his voice,
And so stole the glory of Orpheus' triumph.
Then they turned on the singer with bloody hands,
Gathering like birds when they spot a night owl
Wandering in the daylight; and he is like a deer
In an amphitheater, soon to perish on the morning sand
As the dogs close in. They rushed at the poet, hurling
Their green-leaved thyrsi, made not for this use.
Some threw clods of earth, some branches ripped from trees,
Some stones. But more substantial weapons were at hand.   30
It happened that yokes of oxen were plowing the soil,
And, nearby, sturdy peasants were digging up fields,
Their arms glistening with sweat. When they saw
The advancing women, they ran, leaving behind
The tools of their trade. Scattered through the empty fields

Lay grub hoes, heavy pick-axes, long mattocks;
The savage women made off with these, and after
Tearing apart the oxen threatening them with their horns,
They rushed back to attend to the fate of the poet,
And as he stretched out his hands, speaking for the first time   40
To no effect and moving them not a bit with his voice,
The sacrilegious women undid him, and—O God—
Through that mouth, heard by rocks and understood by beasts,
His soul was exhaled and drifted off in the air.

The mourning birds wept for you, Orpheus,
The throngs of animals, the flinty rocks,
And the woods that had so often followed your songs,
The trees shedding their leaves as they grieved for you
With heads shorn. They say that rivers were swollen
With their own tears, and that nymphs of wood and stream   50
Wore black and grey and kept their hair disheveled.
His limbs lay all over the fields, but his head and lyre
Were received by you, O Hebrus, and as they floated
Downstream, his lyre—it was a miracle—
Played mournful notes, and his lifeless tongue
Murmured mournfully, and mournfully the banks replied.
And now, borne onto the sea, they left their native stream
And came ashore near Methymna on Lesbos.
As the severed head lay on that foreign beach,
Its hair still dripping with the spume of the sea,   60
A serpent attacked it. But Apollo appeared
And fended the serpent off in midstrike, turning
Its wide open jaws, just as they were, into stone.

The poet's shade went beneath the earth,
And all that he had seen before he recognized now.
Searching through the Fields of the Blessed
He found Eurydice and caught her up
In his eager arms. Now they walk together,
Matching steps. Sometimes she is in front,

Sometimes he takes the lead, and Orpheus 70
Can always look back at his Eurydice.

But Bacchus saw that this crime was avenged.
Grieved at the loss of his sacred poet,
He bound all of those Thracian women
Who witnessed the outrage with twisted roots.
The path that each of them took through the woods
Would tug at her toes and jam their tips
Into the solid earth. It was just like a bird
Who has got its leg caught in a snare
A cunning fowler has set; it flaps its wings, 80
And by its struggles draws the noose tighter.
So too these women, fixed in the clinging soil,
Desperately tried to break free, but the tough roots
Held them in place no matter their struggles.
And when they looked to see where their toes were,
Their feet, their nails, they saw the wood
Creep up their shapely legs. When they tried
To smack their thighs with grieving hands
They hit hard oak. Their breasts too became oak,
And oaken their shoulders. You would think their arms 90
Had become real branches, and you would not be wrong.

Midas

But not even this was enough for Bacchus.
He left those fields with a worthier retinue
And made for the vineyards near his own waters,
The Timolus River and the Pactolus,
Although the latter was not yet a golden stream
Envied for its precious sand. His usual crew,
Satyrs and Bacchants, were with him in droves,
But Silenus was not there. Some Phrygian peasants
Had captured him while he was stumbling along 100
Under the influence of old age and wine.
They bound him with wreaths and led him to Midas,

Their king, whom Thracian Orpheus had taught,
Along with Eumolpus, the rituals of Bacchus.
When Midas saw it was his old companion
In the Bacchic orgies, he held a festival
To celebrate his honored guest's arrival,
And they feasted nonstop for ten days and nights.
When the eleventh dawn banished the ranking stars
The king rode merrily to the Lydian fields   110
And gave Silenus back to the youthful god
Who once was his ward. Bacchus was happy
To have his foster father back and as a reward
Granted Midas whatever he wanted,
A pleasing gift but not one that the king
Would use at all well.
                    "Grant," he said
That whatever I touch will turn to gold."

The god nodded and gave him the harm he asked for,
Sorry he hadn't seen fit to request something better.

Our hero went off pleased with his fatal gift   120
And tried it by touching things one at a time.
Not really believing, he broke off a green twig
From a hanging oak branch. The twig became gold.
He picked up a stone, and it blanched into gold.
He touched a clod of earth, and at his potent touch
It became a lump of gold. He plucked some ripe
Ears of wheat. It was a golden harvest.
He picked an apple from a tree. You would think
That it came from the garden of the Hesperides.
If he brushed his fingers on the soaring columns   130
The columns gleamed. When he washed his hands,
The water could delude a Danaë. His mind
Could hardly contain his hopes, imagining
That everything was gold. Deliriously happy,
He sat down at a table on which his servants
Had set out an elaborate feast, but when he picked up
A piece of bread, the bounty of Ceres

Became stiff and hard in his hand. If he tried to bite
Any piece of food, his teeth only closed on
A hard layer of gold. Water mingled with wine,   140
The wine of Bacchus who gave him his gift,
Flowed into his mouth as molten gold.

This was an alarming turn of events. Rich
And yet wretched, he yearns to flee his wealth,
And he hates what he asked for. No amount of food
Can relieve his hunger. His throat burns with thirst,
And he is, through his own fault, tortured by gold.
Lifting his hands and glistening arms to heaven,
He cried,
           "Forgive me, Father Lenaeus,
For I have sinned. Have mercy upon me,   150
And save me from this glittering curse!"

The gods are kind. Because he confessed his sin,
Bacchus restored him to what he was before
And rescinded the pledged gift. And he said,

"So you will not remain circumscribed by gold
That you so foolishly desired, go to the river
That laps great Sardis and work your way upstream
Against the current until you come to its source.
There you must submerge your head and body
In the gushing water, and so wash away your guilt."   160

Midas went to the water and did as directed,
And the golden touch suffused the whole river,
Passing from the man's body into the stream.
And even today the river's ancient vein
Still seeds the bordering fields with gold,
Their moistened soil turning hard and yellow.

Midas now despised wealth and lived in the woods
And fields, worshipping Pan, whose haunts
Are caves in the hills. But he remained dull-witted

And his mind would be his worst enemy once more.   170
Tmolus, a high peak, looks out over the sea,
One steep slope extending down to Sardis,
The other down to little Hypaepae, where Pan,
Impressing some young nymphs with his music,
Played gentle airs on his wax-joined reed pipe.
He went too far when he slighted Apollo's songs
In comparison with his own and wound up
Outmatched in a contest judged by Tmolus.

The old judge sat on his own mountain top
And shook his ears free from the trees. He wore   180
Only an oak wreath on his dark blue hair,
And acorns hung around his hollow temples,
Looking at the pastoral deity he said,
"There is no delay on the part of the judge."
Then Pan began to play on his rustic pipes
And the foreign melody charmed Midas' ears
(He happened to be nearby). When Pan was done,
Venerable Tmolus turned his face toward Phoebus,
And his whole forest turned with his face.
Phoebus Apollo's golden head was wreathed   190
With laurel from Parnassus, and his mantle,
Dyed deep Tyrian purple, swept the ground.
In his left hand was his lyre, inlaid with gems
And Indian ivory, and his plectrum
Was in his right. His very pose was an artist's.
When his trained thumb swept the strings, the sweet music
So charmed Tmolus that he ordered Pan
To lower his reeds before the lyre.

The holy mountain's verdict pleased everyone
Except for Midas, who called it unjust.   200
Apollo did not allow ears so insensitive
To keep their human form. He stretched them out
And covered them with coarse grey hair,
Great floppy things with the power to move.
Human otherwise, he now had the one deficit

Of wearing the ears of a slow-moving ass.
Desperate for a disguise, he tried to soften
The shame of his temples with a purple turban,
But the slave who cut his hair saw his disgrace.
He did not dare reveal it, but could not keep quiet,   210
And so he went off and dug a hole in the ground
And whispered into the excavation
What kind of ears he had seen on his master.
Then he filled the hole up, burying there
His testimony, and then went quietly home.
But a thick stand of reeds began to grow there
And when they reached full size at the end of the year,
They betrayed the digger, for, stirred by a breeze,
The reeds repeated the words he had buried
And revealed the truth about his master's ears.   220

Laomedon

Fully avenged, Apollo left Mount Tmolus
And rode through the liquid air, staying south
Of the Straits of Helle (daughter of Nephele),
Until he came down in Laomedon's land.
Midway between the promontories of Sigeum
And Rhoeteum there was an ancient altar
Dedicated to the Panomphaeum Thunderer.
There Apollo saw Laomedon at work
Building the walls of his new city, Troy.
He saw, too, that this massive undertaking   230
Was progressing with great difficulty
And required no slight resources. So Apollo
Teamed up with the trident-bearing sea god,
Neptune. The two of them assumed mortal form
And contracted with the Phrygian king
To build the walls for a certain sum of gold.
The walls were built. But Laomedon
Refused to pay, and to top off his duplicity,
He swore that he never agreed to the deal.
"You will pay for this," said the Lord of Ocean,   240

And he turned all his water against miserly Troy,
Flooding the land until it looked like a sea,
Sweeping away all of the farmers' crops,
And drowning their fields beneath his water.
Nor was this punishment enough. A monster
From the deep attacked the king's daughter
Who was bound to flinty rocks until Hercules
Came to her rescue. He then demanded his reward,
A certain team of horses he had bargained for,
But this labor too went uncompensated.   250
And so the great hero conquered the walls
Of twice-perjured Troy. Telamon, too,
Hercules' partner in this campaign,
Had his reward, taking Hesione as his own.
For Peleus, who had also assisted the hero,
Was honored with an immortal goddess
For his own bride; and he was not more proud
Of his grandfather's name than his father-in-law's,
For he was hardly the only grandson of Jove,
But only he had a goddess for his wife.   260

Peleus and Thetis

It happened this way. Old Proteus had told
His daughter, Thetis,
                    "Goddess of the sea, conceive.
You will be the mother of a great hero
Who will surpass his father and all his deeds."

To prevent the world from having anything greater
Than himself, Jove stayed away from Thetis' embrace,
Even though he had strong feelings for her,
And told Peleus, his grandson through Aeacus,
To stand in for him, act as his surrogate,
And find a way into this marine virgin's arms.   270

There is a bay where the Thessalian coast
Curves like a sickle with two arms running out,

A good harbor if the water were deeper.
It has a shelving shore; the sand is firm
And takes no footprints, free from seaweed
And easy to walk on. A stand of myrtles
With bicolored berries comes up to the beach,
And within this grove had been fashioned a grotto,
By art or by nature is difficult to say,
But one would say by art. This is where you,   280
Thetis, would often come, riding naked
On your bridled dolphin, and this is where
Peleus seized you when you were wrapped in sleep,
And since you rejected his proffered advances
He resorted to force, twining both of his arms
Around your neck, and would have had his way
Had you not resorted to your usual tricks.
When you changed to a bird, he held on to the bird;
Then you were a tree, and Peleus clung to the tree;
But your third change was into a spotted tigress,   290
And Aeacus' terrified son released you.
But then he prayed to the gods of the deep,
Pouring wine on the water, and supplicating them
With burnt sacrifice and the smoke of incense
Until Proteus rose from the depths and said,

"Peleus, you will win the one you desire.
All you have to do is tie her down tightly
When she is asleep unawares in the rocky cave.
And even if she assumes a hundred false forms
Don't let her get away, whatever she turns to,   300
Until she resumes her original form."

As Proteus spoke he hid his face in the waves
And let the water close over his final words.

Now the Titan Sun was slanting his chariot
Down to the western sea, when the lovely Nereid
Came out of the water to where she loved to rest.
Peleus had just got a good hold on her virgin limbs

And the goddess had begun to assume new forms
When she realized she was tied down and her arms
Pinned wide apart. She gave a long groan and said,   310
"Some god helped you with this," and showed herself
As Thetis. The hero embraced the goddess,
Fulfilled his desire, and filled her with Achilles.

Peleus and the Wolf of the Marsh

Peleus was fortunate in his son and his wife
And everything else, except for the crime
Of murdering Phocus, his brother. Their father
Drove Peleus out with blood on his hands.
He took refuge in Trachinia, where Ceyx,
A resplendent son of the Morning Star,
Ruled peacefully and without shedding blood. Ceyx   320
Was in mourning then, sad and unlike himself,
Grieving the loss of his own brother. Peleus
Came to him weary from his hard travels
And entered the city with his few companions.
He left the flocks of sheep and cattle he had brought
In a shady valley not far outside the walls.
When he was granted an audience with the king
He held out a wreath in his suppliant hand
And told Ceyx his name and that of his father,
Hiding only his crime and why he was on the run.   330
He asked to support himself in town or field,
And the Trachinian responded benevolently,

"Our resources are here even for ordinary folk,
And you bring to our spirit of generosity
An illustrious name in the line of Jupiter.
Don't waste your time asking. You will have
All that you want, and consider everything you see
As yours to share in. I wish it were better."

And then he wept. When Peleus and his friends
Asked him the cause of his great grief, he said,   340

Daedalion and Chione

"Perhaps you think that bird, a raptor
Who terrorizes all other birds, was always
A feathered creature. He was once a man,
And even then—character being a persistent thing—
He liked to fight and was prone to violence.
His name was Daedalion. He and I were born
From the star that wakes the dawn and is the last
To leave the sky. I was always the peaceful one.
I care about preserving peace and about my wife.
But my brother liked war, and his fighting spirit   350
Subdued kings and nations. Now, transformed,
His fighting spirit pursues the doves of Thisbe.
He had a daughter, Chione, a beautiful girl
Who had a thousand suitors when she turned fourteen
And was ready to marry. It happened that Phoebus
And Mercury, one returning from Delphi,
The other from the peaks of Cyllene,
Both saw her at once and both fell in love.
Apollo put off his hope of love until that night,
But Mercury wasted no time and touched the girl   360
On her face with his soporific wand. So touched,
She lay passively beneath the powerful god.
And when night had sprinkled the sky with stars,
Apollo, disguised as an old woman,
Took his postponed pleasure. In the ripeness of time
A son was born to the winged-footed god,
Autolycus, clever at every kind of deception,
Who could make black white and white black,
A worthy successor to his father in art.
A son was born to Phoebus too (it was a twin birth)   370
Philammon, famous for his songs and his lyre.
But did it do Chione any good that she had
Two sons, was loved by two gods, was herself born
Of a brave father and a resplendent grandfather?
Glory is often a curse, and it was a curse for her,
For she set herself above Diana and had the nerve

To criticize the goddess' beauty. Furious,
Diana said, 'We'll see how you like this,'
As she bent her bow and sent an arrow whizzing
Into the girl's blasphemous tongue, a tongue   380
That said no more. Even as she tried to speak
Her life oozed out with her blood. In my sorrow
I embraced her, and felt her father's grief
In my own heart, and spoke to my dear brother
Words of comfort, but he no more heard them
Than rocky crags hear the murmuring sea,
And he kept lamenting the child he had lost.
But when he saw her on the pyre, three times
He tried to rush into the flames. Turned back
A fourth time, he bolted like a maddened bull   390
Whose neck has been stung by hornets
And rushed wildly where there was no path.
Even then it seemed to me that he was running
Faster than a human could, and you would have thought
That his feet had grown wings. So he left us all
And, wanting to die, had soon reached the topmost
Ridge of Parnassus. Apollo pitied him,
And when Daedalion had thrown himself
From that high cliff, the god transformed him
Into a bird, and held him suspended there   400
On sudden wings, and gave him a hooked beak
And curving talons, but left his courage intact
And his body's great strength. Now as a hawk,
Friendly to no one, he savages other birds,
And suffering himself makes others suffer too."

While Ceyx was telling this fascinating story
About his brother, Peleus' herdsman
Came running up, breathing hard and crying,
"Peleus! Peleus! I have terrible news."
Peleus told him to go on. Ceyx himself   410
Anxiously awaited the news. The herdsman
Went on with his story:

                    "I had driven

The weary cattle down to the curving shore
When the sun was at its highest, looking back
At as much as still was ahead in his drive.
Part of the herd had kneeled down in the sand
And lying there looked out on the broad, flat sea;
Part was wandering about with slow, shambling gait;
Others were swimming in water up to their necks.
There is a temple near the sea, nothing adorned   420
With marble and gold, just good, heavy timbers,
And shaded by an ancient grove. The tenants
Are Nereus and the Nereids. A sailor told me,
While he was drying his nets on the shore,
That these are the local gods of that sea.
Close to the temple there was a willow marsh
Formed by backwash from the sea, and from here
A huge beast came out, a wolf, just raging
In the swampy undergrowth, a real terror
With flashing jaws slimy with foam and blood   430
And eyes like red-hot coals. He was rabid with rage
And hunger, but more with rage. He didn't bother
To fill his belly with the cattle he slaughtered
But went on mangling the herd out of sheer malice.
We tried to drive him off, and some of us
Were badly wounded by his fangs and died.
The shore, the shallows, and the marsh were filled
With the bellowing of the cattle, and red with blood.
Delay is fatal, and we don't have much time.
While there's still something left, let's grab our weapons   440
And attack this wolf with everything we have!"

The herdsman finished. Peleus did not react
To his losses. Conscious of his crime, he knew
That the Nereid mother of Phocus was sending
This disaster upon him as a funeral offering
To her deceased son. Ceyx ordered his men
To arm themselves, and he was doing the same
When his wife Alcyone, roused by the tumult,
Came rushing in, her hair not quite done yet

And then flying free as she threw her arms   450
Around her husband's neck and begged him
With tears in her eyes not to go himself
On the mission, and so save two lives in one.
But Peleus said to her,
                          "Your devotion
To your husband is becoming, but have no fear.
I appreciate the aid you are offering,
But I don't want anyone to fight this monster
On my behalf. I must pray to the sea goddess."

There was a lighthouse high on the citadel,
A landmark welcome to weary sailors.   460
They climbed up to the top and cried aloud
When they looked down and saw the cattle
Lying dead on the shore, and the killer wolf
With jaws bloody and shaggy hair stained red.
Then Peleus stretched his arms out toward the sea
And beseeched the Nereid Psamathe
To cease her anger and come to his aid.
The sea-blue goddess was not moved by his prayers,
But Thetis interceded for her husband's sake
And obtained the nymph's forgiveness. The wolf,   470
Though ordered to stop, kept on with his slaughter,
Mad with bloodlust, until, just as he was
Closing his jaws on a heifer's torn neck, the nymph
Turned him into marble. Everything about him
Stayed the same but his color, and the stone's color
Announced that this wolf need no longer be feared.
Still, the Fates did not permit the banished Peleus
To stay in this land. He wandered in exile
To Magnesia, and there he obtained
Absolution of his bloodguilt from King Acastus.   480

Ceyx and Alcyone

Ceyx had now become increasingly disturbed,
Not only because of his brother's strange fate,

But what had happened since then as well.
And so, as men do in time of trouble,
He decided to consult a sacred oracle
And prepared a voyage to the god in Claros,
For the journey to Delphi had been made unsafe
By the rogue Phorbas and Phlegyas' followers.
But first he shared his plan with you, Alcyone,
His most faithful wife. She felt a sudden chill   490
Deep in her bones; her face turned as pale
As boxwood, and her cheeks were wet with tears.
Three times she tried to speak, and three times
The tears ran down. At last she sobbed out
Her wifely complaints, saying,
                    "What have I done,
My dear husband, to bring you to this? What happened
To the care you once had for me, putting me first?
Can you really abandon your Alcyone like this,
Without a thought for me? Do you really want
To go on a long journey? Am I dearer to you   500
When you are away? At least, I suppose,
You are traveling by land, and although I will grieve,
I need not fear for you and live in constant terror.
The sea terrifies me, the grim face of the deep.
Just recently I saw splintered planks on the shore,
And I have often read names on empty tombs.
And don't be overconfident because Aeolus
Is your father-in-law, who holds the winds behind bars
And can keep the sea calm. Once the winds are loose
On the open water, no power can stop them,   510
And every land and sea is theirs to harass,
Even the clouds of heaven, and their wild collisions
Rouse the red lightning. The more I know them,
And I do—I saw them often when I was a child
In my father's house—the more dangerous they seem.
But if you are not going to listen to prayers
And are determined to go, take me with you,
Dear husband. Then we will be storm-tossed together,
And I will fear only what I experience,

And we will bear whatever happens together,   520
And side by side be borne over the water."

The words and tears of Aeolus' daughter
Moved her star-born husband, for love's fire
Burned no less in him. Yet he was unwilling
Either to give up the journey he planned by sea
Or to take Alcyone along to share his perils.
He said all that he could to comfort her,
But she would not approve. Finally he assuaged
His loving wife by promising one more thing:

"Any time apart will seem long to us,   530
But I swear by my father's light, I will return
If Fate allows, before the second full moon."

She took hope at this promise of his return,
And he ordered his ship to be launched and equipped.
When Alcyone saw this it was like an omen to her
Of what was to come. She trembled all over
And again the tears came. In the depths of despair
She embraced her husband, said a sad farewell,
And then collapsed. Ceyx tried to delay
Their departure, but the two rows of young men   540
Were pulling the oars back to their muscular chests
And splitting the water with measured strokes.
Alcyone lifted her wet eyes and saw her husband
Standing on the stern deck waving to her,
And she waved back. When the land fell away
And her eyes could no longer make out his face
She kept her eyes on the fast-receding ship
As long as she could, and when it disappeared
She still watched the sails as they flowed along
At the top of the mast. When she could no longer see   550
Even the sails, she went to her bedroom, distraught,
And lay down on the bed. Bedroom and bed
Renewed her tears, reminding Alcyone
Of the part of her life that was gone from her.

When they pulled out of the harbor the rigging
Began to stir in the wind. The captain
Shipped his oars, ran the yard to the top of the mast,
And spread the sails to catch the following wind.
The ship was cutting through the waves, midway
Or so in the sea, and a long way from either shore,   560
When, at nightfall, the sea began to roughen
With whitecaps, and the East Wind picked up.
"Lower the yard right now," the captain shouted,
"And close reef all sails." He gave the order,
But the wind smothered it, and the heavy seas
Drowned out his voice. Some of the crew
Pulled in the oars on their own, plugged the oar holes
And reefed the sails. Someone bailed out water,
Pouring the sea back into the sea, and someone else
Secured the spars. While all this was being done   570
Helter-skelter, the storm was gaining strength,
And winds were roaring in from every direction,
Agitating the waves. The captain is terrified
And admits he does not know how the ship stands,
What to order or what to forestall, so heavy
Is the impending doom and so beyond his skill.
Men are shouting, the rigging strains and screeches,
Heavy waves slap down waves, thunder crashes.
The sea seems to run up to the sky itself
And touch the scudding clouds with its salt spray.   580
Now the waves churn up yellow sand from the bottom,
Now they are blacker than the waters of Styx
And then flatten out and whiten with hissing foam.
The Trachinian ship is subject to all these sea changes.
Now she seems to stare from a high mountain top
Down into deep valleys and Acheron's pit;
And when the sea lowers her into a deep trough
She seems to gaze up at heaven from the abyss of hell.
The ship's sides boom as thudding waves strike
With the force of a battering ram, or a projectile   590
Launched by a catapult into a fortress.
And just as fierce lions gather their strength

And drive into hunters' leveled spears and chests,
So too the waves, driven on by the winds,
Reared up high and overarched the ship's mast.
And now the hull's wedges begin to give way,
And when their wax coating is lost, cracks appear
And let the lethal waves in. The rain is so heavy
You would think that all of heaven is emptying
Into the sea, and the sea was rising to fill   600
All the zones of heaven. The sails are soaked
With rain, and water thrown up from the sea
Mingles with the rain. No stars shine in the sky,
And the night is black with its own darkness
And the storm's gloom. But fire flashes from the sky,
Splitting the shadows with light, and the rain gleams
In the lightning's glare, which also reveals
Water pouring through the ship's hollow hull.
And as a soldier distinguishes himself
As the first to scale a besieged city wall   610
After repeated efforts, and finally stands out
As one in a thousand, so too among the waves
Battering the ship, the tenth one heaves up
With a mightier effort and does not stop
Until it is over the side of the conquered ship.
So now part of the sea is in the vessel's hold
And the rest of it is still trying to get in.
The whole crew panics, as if enemy forces
Were tunneling under their city's walls
And they were inside trying to defend it.   620
Skill fails, courage ebbs, and deaths as numerous
As the advancing waves seem to crowd in.
One sailor cannot hold back his tears, another
Is struck dumb, another cries out, "Fortunate the man
Who is properly buried." Someone else
Prays to the gods, begging for help, with arms outstretched
To unseen, unanswering heaven; one of them
Thinks of his brothers and his father, another
Of his home and his children, each of them

On what he has left behind. But Ceyx thinks   630
Of Alcyone; upon Ceyx's lips
There is only Alcyone, and although
He longs for her, he is glad she is absent.
He would love to look back at his native shores,
And turn his last gaze in the direction of home,
But he has no idea where he is, for the sea
Seethes in a maelstrom, and the pitch-black clouds
Hide all the sky and double night's darkness.
The mast snaps in a blast of wind; the rudder, too,
Is broken. One last wave, like a victor   640
Gloating over his spoils, coils itself high,
Pauses to look down at the other waves,
And then—as if Athos and Pindus were torn
From their foundations and thrown into the sea—
Falls on the ship with overwhelming force
And plunges it all the way down to the bottom.
Most of the sailors died then and there,
Sucked down into the abyss, never to see
The light of day again. The rest of them clung
To broken bits of the ship. Ceyx himself,   650
With a hand accustomed to holding a scepter,
Held on to a fragment of the wreck, calling upon
His father-in-law and his father, to no avail.
But as he swam it was mostly Alcyone's name
That was on his lips. He thought of her,
Spoke to her, and he prayed that the waves
Would take his dead body into her sight,
So that he could be buried by her own dear hands.
While he can still swim, and as often as the waves
Allow him to open his mouth, he says the name   660
Of his far-off Alycone, and finally murmurs it
Into the waves themselves when a black arc of water
Breaks over him and submerges his head.
The Morning Star was dull that dawn, its light
Unrecognizable. Since he could not leave
The sky, he shrouded his face with dark clouds.

Meanwhile, Aeolus' daughter knew nothing
Of this great calamity. She counted the nights
And hurried to weave the robes he would wear,
And then those she would put on for his return,   670
Imagining a homecoming that could never be.
She dutifully burns incense to all the gods,
But worships Juno more than the others,
Coming to her altars to pray for the man
Who is no more, praying that her husband
Be kept safe from harm, return to his home
And love no other woman more than her.
Of all her prayers only the last could be answered.
But the goddess could no longer endure
These appeals for the dead, and to protect her altar   680
From the hands of a mourner, she called Iris,
Saying,
          "Iris, my faithful messenger,
Go swiftly now to the drowsy house of Sleep
And have him send to Alcyone a vision
Of her dead Ceyx, a dream that will tell her
What his true fate has been."
                                        As Juno spoke,
Iris put on her thousand-hued robe and, trailing
The long arc of a rainbow across the sky, came
To the cloud-capped palace of the King of Sleep.

Near the land of the Cimmerians is a deep cave,   690
A hollow mountain really, that is the inner sanctum
Of lethargic Sleep. Phoebus cannot enter it
With his rising, noon-time, or setting rays. Misty clouds
And half-lit shadows breathe forth from the earth.
No cock crows there to summon the dawn,
And no watchdog disturbs the quiet there,
Nor a goose, more watchful, nor beast, nor cattle,
Nor a branch in the breeze, nor human voices.
That place is home to mute silence only,
And from the cave's bottom the river Lethe flows,   700

Whose water murmuring over its pebbly bed
Invites deep slumber. Before the cave's entrance
Banks of poppies bloom, and countless herbs,
From whose juices dewy Night extracts sleep
And sprinkles it over the darkened earth.
The palace has no doors, lest a turning hinge creak,
And no guard at the threshold. In the central court
Is a high ebony bed spread with dusky blankets,
Downy, soft, and black as midnight. In it lies
The god himself, his limbs relaxed in languor.   710
Around him lie empty dreams, phantom forms
As numerous as ears of grain at harvest,
As leaves in a forest, grains of sand on a shore.

When Iris entered, brushing aside with her hands
The dreams in her way, the sacred space shone
With the light from her robes. Then the god,
Hardly opening his slow, heavy eyelids
And sinking back on his pillow again and again,
His chin knocking his chest as he kept nodding off,
Finally shook himself free of, well, himself,   720
And propped on an elbow asked the goddess,
Whom he now recognized, why she had come.
Iris replied,
            "O Sleep, who quiets all, Sleep,
Mildest of the gods, peace of our souls,
Who puts care to flight, soothes our raveled bodies
And readies them for further ministries—
Send a dream to Alcyone. Make it look like
The king of Trachinia, famous for Hercules,
And have it show her her husband's shipwreck.
By order of Juno."
                  Her mission accomplished,   730
Iris departed, for she could no longer resist
The power of sleep, and when she felt drowsiness
Slipping up on her, she took off and retraced
The long bow on which she had just traveled.

Sleep had a thousand sons, and from that throng
He roused Morpheus, an artful imitator
Of the human form. No one else is more cunning
At representing movement, features, clothing,
The accents of speech. He does humans only.
Another son mimics birds, beasts, and snakes;   740
Gods call him Icelos, and mortals Phobetor.
A third, Phantasos, specializes in illusions
Of inanimate things, earth, stones, rivers, trees.
These three appear at night to kings and such;
The rest pay visits to common citizens.
All these Sleep passed by and chose Morpheus,
Of all his brothers, for Iris' commission.
Then he drifted off again into sweet drowsiness,
And, head nodding, snuggled into his bed.

Flying through night's shadows on soundless wings,   750
Morpheus soon arrived at the Haemonian city.
Shedding his wings, he assumed Ceyx's form,
Pale as death, and stood naked by the bed
Of his unhappy wife. His beard was sodden,
And seawater dripped from his matted hair.
Bending over her, tears streaming down his face,
He said,
          "My poor wife, do you recognize
Your Ceyx, or has my face changed in death?
Look at me. You will know me then, and find
In place of your husband your husband's shade.   760
Your prayers have brought me no help, Alcyone.
I am dead. Do not think I will come back to you.
The stormy South Wind took hold of the ship
In the Aegean and tossing her in strong blasts
Wrecked her there. My lips drank the waves
As I called your name. No dubious messenger
Brings you this news, nor is it a rumor you hear.
I myself, drowned as you see me, tell you my fate.
Then get up and weep for me, wear mourning,
Do not send me unlamented to Tartarus."   770

Morpheus said all this in a voice that Alcyone
Would believe was her husband's; his tears, too,
Seemed to be real, and he moved his hands
The way Ceyx did. Alcyone moaned tearfully
And in her sleep reached out for his body
But embraced only air. She cried out in the dark,

"Wait! Where are you going? We will go together!"

Roused by her own voice and her husband's image,
She awoke suddenly. At first she looked around
To see if he was still there (her attendants,   780
Startled by her cry, had brought in a lamp).
When she didn't find him, she slapped her cheeks
With her hands, tore the clothes from her breast
And then beat her breasts. She tore out her hair
Without bothering to unbind it, and when her nurse
Asked what was wrong, she cried out to her,

"Alcyone is gone, gone, dead with her Ceyx.
Don't try to console me. He's shipwrecked, dead!
I just saw him, knew him, stretched out my arms
As he vanished, wanting to hold him back.   790
It was only a shade, but my husband's true shade,
Clear as can be, not as he used to look
With his bright face, but all pale and naked,
With his hair still dripping. Ah me, I saw him!
The poor thing stood here, on this very spot—"
And she looked to see if there were still any footprints.
"This is just what I feared in my foreboding
And was why I begged you not to sail away
And leave me here. What I should have wished for,
Since you were sailing away to your death,   800
Was for you to take me with you. It would have been
Far better for me to go with you. We would have spent
All of our life together, and not been apart in death.
But now I have died far away from myself;
Far from myself I am tossed on the waves,

And the sea holds me without my being there.
But I won't struggle, O my poor husband,
And I will never leave you. Now at least
I am coming to join you. If not an urn,
Our epitaph will unite us. Our bones   810
Will not touch, but I will touch your name with mine."

Grief stopped her words, which turned into wails
And long moans drawn from her stricken heart.

Morning had broken. She left her house
And went to the seashore to find the spot
From which she had watched him set sail.
She lingered there a while, musing,
"Here he loosened the cable, he kissed me
On the beach here as he was leaving,"
And was recalling details and places   820
And gazing out to sea, when she saw something
That looked like a corpse floating on the water.
She was not sure at first, but as the waves
Washed it closer, but still some distance away,
It was clearly a body, whose she did not know,
But because it was someone who had been shipwrecked,
She was moved by the omen, and as if she would weep
For an unknown sailor, she said,
                                  "I pity you,
Poor man, whoever you are, and I pity your wife,
If you have a wife."
                              The closer the body   830
Was moved by the waves, and the more she looked at it,
The less she could control herself. And now
It was almost ashore, and she could see clearly
Who it was. It was her husband.
                                  "It is he!"
She cried, and tearing her cheeks, her hair
And her clothes all at once, she stretched out
Her trembling hands to Ceyx, saying,

"Is this how you come back, O my dear husband,
Like this, poor thing, you come back to me?"

There was a breakwater extending from the shore,   840
Built to deflect the force of the pounding waves,
And along this Alcyone ran until she leapt
Into the sea. What she did next was a wonder:
She flew, beating the light air with newborn wings,
And as she skimmed the water's surface,
She uttered from her slender beak croaking sounds
Full of plaintive grief. But when she reached
The silent, bloodless body, she embraced
The beloved limbs with her unfamiliar wings
And bestowed cold kisses with her hard, rough beak.   850
Whether Ceyx felt this, or whether it was the waves
That made it seem he lifted his face, we do not know.
But he did feel something, and in the end the gods
Took pity on them, and turned them both into birds.
Suffering the same fate, their love too remained,
Nor were their conjugal bonds dissolved.
They still mate and still produce offspring,
And for seven peaceful days each winter
Alcyone broods upon her nest, floating
In the sea. At that time the waves are still,   860
For Aeolus guards the winds and restrains them,
Keeping the sea calm for his grandsons' sake.

The Bird Sightings

An old man saw these two birds flying together
And praised their love's long perseverance.
Someone nearby, or perhaps the same person,
Pointed to a long-necked diver and said,

Aesacus and Hesperia

"That bird, the one trailing his slender legs
As he skims the water, has a royal pedigree too,

Going all the way back to Jupiter himself
In an unbroken line. You have Ilus next   870
And then Assaracus, Ganymede—the boy
Jupiter abducted—old Laomedon,
And Priam, whose lot was the last days of Troy.
He was Hector's brother, and if he hadn't met
His strange fate when he was young, his name
Would be as famous as Hector's. Hecuba
Was Hector's mother, but this one, Aesacus,
Was born in secret under the shade of Mount Ida
To Alexiroë, daughter of the Granicus River.
The boy hated cities and lived in the country   880
And on remote mountainsides, far away
From gleaming palace halls, and hardly ever
Went into town to mingle with Trojan society.
Not that he was a bumpkin, and he did have a heart
That was vulnerable to love. Many a time
He would chase Hesperia all through the woods.
He had seen her—she was Cebren's daughter—
Drying her hair, which fanned out on her shoulders,
On the banks of her father's river. The nymph
Ran at the sight of him, like a frightened deer   890
Running from a tawny wolf, or like a wild duck
Winging away from a hawk and its abandoned pond.
But the Trojan hero kept after her,
His speed coming from love as hers from fear.
And then, you see, a snake hidden in the grass
Bit her on the foot as she raced along,
And its curved fangs left their poison in her veins.
Her flight ended with her life. The lover,
Out of his mind with grief, held the lifeless body
And cried,

        'O I am sorry, I am sorry   900
I chased you. I didn't think this would happen,
And it wasn't worth so much for me to win you.
We have destroyed you, poor girl, the two of us,
The snake wounded you, but I was the cause!

Let me be called the worse, if my own death
Does not console yours.'
                                        That said, he jumped
Off a high cliff eaten out by the thundering waves
Down into the sea. But Tethys, pitying him,
Brought him down gently, and as he floated
Covered him with feathers, and so denied him   910
The death that he sought. The lover was outraged
At being forced to live, and that his soul was blocked
When it wanted to leave its miserable body.
So as soon as he had his wings on his shoulders,
He flew up high and hurled his body once more
Down to the sea, but his feathers lightened his fall.
So he dove down furiously beneath the water
And endlessly tried to find a way to die.
His passion made him lean. His legs are long
Between the joints, his neck remains long,   920
And his head is far from his body. He loves the sea,
And he has his name because he dives beneath it."

Book 12

The Greeks at Aulis

Priam mourned, unaware that Aesacus lived on
As a bird on the wing, and had his son's name
Inscribed on an empty tomb, where Hector
And his brothers were making funeral offerings.
Only Paris was absent from the services,
Arriving home later with his stolen wife
And bringing to his country a lengthy war.
A coalition of a thousand ships
From every town in Greece soon sailed to Troy,
Nor would vengeance have been delayed   10
Had storms not made the sea impassable
And held up the fleet off Boeotia's coast
At the port of Aulis, teeming with fish. Gathered there,
The Greeks were preparing a sacrifice to Jove
And the ancient altar was glowing with fire
When they saw a dark blue serpent crawling up
A plane tree that stood on the sacred ground.
In the tree's top branches there was a nest
With eight fledglings in it, and these young birds
Together with their mother, who was flitting around   20
Her doomed brood, the serpent devoured
In its greedy maw. The men looked on in wonder,
But Calchas, their augur, prophesied for them,
Saying,
          "Greeks, rejoice! Troy will fall to us,
But the labor will be long."
                              And he foretold
That those nine birds meant nine years of war.
Meanwhile, the serpent had turned into stone,
Just as he was, a rock formation
Coiled like a snake in the tree's green branches.

But the North Wind continued to rage   30
Over the Aonian waters and gave no passage
To the ships of war. Some said that Neptune
Was sparing Troy, whose walls he had built.

But not Calchas, who did not conceal his knowledge
That the virgin goddess must be appeased
With a virgin's blood. When Agamemnon
Put his people's welfare above his own family
And became less of a father and more of a king,
And just as Iphigeneia was standing
Before the altar amid tearful attendants,   40
Ready to shed her chaste blood, Diana
Was moved to pity. She threw up a mist
Before their eyes, and in the confusion
Of the ritual and prayers they say she substituted
A deer on the altar for the Mycenaean girl.
So when Diana's wrath was appeased
With appropriate blood, and the sea's rage
Receded with that of the goddess, the wind
Shifted to the sterns of a thousand ships
That finally made their way to Phrygian shores.   50

The House of Rumor

There is a place in the middle of the world
Where land, sea, and sky meet, the intersection
Of the three realms. From there, wherever a place
Might be, however far away, it is under surveillance.
All that happens there is seen, and every word reaches
Those cavernous ears. Rumor dwells there
In a house she chose on the highest point,
Fitted with innumerable entrances
And a thousand apertures with no doors
To close them. Night and day the house is open.   60
It is built of echoing bronze, and the whole place
Hums with sound, repeated words, and doubles
Of every sound it hears. There is no quiet inside
No silence anywhere, but no clamor either,
Rather only the murmur of small voices,
Like the murmur of the sea heard from afar,
Or thunder as it dies away when Jupiter
Has made the dark clouds clash in the sky.

Crowds fill the hall, people come and go,
And rumors mingle in their thousands, the false   70
With the true. Confused reports flit about,
Filling idle ears with their talk, going everywhere
To tell what they've heard. Stories grow in size
As each new teller makes his own additions.
There lives Credulity, and rash Error,
Premature Joy and nervous Fears,
Sudden Sedition and unattributed Whispers.
Rumor herself observes all that is done
On land and sea and in the heavens
As she scrutinizes the entire world.   80

Cygnus and Achilles

And now she makes it known that the Greek ships
Are coming in force, and so the invasion
Was not unforeseen. The Trojans were steeled
To hold off the Greeks and protect their shores,
And you, Protesilaus, were the first to fall
To Hector's deadly spear. The first pitched battles
Cost the Greeks dearly, as Hector made himself
All too well known, and the Phrygians also
Paid in blood to learn what Achaean arms could do.
The Sigean shores grew red. And now Cygnus,   90
Neptune's son, who had killed a thousand men
Was pressing on, as was Achilles in his chariot,
Taking out whole squadrons with his Pelian spear
But always looking through the lanes of battle
For either Cygnus or Hector, and, Hector's fate
Having been postponed until the war's tenth year,
Met with Cygnus. The snow-white necks
Of Achilles' horses were straining at the yoke.
Achilles shouted to them and drove his chariot
Straight at his enemy, rocking his spear   100
And yelling,
            "May this console you,
Whoever you are: you are about to be killed

By Achilles of Thessaly."
                              Thus Achilles,
And his heavy spear followed his words.
It was a good throw, too, hitting the mark,
But to little effect, the spear's sharp point
Only bruising Cygnus' chest as if it were blunt.
It was Cygnus' turn now.
                              "Well, son of Thetis,"
He said, "I've heard all about your reputation,
But why are you surprised that I have no wound?"   110
(Achilles was clearly amazed.) "This helmet,
With its golden horsehair crest, and this shield
On my left arm are not for protection
But mere decorations, like the armor Mars wears.
Take it all off and I am invulnerable still.
It's something to be the son not of Nereus' daughter,
But of Nereus' lord, who rules the whole sea besides."

Cygnus spoke, and let fly against Achilles,
But his spear only stuck in his curving shield,
Penetrating bronze and nine layers of ox hide   120
But stopped by the tenth. Shaking it off,
Achilles rifled another quivering spear
From his strong hand, and again Cygnus
Was unwounded and whole. A third spear,
Though Cygnus pulled off his armor to receive it,
Didn't even graze him. Achilles was furious,
Like a bull in a bull ring lowering his horns
As it charges a scarlet cloak, the object of his rage,
And finds it forever eludes his attack.
He looked at the spear to make sure that the point   130
Was still attached to the shaft.
                              "Is my arm that weak?"
He asked himself. "Or has its usual strength
Been washed out just this once? It was strong enough
When I tore down Lyrnesos, or made Tenedos
And Eëtion's city run with blood,

Or when the Caïcus flowed red with the blood
Of all the tribes on its banks, or when Telephus
Took two strong hits. Not to mention this field,
Littered with the corpses I made and see now.
My right arm's been strong, and it still is strong." 140

He said this, but as if he were still not sure
He hurled another spear right at Menoetes,
A Lycian soldier, hitting him square in the breastplate
And through to his chest. As Menoetes went down
In a clatter of bronze, Achilles pulled the spear out
From the hot wound and said,
                            "This is the hand,
And this is the spear that I just used. All right,
I'll use them now against Cygnus and pray
I get the same outcome."
                            He got the shot off.
The ash spear flew straight and crashed into 150
The man's left shoulder, but then it rebounded
As if it had hit a wall. Achilles saw a spot of blood
At the point of impact and his spirits soared,
But there was no wound: it was Menoetes' blood.
Filled with rage, Achilles leaped from his chariot
And locked up with his invulnerable enemy,
Saw his bright sword cut through his helmet and shield,
But blunted on the edge of Cygnus' hard body.
The Greek could take no more and began pounding
Cygnus' head and face with the hilt of his sword 160
And his heavy shield, always pushing him back,
Giving him no time to breathe, no time to recover.
Cygnus began to panic; shadows swam in his eyes.
Stepping backward, he stumbled on a stone,
And Achilles smashed him down to the ground.
Kneeling on his chest and pressing down hard
With the edge of his shield, he unbuckled the strap
Of Cygnus' helmet and used it to choke him,
Cutting off both breath and life. But when he started

To strip off the armor, he saw the armor was empty,   170
For Cygnus' divine father had transformed his son
Into a swan, whose name he already had.

Tales from the Truce

After this hard-fought battle a long truce,
Lasting many days, was in order. Each side
Laid down its weapons. Alert sentries patrolled
The walls of Troy, and sharp-eyed guards were posted
Over the Greek trenches. Achilles offered
A heifer to Athena as thanksgiving
For Cygnus' defeat. The entrails were placed
On the blazing altar, and the savor rose up   180
To be received by the gods in heaven,
Who then had their portion, as the men had theirs,
Reclining at tables filled with roast beef
And easing their cares and their thirst with wine.
This evening they were not entertained with the lyre,
Nor by singers, nor the long boxwood flute,
But with their own conversation. Late into the night
They talked about valor, heroism in war,
Battles of their enemies and of their own,
And it was a joy to take turns telling over and over   190
The perils they had been through. What else
Would Achilles talk about, what else would those
In Achilles' presence want to discuss?
They talked mostly about his latest victory
And the downfall of Cygnus. It amazed them all
That a youth could have a body no spear could pierce,
Invulnerable, that could even blunt a sword's edge.

The Origin of Caeneus

Achilles and the others were wondering at this
When Nestor said,
                      "In your generation
There has only been one who scorned cold steel   200

And could not be pierced by any blow—Cygnus.
But I myself once saw someone who could bear
A thousand strokes without injury, a Thessalian
Named Caeneus; yes, Caeneus of Thessaly
Who lived on Mount Othrys, a renowned hero.
And, what made Caeneus more amazing still,
He had been born a woman."

                        Their ears pricked up
And they begged him for more, Achilles saying,

"Tell us! Everyone wants to hear this from you,
Old sir, the age's wisest and most eloquent speaker.   210
Who was this Caeneus, and why was his sex changed?
What campaign brought you together, fighting whom,
And who overcame him, if anyone did?"

Then the old man said,
                  "I'm slowing down with age,
And there are many things I saw when I was young
That escape me now. Still, there is much
I do remember, and through all those years
Of war and peace, nothing sticks in my memory
So well as this. And if advanced age means
You have seen a lot, well, I have lived now   220
For over two centuries, and am in my third.

Elatus' daughter, Caenis, was famed for her beauty,
The loveliest girl in all of the cities
Of Thessaly, including yours, Achilles,
Which is where she was from. She was the despair
Of numerous suitors. Peleus, too, perhaps
Would have tried to win her, but he had either
Wed your mother already, or they were betrothed.
Caenis would not consent to any marriage,
But, as the story goes, while she was walking   230
On a lonely shore, the god of the sea
Had her by force. After Neptune had enjoyed
The pleasure of this new love, he said to her,

'You may now ask for whatever you wish,
And know that your request will not be denied.'

That too is in the story. And Caenis answered,

'The wrong you've done me demands the great prayer
That I never be able to suffer this again. Make me
A woman no longer and you will have given me all.'

She spoke the last words in a huskier voice   240
That seemed like a man's. And so it was,
For the sea god had already answered her prayer
And granted her besides that she could not be wounded
Or fall to any weapon. Caeneus now
Went away happy and spent all his time
Pursuing manly arts in Thessaly's fields.

The Battle of the Lapiths
and the Centaurs

Pirithoüs, son of bold Ixion, now married
Hippodameia, and invited the Centaurs,
Those cloud-born beasts, to the wedding feast.
The tables were set in a shaded grotto,   250
And all the Thessalian heroes were there.
I was there too. The palace was buzzing
With all of the guests, the nuptial hymn was sung,
The great hall smoked with fires, and the bride,
Escorted by matrons and maids of honor,
Made her entrance, beautiful as can be.
We congratulated Pirithoüs on his bride,
Which may have put a jinx on the occasion.
What happened was that Eurytus, the wildest
Of the wild Centaurs, got all hot with wine   260
And lust for the bride, and the two together
Were too much for him. Before you knew it,
The tables were overturned, the whole banquet
Was in an uproar, and there was Eurytus
Dragging Hippodameia away by her hair.

Each of the other Centaurs grabbed
Whichever woman he wanted, or whichever
He could lay his hands on, and the whole scene
Looked like a city being sacked. The hall
Resounded with the women's shrieks. We men   270
All jumped to our feet, and Theseus called out,

'Are you mad, Eurytus? Move against Pirithoüs
And you have two enemies in one as long as I live.'

And the great hero, to back up his threat,
Pushed through the Centaurs to rescue the bride.
Eurytus, with nothing to say that could justify
What he had done, charged at his avenger,
Raining down fists on his face and noble chest.
Nearby was an enormous antique mixing bowl,
Heavily embossed, and as huge as it was   280
Theseus was huger. The hero snatched it up
And smashed it into the face of the Centaur,
Who spewed out gobs of brain, blood, and wine
From his mouth and gaping wound. He reeled backward,
Kicking the reeking ground with all four of his hooves.
His hybrid brothers were enraged at his death
And outdid each other yelling, 'A fight, a fight!'
Wine gave them courage, and in the first onslaught
Cups and brittle flasks and bowls went flying,
Festal utensils now adapted to warfare.   290

First off, Ophion's son Amycus had the cheek
To loot the sanctuary, ripping out of the shrine
A chandelier bristling with glittering lamps.
Lifting it high as if it were an axe
About to come down on a bull's glossy neck,
He brought it down hard onto the head of Celadon,
One of the Lapiths, obliterating his face.
His eyes spurted out of their sockets, the bones
Of his face splintered wide, and his nose was driven
Into his throat. But Pelates of Pella,   300

Wrenching off the leg of a maple-wood table,
Laid Amycus low, and as he slumped on the ground
With his chin on his chest, spitting out teeth
Along with his blood, his enemy hit him again,
Sending him down to the shades of Tartarus.

Then Gryneus, eyeing a smoking altar
That stood next to him, shouted, 'Why not use this?'
And hoisting up the altar, fire and all,
He heaved it into a crowd of Lapiths,
Crushing two, Broteas and Orios.   310
(Orios' mother was Mycale, a witch
Whose incantations were known to draw down
The crescent of the reluctant moon.) Exadius
Now cried, 'You won't get away with this,
If I can only find a weapon!' He found one
In the antlers of a stag hanging from a tall pine
As a votive offering. Gryneus' eyes were pierced
By the branching rack, and his eyeballs
Were both gouged out, one of them sticking
On the tip of a horn, while the other rolled down   320
And hung up on the bloodied clot of his beard.

Then Rhoetus snatched up a flaming torch
Made of plum wood and whirled it around
Plumb into the temples of Charaxus' head, setting
His blond hair on fire with its rapacious flames.
The Lapith's hair burned like a field of dry grain,
And the scorched blood sizzled in the open wound,
Making a horrible sound, hissing like a bar
Of red-hot iron when a smith takes his tongs
And plunges it into a tub of water; the iron shrieks   330
As it sinks in a burst of steam. The injured Lapith
Shook the fire out of his shaggy hair
And shouldered a stone used as a threshold,
A weight more suited to a team of oxen
And too heavy in fact to make it to Rhoetus.

The massive stone did reach Cometes, however,
A friend of Charaxus who was standing closer,
And crushed him. Rhoetus was overjoyed
And said, 'May all of you have strength like that.'
And he renewed his attack with the half-burned brand,   340
Raining down blows until he split the skull's sutures
And the bones sank down into the mushy brain.

After this victory Rhoetus turned against
Euagrus, Corythus, and Dryas. When Corythus,
Whose cheeks were touched with down, pitched forward,
Dead, Euagrus cried, 'What glory is there in killing a boy?'
Rhoetus didn't give him a chance to say any more,
Shoving the flaming torch down his throat
While he was still speaking. He chased you also,
Dryas, but with different results. As he came on   350
Swimming in glory from his killing spree,
You ran him through with a charred stake
Where the neck meets the shoulder. Rhoetus yelped,
Wrenching the stake free from his collarbone,
And ran off reeking with blood. Oneus fled too,
As did Lycabas and Medon, whose right shoulder
Was wounded, along with Thaumas and Pisenor.
Mermeros, who had been the fastest Centaur alive,
Was slower now because of the hit he had taken.
Pholus galloped off too, and Melaneus and Abas,   360
Who hunted wild boar, and Asbolus, the augur,
Who had tried to talk his friends out of the fight.
He said to Nessus, who was running with him
To avoid being wounded, 'You don't have to run;
You're being saved for Hercules' arrow.'
But Eurynomus and Lycidas, Areos
And Imbreus did not escape death. Dryas
Cut them all down as they stood to confront him.
You fell that way too, Crenaeus, even though
You had already turned to run. Looking back,   370
You took a javelin right between the eyes.

In the middle of all this uproar Aphidas
Lay sound asleep, still holding his cup of wine
As he slumbered stretched out on an Ossaean bearskin.
He had done nothing at all in the fight
When Phorbas spotted him from a distance,
And slipping his fingers into his javelin's thong
He cried, 'You can drink your wine mixed with the Styx!'
And he got the shot off. The iron-tipped ash wood
Punched through the youth's neck as he lay asleep   380
With his head thrown back. Death came with no feeling,
And from his engorged throat dark blood spurted out
Onto the couch and into the wine cup itself.

I saw Petraeus trying to uproot an oak tree
Laden with acorns. He had both hands around it,
Working it this way and that, and just as he was
Wrenching out the loosened trunk, Pirithoüs
Sent a spear clear through the Centaur's ribs
And pinned him squirming against the hard oak.
Pirithoüs was the man, they say, killing Lycus;   390
Pirithoüs was the man, dispatching Chromis,
But Dictys and Helops pumped up the hero's fame
More than either of these, as Helops was pierced
By the spear of Pirithoüs sailing right through
The Centaur's right temple and out his right ear,
While Dictys was pursued so hard by Pirithoüs
That he stumbled and fell from a high precipice
And was impaled through his groin on an ash tree's limbs.

Aphareus was there to avenge him,
But as he prepared to heave a rock he had torn   400
Out of the mountain, Theseus whacked him
With an oaken club and shattered his elbow.
With neither the time nor the inclination
To finish off his maimed body, Theseus
Vaulted up onto Bienor, who had never
Carried anyone except himself on his back.
Pressing his knees into the Centaur's flanks

And with his left hand clutching his mane,
He clubbed his temples and blustering mouth
With the knotted oak, crushing all the bones.   410
Theseus went on to kill Nedymnus
And Lycopes, known for his javelin throws,
Hipassus, his long beard fanning over his chest,
And Ripheus, rearing up as tall as the trees;
Thereus too, who used to catch bears
In the mountains of Thessaly and bring them
Back home, alive and unhappy. Demoleon
Was fed up with all of Theseus' successes.
Unable to uproot a pine tree, he snapped it off
And threw it at the hero, who saw it coming   420
And drew out of range, prompted by Athena,
Or so he wanted us all to believe.

But the tree trunk fell to no small effect,
Shearing off Crantor's entire right shoulder.
He had served as armor-bearer, Achilles,
To your father, given to Peleus
By Amyntor, king of the Dolopians,
As a peace pledge after being conquered in war.
When Peleus saw him so foully disfigured,
He cried,
                   'Accept this funeral offering,   430
Crantor, most beloved youth.'
                                     Saying this,
Peleus hurled his ash spear with all his might
At Demoleon, exploding his ribcage
And leaving the shaft quivering in his bones.
The Centaur managed to pull the shaft out
And felt around for the point, but it was lodged
Deep in his lungs. Pain gave him courage,
And wounded as he was, he reared up high
And with his forelegs beat Peleus down,
But the hero received the blows from his hooves   440
On his helmet and shield. Hunkered down,
He kept his spear ready and ran the Centaur through

In his torso where his two natures blended.
Peleus had already killed Phlegraeos and Hyles
With shots from long range, and had taken down
Iphinoüs and Clanis in hand-to-hand combat.
Now he added Dorylas, who wore a wolf-skin cap
And instead of a spear carried a pair
Of curving bull's horns stained red with blood.
My courage gave me strength, and I said to him,   450
'Let's see how your horns hold up to my spear.'
I hurled my spear, and since he could not duck it
He put up his right hand to protect his face,
And my spear pinned it to his forehead. Peleus
Was right there, and in the hubbub slashed his sword
Across the Centaur's belly. This made him lurch forward,
Trailing his entrails, which he trod upon,
Bursting them, tangling his legs in his guts,
And finally falling with an emptied stomach.

And, Cyllarus, your beauty did not save you then   460
(If one can grant beauty to that kind of creature).
His beard was just coming in, fuzzy and golden,
And long gold hair fell down past his shoulders
To the middle of his flanks. He had a pleasing
And lively face; his neck, shoulders, chest, and hands,
All his human parts, neared artistic perfection,
And his equine parts, too, absolutely unblemished,
Were no less perfect. Give him a horse's head
And a neck, and he would have been worthy of Castor,
His back was so straight, his chest so muscled.   470
His body was pitch-black, but his tail white as snow,
As were his legs. Many female Centaurs
Had wooed him, but Hylonome alone,
Loveliest lady Centaur in all the deep woods,
Had won him. With tender words, by loving him
And confessing her love, she alone possessed
Her Cyllarus—and also by the care she took
To look her best, as far as Centaurs can.

She would comb her long hair, entwining it
With rosemary or violets, or sometimes roses   480
And white lilies. Twice each day she bathed her face
In a brook that tumbled from the wooded heights
Of Pagasa, and dipped her body twice in the stream.
Her left shoulder and her flank were graced
With only the choicest pelts. They were both in love,
Wandering the mountains together, and resting
Together in caves. Together they had come
To the Lapiths' palace, and now they were fighting
Side by side, when a javelin came from the left
(No one knows who threw it) and pierced Cyllarus   490
In the middle of his chest. The heart was just grazed
But it grew cold, and the whole body also,
When the weapon was withdrawn. Hylonome
Embraced his dying body, soothed the wound
With her hand, and with her lips tried to keep
His last breath from passing. When she saw he was dead,
Saying some words drowned out by the noise,
She fell on the spear that had pierced Cyllarus
And lay with her lover in a dying embrace.

I can still see Phaeocomes, who had tied   500
The skins of six lions together with knotted cords
As body armor for both man and horse.
He hurled a log that could have hardly been moved
By two teams of oxen and crushed in the head
Of Tectaphos, Olenus' son. His skull's dome
Was shattered and his brain oozed out through his eyes
His ears and his nostrils, the way curdled milk
Or some other soft mass is forced out through a sieve.
But just as Phaecomes was about to strip
The armor from the fallen man, I shoved my sword deep   510
(As your father knows well) into his thigh.
Chthonius and Teleboas also fell to my sword.
One carried a forked branch, the other a spear,
With which I was wounded—if you look here

You can still see the old scar! Back in those days
I should have been shipped off to Troy.
I could have given Hector all the fun he wanted,
If not taken him down. But Hector was a child then
Or not even born, and age has weakened me now.

Why tell you how Periphas beat up Pyraethus,   520
Both man and horse? Or how Ampyx drove
A cornel-wood spear that had lost its tip
Into the face of four-footed Echechlus?
Macarius killed Pelethronian Erigdupus
By smashing a crowbar into his chest,
And I remember Nessus planting a javelin
In Cymelus' groin. And Mopsus made it clear
He was more than a prophet by how he handled
The Centaur Hodites, who was trying to speak
When Mopsus' spear nailed his tongue to his throat.   530

Caeneus had killed five Centaurs by now:
Styphelos, Bromus, Antimachus, Elymus,
And Pyracmos, who was armed with a battle-axe.
I don't remember their wounds, but I do recall
Their number and names. Then Latreus rushed up,
A huge Centaur armed with the spoils of Halesus,
Whom he had just killed. Latreus was middle-aged,
But had the strength of youth though his hair was grey.
He pranced around between the two battle lines,
Showing off his Macedonian lance,   540
His helmet and shield, clashing his weapons
And pouring out big talk into the empty air:

'What are you doing here, Caenis? You'll always be
A woman to me, Caenis. Don't you remember
What you were born as, or what you did to get
This phony look of a man? Think about
Your natural sex and the rape you suffered,
And go pick up your distaff and basket of wool,
Go spin thread with your thumb, and leave war to men!'

At this Caeneus' spear ploughed a deep furrow   550
Into the galloping Centaur's side, where horse met man.
Maddened with pain, Latreus hurled his lance
Into Caeneus' unprotected face, but it bounced off
Like a hailstone from a tile roof, or a pebble
From a drum's taut hide. Then he moved in close
And tried to thrust his sword into his enemy's
Impenetrable side, but the sword failed to enter.
The Centaur shouted, 'Even so, you're not getting away!
I'll kill you with the edge if the point is blunt.'
And he sliced at Caeneus' loins with his long right arm,   560
But the sword clanged as if it had struck marble,
And the blade shattered as it hit the too solid flesh.

When he had exposed his unwounded body
Long enough to his enemy's wonder,
Caeneus said, 'Now let's see what my sword
Can do to your body.' As he spoke, he drove
His lethal weapon into the Centaur's flank,
Twisting the blade as he buried it in his guts
To redouble the trauma. The Centaurs now
Went berserk with rage, and all of them threw   570
Their spears at one man, but their weapons only
Rebounded off him and lay blunted on the ground,
While Caeneus stood there, unbowed and unbloodied
Despite their best efforts. The Centaurs were stunned.

'Oh, the shame of it,' Monychus shouted,
'Our race defeated by someone barely a man,
Yet he is a man, and with our feeble attempts
We are what he once was! What is the use
Of having super-bodies, of possessing twin powers,
Natures combining the strongest two beings?   580
We are not after all the sons of a goddess,
Or of Ixion, who aspired to be Juno's mate.
We are undone by an enemy who is half a man!
Let's roll down boulders and tree trunks on him,
Whole mountainsides, and crush the life out of him

Under a piled–up forest, a mass that will choke him.
If we can't wound him, let weight be our weapon.'

He spoke, and latching onto the trunk of a tree
Blown over by a storm, threw it at Caeneus.
The others followed suit; in no time Othrys   590
Was stripped of its trees, and Pelion lost its shade.
Buried under a huge pile, Caeneus strained
Against the weight of the trees, bearing the oaken mass
Upon his strong shoulders. But when it rose higher
Than his mouth and head, he ran out of air.
Gasping for breath, he tried to get his head up
Into the air and throw off the heaped forest,
Moving at times the way Ida's steep mass
Trembles in an earthquake. His end is uncertain.
Some said the weight of the woods thrust him down   600
Into Tartarus' pit. But Mopsus denied this,
For he saw a bird with golden wings rise up
From the middle of the pile, and fly through the air.
I saw it too, for the first and last time.

As Mopsus watched it wheeling round the camp
In lazy circles, and caught the sound of its wings,
He followed it with his soul as well as his senses
And said,
              'Hail to thee, blithe Caeneus, glory
Of the Lapith race, once a great hero,
And now the only bird of your kind!'   610
This story gained credence from its teller.
As for us, our grief increased our wrath.
We took it hard that so many had ganged up
To overwhelm one man, and we kept up our killing rage
Until half of our enemies were dead,
And the rest escaped into the dark of night."

Hercules and Periclymenus

As Nestor told the story of the battle
Between the Lapiths and the half-human Centaurs,

Tlepolemus could not contain his resentment
That Hercules had been passed over, and said,   620

"Old sir, I find it odd that Hercules received
No praise in your story. My father often told me
Of the cloud-born Centaurs he had overcome."

Nestor responded grimly,
                          "Why do you ask me
To remember past grievances, to reopen
Sorrows long buried, and to dredge up the injuries
That make me hate your father? He has done deeds
Beyond belief, God knows, and filled the earth
With well-deserved praise, which I wish I could deny.
But we don't praise Deïphobus, or Polydamas,   630
Or even Hector. Who praises his enemy?
That father of yours once destroyed Messene
And the innocent cities of Elis and Pylos,
And laid waste my own home with fire and sword.
To say nothing of the others whose lives he ended,
There were twelve of us sons of Neleus,
And Hercules killed all twelve except me,
A fine brood of young men. Well, their deaths
Had to be borne, but Periclymenus' death
Was strange indeed. Neleus' father was Neptune,   640
And he had given to Periclymenus the power
To assume any form that he wished, and then
Resume his human shape once more. In this battle
None of his forms were doing any good
So he changed into an eagle, the bird
Whose hooked talons carry the thunderbolts
And is most dear to Jove, the king of the gods.
Using his strong wings, his talons, and beak,
He savaged Hercules' face. But then the hero
Took aim with his bow as Periclymenus   650
Floated high in the clouds, and the arrow hit
Where the wing joins the side, not a grave wound
But the sinew was cut and wouldn't let his wing beat.

He fell to the ground, where the weight of his body
Forced the arrow to go up through his breast
And into his throat. So now, my handsome captain
Of the Rhodian fleet, what cause do I have
To sing the praises your Hercules? And yet,
My only vengeance is to ignore his deeds.
My friendship with you is as solid as ever."   660

When Nestor, whose words were like honey,
Finishéd this story, they drank one more round,
Rose from their couches, and went to bed for the night.

The Death of Achilles

But the god who governs the sea with his trident
Was still filled with grief for his son, whose body
He had changed into a swan, and his hatred
For Achilles knew no bounds. The war had dragged on
For almost ten years now when he addressed
The unshorn lord of Smintheus, Apollo:

"By far the favorite son of my brother,   670
You built with me the walls of Troy, Apollo,
So does it not grieve you to see they will fall,
And that thousands have died defending them?
No need to mention them all; just think of Hector,
Dragged in death around his Pergamum's walls.
And yet Achilles, more cruel than war itself,
Still lives, the man who destroyed our work.
Just let him come near me. I'll make him feel
What my trident can do. But since I may not meet
My enemy face to face, give him a surprise   680
And kill him with an invisible arrow."

The god of Delos nodded in assent
And indulging equally his uncle's desire
And his own, he came to the Trojan lines
Wrapped in mist. There, in the bloody toil

Of heroes, he saw Paris taking potshots
Into the crowd and, manifesting divinity,
Said to him,
                    "Why are you wasting arrows
On the rabble? If you care about your people,
Aim at Achilles and avenge your brothers' deaths."   690
And pointing to where the son of Peleus
Was mowing down Trojans, he turned the bow
In the right direction and guided the arrow
With his deadly hand. This was the first joy
That Priam felt since the death of Hector.
And so, Achilles, you conquered everyone
But you yourself were conquered by a coward
Who abducted a married Greek woman. If you were
Fated to be killed by a woman warrior,
You would have gladly fallen to the Amazon's axe.   700

And now the terror of Troy, the great bulwark
And splendor of the Greeks, the grandson of Aeacus,
The invincible hero, was burned on the pyre.
The same god who had given him his armor
Consumed him as well, and now Achilles,
Once so great, is only dust and ashes,
Barely enough to fill an urn. But his glory lives on,
Enough to fill the whole world, and this is how
The man must be measured. By this the son of Peleus
Is still himself, and disdains Tartarus' pit.   710
Even his shield still wages war, and for his arms
Arms are taken up. You should hear the story
Of who came to own them. Neither Diomedes
Nor Oïlean Ajax dared to claim them,
Not Agamemnon nor Menelaus, nor anyone
Except Odysseus and Telamonian Ajax
Were bold enough to lay claim to this prize.
To avoid acrimony Agamemnon assembled
All the Greek captains and had them decide.

Book 13

The Contest for Achilles' Arms

The Greek leaders took their seats, the rank and file
Standing in a circle around them. Up rose Ajax,
Lord of the sevenfold shield, barely able
To control his anger. His scowling gaze scanned
The Sigean shoreline, and stretching his hand
Toward the beached ships he said:

Ajax's Speech

                              "I plead my case
In the presence of these ships and Jupiter himself.
Ulysses opposes me. But did he oppose Hector
When he came to burn our ships? No, I did,
Standing up to the smoke and flames, I drove   10
The Trojans away from the fleet. Far safer to fight
With lies than with your hands. I am less ready
To speak, as he is to act, and I am as much
His master in war as he is mine in speech.
As for what I have done, I don't need to tell you,
Because you saw it all yourself. Let Ulysses tell
What he has done, unseen and in the dark of night.
It is a great prize, I admit, that I contend for,
But a rival like this diminishes its honor.
It is no honor for Ajax to win a prize,   20
However great, that Ulysses has hoped for.
He already has his prize: when he is beaten,
He can say that he competed with me.

And even if my valor were open to question,
I am nobler in birth. My father was Telamon,
Who with great Hercules captured Troy
And sailed on the Argo. Aeacus was his father,
Who is now a judge in the silent world
Where Sisyphus strains at his heavy stone;
And Jupiter most high acknowledges Aeacus   30
To be his own son. Ajax is therefore
Three removes from Jove. But this lineage

Would not help my cause, if I did not, Achaeans,
Hold it in common with the great Achilles.
He was my cousin; I seek a cousin's arms.
Why do you, the son of Sisyphus, and just like him
When it comes to trickery, try to link
The line of Aeacus with a foreign family?

Is it because I took up arms freely,
Without coercion, that I am now denied arms?   40
And will they be given to one who feigned madness
To dodge the war and had to be exposed
By someone shrewder? Little good it did him.
It took Palamedes, the son of Nauplius,
To uncover this coward's scam and drag him out
To the arms he shirked. Will he take the best
Because he wanted to take up none? And will I
Go unhonored and be deprived of my cousin's arms
Because I was the first to meet this danger head on?

It would have been better had his madness been real   50
Or gone undetected, and that this evil counselor
Would not have come with us to fight the Phyrgians.
Then, Philoctetes, you would not be marooned
On the island of Lemnos, to our criminal shame,
Hiding in the woods and making the very stones
Weep with your groans as you curse Ulysses,
Curses he deserves and that, if there are gods,
Will not be in vain. But now this man, who swore
The oath with us for this war, one of our leaders,
Heir to the bow of Hercules, is wasted by disease   60
And hunger, hunting birds for food and clothing,
Using the arrows that fate intended for Troy.
At least he is still alive, since Ulysses is not there.
Poor Palamedes would prefer being left behind.
He would still be alive, or at least would have died
Without dishonor. Ulysses, remembering
How he had been exposed by the man, accused him

Of being a traitor, and got him convicted
Of this false charge by planting gold in his tent.
So Ulysses has, by either execution or exile,   70
Been depleting our strength. That's how he fights,
And that's why Ulysses has to be feared.

Even if he were more eloquent than Nestor
He could never convince me it was not criminal
When he deserted Nestor. His horse wounded
And himself slow with age, he appealed to Ulysses
And was abandoned by his comrade in arms.
Diomedes knows I am not making this up,
For he kept calling his cowardly friend by name
And rebuking him. But the gods are righteous,   80
And they aren't blind. Before long he needed aid,
Having rendered none. And as he abandoned another,
So should he have been abandoned, by the precedent
He himself had set. He was crying for his friends.
I came over and saw him all trembling and pale,
So scared of dying. I covered him with my shield
And saved his lame soul—big deal that was!
If you want to keep disputing this, let's go back
To the same spot, bring back the enemy, your wound,
And your usual fear. Hide behind my shield   90
And argue with me there. And after I rescued him,
So badly injured he could hardly stand,
He ran away not slowed at all by his wounds.

And then there's Hector, who comes into battle
With gods on his side, and when he charges
He terrifies not just you, Ulysses,
But brave men too. That's how scary he is.
He was riding high when I knocked him on his ass
With a huge stone I heaved from long range.
And when he challenged us to one-on-one combat,   100
It fell upon me. You were all praying, Achaeans,
The lot would be mine. Your prayers were heard.

If you want to know the outcome, at the very least
I did not lose. And when the Trojans came
With fire and sword, and with Jove on their side,
To attack our ships, where was Ulysses then
With all of his speeches? My chest was the wall
For a thousand ships, your only hope of return.
You should grant me the arms for all of those ships.

But the truth is, this is not about my honor   110
But about giving these arms their due. Our glory
Is linked, but the arms need Ajax, not Ajax the arms.
Let the smart Ithacan put up for comparison
His snoring Rhesus, his pitiful Dolon, his Helenus,
Priam's captured son, and the stolen Palladium,
None of it done in the light of the day
Or without Diomedes. If you award the armor
For such cheap exploits, divide it up
And give Diomedes the greater share.

But why give them to the Ithacan, who operates   120
Unarmed, by stealth, and by tricking the enemy?
The glint of gold on Achilles' helmet would only
Give away his hiding place, not that his head
Could ever bear the weight. Nor would the spear,
Whose shaft was cut on Pelion, ever be more
Than a dead weight on his unwarlike arm.
And Achilles' shield, engraved with an image
Of the entire universe, would not suit a left hand
Born for petty theft. For shame, Ulysses,
Seeking a prize that would only wear you out,   130
A prize that, if the Greeks made the mistake
Of handing it over to you, would give the enemy
A reason to despoil but not to fear you.
Then too, retreat, your cowardly specialty,
Would only be slowed if you bore such a weight.
And remember that your own shield, so rarely used,
Is as good as new, but mine has been hit
A thousand times and needs to be replaced.

Finally, why talk about it? Throw Achilles' arms
Into the enemy's ranks, and then award them   140
To whichever hero can recover them."

As the son of Telamon finished his speech
The crowd murmured approval, until Ulysses,
Laertes' heroic son, rose up. He held his eyes
Fixed on the ground for a short while, and then
Lifted them to the captains and made the speech
They awaited. His eloquence did not disappoint:

Ulysses' Speech

"If my prayers and yours had been answered,
Pelasgian lords, there would be no need
For us to be deciding who should now possess   150
The arms of Achilles. You would still have them,
Achilles, and we would still have you. But since
An unjust fate has denied him to me and to you"
(Here he pretended to wipe a tear from his eye),
"Who should better follow the great Achilles
Than the man whom the great Achilles followed
When he came to the Greeks? All I ask is that Ajax
Not profit from seeming to be, as indeed he is,
Slow of wit, and that I not be disadvantaged
Because I have always used my intelligence   160
To your benefit. And my eloquence, such as it is,
That now speaks for its owner but has often
Been deployed in the past on your behalf,
Should not be held against me. Rather, let each man
Acknowledge and use the gifts that he has.

Now, I do not count a noble lineage
As one's own accomplishment, but since Ajax
Tells us that he is the great-grandson of Jove,
I will say that Jove is my ancestor as well,
And at the same remove. For my father   170
Is Laertes and his was Arcesius,
And Arcesius was, in fact, Jupiter's son,

Nor is there in this bloodline of mine
Even one exiled criminal. On my mother's side
Our nobility is enhanced by Mercury's blood.
I am of divine descent through both my parents.
But it is not because my mother is nobly born
Nor my father innocent of his brother's blood
That I seek the armor that lies before us here.
Decide this case on merit alone. It is not   180
Ajax's merit that Telamon and Peleus
Were brothers, and you should not consider
Bloodlines, only valor, in making this award.
Or if you wish to consider close relatives, Peleus
Is Achilles' father and Pyrrhus his son,
So ship the arms off to Phthia or Scyros.
And Teucer is as much Achilles' cousin
As Ajax is, but does he lay claim to the arms?
And if he did, would he get them? So then,
It comes down to a simple contest of deeds,   190
And I have done more than I could recount
Off the top of my head. But I'll start with the first.

Achilles' Nereid mother, Thetis, foreseeing
The death of her son, had disguised him as a girl
And dressed him so deceptively that everyone,
Including Ajax, was taken in. But I inserted
Among the women's paraphernalia some items
That would attract a man's eye. The hero
Was still disguised as a girl when his hand
Drifted to a spear and a shield, and I said to him,   200
'Son of Thetis, Troy is waiting to fall to you.
What are you waiting for?' And I laid my hand
On the warrior and sent him forth to brave deeds.
Therefore, all that he did after is due to me.
It was I who wounded Telephus and then
Healed his wound when he begged for aid. Thebes fell
To me; give me credit for Tenedos, Chrsye, and Cilla,
All cities of Apollo, and Scyros too.
Consider that I broke through Lyrnesus' walls

And threw them down. And I brought the man 210
Who killed, not to mention others, ferocious Hector.
Yes, it is through me that glorious Hector
Lies in his grave. I lay claim to these weapons
In return for those by which Achilles was found.
I gave the living arms, I ask them back after death.

When one man's grief came to all the Greeks
And a thousand ships were assembled at Aulis,
The long awaited winds blew contrary
Or not all. Then a cruel oracle ordered Agamemnon
To sacrifice his innocent daughter 220
To heartless Diana. Agamemnon refused
And raged at the gods themselves, for although
He was king, he was still a father. With my words
I was the one who turned his father's kind heart
To what was best for his people. This was not
An easy case, I confess (and may Agamemnon
Forgive me as I confess), and before a judge
Who was hardly impartial. But the people's good,
His brother, and his responsibilities
As commander in chief persuaded him 230
To balance approbation with blood.
Then I was sent to Clytemnestra, the mother,
Who was not to be exhorted but to be conned.
If Ajax had gone, we would never have sailed,
And the ships would still be there, utterly becalmed.

I was also sent as a bold ambassador
To Ilium's citadel and Troy's senate house,
When it was still full of heroes. Unafraid,
I pleaded for what had been entrusted to me,
The Greek common cause, denouncing Paris 240
And demanding both the return of Helen
And full restitution. I won over Priam
And Antenor with Priam, but Paris,
His brothers, and his marauding underlings
Could hardly restrain their impious hands

(You know this, Menelaus) from violence.
That was the first of all the dangerous days
I shared with you. It would take a long time
To tell all that I did for you both in council
And in battle. The war dragged on. The Trojans   250
Stayed within their walls after the first encounter
And there was no chance for open combat.
At last, in the tenth year, we fought again.
Where were you all that time? Sure, you can fight,
But what other service did you perform?
If you ask me what I was doing, I'll tell you.
I laid traps for the enemy, I surrounded
Our fortifications with a trench, I kept up
Our allies' morale in a long, tedious war,
I advised on supply lines and provisions,   260
And I was sent out on missions as needed.

And then Jove sent a lying dream in the night
To tell Agamemnon to abandon the war.
The king can defend the order he gave
On such authority. But what did Ajax do?
He could have halted the retreat, demanded
Troy be destroyed, started fighting, since that is all
He knows how to do. Why didn't he stop the men
From leaving, take up arms and give the mob
Someone to follow? Was this too much to ask   270
From someone who only speaks when he boasts?
But what about this? He himself ran! I saw you,
And I was ashamed to see you, turning your back
And getting ready to hoist your dishonorable sails.

'What are you doing?' I yelled. 'This is madness,
Abandoning Troy, which is already seized.
What are you taking home after ten years here
Except disgrace?'
                    Grief made me eloquent;
My words turned them around and brought them back.
Agamemnon assembled all the troops,   280

Who were still agitated, and even then Ajax
Didn't open his mouth. But Thersites did,
And heckled the kings but, thanks to me,
Did not get off unpunished. I stood up and urged
My trembling comrades to take on the enemy,
And my words restored their faltering courage.
From that time on, whatever act of bravery
This man did is due to me, who halted his flight.

Finally, which of the Greeks wants to be your friend?
Diomedes does everything with me,   290
Approves of me and wants me to be at his side.
It is something to be chosen by Diomedes
Out of thousands of Greeks. And no one cast lots
When we went on a night raid and fell upon Dolon,
Who was on the same kind of dangerous mission,
But I didn't kill him before I had forced out of him
All of Troy's treacherous plans. Once I learned that
I had no more need for espionage
And could have returned with honor. Instead,
I went to Rhesus' tents, killed the captain   300
And all his men, and then, all my prayers answered,
Came back victorious in a captured chariot
As if celebrating a triumph. Deny to me now
The arms of the man whose horses Hector
Had promised to Dolon for his work that night,
And you will let Ajax, with his specious proposal,
Begin to seem more generous than you.

Do I have to mention how I cut to ribbons
The ranks of Sarpedon? How I slaughtered
Coeranus, the son of Iphitus? Alastor,   310
Chromius, Alcander, Halius, Noemon,
And Prytanis? Killed Thoön and Chersidamas,
Charops and Ennomos, all of them doomed?
And others less famous fell by my hand
Beneath their city's walls. I have wounds too,
My friends, all in the right place. No need to trust

Words in the air. Look!" He opened his tunic.
"Here is my chest and all it has been through
On your behalf. But the son of Telamon here
In all these years has lost not an ounce of blood   320
On behalf of his friends, has not even been scratched.

What is the point of his declaration
That he fought the Trojans and Jove himself?
I agree he did fight, since I do not discount
Meritorious action, but do not allow him
To lay sole claim to an honor that is shared,
And do insist that he show you some respect.
It was Patroclus, in the protective disguise
Of Achilles' armor, who pushed the Trojans
Back from the ships, which would have otherwise   330
Gone up in flames with their defender, Ajax.
And he thinks that he was the only one who dared
To face Hector in a duel, forgetting that the king,
The other captains and myself all volunteered.
He was the ninth to step forward then
And was only selected by the luck of the draw.
And what was the outcome, O mightiest hero?
Hector withdrew without receiving a wound.

And now I am forced to recall with sadness
That time when Achilles, Achaea's defense,   340
Fell in battle. Yet neither grief nor fear
Prevented me from lifting up his body
And carrying it upon these very shoulders
Along with all of the armor and weapons
That now I wish to carry again. I have the strength
To bear these arms, and the mind to appreciate
What an honor it is. Do you think that Thetis,
The sea goddess who was the hero's mother,
Wanted her heavenly gifts, the divine armor
That she gave her son, a work of heavenly art,   350
To grace the shoulders of an oaf like this?

He knows nothing of what is carved on this shield,
The sea, the lands, the stars in the deep sky,
The Pleiades, the Hyades, the Great Bear
That is aloof from the sea, and opposite her
Orion wheeling with his glittering sword.
He's asking for armor he can't understand.

He gives me a hard time for trying to shun
The trials of war and for coming to it late.
Doesn't he grasp that he is also censuring   360
The great Achilles? If pretending is a crime,
Well, we both pretended. If delay is wrong,
Of the two of us I arrived earlier.
A loving wife held me back, a loving mother
Detained Achilles. We spent our first time with them,
The rest with you. I hardly fear a charge,
Even if I cannot defend against it,
That I have in common with such a great man. Ulysses
Outwitted Achilles, but not Ajax Ulysses.

We should not wonder that his ignorant mouth   370
Spews out insults against me, when he even tries
To heap shame upon you. If it was dishonorable
For me to accuse Palamedes falsely,
Was it honorable for you to have condemned him?
But Palamedes was not able to clear himself
Of a charge based on evidence so clear,
Nor did you just hear the charge; you saw the proof.
The patent bribe is what convicted him.

Nor should I be blamed because the island of Lemnos
Detains Philoctetes. Defend your own decision,   380
For you agreed to the plan. I will not deny
That I advised him to absent himself
From the long journey and the toil of war
And recuperate from his terrible pain.
He took the advice—and he is still alive.

Not only was the advice given in good faith,
It also worked out well, though it should be enough
That it was given in good faith. Now the seers say
That Troy will not fall unless he is brought back.
Don't give that job to me! The son of Telamon   390
Should be the one to go and calm the hero,
Raging mad and ill, with his eloquent speech,
Or bring him back to us by a clever trick.
The Simoïs will flow backward, Ida stand leafless,
And Greece will send foreign aid to Troy
Before Ajax's cunning could help the Greeks,
Should you be deprived of my good services.
You are a hard man, Philoctetes, and you hate
The Greeks, the kings, and me myself. Even so,
Although you heap endless curses on my head,   400
And you wish I were handed over to you
So you could drink my blood, wish that just as I
Had a shot at you, you could have a shot at me—
I would still go and try to bring you back,
And, with a little luck, I would get your arrows,
Just as I captured the Dardanian seer,
Just as I discovered the Trojan oracles,
Just as I stole the statue of Minerva
From her shrine deep in enemy territory.
And Ajax wants to be compared to me?   410
The Fates declared that we could not take Troy
Without this statue. Where does that leave Ajax,
The mighty hero, and all his big talk?
What's there to be afraid of at a time like that?
Why does Ulysses dare to entrust himself
To the darkness of night, go beyond the sentinels
Through enemy lines, not only break into
The walls of Troy, but steal the goddess from her shrine
And bear it away through a hostile force?
If I hadn't done this, the son of Telamon   420
Would bear his sevenfold ox-hide shield in vain.
That night I secured our victory over Troy,
Conquering it by making conquest possible.

And you can stop grumbling that Diomedes
Is my partner. He has his share of praise.
You had partners too when your shield defended
The Argive fleet, a crowd of them. I had one.
And if Diomedes did not know that a soldier
Is worth less than a strategist, and that this prize
Should not go to mere strength, or even   430
Indomitable strength, he would seek it himself.
So would the lesser Ajax, Eurypylus,
Thoas, Idomeneus, and his countryman,
Meriones, and Menelaus too. All of them
Are brave and strong and my match in battle,
But all of them have yielded to my counsels.
Your strong arms serve you well; it is your mind
That needs my guidance. You have brute strength
But no intelligence, whereas my concern
Is for what happens next. You fight well, it's true,   440
But I help Agamemnon choose when to fight.
Your total worth is all in your bulk, mine in my mind.
And as much as the pilot surpasses the rower,
As much as the general exceeds the soldier,
So much greater am I than you. In our lives
The head counts for more than the hand,
And in our intelligence our existence lies.

Award, captains, the prize to your sentry,
And reward my long years of watchful service
With this fitting honor. My work has come to an end.   450
I have removed the fated obstructions
And by making it possible to take tall Troy
I have taken her. Now, by our common hopes,
By the walls of Troy doomed to fall, by the gods
That I have just now taken from our enemy,
And by any other hazardous mission
That remains to be done with wisdom and tact
(If you think Troy's fate requires still more)
Be mindful of me. Otherwise, give the arms to her!"
And he pointed to Minerva's fateful statue.   460

The captains were swayed by Ulysses' eloquence,
And the smooth talker bore off the hero's arms.
Then Ajax, who had so often borne all alone
Fire and sword, Hector's might and Jove's,
Could not bear his own anger, and grief conquered
The unconquered hero. Drawing his sword, he said,

"This at least is mine, or does Ulysses demand it
For himself? I will use it myself, on myself,
And so this blade, so often wet with Phrygian blood,
Will be wet with its master's, so that no one   470
But Ajax will be able to defeat Ajax."

He spoke, and buried the lethal sword's full length
Deep in his chest, the first wound it had suffered.
No human hand had the strength to extract
The infixed weapon. The blood itself expelled it
And soaked the ground, and from the green sod
A purple flower grew, the same that had sprung up
From Hyacinthus' blood, its petals inscribed
With letters common to the boy and the hero,
The former's lament and the latter's name.   480

The Fall of Troy

Victorious Ulysses sailed off to Lemnos,
Hypsipyle's island, famous for its women
Murdering their men, and brought back Hercules' bow
And poisoned arrows, along with Philoctetes,
Who owned them now. This was the final touch
In the long war. Troy fell, and Priam with it.
Priam's wife Hecuba, when she had lost all else,
Lost her human form too, and her strange barking
Filled the alien air of the Hellespont's shore.
Ilium was burning, and the flames   490
Had not yet died down; Jupiter's altar
Had drunk Priam's thin stream of blood;
And Cassandra, priestess of Apollo

Was stretching her unavailing arms to heaven
As she was being dragged by the hair.
The Trojan women, thronging the half-burnt temples
And clutching the statues of their country's gods
While they still could, were carried off
By the conquering Greeks as valuable prizes.
Astyanax was thrown down from the tower   500
Where he used to stand with Andromache
As she pointed out to him his father, Hector,
Fighting for him and his ancestral kingdom.
The North Wind picks up, filling the sails
With a favorable breeze. It is time to go.
The Trojan women kiss their native soil. "Troy,
Farewell! We are leaving against our will,"
The last to board was Hecuba. The pitiful thing
Was found among the tombs of her sons, clinging
To their graves, trying to kiss their remains.   510
Ulysses dragged her away, but not before
She emptied one tomb, clutching at her breast
The ashes of Hector. The urn lay empty,
And on the grave of her son she left an offering,
A few wisps of grey hair, grey hair and tears.

Polydorus and Polyxena

Across from Troy is the land of the Bistones,
Where Polymestor had his royal court.
This was where Priam sent his son Polydorus,
To be reared in secret away from the war,
A wise plan if Priam had not sent with him   520
A treasure large enough to reward criminality
And tempt the greedy. When Troy's fortunes waned,
Polymestor slit his foster child's throat
And threw the body from a cliff into the sea,
As if murder and corpse could be jointly disposed of.

It was on this Thracian coast that Agamemnon
Moored his fleet to wait out a storm. Suddenly,

The earth split open and the ghost of Achilles
Rose up, as large as life and looking just as he did
On the day when he threatened Agamemnon,   530
Unjustly pulling his sword on the king.

"So, you are leaving, Achaeans," he cried out,
"Forgetting me; your gratitude for my courage
Is buried with me. Do not do this! Honor
My tomb by sacrificing Polyxena
And so appease the shade of Achilles."

His old comrades obeyed the pitiless ghost.
Polyxena, her mother's sole consolation,
Was torn from her arms, an ill-fated girl
Braver than any grown woman. She was led   540
To Achilles' funeral mound, there to become
A sacrificial victim. She never forgot
Who she was, even when she was placed
Before the grim altar and understood
That the savage rites were being prepared for her.
When she saw Neoptolemus standing there
And staring at her with sword in hand, she said,

"Avail yourself of my noble blood. Go ahead,
No need to wait. Just sink your sword deep
Into my throat or my breast." And she bared   550
Her throat and her breast. "Polyxena
Will not be a slave to any man, nor will you
Placate any god with a rite such as this.
I only wish that my mother not know of my death;
My mother diminishes my joy in death,
But my death should not be as dreadful to her
As her own life. All I ask, if my request is just,
Is that you move away, so that I may go freely
To the Stygian shades. Do not let a man's hands
Touch my virgin flesh. My blood pure and free   560
Will be more acceptable to whoever it is
You are trying to appease by slaughtering me.

And if my last words still move any of you
(The daughter of Priam, no captive asks you),
Return my body to my mother unransomed.
Let her pay with tears, not gold, for the sad right
Of burying me. She paid with gold when she could."

She spoke, and the people could not restrain
Their tears, as she could hers. The priest too wept
And driving the sword in against his will   570
Pierced her proffered breast. Her knees buckled,
And as she sank to the earth she kept to the end
Her look of fearless courage, taking care
Even as she fell to keep herself covered
And guard the honor of her chastity.

Hecuba

The Trojan women gathered her up
And counted how many children of Priam
There were to lament. And they wept for you also,
Hecuba, who just yesterday were called
The queen consort, the royal mother,   580
The very image of a flourishing Asia.
But now you are wretched even for a captive,
Unwanted by victorious Ulysses
Except that you had given birth to Hector,
Who never imagined such a lord for his mother.
Now, embracing the body left empty
Of that brave spirit, she bestows upon it
The tears she has shed so often for her country,
Her sons, and for her husband, pouring them
Into her daughter's wound, covering her lips   590
With kisses, and beating again her bruised breasts.
Then, sweeping her white hair in the congealed blood,
She uttered these words and more from her torn breast:

"My child, the last cause for your mother to grieve—
For what else is left?—here you lie, and I see your wound,

My wound, which you have so I would not lose
Even one of my children without any bloodshed.
Because you were a woman I thought that you
Would be safe from the sword, but you, a woman,
Have died by the sword, and the same Achilles   600
Who has destroyed Troy and made me childless,
Killing so many of your brothers, has now killed you.
When he fell to Paris' and Apollo's arrows,
I said that Achilles need no longer be feared,
But I still have to fear him. Although he is buried,
His very ashes rage against our race,
We feel him as an enemy even in his tomb.
I have borne my children for Aeacus' grandson!
Great Troy has fallen; our nation has come
To an awful end. But it did come to an end.   610
For me alone Ilium still survives,
And my troubles go on. Not long ago
I had everything, so many sons and daughters
And their husbands and wives, and my husband.
Now I am exiled, ragged, torn from the graves
Of my loved ones, dragged off to be a prize
For Penelope. She will point me out
To the Ithacan women as I spin her wool
And say, 'That is the famous mother of Hector,
Priam's queen.' Now you, my Polyxena,   620
The only one left, after so many were lost,
To comfort my grief, you have been sacrificed
On an enemy tomb, and I have given birth
To a funeral offering for the enemy dead.
Why should I go on living, numb with sorrow,
Why cling to life, preserved in wrinkled old age?
Why cruel gods, prolong an old woman's life,
Unless to see more funerals? Who would think
That Priam could be happy when Ilium fell?
In death he is happy. He does not see you dead,   630
My daughter, and he left his life and his kingdom
At the same time. What a splendid funeral

You will have, a royal maiden buried
In her ancestral tomb! This is no longer
The fortune of our house. Your funeral offerings
Will be your mother's tears, and a handful
Of foreign sand. I have lost everything,
But I still have some reason to live, to endure
A little while longer: his mother's dearest
And now only child, once my youngest son,   640
My Polydorus, sent to the Thracian king
Who rules these shores. But why do I delay
To cleanse your wound and wash your face of blood?"

Hecuba spoke, and the old woman stumbled
Down to the shore, tearing her white hair as she went.
"Give me an urn, Trojan women," she said,
Intending to draw some water from the sea.
There she saw the body of Polydorus
Cast up on the shore, rent with gaping wounds
By Thracian weapons. The Trojan women   650
Cried aloud, but Hecuba was dumb with a grief
That blocked not only her voice but her rising tears.
She stood like a stone, her eyes fixed
Sometimes on the ground, sometimes lifted
In horror to the sky, and at times resting
On the face of her son and upon his wounds.
And as she looked more and more at his wounds
Her rage became lethal, finally blazing forth
As if she were still the queen, bent on vengeance
And wholly absorbed in thoughts of punishment.   660
And just as a lioness who has had her suckling cub
Stolen from her and tracks down her unseen enemy
In silent fury, so too Hecuba, mingling grief
With wrath, forgetting her years but not her spite,
Went straight to Polymestor, the murder's architect,
And got an audience with him, pretending she had
A hoard of gold to reveal, as a bequest to her son.
The Thracian king, habituated to greed,

Was taken in and came to the hiding place,
Saying with smooth, practiced cunning,

                "Quickly, Hecuba,   670
Give me the treasure for your son. All will be his,
What you give now and what you gave before,
I swear by the gods above."

                She snarled at him
As he swore his lying oath, and then her rage
Boiled over. Calling the captive women in,
She seized the man and, digging her fingers
Into his lying eyes, she gouged them out.
Anger lent her strength, and plunging her hands
Deep inside, grimy with his guilty blood,
She sucked out not his eyes, for they were gone,   680
But the sockets themselves. The Thracian men,
Enraged by the slaughter of their king, attacked
The Trojan woman, hurling stones and weapons,
But she growled and snapped at the stones they threw,
And when she set her jaws to speak could only bark.
The place is still there and takes its name, Cynossema,
The Bitch's Tomb, from what happened there,
And for a long time she howled mournfully
Through the Sithonian plains, remembering
Her ancient wrongs. Her fate moved the Trojans   690
And her enemies the Greeks, and it moved the gods,
All the gods, for even Juno, Jove's sister and wife,
Said Hecuba had never deserved such an end.

Memnon

But Aurora was not free to be moved
By Hecuba's ruin and Troy's. She had aided
The city in war, but now she was tormented
By a private grief, the loss of her son, Memnon,
Whom the glowing goddess had seen go down
At the hands of Achilles on Troy's wide plain.
When she saw his death, the amethyst morning   700
Paled to white, and sky was covered with clouds.

She could not bear to look at his body
On top of the pyre, but went just as she was,
With her hair disheveled, to fall at the feet
Of almighty Jove, and salted her words with tears:

"The least of those whom golden heaven sustains
(Temples to me are exceedingly rare)
I come to you nonetheless as a goddess,
Not to ask for more shrines or festival days
Or altars aflame with sacrificial fires.   710
Yet if you consider my services to you,
As a mere woman, keeping night's borders
At each new dawn, you would see I deserve
Some kind of reward. But it is not my concern,
Nor Aurora's business, to ask for honors
However well deserved. I come because I am
Bereft of my Memnon, who bravely bore arms
For Priam, his uncle, and had his life cut short
By mighty Achilles, for such was your will.
I beg you now, O lord of Olympus,   720
To grant him some honor as solace for death
And lessen also the pain of his mother."

Jupiter nodded, as Memnon's great pyre
Collapsed in flames, and whorls of smoke
Stained the daylight dark, as when from her river
A naiad exhales thick swirling fog, cloaking
The sun and allowing no light to come through.
Black ash whirled up to the sky, congealing there
Into a shape that took life from the fire
And whose own lightness furnished it wings.   730
At first it was only the semblance of a bird
And then a real bird, clapping its wings,
And soon it was joined by innumerable sisters
From the same natal source, all in noisy flight.
Three times they circled the funeral pyre,
And three times their clamor rose as one sound
Into the air. On the fourth flight around

The flock divided into two warring camps
That attacked each other with talon and beak,
Their wings growing weary until they spun down   740
As kinship offerings to the buried ashes,
Remembering the hero from which they had sprung.
The source of this sudden avian creation
Gave these birds their name. They are called
Memnonides; and every year, when the sun
Has transited the twelve signs of the zodiac,
They fight again and die in their father's memory.
And so as others wept while Hecuba bayed,
Aurora was lost in her personal grief,
And even to this day she sheds pious tears   750
And wets the whole world with morning's dew.

Aeneas Comes to Delos

Fate did not allow Troy's promise to perish
Along with her walls. Venus' heroic son,
Aeneas, bore away on his shoulders
Her sacred icons and something even more holy,
His father, a venerable burden,
Piously choosing that treasure from all his riches.
He took with him also his son, Ascanius,
And sailed with his exiled fleet from Antandros,
Leaving behind the sinful shores of Thrace   760
And the beach drenched with Polydorus' blood
Until, with favorable winds and tides, he came
With all his companions to Apollo's Delos.
There Anius, both king and priest of Apollo,
Received him in his temple and his palace.
He showed him the city and the sanctuary,
And the twin palms upon which Latona leaned
When she gave birth. They lit incense at the altar
And doused it with wine, and observed the ritual
Of burning the entrails of slaughtered oxen.   770
Then they retired to the royal palace,

Where they reclined on high couches to dine on
Ceres' munificence and drink Bacchus' wine.

The Daughters of Anius

Then pious Anchises said,
               "Priest of Phoebus,
Am I mistaken, or did you not have a son
When I first saw your city, and four daughters too?"

Anius shook his head, bound with white fillets,
And sadly replied,
             "You are not mistaken,
Greatest of heroes. You saw me back then
A father of five, but men's fortunes shift,   780
And now you see me as practically childless.
What help to me is my absent son, who rules
The island of Andros, named after him,
In his father's place? Delian Apollo
Gave to my son the power of prophecy,
But Bacchus gave my daughters quite other gifts,
Greater than any they could have ever hoped for.
Everything they touched turned into grain or wine
Or Minerva's grey olives, richly profitable.
When Agamemnon, destroyer of Ilium,   790
Heard of this (so you may see that we too felt
Some of the force of the storm you faced),
He sent his men to drag my unwilling daughters
From their father's arms, commanding them to feed
The Greek army with their heavenly gift.
They escaped, each as she could. Two of them
Took refuge in Euboea; the other two went
To their brother in Andros, but armed men came
And threatened war if they were not surrendered.
Fear conquered a brother's love, and he gave up   800
His own sisters. You could pardon his timidity
For Andros had no Aeneas or Hector,

Through whom you held on for ten long years.
They were preparing shackles for the captives
When my girls stretched their arms, still free,
To heaven and prayed, 'Help, Father Bacchus!'
And the god that gave them their gift came to their aid,
If you can call it aid to lose your human form.
I never knew and so cannot now describe
How, in what strange way, they lost their form,   810
But I do know how this terrible thing turned out.
Feathers covered their bodies, and they were changed
Into snow-white doves, the birds of Venus, your wife."

And so they garnished their banquet with talk
And then left the table to retire for the night.
In the morning they went to Phoebus' oracle,
Which advised them to seek their ancient mother
And kindred shores. Anius went with them
As they prepared to cast off, and gave them parting gifts,
A scepter for Anchises, and for his grandson   820
A robe and a quiver. To Aeneas he gave
A goblet that a guest, Ismenian Therses,
Had brought to the king from Aonia,
The work of Alcon of Lindos, who had engraved
A long story on the metal cup's surface.
There was a city, which you could tell was Thebes
From its seven gates, and before the city
There were funeral rites, with blazing pyres
And mounds, and women with disheveled hair
And breasts naked in grief. There were nymphs too,   830
Who seemed to bewail their dried-up springs, trees
That stood bare and leafless, and goats grazing
In dry rocky fields. But look! you can see that the artist
Has pictured in Thebes' streets Orion's daughters,
Wounding themselves with more than womanly courage,
Cutting their throats, piercing their brave hearts with swords,
Lying dead for the sake of their people, borne
In beautiful processions throughout the town,
And burned on pyres among crowds of mourners.

And then, so their race would not perish, twin youths, 840
Known as Coronae, rose from the virgin embers
And led the ritual due to their mothers' ashes.
The ancient bronze gleamed with these storied figures,
And golden acanthus twined along the cup's rim.
The Trojans made presents that were no less precious,
An incense casket for the priest, a bowl for libation,
And a crown that glistened with gemstones and gold.

Aeneas Comes to Scylla and Charybdis

Remembering that their ancestor was Teucer,
The Trojans sailed to Crete, but unable to endure
The troubles Jove sent them, they left the island 850
Of a hundred cities and headed for the harbors
Of Italy. Storms at sea forced them to take refuge
In the Strophades, where they were terrorized
By Aello, the Harpy. From there they sailed past
The port of Dulichium, past Same and Neritos
And past Ithaca, cunning Ulysses' kingdom.
They saw Ambracia, which is now renowned
For the temple of Apollo at Actium
But was once the object of heavenly strife,
And saw there the judge who was turned to stone. 860
They scanned Dodona with its oracle oak,
And the Chaonian bay, where King Molossus' sons
Escaped from the impious fires on wings.

They then headed toward the Phaeacians' land,
Rich in orchards, but put in at Buthrotis,
A miniature Troy ruled by Helenus,
The Trojan seer. Forewarned by the prophecies
Of Priam's son, they entered the waters
Of Sicily, whose three broad capes run into the sea.
Pachynos faces the rainy south, Lilybaeon 870
Catches the western winds, and Peloros looks
To the northern Bears that never touch the waves.
The Trojans rowed in here, and a favorable tide

Brought them at nightfall to the beach at Zancle.
Here Scylla plagues the coast on the right
And Charybdis on the left, sucking down ships
And spitting them out, while the wild dogs bark
Around Scylla's dark loins. She has a girl's face,
And if what poets say is not wholly made up,
She once was a girl. Many suitors sought her   880
But she rejected them all and spent her time
With the ocean nymphs, for the nymphs of the ocean
Were very fond of her. She would tell them
All about her disappointed lovers. Once,
While she was combing Galatea's hair,
The nymph kept sighing, and finally said,

"At least, virgin Scylla, you are being wooed
By a gentler sort of man, whom you can reject,
As you do, without any fear. But I,
Daughter of Nereus and sea-green Doris,   890
And with a cadre of sisters, could not shun
The Cyclops' love without bitter grief."

She became choked up with tears, which Scylla
Stroked away with her delicate white fingers
As she consoled the nymph and said to her,

"Tell me, my dearest, the cause of your grief.
Don't hide anything. You know you can trust me."

And this is what the Nereid told her:

Galatea and Polyphemus

"Faunus had a son by the nymph Symaethis.
Acis was his name, and he was a great delight   900
To his father and mother, but more so to me,
Since he and I loved only each other.
He was handsome, just sixteen, a faint down
On his tender cheeks. While I only went for him,
The Cyclops only went for me, relentlessly.

If you asked me I could not say whether
Love for Acis or hatred of the Cyclops
Was stronger in me. Both were just as strong.
O sweet Venus, how powerfully you rule us.
That savage, a horror to the woods themselves,   910
Whom no stranger has ever laid eyes on
Without getting hurt, who scorns great Olympus
And its gods, how strongly he feels just what love is,
How he burns, a prisoner of desire so passionate
He forgets his cave and his flocks. Now, Polyphemus,
You care about how you look, anxious to please.
Now you comb your bristling hair with a rake
And trim your rough beard with a scythe, gazing
At your face in a farm pond and taking care
To compose your expression. Your love of killing,   920
Your ferocity, your immense thirst for blood
Are gone, and ships now can sail by in safety.

During this time Telemus had traveled
To Sicilian Aetna, Telemus Eurymides,
Who knew what meaning every bird portended.
This augur addressed Polyphemus and said,
'That one eye in the middle of your forehead—
Ulysses will steal it.' The Cyclops laughed, saying
'Stupid seer, someone has already stolen it.'
Scoffing at the man who had tried to warn him,   930
He plodded heavily along the seashore
Or returned wearily to his shadowy cave.
There was a wedge-shaped hill with a high ridge
Jutting into the sea, washed by waves on both sides.
The beastly Cyclops climbed up to the top
And sat himself down. His sheep followed him
All on their own. Then, laying at his feet
The trunk of a pine that served as his staff,
Big as a ship's mast, he picked up his pipe
Made of a hundred bound reeds. All the mountains   940
Felt the sound of his pastoral pipings,
And the waves felt it too. I heard it myself

From a faraway cliff as I lay with my head
In Acis' lap, and I remember his song:

Polyphemus' Song to Galatea

'Galatea, whiter than privet petals,
Slimmer than an alder, more in bloom
Than a meadow, friskier than a kid,
More radiant than crystal, smoother than shells
Polished by the tide, more welcome than shade
In the summer, than sunshine in winter,   950
Prettier than a plane tree, nimbler than a gazelle,
More sparkling than ice, sweeter than ripe grapes,
Softer than swan's down or curdled milk,
Lovelier than a watered garden, if you did not flee.

Galatea, wilder than an untamed heifer,
Harder than old oak, more slippery than water,
Tougher than willow or twisting vines,
More stubborn than cliffs, roiling more than a river,
Vainer than a peacock, fiercer than fire,
Meaner than a pregnant bear, pricklier   960
Than thistles, deafer than the sea, more vicious
Than a snake that's been stepped on and kicked;
And what I wish I could change most of all,
Swifter than a deer driven on by loud baying,
Swifter than the wind or a fleeting breeze.

But if you really knew me, O Galatea,
You'd be sorry you ran, renounce putting me off
And try your best to hold on to me.
I have most of a mountain, with deep caves
Where you don't feel the heat of the sun in summer   970
Nor winter's cold. I have apples weighing down
Their branches, golden grapes on long trailing vines,
Purple grapes too. I'm keeping both kinds for you.
You can pick ripe strawberries in the shady woods,
Cherries in the autumn, and plums, purple-black
And juicy, and the large yellow kind, yellow as wax.

If I can just be your man, you will have chestnuts too,
And arbute berries. Every tree will serve you.

And this whole flock is mine, many more too,
Browsing the valleys and wandering the woods,   980
And still others safe in their folds in the caves.
Don't ask me how many, I could not tell you
How many. Only poor people count up their flocks.
You don't have to believe me, you can see for yourself
How fine they are, how they can hardly walk
With their swollen udders. And I have lambs
In their warm pens, and kids too, all the same ages
Kept in separate pens. There's always plenty of milk,
White as snow, some of it kept for drinking,
And some of it rennet hardens into curds.   990

And you will not have any ordinary pets
Like does, rabbits, goats, a pair of doves
Or a nest from a treetop. I just found
A pair of bear cubs up on the mountain
For you to play with, so much alike
You can hardly tell them apart. When I found them
I said, "These I'll save for my mistress."

Just raise your glistening head, Galatea,
From the deep blue sea and come to me!
Don't hate my gifts. I know what I look like. I saw   1000
My reflection in a clear pool, and I liked what I saw.
Just look how big I am! Jupiter's no bigger,
Since you're always talking about some Jupiter
Who rules up in the sky. I have lots of hair
On my fierce looking face, down to my shoulders
Like a shady grove. And don't think I am ugly
Because my whole body bristles with hair.
A tree without any leaves is ugly, a horse
Is ugly without a golden mane on its neck;
Feathers cover birds; wool looks nice on sheep,   1010
And a beard and long hair look nice on a man.

I have only one eye in my forehead's middle,
But it's a big eye, as big as a shield! So?
Doesn't the Sun see all there is from the sky?
And doesn't the Sun have only one eye?
More, my father, Neptune, rules your waters,
And I'm giving him to you as a father-in-law.
Just pity me and hear my humble prayer,
For I bend my knee to you alone. I,
Who scorn Jupiter, his sky, and his thunderbolt,   1020
Fear you alone, O Nereid! Your anger
Is fiercer than lightning. And I could endure
Your contempt more easily if you also scorned
Your other suitors as well. Tell me why,
When you turn your back on Cyclops, you love
Acis, and why do you prefer his embrace to mine?
He can please himself, and what I don't like,
Galatea, please you as well. Just let me at him!
He'll find out I'm as strong as I am big.
I'll rip his guts out alive, and tear him apart   1030
Limb from limb, and scatter the pieces
All over the fields and over your waves.
Let him mate with you then! Oh, I'm burning up,
Just boiling mad. I feel like I have Aetna
Pent up inside me, with all of its power,
And you, Galatea, you don't even care!'

He went on with this drivel and then rose
Like a bull that is furious (I saw all of this)
Because his cow has been taken away.
Restless, he wandered the woods and pastures,   1040
Until, to my utter surprise, the big brute
Caught sight of me with Acis. 'I see you,' he said,
'And I'll fix it so this is the last time you make love.'
His voice was as loud and as awful
As only a Cyclops' voice can be. Aetna
Trembled at the sound. As for me, I panicked
And dove into the sea. My hero, Symaethis' son,
Had already turned his back and started to run,

Crying,
      'Galatea, help me! Mother and Father,
I am about to die, take me into your world!'   1050

Cyclops stayed on him and hurled a rock
He had wrenched from the mountain. Although
The rock's very tip was all that hit Acis,
It was enough to bury the boy completely.
I did the only thing the fates allowed me to do,
Caused Acis to assume his ancestral powers.
Crimson blood seeped out from the massive rock,
And in a little while the color began to fade,
Looking at first like a rain-swollen river
And then slowly running clear. Then the rock   1060
Split open. A tall green reed grew from the crack,
And leaping waters resounded in a cavity
That formed in the stone, and then, more wonderful still,
A youth stood waist-deep in the water, his new horns
Wreathed with rushes. Though he was bigger,
And his face was deep blue, it could have been Acis,
And in fact it was Acis, changed to a river god,
And his waters retained his name of old."

Glaucus' Transformation

Galatea finished, and the Nereids
Swam their separate ways on the placid water.   1070
Scylla didn't dare to go out on the deep,
So she returned to the shore and either
Wandered on the soft sand without any clothes,
Or, when she was tired, found a sheltered pool
Where she could refresh herself.
                    And now Glaucus
Comes skimming along the sea, the latest
Deep-water denizen, having just undergone
A marine transformation near Euboean Anthedon.
He saw Scylla and was inflamed with love,
And he said whatever he thought might keep her   1080
From running away. She ran anyway.

Fear increased her speed and took her to the top
Of a hill near the shore, a very high hill
Facing the sea and with a shady summit
That leaned over the water. Scylla sat there,
Feeling protected because she had the high ground.
She wondered whether he was a monster
Or some kind of god. His color amazed her,
His hair covered his shoulders and back,
And his loins merged into a coiling fish tail.   1090
He saw her, and leaning on a convenient rock,
He said,

      "I am no monster or wild thing, maiden.
I am a sea god, and neither Proteus, nor Triton,
Nor Palaemon is more potent in the deep
Than yours truly. I was a mortal man once,
But my destiny has always been the sea,
And I spent my life there, hauling in nets
Teeming with fish or sitting on some pier
With rod and line.

      There is a certain shore
That borders on a green meadow, lapped by waves   1100
On one side and herbage on the other, a grassland
Where cattle have never grazed, nor peaceful sheep
Or hairy goats browsed. No busy bee ever
Gathered pollen from there, flowers for wreaths
Were never picked in that meadow, and no sickles
Ever mowed its grass. I was the first to sit down
On that virgin turf, drying my lines and spreading out,
So I could count them, the fish I had caught
Either by chance in my nets or by guile on my hook.
Now this may sound crazy, but why should I lie?   1110
After nibbling on the grass, the floundering fish
Began to move on land as if it were the sea,
And while I stood there absolutely amazed
My whole catch of fish slithered off the shore
And into their native waters. I stood there a long time
Trying to figure it out. Had some god done this,
Or was it the grass? 'But how could any grass

Have this kind of power?' I asked myself,
As I plucked a bit of it and started to chew.
When I swallowed the strange juice, I felt my heart   1120
Pounding inside, and felt an overwhelming desire
For another nature. Unable to resist it,
I cried, 'Farewell Earth, I will never return!'
And I dove into the waves. The sea gods
All welcomed me and thought me worthy of the deep.
They asked Oceanus and Tethys to purge
What was mortal in me. And so I was purified,
First with an incantation repeated nine times
To wash away my sins, and then by bathing
In a hundred streams. All of the rivers   1130
That flow into the sea poured their waters
Onto my head. Up to this point I can remember
What happened, and tell it to you, but my mind
Did not perceive the rest. When my senses returned
I was completely different in body and mind.
That was when I first noticed this rust-green beard,
This hair that sweeps out over the billows,
These huge shoulders and deep blue arms, these legs
That curve into the tail of a fish. And yet,
What does it matter that I have this form,   1140
That I pleased the sea gods and became a god myself,
If you are not somehow moved by all this?"

                                   As he spoke

And was about to say more, Scylla took flight.
Furious at being rejected, Glaucus sought out
The wondrous halls of Circe, daughter of the Sun.

Book 14

Glaucus, Circe, Scylla

And now Glaucus, the Euboean sea god,
Had left behind Aetna, the volcano that vents
The breath of a giant, and the Cyclopes' fields
That knew nothing of mattocks or yoked oxen,
Forever unplowed. The city of Zancle
Was also behind him, and the walls of Rhegium
On the opposite coast, and the narrow graveyard of ships
That divides Italian from Sicilian shores.
Then, swimming strongly through the Tyrrhenian Sea,
He came to the herb-bearing hills of Circe   10
And her courtyards teeming with all sorts of beasts.
As soon as he saw the daughter of the Sun
And salutations had been exchanged, he said,

"Goddess, pity a god! Only you can help me,
If you think me worthy, with this love of mine.
No one knows better than I the power of herbs,
Titaness, for I myself was changed by them.
But let me tell you how I fell so madly in love.
Opposite Messina, on the Italian coast there,
I saw Scylla, and I'm embarrassed to tell you   20
All the promises and prayers I made,
All the sweet things I said—all of them scorned.
If a spell would work here, utter a spell
From your sacred lips, or if herbs would work better
Use a good, proven one. I am not asking
To be cured of my wound; my love need not end!
Just make her feel some of this passion."

No one was more vulnerable than Circe
To this kind of passion. It may have been just her,
Or perhaps Venus, upset with the tattling   30
Of Circe's father, the Sun, took it out on her.

"You would do better," she answered, "to chase someone
More sympathetic, one who loves you as much

As you love her. You are well worth pursuing,
And if you offer encouragement, believe it,
You will be pursued. If you doubt your charms,
Well, I am a goddess, a daughter of the Sun,
And a powerful witch with my spells and herbs—
And I am yours. Spurn the spurner, reward
The admirer, and in one stroke be doubly avenged."   40

To these enticements Glaucus responded,

"Trees will grow on the ocean and seaweed on hills
Before my love will change, as long as Scylla lives."

Circe was furious, and since she could not harm
The god (nor wanted to), she vented her anger
On the girl who was preferred to her. In a pique,
She ground up a batch of notorious herbs, muttering
Hecate's spells as she worked. Wrapping herself
In a slate-blue cloak, she moved through the throng
Of fawning beasts in her palace and made her way   50
To Rhegium, opposite the cliffs of Zancle,
Traveling with dry feet over the seething surf
As if she walked on solid ground. There was a pool,
A quiet crescent of water that Scylla loved,
Her retreat when the sun burned high and strong
At the sky's zenith, and shadows were shortest.
Before this hour came, the goddess tainted the pool,
Contaminated it with her freakish poison,
Sprinkling it with juice squeezed from toxic roots
And muttering dark spells, a mysterious maze   60
Of magical words repeated thrice nine times.

Scylla came to the pool, and had waded in
Up to her waist when she saw that her groin
Was infested with a brood of yowling monsters.
Not realizing at first that they were part
Of her own body, she cringed at their snarling muzzles
And tried to push them away, tried to run off,

But what she avoided she took along with her,
And when she looked down for her thighs and shins,
She found instead snapping jaws not unlike those   70
Of Cerberus, a welter of rabid dogs, from which
Her truncated thighs and belly emerged.

Her lover Glaucus wept, shunning the embrace
Of Circe, who had been far too hostile
In her use of magic herbs. Scylla remained
Where she was and as soon as she could took revenge
On Circe by robbing Ulysses of his companions.
Later, she would have destroyed the Trojan ships,
But by then she had been transmuted to stone,
A rock still to be seen and that sailors avoid.   80

Aeneas Comes to Cumae

When the Trojan fleet had managed to avoid
Scylla and Charybdis, and had almost reached
The shores of Italy, storm winds blew them
To the coast of Libya. Here Phoenician Dido
Received Aeneas into her heart and home,
But when her Trojan mate left, she could not
Endure it, turning his sword on her own breast
On top of the pyre built for a fictive ritual,
Deceiving all as she had been deceived herself.

Sailing away from the new city of Carthage   90
And its sandy shores, Aeneas now returned
To Sicily and his half brother Acestes,
Son of Venus of Eryx, and offered sacrifice,
Honoring the tomb of his father, Anchises.
Then he set sail again with the ships that Iris,
At Juno's command, had almost destroyed by fire,
And passed the Aeolian Islands, smoking with hot,
Sulphurous clouds, the home of Aeolus,
And passed also the rocky isle of the Sirens.

When his ship had lost Palinurus, her pilot,   100
He followed the coastline. Inarime went by,
Prochyte too, and then Pithecusae, stuck
Up on its barren hill, a city aptly named
After its inhabitants, who looked like small apes.
These people had once lived in far-off Lydia
And were called the Cercopes. Jupiter hated
Their lies and their treachery, and so transformed them
Into disgusting creatures that were both like
And unlike men. He contracted their bodies,
Blunted their noses, and furrowed their faces   110
With wrinkles usually due to old age.
Then he sent them off as monkeys, their bodies
Covered with yellow hair, to this place,
First depriving them of the power of speech
And the tongues with which they told terrible lies.
Now they can only complain with raucous shrieks.

Aeneas sailed on, leaving Parthenope
On the right, and Misenus' mound on the left,
And coming up to Cumae's marshy shores.
There he entered the grotto of the Sibyl   120
And prayed to descend down through Avernus
To see his father's shade. The Sibyl kept her eyes
Fixed on the earth a long time, then lifted them,
Stung with divine frenzy, and said,
                                        "Great things you seek,
O mightiest hero, whose hand has been tried
By steel, whose piety has been tested by fire.
Have no fear, Trojan, you will have what you seek,
And see with my guidance Elysium's halls
And the world's last realms, and you shall know
Your dear father's shade. No road is closed to virtue."   130

She spoke, and showed him deep in a grove
Of Proserpina, the underworld's Juno, a bough
Gleaming with gold, and told him to pluck it.
Aeneas obeyed, and saw the riches of terrible Orcus,

And his ancestral shades, and the aged ghost
Of great-hearted Anchises. He learned also
The laws of those places, and all the perils
Of wars yet to be fought. As he retraced
His weary steps, he eased the toil by talking
With his Cumaean guide, and picking his way   140
Along the unnerving, crepuscular road,
He said to her,
           "Whether you are a goddess
Or simply a woman most pleasing to the gods,
You will always seem divine to me, and I will
Always proclaim that I owe you my life.
Through your grace I have seen the world of death
And escaped from that world. For what you have done
I vow, when I return to the regions above,
To build a temple to you and offer sacred incense."

Phoebus and the Sibyl of Cumae

The Sibyl looked at him, sighed deeply, and said,   150

"I am no goddess, nor does any mortal deserve
To be honored with incense. But so you will know,
Eternal life without end was offered to me,
Had my virginity been offered to Apollo's love.
While he still hoped for this, while he still longed
To break me down with gifts, he said,
                  'Choose what you will,
Virgin of Cumae, and you will have what you choose.'

I pointed to a heap of sand and foolishly asked
To have as many years as there were grains in that pile.
But I forgot to ask that the years of my life   160
Be forever young. He promised me the years,
And promised endless youth too, on the condition
That I would yield to love. I refused Phoebus' gift
And am still unmarried. Now I'm saying good-bye
To the better part of my life, and tottering along

In weak old age that I must long endure.
I have already lived for seven centuries,
But before my years measure up to the sand,
I must see three hundred more harvests and vintages.
The time will come when age will shrivel me   170
To a tiny thing, and my withered body will weigh
No more than a feather. Then it will seem that I
Was never lovely, never could have pleased a god,
And Phoebus would not know me if he saw me,
Nor would admit that he ever loved me. Such changes
Await me, and although I will no longer be seen,
I will be heard. The Fates will leave me my voice."

Two of Ulysses' Crewmembers Reunite

The Sibyl told her story as they made their way
Up the tunneled path, and they emerged from the gloom
Near the city of Cumae. Having sacrificed there,   180
Trojan Aeneas next landed on the shore
Not yet named after his nurse, Caieta.
One of Ulysses' men had stayed behind here,
Macareus of Neritos, too weary to go on.
He recognized among Aeneas' companions
Achaemenides, whom Ulysses and his crew
Had long since abandoned on Aetna's slopes.
Amazed to find him still alive, he said,

"What stroke of luck, or what god has saved you,
Achaemenides? What is a Greek doing   190
On a Trojan ship? What's your vessel's next port?"

And Achaemenides, no longer in rags
Pinned with thorns, his own man once more, replied,

Stranded on the Isle of the Cyclopes

"May I look once more upon Polyphemus' jaws
Dripping with human gore, if I would rather be

Home on Ithaca than on this ship, or if I revere
Aeneas less than my own father. I could never
Thank him enough. That I can speak and breathe
And see the sky, see the stars and the sun,
I owe to him, so could I ever forget or become   200
Ungrateful? It is because of Aeneas
That my life did not end in the Cyclops' jaws,
And even if I should now leave the light
I would be buried in a tomb, not that monster's maw.
How did I feel then, when I was left behind
And saw all of my shipmates headed out to sea?
I could only feel numb, seized with stark terror.
I wanted to call out to you but was afraid
Of revealing myself to the enemy.
Ulysses did call out, and almost brought destruction   210
On your ship. I saw it when the Cyclops
Heaved half of a mountain far out to sea.
I saw him hurling stones with his gigantic arms
As if he were a catapult, and I was terrified
That the splashes would sink the ship, forgetting
I was not aboard. And then, when you escaped
From certain death, he went groaning and stumbling
All over Aetna, groping blindly through the woods
Crashing into rocks, bereft of his eye. And then
He would stretch his blood-grimed arms out to sea   220
And rain curses down on the whole Greek race,
Saying,
            'Just let Ulysses or one of his friends
Come back to me, so I could take it out on him,
Tear him up alive, gulp down his guts and his blood,
Feel his crushed body quiver between my teeth.
Then I wouldn't mind that I have lost my sight.'

The savage said this and much more. My skin crawled
As I looked at his face, still smeared with blood,
His cruel hands, his dark eye socket, and his beard
Matted with human gore. Death was before my eyes   230

But was the least of my worries. I kept thinking
He was about to catch me and chew me up,
And the picture stuck in my mind of that time
When I saw him seize two of my friends at once
And dash them again and again on the ground
And then crouch above them as if he were a lion
And glut himself on their entrails and flesh,
Their bones' white marrow and their twitching limbs.
I remembered standing there, stricken with grief,
As I watched him chew up his horrid blood feast   240
And then vomit it out in gobs mixed with wine.
This is what I pictured would happen to me.
I hid out for days on end, spooked by every sound,
Fearing death and yet longing to die, fending off
Hunger by eating acorns, grass mixed with leaves,
All alone, helpless and hopeless, abandoned
To suffer and die. And then, after a long time,
I saw this ship off in the distance and signaled it
To come rescue me. Running down to the shore
I moved them to pity, and a Trojan ship   250
Welcomed a Greek aboard.
                 And now tell me,
Old friend, what you have been through, as well as
The captain and crew with whom you put out to sea."

Aeolus, The Laestrygonians, and Circe

Then Macareus told him how Aeolus,
Son of Hippotes, ruled the Tuscan waters
And kept the winds confined; and how Ulysses
Was given these winds in a leather bag,
A memorable gift, and sailed for nine days
With a following breeze and the land they sought
Rose into view, but as the tenth day dawned   260
His crew gave in to envy and greed
And opened the bag, thinking it filled with gold.
When they untied the strings the winds escaped
And blew the vessel back over the waves
Until they came again to Aeolus' harbor.

"After that," he went on, "we came to Lamus,
The ancient Laestrygonian city
Ruled by Antiphates. I was sent to him
With two companions, one of which managed
To escape with me, but the other one stained   270
The impious mouths of the Laestrygonians
With his blood. Antiphates pursued us,
Urging on a mob that pelted us with stones
And timbers that sank our ships and their crews.
Only one ship escaped, the one that I sailed in
Along with Ulysses. Grieving for our dead
And lamenting our own pains, we pulled in
At last to the land you see way over there,
And, believe me, it's an island best viewed
At a distance. And you, most righteous Trojan,   280
Son of Venus (for since the war is over
You are no longer to be called an enemy,
Aeneas), I warn you, keep your distance
From the shores of Circe. Remembering Antiphates,
And the Cyclops' cruelty, we refused to go farther
Than the shore where our ship stood pulled up there.
But we drew lots anyway to explore the island,
And I was sent out with trusty Polites,
Eurylochus also, and Elpenor,
Who liked his wine too much, and eighteen others.   290
When we arrived at Circe's walls and stood
In her courtyard, a thousand wolves, bears, and lions
Came careening at us in a confused throng,
Filling us with terror. But there was nothing to fear.
None of these animals would so much as scratch us.
They all wagged their tails and fawned upon us,
Trotting along until some female attendants
Took us in tow and led us through the marble halls
And into their mistress' presence. She sat
On a stately throne in a beautiful alcove,   300
Clad in a lustrous purple robe, a gold veil on her head.
Her attendants were Nereids and nymphs.
Instead of carding fleece and spinning wool,

Their only household task was sorting plants,
Picking out flowers and herbs of different colors
From a jumbled mass and placing them in baskets.
Circe herself supervised the work; she understood
The use of each leaf and how ingredients blend,
And carefully weighed and examined them all.
When she saw us, and greetings had been exchanged,   310
She smiled upon us and seemed hospitable enough,
Ordering her servants to lay out a feast
Of toasted barley bread, honey, and strong wine
With curdled milk, stealthily lacing the sweet drink
With certain juices. We each took the sacred cup
Offered by the goddess' hand, and when our thirst
Had been quenched, the witch touched our heads
With a magic wand. I am ashamed to tell you
What happened next, but I will. I began to bristle
With coarse hair, and I could no longer speak,   320
Producing grunts instead of words. My face began
To bend toward the ground, and I could feel my mouth
Stiffening into a wide snout, and my neck swelling
Into ringed folds, and my hands, that had just now
Picked up the goblet, made tracks in the ground.
Then I was penned up along with the others
Who had undergone the same change (Oh, drugs
Have such power!). We saw that only Eurylochus
Did not have pig form, for he alone
Had refused the cup. If he had not refused it,   330
Ulysses would have never been informed
Of our calamity and never would have come
To save us from Circe, and I would still be part
Of that bristly herd. Mercury the peacemaker
Gave him a white flower with a black root
That the gods call moly. Protected by this,
And by the instructions the god had given him,
The hero entered Circe's palace, and when
He was offered the fatal cup, he knocked aside
The wand she was lifting to stroke his hair   340

And drew his sword on the now trembling goddess.
They came to an understanding and, Ulysses,
Now in her bedroom, demanded as a wedding gift
The bodies of his friends. We were sprinkled
With the restorative juices of some strange herb,
Our heads were struck with the reversed magic wand,
And a counterspell was pronounced over us.
As she chanted it we stood more and more erect,
Our bristles fell away, our feet lost their hooves,
And our shoulders and arms came back into shape.   350
Weeping, we embraced our captain, and he wept too
As we clung to his neck, and the very first words
That came from our lips expressed our deep thanks.
We lingered a year on the island, and in that time
I saw many things, and heard many more.
Here is one of the many tales that were told
In private to me by one of the four attendants
Employed in the witch's service. This nymph,
While Circe dallied alone with Ulysses,
Pointed out to me a white marble statue   360
Of a youth with a woodpecker perched on his head.
The statue was set in a sacred shrine
And marked as special by the many wreaths there.
I asked who it was and why he was worshipped
In that holy shrine, and why he had that bird,
And she said to me,
                    'Listen, Macareus,
And this too can teach you how powerful
My mistress is. Pay attention to my words!

Picus

Picus, a son of Saturn, ruled over
All of Italy and was keen on horses   370
Fit for war. The hero looked just as you see him,
But if you could see his living beauty
This copy would pale beside his true form.
His spirit matched his looks. He could not have seen

Four Olympic Games, but already his beauty
Had attracted all the Dryads that haunted
The verdant hills of Latium. The nymphs
Of the springs also yearned for him, and the naiads
Who lived in the Albula, and those beneath
The rills of Numicus and the Anio,   380
In the Almo's short run, in the rushing Nar
And the shady waters of the Farfarus,
Not to mention those in the forest pool
Of Scythian Diana and the lakes nearby.
But spurning all these he loved only one,
A nymph whom Venilia is said to have borne
To two-headed Janus on the Palatine Hill.
When she was ripe for marriage, Picus was preferred
To all other suitors. Her beauty was rare
But rarer still was her gift for singing,   390
And so her name was Canens. Her sweet songs
Moved the woods and the hills, tamed wild beasts,
Stopped the flow of rivers and the wandering birds.
Once when she sang in her clear virgin tones,
Picus had ridden out into the Laurentian fields
To hunt the native boar. He was mounted upon
A spirited stallion, holding a brace of spears
And wearing a purple mantle clasped with gold.
The daughter of the Sun had come to those very woods,
Leaving her own Circaean fields that day   400
To gather fresh herbs on the fertile hills.
When she saw Picus from where she stood
In the forest's shade, she was astonished.
The herbs she had gathered fell from her hands,
And a burning fire seemed to creep through her bones.
She had her emotions barely under control
And was just about to announce her desire,
When his swift horse and the whole hunting party
Galloped by and prevented her approach.

"You won't get past me like that," she cried out,   410
"Even if the wind itself whisked you away,

Unless my herbal magic has vanished completely
And all my spells have deserted me."

She spoke, and conjured up the spectral image
Of a boar, ordering it to bolt across the trail
Before the king's eyes, then seem to take cover
In a dense thicket where a horse could not go.
In a moment the unsuspecting Picus
Was hot on his shadowy prey, quickly dismounting
His foaming steed and blundering on foot   420
Into the deep woods after the phantom bait.
Circe applied herself to prayers and spells,
Worshipping her strange gods with a strange chant
That she used to confound the moon's white face
Or hide her father's face in mist and cloud.
So now too her incantation darkens the sky
And the earth exhales fog, while the king's men
Wander dim and distant trails and cannot defend him.
When the time and the place suited her, she said,

"O, by those eyes, which have entranced my own,   430
And by that beauty, O loveliest of youths,
That has made me, a goddess, your suppliant,
Smile upon my passion, accept the all-seeing Sun
As your father-in-law, soften your heart
And do not reject the Titaness Circe."

He did reject her, saying to her sternly,

"Whoever you are, I am not for you.
Another has taken me; she holds me now,
And I pray she will hold me to the end of time.
I will not break my pledge by loving another,   440
As long as Janus' daughter, my Canens, shall live."

None of the Titaness' repeated prayers worked,
And finally she exclaimed,
                              "But you will not

Go unpunished, and your Canens will never
Hold you again! And you will learn from this
What a scorned lover and a woman can do,
And Circe is a lover scorned, and a woman!"

Then she turned around twice to the west
And twice to the east; and she touched Picus
Three times with her wand and chanted her spells   450
Three times too. He turned to run and was amazed
At his sudden burst of speed, and then he saw wings
Attached to his own body. Enraged at his mutation
Into a strange bird in his own Latian woods,
He pecked at the oak trees with his hard beak,
Wounding their long branches to express his anger.
His wings took on the color of his purple cloak,
And its golden brooch was itself transformed
To a golden band of feathers around his neck,
And nothing remained of Picus except his name.   460

His companions, meanwhile, had been calling him
And searching the countryside to no avail
When they came upon Circe, who by now
Had clarified the air, allowing the mists
To be dispelled by the wind and the sun.
They charged her with Picus' disappearance
And demanded their king back, threatening
Violence and leveling at her their hunting spears.
She sprinkled them all with a noxious poison
And summoned Night and Night's deities   470
From Erebus and Chaos, and she called upon
Hecate with long, eerie wails. The woods—
To report a miracle—leaped from the ground,
While the ground itself groaned, the trees all around
Blanched, and the plants where her poison fell
Were stained with drops of blood. Even the stones
Seemed to emit a grating bellow, dogs howled,
The earth was fetid with dark slithering things,

And thin shades of the dead flitted about.
The young men cringed at these monstrosities,   480
And then Circe touched their astonished faces
With her magic wand, and horrid bestial forms
Came over them; not one kept his own looks.

The setting sun had touched the Tartessian shores,
And Canens was still looking with her eyes and heart
For her husband's return. Her servants and her people
Were scouring the woods, carrying torches
To light his way home. Nor was the nymph content
Merely to weep, tear her hair out, or beat her breasts
(Although she did all these things). She rushed forth   490
And wandered distraught through the fields of Latium.
Six nights and as many returning dawns
Saw her drifting through the hills, sleepless, fasting,
And down through valleys, wherever chance took her.
The Tiber was the last to see her, all forspent,
Laying down her body on the long riverbank.
Weeping, she poured out words tuned to her grief
In a thin, mournful tone, just as a dying swan
Chants a last funeral song. She finally melted away
From sorrow, and slowly vanished into the air.   500
But her story has been memorialized
By that place on the Tiber. From this nymph's name
The ancient Camenae have called it Canens.'

I heard many such things during that year.
At last, when we had grown fat and lazy
From lying around, we were ordered to go
And sail the sea once more. Circe had told us
Of all of the perils we still had to face,
But, I admit, I was afraid to face them,
And when we reached this shore, I stayed behind."   510

Macareus had finished his story. Meanwhile,
Aeneas' old nurse, buried in a marble urn,

Was memorialized with this epitaph:

CAIETA

BY MY PIOUS WARD SAVED FROM TROY'S CONFLAGRATION,
I RECEIVED FROM HIM HERE A PROPER CREMATION.

Casting off from the grassy shoreline
They steered clear of the treacherous island
That was home to the goddess of ill repute,
And headed for the groves along the coast
Where the shady Tiber pours into the sea   520
Its flood of yellow sand and silt.

Aeneas Comes to Latium

                              There Aeneas won
The daughter and the throne of King Latinus,
Son of Faunus, but not without fighting a war
With a fierce people. Turnus fought madly
For his promised bride, and all Etruria
Clashed with Latium, and the long, hard struggle
For victory began. Each side enlisted
Outside aid, and many defended the Rutulian,
Many the Trojan camp. Aeneas had not returned
Empty-handed from Evander's city,   530
But Venulus had gone in vain to Diomedes,
Who in exile had founded a large city
Within the realm of Iapygian Daunus
And ruled the lands he had received in marriage.
When Venulus arrived with Turnus' request
For assistance in war, the Greek hero
Excused himself, saying he was not willing
To commit himself or his father-in-law
And that neither had the required manpower.

Acmon

"And so you will not think this a lame excuse,"   540
The hero went on, "although recalling my trials

Renews old grief, I will recount them to you.
After tall Troy had been burned, and after Minerva,
A virgin goddess in defense of a ravaged virgin,
Had punished us all for Ajax's rape of Cassandra,
Winds scattered the Greeks over hostile seas,
And we endured lightning, darkness, storms,
The anger of sea and sky, and, topping it all,
The disaster at Cape Caphereus.
Not to bore you with a litany of our misfortunes,   550
Greece then could have moved even Priam to tears.
Minerva, goddess of war, saved me from the waves,
But I was driven again from my native fields,
For Venus had not forgotten the old wound
I had given her, and exacted vengeance now.
I suffered so much on the sea and in war
That I often called all those men blessed
Who had drowned in the waters off Caphereus,
And I wished that I too had gone down with them.

My men at last had endured all that they could   560
At sea and in war. Morale was sinking,
And they begged me to end all our wandering.
One of them, Acmon, a hothead exasperated
With our run of bad luck, said to the crew,

'Is there anything left, men, that you would
Not put up with? What more could Venus do
If she set her mind to it? When we fear the worst
There is room for prayer, but when the worst is here
Fear goes out the window. At the height of misfortune
We become indifferent. Even if she hears me,   570
Even if she hates, as I'm sure she does, all of us
Under Diomedes' command, what do we care?
Great powers are anything but great to us.'

With insults like this Acmon goaded the goddess
And rekindled her old anger. Few of us
Approved what he said, and most of his friends

Rebuked him for it. But when he tried to answer
His voice and throat grew thin; his hair became
Feathers that covered his newly formed neck,
His breast and his back. Larger feathers grew   580
All over his arms, and his elbows curved
To form buoyant wings; his feet became webbed,
His face stiffened with horn sharpened into a beak.
Lycus looked at him in wonder, as did Idas,
Rhexenor and Nycteus, and Abas too;
And as they looked they took on the same form.
The better part of them rose up in a flock
And circled the rowers with flapping wings.
And if you're curious about the species
Of this new kind of bird, they're not really swans,   590
But they are white as snow and much like swans.
Now I am the son-in-law of Iapygian Daunus,
And it's all I can do to hold this place together,
These dry fields, with what's left of my friends."

The Apulian Shepherd

Diomedes finished, and Venulus left
That Calydonian realm, sailing past
The Peucetian Bay and the fields of Messapia,
Where he saw a cavern clouded with woods
And dripping with gentle dew. The half-goat Pan
Now haunts the place, but nymphs used to live there. 600
An Apulian shepherd once surprised them
And frightened them away, but when they looked back
And saw who it was, they were filled with scorn
And soon resumed their light, fantastic dance.
But the shepherd started to mock them, aping their steps
And taunting them with backwoods obscenities,
Nor did he shut his mouth until he felt a tree
Clogging his throat, and that's what he is now,
A tree. You can identify the species
By the taste of its fruit, for the wild olive   610
Still retains traces of this shepherd's tongue
In its bitter berries, as sharp as his words.

Aeneas' Ships

When the ambassadors returned with the news
There would be no Aetolian aid, the Rutulians
Pressed on with the war alone. Both sides
Took heavy casualties. Turnus attacked
The pinewood ships with fire, and the Trojans feared
That flames would destroy what the sea had spared.
The pitch and other inflammables were burning,
Flames licked the sails, and the thwarts were smoldering   620
When Cybele, the gods' sacred mother, remembered
That these pines had been felled on Mount Ida.
The air was filled with the clash of bronze cymbals
And the trilling of boxwood flutes, as the goddess,
Drawn through the sky by her pair of yoked lions, cried out,

"You're throwing those impious torches for nothing,
Turnus! I'm here to the rescue, and I'll never let
Greedy fire devour masts and planks from my woods."

The sky thundered while she spoke, and the thunder
Was followed by a heavy rainfall mixed with hail,   630
While the winds, sons of Astraea, rolled into battle,
Brother against brother, roiling the sky and the sea,
The Mother made use of one of these winds
To break the hemp cables of the Phrygian ships,
And then forced their prows down into the waves.
The wood softened immediately and turned to flesh,
The curved prows became heads, the oars became toes
And swimming legs; the ships' ribs were still ribs,
But the keels at the bottom now served as spine,
The rigging became hair, and their spars became arms,   640
While the sea-green color was still the same. They were
Naiads now, and they loved to play in the waters
That they feared before, and though mountain-bred
They frolicked in the sea, with not a trace left
Of their former state. Remembering how they suffered
Out on the deep, they often lend helping hands
To storm-tossed ships, but not those bearing Greeks,

For they haven't forgotten what happened at Troy
And they hate all Pelasgians, delighted when they saw
The flotsam that had been Ulysses' ship, and when   650
Alcinous' vessel turned from wood to stone.

Ardea

After the fleet had been ensouled as water nymphs,
There was hope that the Rutulians, in awe
Of this portent, would withdraw from the war.
But each side persisted, and each side had their gods,
And, what is as good as gods, they had courage too.
And now they fought not for a kingdom as dowry,
Not for a son-in-law's scepter, nor for you, virgin
Lavinia, but for victory alone, and to avoid
The shame of surrender. In the end, Venus saw   660
Her son's arms victorious and Turnus fallen.
Ardea fell, counted a powerful city
While Turnus still lived. But after the invader
Burnt it down and the embers were still warm,
A bird rose from the ruins, a bird of a kind
Never seen before, its wings fanning the ashes.
Its call, its meager look, its pallor, and everything
That belonged to the captured city, even its name,
Stayed with the bird, the first heron, and Ardea
Is itself lamented when the bird beats its wings.   670

The Death of Aeneas

Aeneas' virtue had now moved all the gods,
Even Juno herself, to set aside their old grudges,
And since his son, Iulus, was growing up
And his fortunes well established, the time was ripe
For Venus' heroic son to enter heaven.
She had lobbied all the gods, and throwing her arms
Around her father's neck she said,

                       "O Father,
You have never been harsh to me, and I pray

That you will be most kind now. Grant my Aeneas—
Your grandson, O Supreme Lord, and of our blood— 680
Some divinity, however slight, but some at least.
Once is enough for him to have looked upon
That unlovely realm, to have crossed the Styx once."

And Father Jupiter replied,
                "You are worthy
Of such divine favor, both you and he for whom
You ask. You may have what you desire, daughter."

Venus was exultant. She thanked her father
And then, borne through the air by her doves,
Came to the coast where the Numicius
Winds through reeds and pours its fresh water 690
Into the Laurentian sea. She asked the river god
To wash away all of Aeneas' mortality
And carry it in his silent stream into the deep.
The horned god obeyed, and he cleansed Aeneas
Of all that was mortal. His best part remained.
His mother anointed him with divine perfume,
Touched his lips with ambrosia and nectar
And so made him a god. The Romans called him
Indiges, and honored him with a temple and altars.

Under Ascanius the state was called both 700
Alban and Latin. Silvius succeeded him,
And his son, Latinus, took the name inherited
With the ancient scepter. Illustrious Alba
Succeeded Latinus; Epytus was next,
And then, in order, Capys and Capetus.
Tiberinus received the kingdom from them,
And when he drowned in the old Tuscan stream
He gave the river his name. His sons were called
Remulus and Acrota. Remulus, the elder,
Was struck by lightning while he was trying 710
To imitate thunder. Acrota, less arrogant,
Passed on the scepter to brave Aventinus,

Who lies buried on the hill where he had his palace
And that still bears his name. And now it was Proca
Who reigned supreme over the Palatine race.

Pomona and Vertumnus

Pomona lived under this king. No other
Latian wood nymph knew more about gardens
Or was more zealous in tending an orchard,
Whence her name. She was not interested
In forests or rivers; she loved the fields   720
And trees laden with delicious ripe fruit.
Her hand held no javelin, but a pruning hook
With which she restrained luxuriant growth,
Cut back spreading branches, or made in the bark
An incision for grafting a twig in a branch
To give it fresh sap. She kept all her trees
Well watered, irrigating their thirsty roots.
This was her love, this was all her desire,
And she had no interest in Venus at all.
But she did fear rape, and shut herself up   730
Inside her orchard, keeping men at a distance.
The dancing satyrs did everything they could
To win her hand, as did the pine-wreathed Pans.
And Silvanus, always younger than his age,
And Priapus, who scares off thieves with his sickle
Or his virile shaft. Vertumnus outdid them all
In the art of love, but came off no better.
How many times did he come dressed as a reaper
And bring her a basket full of barley ears?
And he would really look like a reaper, too.   740
Or he would come with fresh hay wreathing his head,
And you would think he had just been turning
The new-mown grass. Or he would have an ox-goad
In his calloused hand, and you would swear
He had just unyoked his weary team. He would be
A vine-dresser carrying a pruning hook,
Or show up with a ladder, so you would think

He was going to pick apples. He could be
A soldier with a sword, a fisherman with a pole.
With all these disguises he got to see her a lot,   750
And he loved the beauty he saw. Once he put on
A wig of grey hair, bound with a colorful scarf,
And leaning on a staff came as an old woman
Into the immaculate orchard, and said,
As he admired the fruit, "But you are much better."
And he kissed her two or three times, kisses such as
No real old woman would ever have given.
Then, all hunched over, he sat on the grass
And gazed at the branches heavy with autumn's fruit.
There was a shapely elm opposite, draped   760
With gleaming clusters of grapes. He looked at the tree
And its companion vine with an approving eye
And then said,
              "You know, if that tree stood there
Unwed to the vine, it would only have leaves,
Not much use; and the vine, that now clings to the elm
And rests nicely there, if it were not mated
To the tree, would just lie flat on the ground.
But you don't take the vine's example, do you?
You shun wedlock and don't care about a mate.
I wish you did. Then you would have more suitors   770
Than Helen had, or than Hippodameia,
For whom the Lapiths fought, or Penelope,
The wife of the late-returning Ulysses.
Even now, although you hold them in contempt,
A thousand men want you, and all the gods,
Spirits, and demigods that haunt the Alban hills.
But if you are wise and want to make a good match
And would listen to this old woman—who loves you
More than all the rest, more than you can believe—
You would reject all the common offers of marriage   780
And choose Vertumnus for your bedmate.
I can vouch for him, for he is not better known
Even to himself than he is to me.
He doesn't wander the wide world, but stays here

In this neighborhood. Nor does he fall in love
With whatever he sees, unlike most of your suitors.
You will be his first love and his last; you will be
The love of his life. Then too, he is young,
Charming, and can assume any form he likes
And whatever form you want. Moreover,   790
You like the same things, and he is the first to have
Your favorite fruit, and he lights up at your gifts.
But it is neither the fruit from your trees,
Nor the juicy greens that you grow in your garden
Nor anything else except you he desires.
Pity the lover, and believe that he himself
Is courting you through the words I am speaking.
And do respect the avenging gods, and Venus,
Who detests the hard-hearted, and Nemesis,
Who never forgets. And so you will respect them more,   800
Let me tell you (I've learned a thing or two in my time)
A story that is well known all over Cyprus.
It may teach you to bend and to be softer of heart.

Iphis and Anaxarete

Iphis, a boy of humble birth, chanced to see
Anaxarete once, a girl from the old family
Of Teucer in Salamis. As soon as he saw her
Love's fire shot through his bones. He fought it,
But when reason failed to overcome his passion,
He came to her door as a suppliant. First he confided
In the nurse, confessing his love and begging her   810
In the name of all her hopes for her foster child
Not to be hard on him. Then he tried to coax
The servants to put in a good word for him,
Writing sweet talk on tablets for them to pass on.
Sometimes he would hang garlands of flowers
On her door, first wetting them with his tears,
And then lay his soft body on her hard threshold
And utter complaints to her door's grim bars.
Harsher than the sea surge when the Goat Stars set,

Harder than steel tempered in a Noric forge   820
Or than living rock embedded in the earth,
She spurns him and mocks him, adding insults
And abusive language to heartless rejection,
And leaves her lover utterly deprived of hope.
Unable to endure the torment any longer,
Iphis called out his last words before her door:

'You win, Anaxarete; you won't have to put up
With me any longer. Celebrate your victory,
Sing songs of triumph, wear a laurel wreath
On your head, for you have really won,   830
And I will gladly die. Let your iron heart rejoice.
You will be compelled to praise something about me,
Some way I was pleasing, some merit I had.
But remember, my love did not end before my life
And I lost two lights at once. No rumor
Will bring you news of my death. I will be there
In person, so you can feast your cruel eyes
On my lifeless corpse.
                    And yet, O gods,
If you see what mortals do, let me be
Remembered (I cannot bear to ask for more),   840
Let my story be told in future ages
And add to my fame the years you took from my life.'

Iphis said these things, and lifted his tear-filled eyes
To the doorposts on which he had often hung
Garlands of flowers, and raising his pale arms
He tied a rope to the crossbeam, saying,
'This wreath will please you, cruel as you are.'
Then he put his head in the noose, which soon
Crushed his windpipe. And even as he hung there,
The pitiful weight of his body turned slowly   850
To face her, and his feet knocked against the door
As if he were requesting to enter; and when
The door was opened, it revealed what he had done.

The servants shrieked, and lifted him from the noose,
But all in vain. Then they carried his body
To his mother's house, since his father was dead,
And she took him to her breast, enfolding her arms
Around her son's cold limbs. And when she had said
All the things that distraught parents would say,
And done all the things distraught mothers do, 860
His funeral procession wound through the city's streets
As she took his pale corpse on a bier to the pyre.

The sad procession happened to pass the house
Of Anaxarete, and the sound of mourning
Rose to her ears. It must have been some vengeful god
Who roused her stony heart, but she was roused
And said, 'Let's take a look at this wretched funeral,'
As she went to a rooftop room with a view.
She had barely caught sight of Iphis on the pallet,
When her eyes became fixed, and the blood drained 870
From her pallid body. She tried to step back
But was rooted to the spot and could not even
Turn her face away. The stoniness that had long
Been deep in her heart now slowly crept over
Her body as well. If you think this is only
An old wives' tale, there is still in Salamis
A statue of the woman, as well as a temple
Of Gazing Venus. Keep all this in mind,
O nymph of mine. Put aside your stubborn pride
And embrace your lover. That way you'll be sure 880
That the frost won't nip your apples in the bud,
Nor the storm winds scatter your peach blossoms."

Vertumnus said all this dressed as an old woman,
But to no effect. He then threw off his disguise
And became himself again, appearing to Pomona
As a shining youth. It was as if the sun
Had emerged resplendent from a bank of clouds
And shone unblemished in the sky. He was ready

To force her, but no force was needed. The nymph
Responded to the god with an equal passion.   890

The Sabines

Amulius now rules Italy, with unjust use
Of military might, and then old Numitor
Aided by his grandson Romulus, retakes
His lost kingdom, and Rome is founded
On the feast day of Pales, god of shepherds.

The Sabines under Tatius wage war on Rome,
And Tarpeia, who opened the city to them,
Loses her life under a crush of weapons.

Then while the Romans lie buried in sleep,
The men of Cures, like silent wolves, advance   900
With hushed voices and try the city's gates
That Romulus has barred. Juno herself
Unfastens one of these, and the gate swings open
Without a sound. Venus alone perceived
That the bar had fallen and would have replaced it,
But a god may not undo another god's deed.
Right next to Janus' shrine, though, the Ausonian nymphs
Had a spot where a cold spring bubbled up.
Venus enlisted their aid, and the nymphs complied,
Opening their spring's channels. Up until then   910
The pass of Janus had never been closed
Or the road blocked by water, but now the nymphs
Stoked the source of their spring with yellow sulphur
And heated the channels with burning pitch,
So that the pool was steaming down to its depths,
And the water that had been as cold as the Alps
Was as hot as fire. The gateposts smoldered
Under a fiery spray, and the gate itself,
By which the tough Sabines had thought to enter
Was impassable with water, giving the Romans   920

Time to arm themselves. Then Romulus attacked,
And soon the Roman fields were strewn with Sabine dead
As well as the bodies of their native sons,
And those impious swords mingled the blood of Romans
With the Sabine blood of their wives' fathers.
But the war ended with a truce, and it was agreed
That Tatius would share the Roman throne.

Romulus

When Tatius died, you, Romulus, governed
Both peoples with equal justice. Then Mars set aside
His gleaming helmet and in these words addressed   930
The Father of Gods and Men:
                              "The time has come,
Father, since Rome now stands on firm foundations
And does not depend on just one man, for you to grant
The promised reward to me and your grandson,
To free his spirit and set him in the heavens.
You once spoke to me at a council of the gods
Gracious words I remember and keep in my mind,
'There will be one you will raise to heaven's azure.'
Now let the sum of your words at last be fulfilled."

Almighty Jupiter nodded, and veiling the sky   940
With dark clouds, he terrified the men on earth
With thunder and lightning. Mars recognized this
As a sign of the promised ascension to heaven,
And leaning on his spear, he vaulted fearlessly
Into his bloodstained chariot and cracked the whip
Above the straining horses. Gliding steeply down,
He landed on the Palatine's wooded summit.
There, as Ilia's son was dealing royal justice,
Mars caught him up. His mortal body dissipated
Into thin air, the way a lead bullet hurled   950
By a sling can melt into the endless sky.
Beautiful now, he is Quirinus, robed and worthier
To take his place at the gods' high couches.

Hersilia

His wife, Hersilia, mourned him as lost
Until royal Juno ordered Iris to go down
On her curving path and bear this message
To the grieving widow:
                "O glory of both
The Latin and the Sabine people, worthy
To have been the wife of so great a hero
And now of Quirinus, dry your tears,   960
And if you desire to see your husband,
Follow me to the grove on the Quirinal Hill
That shades the temple of the king of Rome."

Iris obeyed and, gliding down to earth
Along the arch of her iridescent bow,
She delivered the message to Hersilia,
Who barely lifted her eyes when she answered,

"Goddess—I cannot easily tell who you are,
But you are clearly a goddess—lead on,
Oh, lead on, and show me my husband's face.   970
If the Fates allow me to see him just once,
I will declare that he has been taken to heaven."

And without delay she went with Thaumas' daughter
To the hill of Romulus, where a star fell,
Gliding down to earth through the pure sky,
And Hersilia, her hair bursting into flames
From its light, disappeared up into the air
Along with the star. The founder of Rome
Enfolded her in his familiar embrace
And changed her in body and name, calling her   980
Hora, a goddess united with her Quirinus.

Book 15

Numa

The search was on for someone who could sustain
Such a massive burden and succeed so great a king.
Rumor, that herald of truth, suggested Numa
For the throne. Not thinking it was enough
To know the old Sabine ways, he set his great mind
On something larger, the nature of the universe.
Pursuit of this passion caused him to leave
His native Cures and make his way to Croton,
The city that once had Hercules as its guest.
When Numa asked who had founded this Greek city   10
On the shores of Italy, one of the elders
Who was well-versed in the city's ancient lore
Answered him:

The Founding of Croton

"It is said that Hercules,
On his way back from Ocean with the herd
He had acquired in Spain, arrived auspiciously
In Lacinium, and while his cattle grazed
On the tender grass, he was given hospitality
In the house of the great Croton, where he rested
After his long labor. Refreshed and ready to leave,
He said,
          'Here the city of your descendants shall stand   20
In future ages.'
          The words proved to be true.
It happened this way. There was a man from Argos
Called Myscelus, most acceptable of all living men
In the eyes of the gods. As he was wrapped in slumber
Hercules stood over him with his club and said,

'Go, leave your native land and seek the stony waters
Of the far Aesar River.'
          And he threatened him
With many horrible things if he did not obey.
Having said this, the god left when sleep did.

Myscelus arose and mused over the dream,   30
Still vivid in his mind, and agonized over it
For a long time. The god ordered him to leave;
His country's laws forbade him to depart.
Death was the penalty for anyone who tried
To move to a new country. The sun went down
Beneath the sea, and Night lifted her starry face.
The same god seemed to be there again, issuing
The same commands, and even more dire threats
If disobeyed. Myscelus was terrified.
As soon as he prepared to move his household   40
To a new location, word got around the city
And he was brought to trial as a scofflaw.
When the prosecution rested, and the charge
Was proved without any testimony,
The wretched defendant lifted his face
And hands to heaven, crying,
                              'O Thou,
Whose twelve great labors earned you heaven,
Help me now, for you caused my transgression.'

There was an ancient custom to use black pebbles
To condemn prisoners and white to acquit them,   50
And the death penalty was decided the same way.
Every pebble dropped into the merciless urn
Was black, but when the urn was tipped over
And the pebbles poured out, all of them were white.
And so, by the will of Hercules, the verdict
Was changed to acquittal, and Myscelus was released.
After giving thanks to his patron, Amphitryon's son,
He sailed with the wind across the Ionian Sea,
Passed by Salentine Neretum, by Sybaris,
Spartan Tarentum, the Bay of Siris,   60
Crimisa, and the Iapygian coast.
He had just scanned those shores when he reached
The destined mouth of the Aesar. Nearby,
An earthen mound held Croton's sacred bones.
There, as the god had ordered, he laid out

The walls of his city, and he named it after
The hero buried there."
                              That was the ancient story
Of the Greek city's foundation on Italian soil.

The Teachings of Pythagoras

There was a man there, a Samian by birth
Who had fled Samos and its tyrannical rulers   70
And lived in voluntary exile. Though his gods
Were far away, he visited their region of the sky
In his mind, and things that nature denied
To human vision he took in with his inner eye.
When he had looked carefully into everything
With his awakened heart, he began to teach
The silent crowds, who listened in wonder
As he described the origin of the universe,
The causes of things, what the natural world is
And what gods are, where snow comes from,   80
And lightning, whether it's Jupiter, or winds
That make thunder roll from colliding clouds,
What causes earthquakes, how the stars move,
And whatever else is hidden. And he was the first
To denounce serving animal flesh at table,
The first—wise beyond doubt but not believed—
To open his mouth and say things such as this:

"Stop desecrating your bodies, mortals,
With impious food! Grains grow in the fields, apples
Weigh down branches, grapes swell on the vines.   90
There are salad greens and vegetables to boil.
You do not lack milk or honey redolent
With flowering thyme. The earth is prodigal
Of its wealth and supplies mild sustenance,
Provides feasts for you without bloody slaughter.
Wild animals satisfy their hunger with flesh—
Not all of them, since horses and cattle and sheep
Live on grasses—but wild, savage beasts,

Armenian tigers and raging lions,
Wolves and bears enjoy food dripping with blood.   100
Oh, how wrong for flesh to become other flesh,
For a greedy body to fatten on a swallowed body,
For one creature to live on another's death!
Surrounded with riches that the best of mothers,
Earth herself, yields, nothing makes you happy
But your cruel teeth tearing at pitiful wounds,
And like the Cyclops you cannot satisfy
Your voracious appetite without destroying another!

But that former age, the one we call Golden,
Blessed itself with fruit from the trees, plants   110
The soil bore, and did not defile its lips with blood.
Birds winged their way safe through the air then,
Hares wandered unafraid through fields, and fish
Were not hooked by their gullibility. The whole world,
Free from trickery and snares, with no fraud to fear,
Was filled with peace. But then some useless person
Started to envy lions for their victims
And stuffed his greedy belly with flesh,
Blazing a trail for sin. It is possible
That weapons were first warm and bloodstained   120
From killing beasts. That should have been enough.
I admit that creatures that try to kill us
May themselves be killed without incurring guilt.
But while they may be killed, they should not be eaten.

The wickedness spread out from there. The pig
May have been the first victim considered
To deserve death, because it rooted up seeds
With its broad snout and ruined the harvest's hopes.
The goat was led to slaughter at the avenging altar
Because it browsed Bacchus' vines. These two   130
Paid for their guilt. But what did you sheep do,
Peaceful flocks born to serve men, udders full
Of sweet milk you give us, who give us your wool

For soft clothing, and are worth more living than dead?
And what have oxen done, guileless animals,
Harmless and simple, born to endure labor?
Truly thankless, and undeserving of the gift
Of grain, is the man who could unhitch the heavy plow
And a moment later kill his laborer, striking
With his axe the toil-worn neck that has helped   140
Renew the hard earth for every harvest ever.
It's not enough to commit sins like these:
They enlist the gods in crime, believing that heaven
Delights in the slaughter of suffering oxen.
An unblemished victim of outstanding beauty
(A liability) gilded and garlanded
Is placed in front of the altar, hears the prayers
Uncomprehending, sees the grain it cultivated
Sprinkled between its horns, and, struck down,
Stains with its blood the knives that it has, perhaps,   150
Already seen in the clear water's reflection.
Immediately they inspect the lungs, ripped
From the living chest, and read the gods' will.
This is where—monumental mortal hunger
For forbidden food!—you dare feed, O humans.
Do not, I beg you. Turn your minds instead
To my admonitions, and when you put the flesh
Of slaughtered cattle into your mouths, know
And feel you are devouring your fellows.

And now, since a god moves me to speak, I will   160
Follow the god, open up Delphi and heaven itself,
And unlock the oracles of the sublime intellect.
I will sing of great things never investigated
By earlier minds, things that long lay hidden.
It is a joy to travel among the exalted stars,
And, leaving earth and its dull regions behind,
To ride on a cloud, to stand on Atlas' shoulders,
And seeing men wandering far below, witless,
Anxious, and in fear of the beyond,
To exhort them and unroll the scroll of Fate.   170

O people stunned with the cold fear of death,
Why do you dread the Styx, the shades, empty names,
The stuff of poets, perils of a false world?
Corpses, you must know, whether the pyre's flames
Or time's decay consume them, cannot suffer any ills.
Our souls do not die, and when they leave
A former residence they always move into
A new receptacle and go on living there.
I myself—I remember this—at the time
Of the Trojan War, was Euphorbus,   180
Whose chest Menelaus' heavy spear transfixed.
Just recently, in Juno's temple in Argos,
I recognized the shield my left arm bore.
All things are changing; nothing dies. The spirit
Wanders here and there and occupies
Whatever set of limbs it pleases, moving
From an animal into a human body
And back again, but at no time perishes.
Just as soft wax stamped with a new design
Does not stay as it was or keep its shape   190
But is still the same wax, so I teach that the soul
Is always the same but migrates into new forms.
And so, to keep your sanctity from being vanquished
By your stomach's greed, abstain—I speak as a seer—
From driving out kindred souls with unholy slaughter,
And do not let blood be nourished by blood.

And since my sails are bellying in the wind
On this great ocean: there is nothing in the whole world
That is static. Everything flows, is a vagrant form.
Time itself glides on in constant motion,   200
Just like a river. A river cannot stand still,
Nor can a wispy hour. As a wave is pushed by a wave,
Pushed on as it comes and pushing on the one before,
So moments of time run on and follow
And are always new. What was before is left behind
And what wasn't becomes, renewed every moment.

You see also that nights travel on into light
And how the day's brilliance gives way to dusk.
Nor is the sky colored the same when everything rests
In midnight quiet as when the bright Morning Star   210
Appears on his white stallion; and it is different again
When Aurora, herald of the day, tints the world
That she passes on to Phoebus. And that god's shield,
When it lifts above the horizon, is morning-red,
And red again when it sinks down in the west,
But it is incandescent when at the zenith
In the pure upper air, far from earth's contagion.
And Diana the Moon can never exhibit
The same phase today as tomorrow night,
Smaller today when waxing, greater when waning.   220

And how could you not notice that the year passes
In four seasons that resemble our passage through life?
Tender spring, flowing with sap, is very much like
Human childhood, the delicate sprouts swelling,
Unsubstantial as yet, but giving farmers hope.
Then everything blossoms, and the mothering fields
Are colored with flowers, though the leaves are still weak.
From spring the year, now grown more robust,
Moves into summer and becomes a sturdy youth.
No season is heartier or more ardent than this.   230
Autumn takes over when that ardor has faded,
A ripe, mellow season between youth and old age,
Mild, with a sprinkling of grey hairs on his head.
Then old winter totters in, shaking and trembling,
What little hair he has left now all turned white.

Our own bodies, too, are always changing,
Without any rest, and what we once were or are now
We will not be tomorrow. There once was a time
When we, the mere seed and promise of humans,
Were hidden in our mother's womb. Nature   240
Was unwilling for our bodies to remain cramped

In a mother's swollen belly, and so applied
Her skillful hands and moved us out into the air.
Born into the light, there lies the weak infant,
But it soon is crawling on all fours like an animal,
And then gradually starts to stand, supported
At first in a little sling, on its still shaky legs.
Then, grown strong and swift, it passes through
Its span of youth, and when the middle years too
Are past, life goes downhill and into old age,   250
Which demolishes all of life's former strength.
Milon, the great wrestler, now grown old
Sheds tears when he looks at his weak, flabby arms,
Once solid muscle like those of Hercules.
And Helen, daughter of Tyndareus, weeps
When she looks at her wrinkles in the mirror
And asks herself why she has been ravaged twice.
Devouring Time, and you, jealous Age,
Destroy everything, gnawing at life's ruins
And consuming it in the slow maw of death.   260

Not even what we call the elements persist.
Concentrate, and I will teach you the changes
That they undergo. The everlasting universe
Contains four generative bodies, or elements,
Of which two, earth and water, are ponderous
And sink down by their own weight. The other two
Lack weight, and if nothing presses them down
They ascend, air, and purer than air, fire.
Though they are distinct in space, they all derive
From each other and resolve into each other.   270
Earth dissolves and rarifies into pure water,
And moisture evaporates into the atmosphere;
Then the air lightens into the upper regions
And shines forth as fire, the most tenuous of all.
Then the whole process reverses, and fire
Condenses into air, air into water,
And water contracts and congeals into earth.

Nothing keeps its own shape, and Nature renews
By recycling one form into another.
Nothing dies, believe me, in the world as a whole   280
But only changes its looks. What we call birth
Is a new beginning of what was before,
As death is an ending of a former state.
Although that over there may be transferred here,
And this over there, the sum remains constant.

I do believe that nothing at all lasts for long
In the same form. The ages changed from gold to iron,
And locales too have seen their fortunes altered.
I have seen myself what was once solid land
Become sea, and have seen land replace water.   290
Seashells can be found lying far from any shore,
And ancient anchors on mountains. Flowing water
Has turned plains into valleys; floods have washed hills
Into the sea; swamps have dried up into sand;
And dry, thirsty earth has become stagnant marsh.
Nature spurts out springs here, seals them up there;
And rivers, disturbed by tremors deep in the earth,
Burst to the surface or dry up and sink.
In this way the Lycus, swallowed by a chasm,
Emerges far off, reborn from a different source;   300
And the mighty Erasinus, sucked underground,
Flows hidden and reappears in the fields of Argos.
And they say that the Mysus, ashamed of its headwaters,
Now flows elsewhere as the Caïcus River.
And does not the Amenanus churn Sicilian sand
Only to stop flowing, its springs run dry?
Once a drinkable river, now the Anigrus
Flows with water you would not want to touch,
Unless we cannot believe the poets who say
That the Centaurs used it to wash the wounds   310
Inflicted upon them by Hercules' club and bow.
And the Hypanis, rising in the Scythian mountains—
Wasn't it once sweet but now bitter and salty?

Antissa, Pharos, and Phoenician Tyre
Were once surrounded by sea: none is an island now.
Leucas, formerly a peninsula, is now
Circled by waves. Zancle is said to have been
Joined to Italy, until the surf washed away
The border, and the sea pushed back the land.
If you look for the Achaean cities Helice   320
And Buris, you will find them underwater;
Sailors still point out the sunken town walls.
There is a mound near Troezen, Pittheus' town,
Treeless and steep, once the plain's flattest part,
A tumulus now. The eerie story is told
That the wild winds, imprisoned in a dark cave,
Desperately wanted somewhere to breathe,
To enjoy the free, open sky, and since their cave
Was airtight, without a crack for breath to escape,
They inflated the ground, the way a man blows up   330
A bladder or the skin of a double-pronged goat.
The swelling remains there and has the appearance
Of a high hill grown solid with the passing of time.

Of many other examples that come to mind
I will mention a few more. Does not water also
Give and take new forms? Your stream, horned Ammon,
Is cold at noon, warm at evening and dawn;
And the Athamanians set fire to wood,
The story goes, by pouring your water over it
When the moon wanes to her smallest crescent.   340
The Ciconians have a stream whose water, when drunk,
Turns inner organs to stone, and will turn to marble
Anything it touches. The Crathis and the Sybaris,
Which flows here on our borders, make hair look like
Amber or gold. And even more amazing
Are waters that change not only bodies but minds.
Who has not heard of the sickening fluids
Of Salmacis' pool or the Ethiopian lakes?
Whoever drinks of these either goes mad
Or falls into an eerily heavy sleep.   350

Whoever slakes his thirst at Clitor's fountain
Avoids wine and enjoys only pure water,
Either because of a quality in the fountain's water
That opposes wine's warmth, or because Melampus,
As the locals claim, after he had saved
Proetus' daughters from madness with spells and herbs,
Threw a mental purgative into the water,
Which thereafter retained an aversion to wine.
The Lyncestius has a quite different effect.
Whoever so much as sips some of that water   360
Stumbles around as if he had drunk straight wine.
There is a place in Arcadia the ancients called Pheneus
Mistrusted for the dual effects of its water:
Drunk at night it is noxious, but not in the light.
So lakes and rivers have various virtues.

There was a time when Ortygia was a floating island;
Now it is fixed. And the Argonauts once feared
The Symplegades colliding with a crash of surf;
Now they stand unmoving and resist the winds.

And Aetna, glowing with sulphurous furnaces,   370
Will not always be fiery, nor has it always been.
For the earth is a living thing, and she has vents
In many places from which she breathes out flame,
And can alter these passages for her breath at will,
Closing some caverns and opening others.
Or, if winds confined in the depths of caves
Blow rocks against rocks or against anything
Containing the seeds of fire, and the friction
Causes Aetna to ignite, the caves will be left cold
When the winds subside. Or, if bituminous substances   380
Are what catch fire, or yellow sulphur
Burning with little smoke, then when the earth
No longer provides rich fuel for the flames,
The resources used up after long ages,
Consuming Nature will no longer be nourished
And, starved and deserted, will desert those fires.

There is a report of men in Hyperborean Pallene
Accustomed to clothe their bodies with plumage
By plunging nine times into Minerva's pool.
I scarcely credit it. Scythian women are said   390
To do the same thing by sprinkling on potions.

But if we should only trust what is proven,
Haven't you seen that whenever corpses
Putrefy over time or in liquefying heat
They turn into tiny creatures? Bury the corpses
Of slaughtered bulls (this is well-known)
Down in a ditch, and honeybees will be born
From the rotting entrails. Like their parents
They are busy in the fields and hope for harvest.

An interred warhorse produces hornets.   400
Remove the hollow claws of a shore crab,
Put the rest in the sand, and from the buried part
Out comes a scorpion with hooked, menacing tail.
And caterpillars that weave their white cocoons
On leafy branches (farmers often see this)
Transform into funereal butterflies.

Mud contains the generative seeds
Of green frogs, and it generates them
Without any legs, soon adding forelegs
That help them swim, and then longer hind legs   410
So that they are adapted to take long leaps.
A newborn bear cub is not really a cub
But a lump of flesh that is barely alive.
The mother forms its body by licking it into
A shape like her own. And haven't you seen
How honeybee larvae, in their hexagonal
Waxen cells, are born as limbless bodies
And acquire legs later, and still later wings?
Juno's peacock, that has stars on its tail,
The eagle that bears Jove's lightning bolt,   420

The doves of Venus, and every species of bird—
Who would believe, if he did not already know
That they are all born from the inside of an egg?
Some believe that when a spine decomposes,
Human marrow turns into a snake in the tomb.

These creatures get their start in life from others,
But there is one that renews and reproduces itself,
A bird Assyrians call the phoenix. It does not subsist
On seeds or berries but on drops of incense
And cardamom. When it has lived five centuries   430
It builds a nest high in a swaying palm tree,
Using only its beak and its talons, and lines it
With cassia bark, smooth spikes of nard,
Crushed cinnamon, and yellow myrrh. Roosting there,
The bird ends its life among the perfumes.
They say that a little phoenix is reborn
From its father's body, destined to live
The same number of years. When it grows up
And is strong enough to carry a burden,
It relieves the high palm of the heavy nest   440
And piously carries what was its cradle
And its father's tomb until it reaches the city
Of Hyperion the Sun, and then sets it down
Before the sacred doors of Hyperion's temple.

If these things seem a bit strange and wondrous,
We might wonder instead at the transformation
Of a female who has just been mounted by a male
And has now herself become a male hyena.
And then there's the creature fed by wind and air
Who takes on the color of whatever it has touched.   450
India, conquered by Bacchus, gave the wine god
Lynxes, and whatever comes out of their bladders
Hardens into stone, they say, when it touches the air.
Coral, too, as soon as it touches the air,
Congeals; it was soft grass when under the waves.

Day will be done, and Phoebus dip his panting horses
Into the sea, before I could put into words
All of the things that undergo transformations.
Times, too, change; we see some nations grow strong
And others decline. Look at Troy, once so great   460
In resources and men, it was able to hold out
For ten long years of bloodshed. Now it is ruins
And instead of wealth shows its ancestors' tombs.
Sparta was once famous, and great Mycenae flourished.
What is Oedipus' Thebes now except a name?
What is left, but a name, of Pandion's Athens?
And now we hear Dardanian Rome is rising,
Laying her foundations with monumental effort
On the banks of the Apennine-fed Tiber River.
She changes form by growing, and, one day,   470
She will be the capital of the boundless world.
So the prophecies run, and the oracles,
And I can recall, when Troy was falling,
What Helenus, one of Priam's sons, said
To the weeping Aeneas, unsure of survival:

'Goddess-born, if you note well my prophecies,
Troy will not wholly fall while you are safe.
Fire and sword will give way to you. You will go
And take Pergamum with you until you reach a land
More friendly to you and Troy than your father's.   480
I see a city that owes you Phrygian descendants,
Greater than which there is none, or ever will be,
Or has ever been. Others will make her powerful
Through the long centuries, but one born of the blood
Of Iulus will make her mistress of the world,
And when the earth has made use of him, heaven
Will enjoy him, and the sky will be his final abode.'

Thus Helenus to Aeneas, the Penates in his arms.
I tell you what I remember, and I rejoice that walls
Related to me are growing, and that the victory   490
Of the Pelasgians has come out well for the Trojans.

But, not to wander off course with horses that forget
To make for the post: the sky and everything beneath
Changes form, as does the earth and all upon it.
We too are a part of the world, and since we are
Not only bodies but winged souls and can reside
In wild animals and lodge in the hearts of cattle,
Let us treat with respect bodies that could have held
The souls of our parents or brothers, or of those
Joined to us by some bond, or of humans at least,   510
And not glut ourselves on Thyestean banquets.
He is forming an evil habit, impiously preparing
To shed human blood, the man who cuts a calf's throat
With a knife and listens to its mooing unmoved,
Or cuts a kid's throat while it cries like a child,
Or feeds on a bird to which he has just given food!
How far short of murder is this? Where does it lead?
Let the ox plow, and owe its death to old age;
Let the sheep protect you against the cold North Wind;
Let nannies give us their full udders to milk.   510
Throw away nets and snares, don't catch birds
With limed twigs, or spook deer with feathers,
Or conceal a barbed hook in treacherous bait.
Kill what harms you, but let killing suffice.
Keep flesh from your lips, take mild nourishment."

Hippolytus and Egeria

They say that Numa returned to his own land
With these and other teachings in his heart,
And when he was asked, he assumed the reins
Of the Latin state. Happy with the nymph Egeria
As his wife, blessed by the Muses of Italy,   520
He made mild a rough people and introduced them
To sacred rituals and the arts of peace.
When he was old and had completed both his reign
And his life, the Latin women, the people,
The elders all mourned their departed Numa.
But his wife fled the city and hid herself

In the deep forests of the Arician valley,
Where she disturbed the worship of Orestean Diana
With her groans and lamentations.

Hippolytus

How often
The nymphs of woods and lakes urged her to refrain   530
And spoke words of consolation to her.
How often did the heroic son of Theseus,
Say to the weeping nymph,
"Stop your crying;
Yours is not the only misfortune to lament.
Think about others who've had just as much suffering
And you'll bear your own more easily. I wish
I didn't have my own example to comfort you
In your grief. But even mine can comfort you.
If you have heard of Hippolytus, how he died
Because of his gullible father and the treachery   540
Of his sinful stepmother, you will be amazed—
And I will have a hard time convincing you—
But that's who I am. Phaedra, daughter of Minos
And Pasiphaë, when she failed to seduce me
And defile my father's bed, falsely accused me
Of doing what she herself wished me to do.
Perhaps she feared discovery, or was offended
At being rejected. At any rate, my father
Drove me from the city although I was innocent
And put a great curse on my head as I left.   550
Banished, I was on my way by chariot
To Troezen, riding along the beach
Of the Bay of Corinth, when the sea surged
Into a huge mound of water, swelling and cresting
To mountainous size, then splitting at the peak
With a bellowing sound. The waves exploded
And a horned bull charged out, chest-high in the sea,
Spouting geysers of water from his nostrils and mouth.
My companions were terrified, but my mind

Preoccupied with exile, remained calm.   560
But then my spirited horses turned their heads
Toward the sea, and, ears pricked, bristled with fear
At the monstrous bull. Off they went, pulling the chariot
At breakneck speed over the rocky path.
Leaning back, I pulled hard on the foam-flecked reins,
And as strong as the horses were in their madness,
I might have controlled them, but the hub of a wheel
Hit a stake in the ground and was torn from the axle.
I was thrown from the car, my legs caught in the reins,
And if you had been there you would have seen   570
My guts trailing out behind the chariot
As my sinews hung to the stake, part of me dragged on,
Part pinned behind, and my bones snapping
As my spirit gasped itself out. There was no body part
You would have recognized, just one great wound.
So now, nymph, can you dare compare
Your calamity with mine? And then, too,
I saw the sunless world of the dead, and washed
My torn body in the waters of Phlegethon.
I would still be there, had not Apollo's son   580
Used his potent medicines to restore my life.
When Paion's healing herbs had revived me,
Much to the dismay of Dis, Diana cloaked me
In a thick mist, so that the sight of me
Would not arouse envy of my gift of life.
And in order for me to go on to be seen
Without fear of retribution, she made me look old
And without recognizable features.
She thought long about whether Crete or Delos
Should be my home, but decided against both   590
And located me here, telling me to drop the name
That would remind me of my horses, saying,
'You were Hippolytus, but now you are Virbius.'
From that time on I have lived in this grove,
A minor deity in the shadow of the godhead
Of my mistress, and one of her followers."

But Egeria's grief would not be comforted
By another's loss. She laid herself down
At the foot of a mountain and melted away
Into tears. Then Diana, moved by her sorrow   600
And fidelity, turned her body into a cool spring,
And her limbs into streams that never fail.

Cipus

The strangeness of it all touched the nymphs,
And the Amazon's son was no less amazed
Than the Tyrrhenian plowman was when he saw
A clod in his fields with a destiny.
First it moved, although no one had touched it.
Soon, no longer dirt, it assumed human form,
And then it opened its newly formed mouth
And spoke things that were to be. The natives   610
Called him Tages; he was the first to teach
The Etruscan race how to unlock the future.
And no less amazed than was Romulus
When he saw the shaft of a spear he had planted
On the Palatine Hill suddenly sprout leaves,
Its iron point in the earth now newly grown roots,
And no longer a spear but a pliant tree, giving
Unexpected shade for those who looked in wonder.
And no less amazed than Cipus when he looked
At his reflection in river water and saw   620
Horns growing out of his forehead. At first he thought
The reflection had fooled him, but lifting his hands
Up to his forehead again and again
He touched what he saw. Rather than stubbornly
Blaming his own eyes, he lifted them to heaven
And raised his arms like a conquering hero,
Crying,
          "Gods, whatever is portended here,
If it is good fortune, let it befall my country
And the people of Romulus; but if it is ill,

Let the ill happen to me."

                     And he built an altar   630
Out of green turf and offered fragrant sacrifice
To appease the gods; then, pouring libations of wine
He consulted the entrails of the slaughtered sheep
To see what they meant for him. When an Etruscan seer
Inspected them, he saw that great things were afoot
But not yet clear. But when he lifted his keen eyes
From the sheep's entrails to the horns on Cipus,
He said,

         "Hail to the king! For to you, Cipus,
To you and your horns, shall Latium's strongholds
And this place be loyal. Only do not delay,   640
Hasten to enter the open gates. Fate commands it.
Received in the city, you will be king
And wield the scepter in safety forever."

He started back, and keeping his frowning face
Away from the city walls, he said,

                        "May the gods
Keep such a fate far from me. Better to live in exile
Than have the Capitol see me crowned."

                           He spoke,
And promptly called an assembly of the Senate
And Roman people. First he hid his horns
In a wreath of laurel, emblem of peace,   650
Then he stood on a mound the army had built,
Uttered the ritual prayers to the ancient gods,
And said,

         "There is one person here who will be,
Unless you expel him from the city, your king.
Who this is I will tell you not by name
But by a sign: he has horns on his forehead.
The augur foretells that if he enters Rome
He will make you slaves. He could have entered
Through the open gates, but I held him off,
Though no one is closer to him than I.   660

Keep this man from the city, Romans,
Or, if he deserves it, bind him in heavy chains,
Or kill the fated tyrant and end your fear."

A murmur swept through the crowd like wind
Through a stand of pines, or waves on a distant sea.
But amid all the confusion of sounds
A single cry rose up: "Who is the man?"
And they looked at everyone's forehead
For the predicted horns. Then Cipus spoke again:
"You have him here." And taking off the wreath   670
(While the people tried to stop him) he showed them
The two horns that distinguished his temples. They all
Lowered their eyes and groaned aloud,
Then looked reluctantly—who could believe this?—
At that illustrious head. Then they replaced the wreath,
Unwilling to leave him unhonored for long.
And since you were forbidden to enter the walls,
The Senate honored you by giving you land,
As much as you could enclose with a team of oxen
From sunrise to sunset. As for the horns,   680
They engraved them on the bronze posts of the gates,
Their wondrous beauty enduring for ages.

Aesculapius

Reveal to me now, Muses, divine ones
Present to poets (for you know, and time
Does not cheat you) how did Aesculapius
Come to the island lapped by the deep Tiber
And be set among the deities of Rome?

Long ago a plague had infected Latium's air,
And the people wasted away with a ghastly disease.
Weary with caring for the dead, and seeing   690
That their human efforts and the physicians' arts
Accomplished nothing, they sought heaven's aid.

Coming to Delphi, the oracle of Phoebus
In the center of the earth, they prayed for a response
That would save them from their suffering and end
The great city's woes. The shrine and the laurel,
And the god's quiver itself, began to tremble,
And the tripod deep in the inner sanctum
Uttered words that made their hearts shake with fear:

"What you seek here, Romans, you should have sought   700
From a closer place. Seek now from some place closer.
Nor do you need Apollo to lessen your troubles,
But Apollo's son, under good auspices sought."

When the Senate in its wisdom heard the oracle,
They found out which city the god's son lived in
And sent an embassy to sail to Epidaurus.
When they had beached their ship on that shore
The ambassadors petitioned the council of elders
To give them the deity whose presence in Rome
Would stop the destruction of the Ausonian race,   710
As the oracle had distinctly pronounced.
The elders held conflicting opinions.
Some thought that the aid should not be denied,
But many advised that they should keep their god
And not surrender the source of their wealth
Or their deity. While they deliberated,
Dusk dispelled the lingering light, and when
Darkness spread shadows all over the world,
The god of healing appeared in your dreams,
O Roman ambassador, standing by your bed   720
Just as he appears in his own temple,
Holding in his left hand a rustic staff
And stroking his flowing beard with his right.
And with a calm presence he uttered these words:

"Have no fear! I will leave my shrine and come.
Just look at this serpent entwining my staff

And fix it in your mind. I will change myself
Into this form, but larger, and will seem as great
As celestial bodies should when they change."

The god left with his voice, and with voice and god   730
The dream left too, and as sleep slipped away
The kindly day dawned and put the stars to flight.
The council, still undecided, assembled
At the magnificent temple of the god in question
And begged him to reveal by signs from heaven
Where he himself wanted to have his home.
They had just finished when the golden god,
In the form of a serpent with a soaring crest,
Signaled his presence by hissing, and at his coming
He shook the statue, the altars, the doors,   740
The marble floor, and the golden rooftop.
Then, arching breast-high in the temple's court,
He surveyed the scene with eyes that flashed fire.
Everyone trembled with fear, but the priest,
His hair bound with a white woolen fillet,
Recognized the divinity and cried,

"The god! Behold the god! Be pure of heart
And observe reverent silence, all who are present.
And, O most beautiful one, may this vision
Be beneficial, and bless all your faithful."   750

The whole congregation worshipped the god,
Repeating the priest's prayer, and the Romans too
Were reverential in the words of their lips
And the meditations of their hearts.
His crest rippled as the god nodded to them
And hissed three times with his flickering tongue
To affirm his pledge. Then he glided down
The polished steps and turned to gaze one last time
Upon the ancient altars he was now leaving,
And he saluted the temple that had long been his home.   760
From there the huge serpent wound his way along

The flower-strewn ground, coiling through the city
To the curved walls of the harbor. Here he paused,
And, with a look of perfect serenity,
Seemed to dismiss his devout throng of followers
Before he boarded the Ausonian ship. It felt
The deity's burden, and the keel sank down
Under the god's weight. The Romans were overjoyed,
And, after sacrificing a bull on the shore,
Wreathed their ship with flowers and then cast off.   770
A light breeze pushed her on. The god rose high,
And resting his neck upon the curved stern,
Gazed down upon the indigo water. Favorable winds
Took him across the Ionian Sea, and the sixth dawn
Saw him reach Italy. He sailed past Juno's temple
On the shore of Lacinium, past Sylaceum,
Left Iapygia behind, and avoiding on portside
The Amphrisian rocks, and on the starboard
The Cocinthian cliffs, skirted Romethium,
Caulon and Narycia, got through the straits   780
Of Sicily and Pelorus' narrows, sailed past
The home of Hippotades, past Temesa
And its copper mines, then made for Leucosia
And the rose gardens of Paestum. From there
He rounded Capreae, Minerva's promontory,
And vineyards on the hills of Surrentum;
Then on to Herculaneum, on to Stabiae
And to Parthenope, the city of Naples,
Founded for pleasure, and from there to the temple
Of the Cumaean Sibyl. Next Baiae's hot springs   790
And the mastic groves of Liternum, and the mouth
Of the Volturnus River, churning with sand;
Then Sinuessa, with its flocks of white doves,
Grim Minturnae, and Caieta, where Aeneas
Buried his nurse; the home of Antiphates,
Marshy Trachas, the land of Circe also,
And the heavily sanded beach of Antium.
The sea was rough when the sailors put in here,
So the god unfolded his coils, and, gliding on

With great sinuous curves, entered the temple 800
Of his father, Apollo, there on the shore.
When the sea was calm again, Aesculapius,
Having enjoyed familial hospitality,
Left his father's altars and furrowed the beach
With his rasping scales, and climbing the rudder
Rested his head on the ship's high stern
Until he came to Castrum, the Tiber's mouth
And the sacred seats of Lavinium.
The entire population came to meet him,
A throng of mothers and fathers, and the virgins 810
Who tend your fires, O Trojan Vesta,
And they greeted the god with joy. As the ship
Floated upstream, incense burned and crackled
On a row of altars built on both banks.
The smoke scented the air; and the blood
Of sacrificial victims warmed the knives at their throats.
And now the ship entered the city of Rome,
Capital of the world. The serpent reared up,
And, resting his head on the top of the mast,
Looked around for a good site for his temple. 820
The river here splits into two branches,
Forming the area known as the Island,
Stretching two equal arms around the land between.
This is where the serpentine son of Phoebus
Disembarked from the Latian ship, and resuming
His celestial form he came to the Romans
As the god who brings health, and ended their sorrows.

The Deification of Caesar

This god came to our shrines from a foreign land,
But Caesar is a god in his own city.
Illustrious in war and peace, his conversion 830
Into a new constellation and into a comet
Was caused not as much by his triumph in war,
Or his civic achievements, or his rise to glory
As by his progeny. For in all Caesar has done,

Nothing is greater than this, that he became
The father of our emperor. For is it greater
To have subdued the island of Britain,
To have led his victorious fleet up the Nile,
To have added the rebellious Numidians,
Libyan Juba, and Pontus shouting "Mithridates!"   840
To the people of Romulus, to have celebrated
Numerous triumphs and deserved many more—
Than to have brought forth such a great man,
The ruler of the world, and your richest blessing,
O gods above, upon the human race?
And so, that his son not have a mortal father,
It was necessary for Caesar to become a god.

When the golden mother of Aeneas saw this,
And saw also that an armed conspiracy
Was plotting the death of the high priest, Caesar,   850
She paled, and cried to each god she met,

"Look at this mountain of treachery upon me,
And the insidious designs upon the one person
Who is all I have left of Dardanian Iulus.
Shall I alone be forever persecuted?
Wounded by Diomedes' Calydonian spear,
The walls of my poorly defended Troy
Falling around me, my son wandering in exile,
Battered on the sea, descending to the realm
Of the silent shades, waging war with Turnus,   860
Or to tell the truth, waging war with Juno!
My present fears do not permit reminiscing.
Look at the impious swords being sharpened.
Stop them! Ward off this crime! Do not extinguish
The fires of Vesta with the blood of her priest!"

Venus flung her anxieties through all of heaven,
But to no effect. Although the gods were moved,
They were powerless against the iron decrees
Of the ancient sisters. Still, they could give

Unmistakable portents of the grief to come.   870
They say that arms clashing in black storm clouds
And the frightening sound of horns in the sky
Forewarned men of the crime. The sun's face dimmed
And gave lurid light upon the troubled lands.
Firebrands were seen burning among stars in the sky,
And drops of blood rained down from the clouds.
The Morning Star darkened and turned dull red,
And the Moon's chariot was stained with blood.
The Stygian owl hooted its mournful omens
In a thousand places, and ivory statues   880
In thousands of places dripped with tears.
Dirges and threats are said to have been heard
In sacred groves. No sacrifices were auspicious.
The liver warned that terrible upheavals
Were about to begin, and its cleft lobe
Was found in the entrails. Dogs howled at night
In the market place, around men's houses
And the temples of the gods; silent shades
Walked abroad, and earthquakes shook the city.
But the gods' warnings were not able to overcome   890
The treachery of men and destiny unfolding.
Naked swords were brought into the sacred Curia,
For no other place in the entire city
Pleased the conspirators for this heinous slaughter.
Then indeed did the Cytherean beat her breast
And tried to hide the descendant of Aeneas
In the same kind of cloud that of old saved Paris
From murderous Menelaus, and that allowed
Aeneas himself to escape Diomedes' sword.
But then Jupiter spoke:
                           "Will you on your own,   900
My child, try to move insuperable Fate?
You may go yourself into the three sisters' house.
There will you see a massive account of the world
Inscribed on tablets of solid iron and brass
That fear in their eternal and total immunity
Neither conflict with heaven, nor lightning's wrath,

Nor any ruin or collapse whatsoever.
And there on everlasting adamant
You will find engraved your descendants' fates.
I have read these myself and made mental note   910
And will now relate them so that you will no longer
Be ignorant of the future.
                    The man, Cytherea,
For whom you struggle has completed the years
He owes to the earth. You will bring about
His entrance to heaven and his worship in temples,
You and his son. He will succeed to the name
And will alone bear the burden placed upon him,
And with ourselves as his allies in war,
Will be his slain father's heroic avenger.
Under his command besieged Mutina   920
Will sue for peace; Pharsalia will feel his power;
The fields of Philippi in Macedonia
Will be drenched in blood again; Sextus Pompeius
Will be defeated off Sicily's coast;
And Cleopatra, the Egyptian mistress
Of a Roman general, her faith misplaced
In their alliance, will fall before the son of Caesar
Despite all her vain threats to transfer our Capitol
To her Canopus.
              I will not mention
The barbarous nations on both shores of the ocean,   930
But every habitable land on earth
Will be under his sway, and the ocean too!
And when peace has been bestowed on all these lands
He will turn his mind to the rights of citizens
And establish laws most just, and by his example
Guide the way men behave. Looking to the future
And generations to come, he will pass on his name
And his burdens as well to the son born to him
And to his chaste wife. And not until he is old
And his years equal his meritorious actions   940
Will he go to heaven and his familial stars.
In the meantime, catch up this Caesar's soul

As it leaves his slain body and make it a star,
So that the divine Julius may ever look forth
Upon our Capitol and Forum from his high temple."

He had scarcely finished when kindly Venus,
Standing in the senate house, invisible to all,
Caught her Caesar's soul as it left his body,
And not allowing it to diffuse in the air,
She bore it upward to the stars of heaven.   950
And while she carried it she felt it glow
And grow warm, and sent it forth from her bosom.
It soared higher than the moon, trailing fire
Behind it, and shone as a star. And now he sees
All his son's good deeds and confesses that
They are greater than his own, and he rejoices
To be surpassed by him. And though the son forbids
His own deeds to be ranked above his father's,
Fame, free and obedient to no one's command,
Puts him forward, only in this opposing his will.   960
So does Atreus yield to his son Agamemnon,
So Aegeus to Theseus, and Peleus to Achilles,
And to cite last an instance that suits them both,
So too is Saturn a lesser god than Jove.
And as Jupiter is in control of high heaven
And the realms of the triple world, the earth
Is under Augustus, as both ruler and sire.

O gods, I pray: comrades of Aeneas,
Before whom fire and sword gave way;
Gods of Italy, and you, Romulus,   970
The father of our city; and Mars,
Invincible sire of Romulus; Vesta,
Revered among Caesar's household gods;
Apollo, worshipped along with Caesar's Vesta;
Jupiter exalted on Tarpeia's rock;
And all other gods to whom it is right and just
For a poet to pray:
                May the day come late

And after our own time, when Augustus,
Abandoning the world he rules, enters
High heaven and hears our prayers from above.   980

Envoi

And now I have completed my work,
Which cannot be undone by the wrath of Jove,
By fire or sword, or corrosive time. That final day,
Which has power only over my body,
May come when it will and end my uncertain
Span of years. The better part of me
Will be borne forever beyond the high stars,
And my name will never die. Wherever Rome
Extends its power over the conquered world
I will be on men's lips, and if a sacred poet   990
Has any power to prophesy the truth,
Throughout the ages I will live on in fame.

Catalog of Transformations

Though it is necessarily interpretive and thus non-definitive, this catalog aims to be as comprehensive and as specific as possible, serving to give the reader a detailed sense of Ovid's expansive view of metamorphosis in his mythological world. Though many transformations fit easily into the chosen categories, some are problematic and have been listed in more than one category (e.g., Acis is listed as both a river and a river god); and several are listed as sui generis (e.g., Philemon's and Baucis' house becoming a temple). The multiple natural transformations referenced in Pythagoras' speech in Book 15 have been subsumed under a single entry.

Line	From	To	Story
Disguise and Shape-Shifting, Temporary Transformations			
Gods Disguised as Humans			
1.218	Jove	a man	Lycaon
1.721–24	Mercury	a shepherd	Io
3.293–300	Juno	Beroë	Jupiter and Semele
4.244–45	Sun God	Eurynome	Leucothoë and the Sun
6.32–33	Minerva	an old woman	Arachne
6.51–52	Minerva as old woman	Minerva as goddess	Arachne
6.123	Jove	Amphitryon	Arachne
6.125	Jove	a shepherd	Arachne
6.134–35	Apollo	a farmer	Arachne
6.136–37	Apollo	a shepherd	Arachne
8.708	Jove	a man	Philemon and Baucis
8.709–10	Mercury	a man	Philemon and Baucis
11.234	Apollo and Neptune	two men	Laomedon

Line	From	To	Story
11.364	Apollo	an old woman	Daedalion and Chione
11.736–39	Morpheus	various humans	Ceyx and Alcyone
11.752	Morpheus	Ceyx	Ceyx and Alcyone

Gods Disguised as Other Gods

2.474	Jove	Diana	Callisto
6.128	Neptune	Enipeus	Arachne and Minerva

Gods Disguised as Animals

2.941–51	Jove	a bull	Jupiter and Europa
3.1	Jove as bull	Jove as god	Jupiter and Europa
5.382	Jove	a ram	Song of Typhoeus
5.384	Apollo	a crow	Song of Typhoeus
5.384	Bacchus	a goat	Song of Typhoeus
5.385	Diana	a cat	Song of Typhoeus
5.385	Juno	a heifer	Song of Typhoeus
5.386	Venus	a fish	Song of Typhoeus
5.386	Mercury	an ibis	Song of Typhoeus
6.115–16	Jove	a bull	Arachne and Minerva
6.119	Jove	an eagle	Arachne and Minerva
6.120	Jove	a swan	Arachne and Minerva
6.121–22	Jove	a satyr (see also Fict.Creatures)	Arachne and Minerva
6.125–26	Jove	a snake	Arachne and Minerva
6.126–27	Neptune	a bull	Arachne and Minerva
6.129	Neptune	a ram	Arachne and Minerva
6.130–31	Neptune	a horse	Arachne and Minerva
6.131–32	Neptune	a bird	Arachne and Minerva
6.133	Neptune	a dolphin	Arachne and Minerva
6.135	Apollo	a hawk	Arachne and Minerva
6.136	Apollo	a lion	Arachne and Minerva

Line	From	To	Story
6.139–40	Saturn	a horse	Arachne and Minerva
9.68–69	Acheloüs	a snake	Acheloüs and Hercules
9.84–85	Acheloüs as snake	a bull	Acheloüs and Hercules
10.165–67	Jove	an eagle	Jupiter and Ganymede
11.288	Thetis	a bird	Peleus and Thetis
11.290	Thetis as tree	a tigress	Peleus and Thetis
11.740–41	Icelos or Phobetor	birds, beasts, and snakes	Ceyx and Alcyone
15.737–41	Aesculapius	serpent	Aesculapius

Humans Disguised as Other Humans

7.794–97	Cephalus	a stranger	Procris and Cephalus
8.961–63	Erysichthon's daughter	a fisherman	Erysichthon
8.980–81	Erysichthon's daughter, as fisherman	a girl	Erysichthon
14.738–53	Vertumnus	various disguises, esp. old woman	Pomona and Vertumnus

Other Disguise and Shape-Shifting

2.9	Proteus	any form	Phaëthon and Phoebus
5.13	Jove	a golden shower	Perseus and Phineus
6.124	Jove	a golden shower	Arachne and Minerva
6.124	Jove	fire	Arachne and Minerva
8.824–31	Proteus	any form	Erysichthon
8.981–84	Erysichthon's daughter	any form	Erysichthon
11.289	Thetis as bird	a tree	Peleus and Thetis
11.742–43	Phantasos	inanimate things	Ceyx and Alcyone
12.640–43	Periclymenus	any form	Hercules and Periclymenus

Line	From	To	Story
12.644–47	Periclymenus	an eagle	Hercules and Periclymenus

Transformations into Animals

Humans and Gods Becoming Birds

Line	From	To	Story
2.411–20	Cygnus	the swan	Phaëthon and Phoebus
2.648–57	Coroneus' daughter	a crow	Apollo and Coronis
2.658–66	Nyctimene	the night owl	Apollo and Coronis
4.55–57	Decretis' daughter	a white pigeon	The Daughters of Minyas
4.621–22	some Theban women	sea birds	Juno and the Theban Women
5.627–36	Ascalaphus	the screech owl	Hymn to Ceres
5.776–87	Pierides	magpies	Muses and the Daughters of Pierus
6.100–103	Pygmy queen	the crane	Arachne and Minerva
6.104–9	Antigone	the stork	Arachne and Minerva
6.770–76	Philomela	the nightingale	Procne and Philomela
6.770–76	Procne	the swallow	Procne and Philomela
6.776–80	Tereus	the hoopoe	Procne and Philomela
7.412–13	Alcidamas' daughter	a dove	Jason and Medea
7.423–25	Cygnus	the swan	Jason and Medea
7.428–29	Combe	a bird	Jason and Medea
7.430–31	Calaurea's king and queen	a bird	Jason and Medea
7.437	Eumelus' son	a bird	Jason and Medea
7.447–50	Phene, Periphas, and Alcyone	birds	Jason and Medea
7.518–21	Arne	the jackdaw	Minos' Embassy to Aegina

Line	From	To	Story
8.175–78	Nisus	the osprey	Nisus and Scylla
8.179–83	Scylla	the ciris	Nisus and Scylla
8.295–303	Daedalus' nephew	the partridge	Daedalus and Icarus
8.620–25	Meleager's sisters	Meleagrides or guinea hens	Meleager and the Calydonian Boar
11.398–405	Daedalion	a hawk	Daedalion and Chione
11.843–62	Ceyx and Alcyone	halcyon birds	Ceyx and Alcyone
11.908–22	Aesacus	a diver bird	Aesacus and Hesperia
12.169–72	Cygnus	the swan	Cygnus and Achilles
12.601–4	Caeneus	a golden bird	Cygnus and Achilles
13.812–13	Anius' daughters	doves	The Daughters of Anius
13.862–63	King Molossus' sons	birds	Galatea and Polyphemus
14.450–60	Picus	the woodpecker	Picus
14.577–91	Acmon, Lycus, Idas, Rhexenor, Nycteus, Abas, and others	swanlike birds	Picus

Other Bird Transformations

Line	From	To	Story
1.775–77	plain peacock	eyed peacock	Pan and Syrinx
2.707–8	white raven	black raven	Apollo and Coronis
13.728–45	Memnon's funeral smoke/ ashes	Memnonides	Memnon
14.663–70	Ardea's ruins/ ashes	heron	Ardea

Humans and Gods Becoming Other Animals

Line	From	To	Story
1.238–46	Lycaon	wolf	Lycaon
1.649–51	Io	cow	Io
2.532–43	Callisto	bear	Callisto

Line	From	To	Story
2.739–55	Ocyrhoë	horse	Ocyrhoë
3.203–13	Actaeon	stag	Diana and Actaeon
3.744–60	Medon, Lycabas, Lybis, and other fishermen	dolphins	Pentheus and Bacchus
4.53–55	Decretis	a fish	The Daughters of Minyas
4.57–59	small boys	a fish	The Daughters of Minyas
4.57–60	naiad	a fish	The Daughters of Minyas
4.444–54	daughters of Minyas	bats	The Daughters of Minyas Become Bats
4.636–43	Cadmus	a snake	Cadmus and Harmonia
4.657–68	Harmonia	a snake	Cadmus and Harmonia
5.525–33	Stellio	the newt	Hymn to Ceres
5.763–65	Lyncus	the lynx	Hymn to Ceres
6.157–62	Arachne	the spider	Arachne and Minerva
6.421–34	Lycian peasants	frogs	Latona and the Lycians
7.434–36	Cephisus' grandson	a seal	Jason and Medea
9.356–64	Galanthis	the weasel	Alcmena and Galanthis
10.255–58	Cerastae	bulls	The Cerastae
10.799–805	Atalanta and Hippomenes	lions	Atalanta and Hippomenes
13.684–90	Hecuba	a bitch	Hecuba
14.106–16	Cercopes	monkeys	Aeneas Comes to Cumae
14.319–25	Macareus and Ulysses's crew	pigs	Aeneas Comes to Cumae
14.481–83	Picus' men	beasts	Picus

Line	From	To	Story

Other Animal Transformations

Line	From	To	Story
4.685–88	drops of Medusa's blood	poisonous vipers	Perseus and Andromeda
4.898–99	Medusa's hair	snakes	Perseus and Andromeda
5.300–301	Medusa's blood	Pegasus (see also Fict. Creatures)	Pegasus and the Spring of the Muses
7.401–2	ox	deer	Jason and Medea

Animals Becoming Humans and Gods

Line	From	To	Story
1.794–802	Io as cow	Io as girl	Pan and Syrinx
7.698–715	ants	Myrmidons	The Myrmidons
14.344–50	Macareus and Ulysses' crew as pigs	men	Aeneas
15.824–27	Aesculapius as serpent	Aesculapius as god	Aesculapius

Inanimate Objects Becoming Humans and Gods

Line	From	To	Story
1.417–31	stones	men and women	Deucalion and Pyrrha
3.110–23	dragon teeth	armed men	Cadmus and the Earthborn People
4.317	storm	Curetes	Clytië
7.144–52	dragon teeth	armed men	Jason and Medea
7.438–40	mushrooms	Corinthian men	Jason and Medea
10.312–22	Pygmalion's statue	girl	Pygmalion
13.840–42	Orion's daughters' ashes	Coronae	The Daughters of Orion
14.636–45	Aeneas' ships	naiads	Aeneas' Ships
15.603–11	dirt clod	Tages	Cipus

Line	From	To	Story

Humans Becoming Gods

Line	From	To	Story
4.597–601	Ino and Melicerta	Leucothoë and Palaemon	Athamas and Ino
9.283–304	Hercules	a god (see also Stars)	The Death of Hercules
13.1055–68	Acis	a river god (see also Water)	Galatea and Polyphemus
13.1120–41 Transformation	Glaucus	a river god	Glaucus'
14.691–99	Aeneas	Indiges	The Death of Aeneas
14.949–53	Romulus	Quirinus	Romulus
14.976–81	Hersilia	Hora	Hersilia
15.579–93	Hippolytus	Virbius	Hippolytus and Egeria
15.948–54	Julius Caesar	a god (see also Stars)	The Deification of Caesar
15.977–80	Augustus Caesar	a god (see also Stars)	The Deification of Caesar
15.986–92	Ovid	a god	Envoi

Transformations into Stone

Humans and Gods Becoming Stone

Line	From	To	Story
2.788–90	Battus	the snitch-stone	Mercury and Battus
2.913–24	Aglauros	a dark statue	Mercury, Herse, and Aglauros
4.309–11	Daphnis' beloved shepherd from Ida	a stone	Clytië and the Sun
4.315	Celmis	adamant	Clytië
4.611–21	some Theban women	a stone	Juno and the Theban Women
4.730–38	Atlas	a mountain (see also Flora)	Perseus and Andromeda

Line	From	To	Story
4.775–76	men seen by Medusa	a stone	Perseus and Andromeda
5.207–39	Theseclus, Ampyx, Nileus, Eryx, Aconteus Astyages, 200 men	stone	Perseus and Andromeda
5.264–70	Phineus	a stone	Perseus and Andromeda
5.288–89	Polydectes	a stone	Perseus and Andromeda
6.97–99	Rhodope and Haemus	mountains	Arachne and Minerva
6.110–12	Cinyras' daughters	temple steps	Arachne and Minerva
6.341–54	Niobe	weeping marble	Niobe and Latona
10.67–70	nameless man who saw Cerberus chained	a stone	Orpheus and Eurydice
10.71–74	Olenus and Lethaea	stones	Orpheus and Eurydice
10.260–65	daughters of Propoetus	flint	The Daughters of Propoetus
13.860	judge in gods' debate	a stone	Galatea and Polyphemus
14.871–75	Anaxarete	a statue	Iphis and Anaxarete

Other Stone Transformations

3.435	Echo's bones	stone	Echo and Narcissus
4.835–43	seaweed tendrils	coral	Perseus and Andromeda
4.775–76	animals seen by Medusa	stone	Perseus and Andromeda
7.399–400	Pitane dragon	stone	Jason and Medea
7.496–99	Sciron's bones	Sciron cliffs	Hymn to Theseus

Line	From	To	Story
7.874–75	Lailaps and monster	marble statues	Procris and Cephalus
11.61–63	serpent	stone	The Death of Orpheus
11.472–76	mad wolf	marble	Daedalion and Chione
12.27–29	dark blue serpent	stone	The Greeks at Aulis
14.78–80	Scylla as monster	rock	Glaucus, Circe, Scylla
14.651	Alcinous' vessel	stone	Aeneas' Ships
15.52–54	black pebbles	white pebbles	Numa

Transformations into Flora

Humans and Gods Becoming Trees

1.575–83	Daphne	the laurel tree	Apollo and Daphne
2.381–404	Phaethousa, Lampetië, and other Heliades	trees	Phaëthon and Phoebus
8.805–13	Philemon and Baucis	a double-trunked tree	Philemon and Baucis
9.391–94	Lotis	the lotus tree	Dryope
9.395–445	Dryope	the lotus tree	Dryope
10.106–9	Attis	a pine tree	Orpheus and Eurydice
10.141–46	Cyparissus	the cypress tree	Cyparissus
10.560–70	Myrrha	the myrrh tree	Myrrha
11.74–91	murdering Bacchants	oak trees	The Death of Orpheus
14.607–12	Apulian shepherd	the olive tree	The Apulian Shepherd

Humans and Gods Becoming Flowers and Plants

1.756–59	Syrinx	reeds	Pan and Syrinx

Line	From	To	Story
3.559–61	Narcissus	the Narcissus flower	Echo and Narcissus
4.283–87	Leucothoë	frankincense	Clytië and the Sun
4.297–302	Clytië	a violet-like flower	Clytië and the Sun
4.318–19	Crocus	the crocus flower	Clytië and the Sun
4.318–19	Smilax	the smilax flower	Clytië and the Sun
10.219–30	Hyacinthus	the hyacinth	Apollo and Hyacinthus
10.834–45	Menthe	the mint plant	Venus and Adonis
10.839–46	Adonis	the anemone	Venus and Adonis

Other Flora Transformations

Line	From	To	Story
4.177–85	white mulberries	dark mulberries	Pyramus and Thisbe
4.431–34	weaving implements	grape leaves, vines, and fruit	The Daughters of Minyas Become Bats
4.732–33	Atlas' hair and beard	trees (see also Stone)	Perseus and Andromeda
7.467–70	Cerberus' drool	aconite	Jason and Medea
10.94–109	stationary trees	ambulatory trees	Orpheus and Eurydice
13.476–80	Ajax's blood	the hyacinth	The Contest for Achilles' Arms
15.614–18	Romulus' spear	tree	Cipus

Transformations into Water

Humans and Gods Becoming Water

Line	From	To	Story
5.493–507	Cyane	water	Hymn to Ceres
5.728–32	Arethusa	a stream	Arethusa and Alpheus

Line	From	To	Story
5.732–35	Alpheus	a stream	Arethusa and Alpheus
7.425–27	Hyrië	a pool	Jason and Medea
9.761–62	Byblis	a spring	Byblis and Her Brother
13.1055–68	Acis	river (see also Humans becoming Gods)	Galatea and Polyphemus
15.597–602	Egeria	a spring and streams	Hippolytus and Egeria

Other Water Transformations

Line	From	To	Story
4.420–24	regular pool	an enervating pool	Salmacis and Hermaphroditus
6.452–57	tears shed for Marsyas	Marsyas stream	Marsyas and Apollo

Transformations of Earth

Line	From	To	Story
1.32–89	Chaos	Earth/Order	Origin of the World
1.115–26	Golden Age	Silver Age	The Four Ages
1.127–29	Silver Age	Bronze Age	The Four Ages
1.129–53	Bronze Age	Iron Age	The Four Ages
1.274–323	dry Earth	flooded Earth	The Flood
1.336–60	flooded Earth	dry Earth	Deucalion and Pyrrha
1.432–53	wet, lifeless soil	dry, fertile, life–filled soil	Deucalion and Pyrrha
2.228–95	normal Earth	scorched Earth	Phaëthon and Apollo
5.552–59	fruitful Sicily	wasteland Sicily	Hymn to Ceres
7.408–10	sights seen by Telchines	blight	Jason and Medea
7.576–69	fruitful Aegina	wasteland Aegina	The Plague

Transformations of Gender

Line	From	To	Story
3.353–54	male Tiresias	female Tiresias	Tiresias

Line	From	To	Story
3.356–59	female Tiresias	male Tiresias	Tiresias
4.313–14	Sithon	"sometimes a woman, sometimes a man"	Clytië and the Sun
4.410–15	Salmacis/ Hermaphroditus	Hermaphrodite	Salmacis and Hermaphroditus
9.903–8	female Iphis	male Iphis	Iphis and Ianthe
12.238–41	Caenis	Caeneus	Cygnus

Transformations in Age

7.322–29	old Aeson	young Aeson	Jason and Medea
7.330–32	Bacchus' old nurses	young nurses	Jason and Medea
7.355–58	old ram	young lamb	Jason and Medea
9.450–53	old Iolaus	young Iolaus	Iolaus and the Bickering of the Gods
9.471–73	Callirhoë's infant sons	warriors	Iolaus and the Bickering of the Gods
14.158–75	young Sibyl infant sons	old Sibyl	Phoebus and the Sibyl of Cumae

Transformations into Stars

2.564–67	Callisto as bear and Arcas	constellations	Callisto
8.214–20	Ariadne's tiara	constellation	Minos and the Minotaur
9.283–304	Hercules	constellation (see also Humans becoming Gods)	The Death of Hercules

Line	From	To	Story
15.948–54	Julius Caesar	comet (see also Humans becoming Gods)	The Deification of Caesar
15.977–80	Augustus Caesar	star (see also Humans becoming Gods)	The Deification of Caesar

Partial Transformations

Line	From	To	Story
5.642–49	Acheloüs' daughters	sirens (see also Fict. Creatures)	Hymn to Ceres
6.822–27	Boreas' sons	winged men	Boreas and Orithyia
11.201–6	Midas' human ears	ass's ears	Midas
14.62–72	Scylla	a monster (see also Fict. Creatures)	Glaucus, Circe, Scylla
15.619–24	Cipus' human head	horned head	Cipus

Transformations into Fictitious Creatures

Line	From	To	Story
5.301	Medusa's blood	Pegasus (see also Animals	Pegasus and the Spring of the Muses
5.642–49	Acheloüs' daughters	Sirens (see also Part. Changes)	Hymn to Ceres
6.121–22	Jove	satyr (see also Disguise)	Arachne and Minerva
14.62–72	Scylla	monster (see also Part. Changes)	Glaucus, Circe, Scylla

Transformations into Bodiless Entities

Line	From	To	Story
3.432–37	Echo	voice only	Echo and Narcissus

Line	From	To	Story
14.175–77	Old Sibyl of Cumae	voice only	Phoebus and the Sibyl of Cumae
14.499–500	Canens	air/nothingness	Picus

Transformations through Enchanted Touch

11.116–34	all that Midas touches	gold	Midas
11.161–66	Pactolus river	a golden river	Midas
13.788–89	all that Anius' daughters touch	food and wine	The Daughters of Anius

Humans and Gods Becoming Islands

8.671–76	five nymphs	Echinades	Acheloüs and the Echinades
8.687–89	Hippodamas' daughter	Peremele	Acheloüs and the Echinades

Other Transformations

8.227	Daedalus	"transformed nature"	Daedalus and Icarus
8.788–92	Philemon and Baucis' house	Temple	Philemon and Baucis
12.701–709	Achilles as man/body	Achilles as glory/legend	The Death of Achilles
15.160–494	"the sky and everything beneath / Changes form, as does the earth and all upon it"		The Teachings of Pythagoras
15.179–83	Euphorbus	Pythagoras	The Teachings of Pythagoras

Glossary of Names

The following glossary includes names of major characters and important place names, some of which correspond to alternative, synonymous names (in parentheses) that occur in the text. For occurrences of such names, see the entry for the corresponding name.

Aces'tes: son of the river god Crinisus, friend of Aeneas; Trojan founder of Segesta, 14.92

Achae'a: northern Peloponnesian region associated with Greece; often refers to the Greeks, 4.672, 5.359, 5.765, 12.89, 13.33, 13.101, 13.340, 13.532, 15.320

Achaemen'ides: member of Odysseus' crew. Accidentally left by Odysseus in flight from the Cyclops; rescued by Aeneas, 14.186, 14.190, 14.192

Ache'loüs: river god with the ability to change form. Father of the Sirens. Host of Theseus; challenger of Hercules, 5.638, 8.694, 9.2, 9.95, 9.103, 9.471

Achil'les: son of Peleus and Thetis; most prominent Greek warrior. Killed by Paris during the Trojan War, 8.355, 9.3, 12.92, 12.98, 12.99, 12.103, 12.111, 12.118, 12.122, 12.126, 12.145, 12.155, 12.165, 12.177, 12.192, 12.193, 12.198, 12.208, 12.224, 12.425, 12.663, 12.676, 12.690, 12.696, 12.705, 13.34, 13.122, 13.127, 13.139, 13.151, 13.152, 13.155, 13.156, 13.185, 13.187, 13.193, 13.214, 13.329, 13.340,. 13.361, 13.365, 13.528, 13.536, 13.541, 13.600, 13.604, 13.699, 13.719, 15.962

A'cis: son of Faunus and Symaethis. Killed by Polyphemus over love for Galatea, 13.900, 13.907, 13.944, 13.1026, 13.1042, 13.1053, 13.1056, 13.1066

Acoe'tes: Etruscan sailor and devotee of Bacchus. Captured by Pentheus; rescued by Bacchus, 3.641, 3.770

Acris'ius: father of Danaë and grandfather of Perseus; king of Argos who resisted Bacchic worship, 3.617, 4.672, 4.678, 5.80, 5.275

Acrop'olis: citadel of Athens and site of Parthenon, 2.803, 7.447

461

Actae'on: son of Autonoë and grandson of Cadmus. Killed by his hounds after seeing Diana as she was bathing, 3.148, 3.153, 3.217, 3.241, 3.256, 3.796, 3.797

Ac'tium: famous promontory of Epirus, site of naval battle between Octavian and Mark Antony, 13.858

Ado'nis: born of his grandfather Cinyras and his sister Myrrha; beloved by Venus. Memorialized as a flower, 10.593, 10.612, 10.624, 10.778, 10.809, 10.821, 10.832, 10.838

Ae'acus: son of Jupiter and Aegina; pious king of the island Aegina, 7.526, 7.531, 7.536, 7.547, 7.554, 7.559, 7.569, 7.731, 7.883, 7.958, 8.4, 9.499, 9.504, 11.268, 11.291, 12.702, 13.27, 13.30, 13.38, 13.608

Aegae'on: a sea god, son of Pontus or Neptune, 2.10

Aegi'na: mother of Aeacus by Jupiter, who carried her away. Her son named an island off the coast of Argolis after her, 6.124, 7.527, 7.538, 7.672

Aene'as: Trojan hero, son of Venus and Anchises; father of Ascanius. Legendary founder of Rome. Led Trojan survivors to Italy, where he was deified as Indiges, 13.751, 13.754, 13.802, 13.821, 14.85, 14.91, 14.117, 14.134, 14.18, 14.185, 14.197, 14.201, 14.283, 14.512, 14.521, 14.529, 14.671, 14.679, 14.692, 14.694, 15.475, 15.488, 15.794, 15.848, 15.896, 15.899, 15.96

Aet'na: see Etna, 5.407, 5.512, 13.924, 13.1034, 13.1045, 14.2, 14.187, 14.218, 15.370, 15.379

Aeto'lia: a country in middle Greece, 14.614

Ae'olus: son of Hippotes; father of Athamas. Warden of the winds, who gave Ulysses the gift of the winds in a bag, 1.274, 4.739, 6.787, 9.582, 11.507, 11.522, 11.667, 11.861, 14.98, 14.254, 14.265

Aes'acus: son of Priam and the nymph Alexiroë. Pursued the nymph Hesperia until she was killed by a snakebite, 11.877, 12.1

Aescula'pius: son of Apollo and Coronis; a mortal deified as the god of healing. Associated with the serpent, 15.685, 15.802

Agamem'non: son of Atreus; Mycenaean king, leader of the Greek forces at Troy. Sacrificed his daughter Iphigenia to appease Diana; killed by Clytemnestra, 12.36, 12.715, 12.718, 13.219, 13.221, 13.226, 13.263, 13.280, 13.441, 13.540, 13.790, 15.961

Aga've: daughter of Cadmus. Killed her son Pentheus during a Bacchic frenzy, 3.802

Age'nor: king of Sidon; son of Neptune. Father of Europa and Cadmus, 2.952, 3.8, 3.86, 3.96, 3.273, 3.334, 4.623, 4.866

Aglau′ros: jealous daughter of Cecrops; sister of Herse and Pandrosos, 2.625, 2.824, 2.835, 2.875, 2.898, 2.924

A′jax: (1: "Lesser Ajax") son of Oileus and Greek leader at Troy. Struck down by Minerva for violating Priam's daughter Cassandra in Minerva's temple, 12.714, 13.432, 14.545; (2) Greek leader at Troy and son of Telamon; half brother of Teucer and cousin of Achilles. Committed suicide when Ulysses was rewarded with the armor of Achilles, 12.716, 13.2, 13.20, 13.31, 13.112, 13.157, 13.167, 13.181, 13.188, 13.196, 13.234, 13.265, 13.281, 13.306, 13.331, 13.369, 13.396, 13.410, 13.412, 13.463, 13.471

Alci′nous: Phaeacian king; gave Ulysses passage home, 14.651

Alcith′oë: blasphemous daughter of Minyas, 4.1, 4.307

Alcme′na: mother of Hercules by Jupiter; wife of Amphitryon, 6.123, 9.27, 9.308, 9.316, 9.352, 9.447

Alcy′one: daughter of Aeolus, husband of Ceyx. Transformed into a kingfisher, 7.450, 11.448, 11.489, 11.498, 11.526, 11.535, 11.543, 11.553, 11.631, 11.632, 11.654, 11.684, 11.727, 11.761, 11.771, 11.774, 11.787, 11.842, 11.859

Aloi′dae: the twin giants Otus and Ephialtes, sons of Neptune and Iphimedeia, 6.128

Alphe′us: primary river of Elis. River god; loved Arethusa, 2.273, 5.560, 5.791, 5.726

Althe′a: wife of Oeneus. Killed her son Meleager by burning the log that contained his soul, 8.504, 8.511, 8.540, 8.583

Am′athus: a city in Cyprus, a sacred site of Venus, 10.234, 10.611

Ambra′cia: a town in Epirus, 13.857

Am′mon: a Middle Eastern ram deity associated with Jupiter, 4.747, 5.20, 5.128, 5.383, 15.336

A′mor: (See Cupid) 1.501, 4.851

Amphiara′us: Greek seer. Sent to his death by his wife, Eriphyle, who had been bribed with a golden necklace. His maddened son Alcmaeon was killed by Phegeus, 8.363, 9.461

Amphitri′te: sea goddess wife of Neptune, mother of Triton, 1.13

Ana′pis: a river god of Sicily; husband of the nymph Cyane, 5.483

Anaxar′ete: girl of noble birth. Rejected the love of Iphis; turned to stone, 14.805, 14.827, 14.864

Anchi′ses: father of the hero Aeneas by Venus; king of the Dardanians, 9.486, 13.774, 13.820, 14.136

Andro'meda: daughter of Cassiopeia and Cepheus. Rescued from chains by Perseus and placed in the stars by Minerva. A northern constellation, 4.748, 4.829, 4.850

An'dros: an island of the Cyclades, 7.522, 13.783, 13.798, 13.802

A'nius: Delian king, priest of Apollo. Father of a prophetic son and four daughters gifted with a touch that turned everything into grain, wine, and olives, 13.764, 13.777, 13.818

Antae'us: Libyan giant, son of Neptune and Ge; rejuvenated by the touch of his mother. Hercules defeated the giant in a wrestling match by holding him off the ground as they fought, 9.207

Ante'nor: Trojan elder; host and protector of Ulysses and Menelaus when they came to retrieve Helen before the Trojan War, 13.243

Anti'ope: mother of twins Amphion and Zethus, punishers of Dirce, 6.122

Anti'phates: ruler of the Laestrygonians, a cannibalistic race of giants, 14.268, 14.272, 14.285, 15.795

Ao'nia: a region of Boeotia containing the mountains Cithaeron and Helicon, sacred to the Muses, 5.388, 7.845, 12.31, 13.823

Apol'lo (Phoe'bus, [occasionally] the Sun): son of Jupiter and Latona, twin brother of Diana. Associated with the oracle at Delphi; god of archery, prophecy, youth, and medicine; occasionally identified, by way of the epithet Phoebus, with the sun god Helius, who is himself sometimes referred to by the name of his father, Hyperion, 1.467, 1.470, 1.494, 1.511, 1.584, 1.600, 2.608, 2.671, 3.10, 3.21, 3.139, 3.460, 5.384, 6.235, 6.299, 7.407, 7.435, 8.16, 8.400, 9.375, 9.508, 9.521, 10.207, 10.223, 10.228, 11.8, 11.61, 11.176, 11.190, 11.221, 11.228, 11.232, 11.3590, 11.364, 11.397, 12.669, 12.671, 13.208, 13.493, 13.603, 13.763, 13.764, 13.784, 13.858, 14.154, 15.580, 15.702, 15.703, 15.801, 15.974

A'ra: southern constellation of the Altar, 2.147

Arach'ne: a famous weaver from Lydia. She lost a weaving contest with Minerva, who transformed her into a spider, 6.6, 6.14, 6.40, 6.54, 6.115, 6.133, 6.145, 6.165

Arca'dia: a central Peloponnesian country, 1.224, 1.739, 2.266, 2.450, 2.514, 2.557, 3.221, 8.362, 8.365, 8.442, 8.482, 9.217, 15.353

Ar'cas: son of Jupiter and Callisto, 2.524, 2.554, 2.559

Ares: See Mars

Arethu'sa: nymph of Elis pursued by Alpheus; transformed into a spring by Diana, 5.474, 5.560, 5.660, 5.690, 5.721, 5.741

Ar'gos: a city in the eastern Peloponnesian region of Argolis, 1.639, 2.262, 2.585, 3.619, 4.674, 6.474, 15.22, 15.182, 15.302

Ar'gus: monstrous son of Arestor. Guarded Io until killed by Mercury, 1.665, 1.666, 1.677, 1.710, 1.718, 1.735, 1.768, 1.773, 2.596

Ariad'ne: daughter of Minos; deserted by Theseus after helping him escape the Labyrinth. The crown constellation, Corona Borealis, was placed in the sky by her rescuer Bacchus in her honor, 8.207.

Aric'ia: a Latian town, southeast of Rome, 15.527

Asca'nius (Iu'lus): son of Aeneas and Creusa; founder of Alba Longa, 13.758, 14.700

Assyr'ia: ancient Middle Eastern empire of Mesopotamia, 5.69, 15.428

Astrae'a: goddess of justice, 1.152, 14.631

Asty'anax: infant son of Hector and Andromache. Killed by the Greeks during the fall of Troy, 13.500

Atalan'ta: daughter of Schoenus; huntress of Arcadia. Married Hippomenes and transformed with him into a lion, 8.365, 8.431, 8.481, 8.486, 10.644, 10.651, 10.687

Ath'amas: son of Aeolus; king of Orchomenus. Husband of Ino. Driven mad by Juno and the Furies, 3.623, 4.460, 4.514, 4.515, 4.519, 4.535, 4.538, 4.545, 4.555, 4.563, 4.569

Athe'na: (See Minerva) 5.290, 6.52, 12.178, 12.421

Athens: Greek city, sacred to Minerva, 2.885, 5.754, 6.80, 6.481, 6.487, 6.510, 7.448, 7.538, 7.545, 7.560, 7.796, 8.306, 8.626, 15.466

A'thos: a mountain in Macedonia, 2.236, 9.643

At'las: son of the Titan Iapetus; father of the Pleiades and Calypso. Holds up the sky, 1.732, 2.323, 2.829, 4.698, 4.700, 4.713, 4.715, 4.717, 4.726, 4.731, 4.868, 6.197, 9.305, 15.167

Augus'tus: (Gaius Julius Caesar Octavianus Augustus) known as Augustus beginning in 27 BCE. Adopted son of Julius Caesar; first emperor of Rome, ruling from 31 BCE to 14 CE, 1.209, 1.595, 15.967, 15.978

Auro'ra: goddess of morning and the dawn, mother of Memnon, 2.119, 2.153, 3.160, 4.699, 5.510, 7.242, 7.770, 7.794, 7.926, 9.481, 13.715, 13.749, 15.212

Auso'nia: southern Italian region, often used to refer to Italy, 5.405, 14.907, 15.710, 15.766

Aus'ter: the South Wind, 1.66

Auto'lycus: cunning son of Mercury by Chione. Son-in-law of Erysichthon; grandfather of Ulysses, 8.832, 9.367

Auto'noë: daughter of Cadmus, mother of Actaeon. Helped destroy her nephew Pentheus, 3.208, 3.796

Aver'nus: entrance into the underworld near Cumae, Italy, 10.55, 14.121

Bab'ylon: capital of the ancient empire in Mesopotamia between the Tigris and the Euphrates, 2.271, 4.53, 4.111

Bac'chus (Li'ber, Diony'sus): son of Jupiter by Semele; sewn into Jupiter's thigh after Semele's death. A god associated with wine, pleasure, and the frenetic revelry of his followers, 3.344, 3.460, 3.570, 3.632, 3.697, 3.765, 4.3, 4.5, 4.14, 4.305, 4.455, 4.588, 4.589, 4.860, 5.384, 6.138, 6.680, 6.689, 6.691, 7.295, 7.330, 7.401, 8.214, 8.319, 11.17, 11.72, 11.92, 11.98, 11.104, 11.106, 11.112, 11.141, 11.153, 13.773, 13.786, 13.806, 15.130, 15.451

Bau'cis: wife of Philemon. She and her husband host Jupiter and Mercury when the gods visit in the guise of mortals, 8.715, 8.725, 8.769, 8.795, 8.806

Bears: Ursa Major, the Great Bear, which includes the group of stars known as the "Big Dipper" and its companion Ursa Minor, the Lesser Bear, which contains the "Little Dipper." Represent Callisto and Arcas, respectively, 2.186, 4.693, 8.247, 10.508, 13.354, 13.872

Bello'na: sister of Mars; goddess of war, 5.180

Be'lus: father of Danaus; an Egyptian king whose granddaughters murdered their husbands and were punished by continuously filling sieves with water in Hades, 4.238, 10.45

Bist'ones: a Thracian people, 13.510

Boeo'tia: region in middle Greece, northwest of Attica, 1.324, 2.261, 3.16, 3.157, 3.369, 5.365, 8.356, 12.12

Boö'tes: the northern Wagon Driver constellation of the nearby Ursa Major, which has often been associated with a wagon. Keeper of the bears, 2.192, 8.247, 10.508

Bo'reas: the North Wind. Father of the Argonauts Zetes and Calaïs by Orithyia, 1.64, 6.788, 6.813, 7.4

Busi'ris: Egyptian king, sacrificed strangers. Killed by Hercules, 9.205

Byb'lis: daughter of Miletus and Cyaneë. Erotically desired her twin brother, Caunus, 9.518, 9.519, 9.520, 9.536, 9.613, 9.667, 9.722, 9.739, 9.745, 9.752, 9.761, 9.765

Cad'mus: exiled brother of Europa, son of Agenor. Founder of Thebes and husband of Harmonia, 3.3, 3.28, 3.58, 3.104, 3.124, 3.140, 3.148, 3.185, 4.518, 4.605, 4.623, 4.632, 4.653, 4.654, 6.201, 6.249

Cae′neus: Thessalian hero who had been born a girl (Caenis), was raped by Neptune, and then transformed by him into an invulnerable man, 8.351, 12.204, 12.206, 12.211, 12.244, 12.531, 12.550, 12.553, 12.560, 12.565, 12.573, 12.589, 12.592, 12.608

Cae′sar: (Gaius Julius Caesar) military and political leader of the Roman republic. Claimed to be a descendant of Venus; adoptive father of Augustus. Deified after his death in 44 BCE, 1.206, 15.829, 15.834, 15.847, 15.850, 15.927, 15.942, 15.948, 15.973, 15.974

Cal′chas: Greek seer, predicted the length of the Trojan War, 12.23, 12.34

Callis′to: Arcadian virgin raped by Jupiter and despised by Juno; mother of Arcas, 2.444, 2.532

Ca′lydon: primary city of Aetolia; site of the Calydonian boar hunt, 6.475, 8.314, 8.317, 8.562, 8.601, 8.603, 8.821, 9.165, 14.596, 15.856

Cap′itoline: one of the seven hills of Rome. Geese in the temple of Juno on the Capitoline were said to have saved Rome from an attack by the Gauls in 390 BCE, 1.594

Carthae′a: a city of the Cycladean island Ceos, 7.411, 10.114

Cenae′um: a promontory in northwestern Euboea, 9.151

Can′cer: zodiacal constellation of the Crab, representing the crab which pinched Hercules' foot during his fight with the Hydra, 2.87, 10.132

Ca′nens: daughter of Janus and Venilia known for her beautiful singing; wife of Picus, 14.391, 14.441, 14.444, 14.485, 14.503

Cano′pus: an Egyptian city close to Alexandria, 15.929

Cap′aneus: one of the Seven against Thebes. Slain by Jupiter's thunderbolt in return for his arrogance as he scaled the city walls, 9.459

Capel′la: "Goat Star," brightest star of the constellation Auriga, 3.653, 14.819

Caphe′reus: promontory on the coast of Euboea, 14.549, 14.558

Ca′ria: a region in southwestern Asia Minor, 4.332, 9.727, 9.738

Cassiopei′a: mother of Andromeda; wife of Cepheus. Punished for arrogance by being chained to a chair in the sky as a northern constellation, 4.750, 4.826

Cas′tor: son of Leda and Tyndareus, king of Sparta; brother of Clytemnestra; half brother of Pollux and Helen of Troy. The two brothers are associated with the constellation Gemini, 8.347, 8.423, 12.469

Cau′casus: an Asian mountain range, 2.245, 5.101, 8.900

Caÿs′ter: Lydian river known for its swans, 2.276, 5.448

Ce'crops: legendary founder of Athens; half serpent, half human in form. Father of three daughters: Pandrosos, Herse, and Aglauros, 2.619, 2.874, 2.889

Ceph'alus: a prince of Athens and grandson of Aeolus; relates the tale of the death of his wife, Procris, 6.787, 7.545, 7.546, 7.554, 7.565, 7.729, 7.736, 7.751, 7.752, 7.880, 7.881, 7.960, 8.4

Ce'pheus: Ethiopian king, father of Andromeda. A northern constellation placed in the stars by Neptune, 4.747, 4.826, 5.14, 5.36, 5.49

Ce'phisus: a river god of Phocis; father of Narcissus, 1.382, 3.22, 3.373, 7.434, 7.492

Cer'berus: three-headed guard dog of Hades. Briefly led from Hades by Hercules, 4.496, 4.550, 7.459, 7.462, 9.210, 14.68

Cer'cyon: Eleusian king, challenged travelers to a fatal wrestling match for his kingdom. Defeated by Theseus, 7.493.

Ce'res (Deme'ter, De'o): goddess of fertility, grain, food; mother of Proserpina by Jupiter, 5.130, 5.396, 5.398, 5.399, 5.437, 5.480, 5.616, 5.659, 5.757, 5.764, 6.130, 8.319, 8.836, 8.869, 8.877, 8.885, 8.916, 9.483, 10.490, 11.137, 13.773

Ce'yx: Trachinian king; brother of Daedalion and husband of Alcyone. Gave refuge to Peleus, 11.318, 11.320, 11.329, 11.406, 11.410, 11.446, 11.481, 11.539, 11.630, 11.631, 11.650, 11.685, 11.752, 11.758, 11.774, 11.787, 11.837, 11.851

Chao'nian: the epithet given to the oaks of Chaonia, at Dodona, 5.188, 10.95, 13.862

Calli'rhoë: daughter of Achelous and wife of the seer Alcmaeon, from whom she demanded the golden necklace of Harmonia, 9.468, 9.471, 9,494

Cha'os: (1) The state of nature prior to the origin of the world, 1.7; (2) a part of the underworld, 10.31, 14.471

Char'iclo: water nymph, mother of Ocyrhoë, 2.713

Charyb'dis: a whirlpool between Sicily and Italy, opposite the monster Scylla, 7.76, 8.145, 13.876, 14.82

Chio'ne: daughter of Daedalion; mother of Mercury's sons Autolycus and Philammon, 11.353, 11.372

Chi'os: island off the coast of Ionia, 3.656

Chi'ron: immortal centaur, son of Saturn and Philyra; father of Ocyrhoë by Chariclo. Caretaker of Aesculapius, 2.706, 2.756, 6.140, 7.394

Cic'ones: a Thracian people, 6.831, 10.2, 11.3, 15.340

Cin'yras: (1) a king of Assyria. His daughters were turned into the steps of Juno's temple as punishment for their pride, 6.110; (2) father of Myrrha and of Adonis by Myrrha, 10.332, 10.377, 10.382, 10.398, 10.403, 10.413, 10.427, 10.498, 10.531, 10.542, 10.815, 10.838

Cir'ce: sorceress daughter of the Sun and the sea nymph Perse. Enchants Ulysses' crew in the *Odyssey,* 4.2290, 13.1145, 14.10, 14.28, 14.31, 14.44, 14.74, 14.77, 14.284, 14.291, 14.307, 14.333, 14.338, 14.359, 14.422, 14.435, 14.447, 14.463, 14.481, 14.507, 15.796

Cithae'ron: a Boeotian mountain, 2.243, 3.777

Cla'ros: an Ionian city, 1.541, 11.486

Cleopa'tra: queen of Egypt and mistress of Mark Antony. Defeated by Octavian (later known as Augustus), 15.925

Clyme'ne: daughter of Oceanus and Tethys; wife of the Ethiopian king Merops; mother of the Heliades, and of Phaëthon by the Sun, 1.823, 2.19, 2.38, 2.44, 2.366, 4.227

Clytemnes'tra: wife of Agamemnon; mother of Iphigenia. Killed Agamemnon when he returned home from the Trojan War, 13.232

Clyt'ië: daughter of Oceanus; infatuated with the Sun, 4.230

Cni'dos: a Carian city, 10.610

Cnos'sus: the primary city of Crete, 9.770

Col'chis: a country east of the Black Sea, 7.141, 7.171, 7.337, 7.390, 7.442

Co'rinth: a city on the western side of the Isthmus of Corinth, 5.472, 6.476, 7.438, 15.5532

Coro'nis: daughter of Thessalian king Phlegyas; mother of Aesculapius by Apollo, 2.605, 2.670

Crete: island southeast of Greece, 3.2, 3.219, 3.234, 7.487, 7.524, 7.542, 8.24, 8.42, 8.45, 8.57, 8.115, 8.141, 8.174, 8.222, 9.766, 9.767, 9.809, 9.827, 9.849, 13.849, 15.589

Croc'ale: one of Diana's attendant nymphs, 3.179

Crom'myon: a town on the Isthmus of Corinth where Theseus killed a monstrous wild sow, 7.488

Cro'nos (See Saturn)

Cro'ton: host of Hercules. Honored after his death by the founding of the city Crotona, 15.18, 15.64

Cu'mae: a city on the coast of Campania in Italy, 14.119, 14.140, 14.157, 14.180, 15.790

Cu′pid (A′mor): god of love. Son of Venus and Mars, 1.471, 1.569, 5.424, 5.442, 9.554, 10.346, 10.591

Cu′res: a primary Sabine city northeast of Rome, 14.900, 15.8

Cya′ne: a nymph of Sicily, bride of Anapis. Transformed into a stream for resisting Proserpina's abduction, 5.474, 5.476, 5.493, 5.537

Cybe′le: Phrygian mother goddess accompanied by lions; desired Attis, 10.108, 10.784, 10.805, 14.621

Cy′clades: island group in the Aegean Sea, 2.288

Cy′clops: (plural **Cy′clopes**): member of a race of giants, sometimes Polyphemus in particular, each with a single eye in the center of the forehead. The Cyclopes forged Jupiter's thunderbolts, 1.270, 3.330, 13.892, 13.905, 13.907, 13.928, 13.935, 13.1025, 13.1045, 13.1051, 14.3, 14.202, 14.211, 14.285, 15.107

Cyg′nus: (1) son of Sthenelus; relative and friend of Phaëthon. Transformed into a swan, 2.405, 2.415; (2) son of Neptune; king of Colonae. Although made invulnerable by Neptune, killed by Achilles and transformed into a swan, 12.90, 12.95, 12.97, 12.107, 12.108, 12.118, 12.122, 12.124, 12.148, 12.160, 12.163, 12.168, 12.171, 12.179, 12.1954, 12.201; (3) Apollo's son by Hyrië; transformed into a swan after jumping off a cliff in anger, 7.415, 7.418, 7.422.

Cylle′ne: Arcadian mountain where Mercury was born, 1.223, 5.699, 7.432, 11.357

Cyn′thia: (See Diana) 7.835

Cyn′thus: Delian mountain and birthplace of Apollo and Diana, 2.241, 6.234

Cyparis′sus: young boy transformed into a tree after he accidentally killed his beloved companion, a tame stag, 10.125, 10.134

Cy′prus: an island in the northeastern Mediterranean Sea and sacred to Venus, 10.234, 10.297, 10.742, 10.824, 14.802

Cythe′ra: an island in the Aegean Sea and sacred to Venus, 4.212, 10.609, 10.822, 15.895

Daeda′lion: brother of Ceyx; father of Chione, 11.346, 11.398

Daed′alus: Athenian artisan, father of Icarus. Uncle of Perdix. Built a wooden cow for Pasiphaë and later the Labyrinth for Minos, 8.191, 8.200, 8.221, 8.279, 8.284, 8.293, 8.304, 9.855

Da′naë: daughter of Acrisius and mother of Perseus by Jupiter after the god came to her as golden rain, 4.676, 4.783, 5.1, 6.124, 11.132

Daph′ne: nymph daughter of Peneus. Pursued by Apollo; transformed into a laurel tree, 1.470, 1.509

Deianei'ra: daughter of Oeneus; one of Meleager's two sisters not transformed into a guinea hen at his death. Courted by Acheloüs and won by Hercules, 8.622, 9.9, 9.120, 9.145, 9.152

Dei''phobus: Trojan hero, son of Priam and Hecuba. Married Helen after Paris' death, 12.630

De'los: Cycladean island where Apollo and Diana were born, 3.655, 5.736, 6.285, 12.682, 13.763, 15.589

Del'phi: city in Phocis, sacred site of the oracle of Apollo, 1.541, 2.757, 9.376, 11.356, 11.486, 15.161, 15.693

Deme'ter: a Greek name for Ceres

De'o: a Greek name for Ceres, 6.125, 8.854

Deuca'lion: pious son of Prometheus; rescued with his wife Pyrrha from a flood sent by Jupiter, 1.330, 1.361, 7.398

Dia'na (Cyn'thia): daughter of Jupiter and Latona, twin sister of Apollo, goddess of fertility, wild animals, archery, the moon. Born on Mount Cynthus in Delos, 1.498, 1.508, 1.745, 2.463, 2.474, 2.492, 2.495, 2.503, 2.507, 2.518, 3.168, 3.184, 3.192, 3.266, 4.339, 5.385, 5.436, 6.235, 6.475, 7.825, 8.316, 8.322, 8.403, 8.447, 8.620, 8.662, 9.96, 10.615, 11.375, 11.377, 12.41, 12.46, 13.221, 14.384, 15.218, 15.528, 15.583, 15.600

Dictyn'na: "goddess of the nets," a Cretan epithet applied to the goddess Britomartis, identified with Diana, 5.713

Di'do: Phoenician queen, founder of Carthage; loved by Aeneas. Committed suicide when Aeneas left Carthage, 14.84

Diome'des: (1) a Thracian king who killed men in order to feed his prized horses, defeated by Hercules, 9.221; (2) son of Tydeus; Greek leader and prominent warrior at Troy, 12.713, 13.78, 13.117, 13.119, 13.290, 13.292, 13.424, 13.428, 14.531, 14.572, 14.595, 15.856, 15.889

Diony'sus: (See Bacchus) 9.737

Dir'ce: cruel wife of the Theban king Lycus; tied to a bull and thus killed by her two stepsons. Bacchus placed a spring in her memory, 2.262

Dis: (See Pluto) 4.481, 15.583

Dodo'na: a city in Epirus where Jupiter's oracle was interpreted from the sound of oak leaves rustling in the wind, 7.681, 13.861

Do'lon: a cowardly Trojan spy captured by Diomedes and Ulysses. Killed by Ulysses, 13.114, 13.294, 13.305

Do'ris: daughter of Oceanus and Tethys, mother of the Nereids, 2.11, 2.292, 13.890

Dra'co: serpentine northern constellation placed in the sky by Minerva, 2.146, 2.188, 3.50

Dry'ope: wife of Andraemon; mother of Amphissus by Apollo. Became a tree, 9.371, 9.379, 9.376, 9.411

Earth: goddess and personification of the earth, whose Greek name is Gaia. Mother of, among others, the Titans, the Cyclopes, the Giants, Python, and Typhoeus, 1.81, 1.87, 1.160, 1.294, 1.409, 1.432, 1.450, 1.454, 2.298, 2.329, 3.134, 4.686, 5.491, 5.578, 6.452, 7.228, 13.1123, 15.105

Echid'na: half-serpent, half-woman mother of Cerberus, 4.550

Echin'ades: an Ionian island group, transformed from nymphs by the angry Acheloüs, 8.675

E'chion: an earthborn hero originating from the serpent's teeth sown by Cadmus. Father of Pentheus; husband of Agave, 3.135, 3.564, 3.579, 8.357, 8.396, 10.785

Ech'o: nymph whose control of her speech was taken away by Juno; smitten by helpless love for Narcissus, 3.390, 3.391, 3.396, 3.401, 3.416, 3.418, 3.422, 3.428, 3.540, 3.549, 3.556

E'lis: city and region in the northwestern Peloponnese, 2.760, 5.570, 5.700, 9.211, 12.633

Eni'peus: a Thessalian river god whose form is briefly assumed by Neptune, 1.616, 6.128

Ep'aphus: son of the deified Io by Jupiter; friend of Phaëthon, 1.805, 1.814

Ephy're: an old name for Corinth, 2.263

Epidau'rus: a city in Argolis, sacred site of Aesculapius, 3.300, 7.489, 15.706

Epi'rus: a region in north-western Greece, 8.328

Er'ebus: a name for the underworld or a part of it, 5.627, 14.471

Erichtho'nius: son of Vulcan and the earth; a king of Athens, 2.617, 2.845, 9.484

Erid'anus: a mythical river of Europe; perhaps the modern Po, 2.356, 2.409

Erig'one: daughter of Icarius; mourning her father's death, she was placed among the stars as the constellation Virgo, 6.138, 10.514

Eryman'thus: river and mountain in Arcadia, 2.266, 5.700

Erysi'chthon: impious Thessalian, punished with everlasting hunger for chopping down a tree of Ceres. Neptune granted Erysichthon's daughter the ability to change her form, 8.832, 8.833, 8.846, 8.863, 8.878, 8.919, 8.927, 8.946

E'ryx: Sicilian mountain, a site of Venus, 2.241, 5.221, 14.93

Ete'ocles: son of Oedipus and Jocasta; brother of Antigone. Died fighting his brother Polynices, 9.460

Ethio'pia: a country in eastern Africa, 1.837, 4.746, 4.858, 5.2, 5.115

Et'na: volcano in Sicily, 2.240, 4.740

Etru'ria: central Italian region of the Etruscan people, 14.525

Eume'lus: father of Antheias, who was killed trying to drive the winged chariot of the god Triptolemus, 7.437

Eumen'ides: (See Furies) 8.547

Eumol'pus: Thracian king; one of the founders of the Eleusinian mystery rites, 11.104

Euphor'bus: Trojan warrior killed by Menelaus. Pythagoras claims to be Euphorbus in a new body, 15.180

Euro'pa: daughter of Agenor, a Phoenician king. In the form of a bull, Jupiter took Europa away on his back, 3.275, 6.115, 8.25, 8.143

Euro'tas: a Laconian river, 2.270, 10.179

Eu'rus: the East Wind, 1.61

Eury'dice: wife of the musician Orpheus, who bargained for her release from Hades after her death, 10.32, 10.50, 11.67, 11.71

Eurypy'lus: king of Cos, killed by Hercules, 7.405, 13.432

Eurys'theus: Mycenaean king, given mastery over Hercules as a result of Juno's treachery. Hercules was required to serve him by performing twelve labors, 9.228, 9.306

Eva'nder: Arcadian founder of Pallantium; ally of Aeneas in the conflict with Turnus, 14.530

Fu'ries (Eume'nides): female spirits of retribution and vengeance; occasionally referred to as the three serpent-haired sisters Allecto, Megaera, and Tisiphone, 4.498, 4.519, 6.591, 6.593, 6.764, 8.546, 9.467, 10.48

Galate'a: nymph daughter of Nereus and Doris; beloved of Acis, but desired by the Cyclops Polyphemus, 13.885, 13.945, 13.955, 13.966, 13.998, 13.1028, 13.1036, 13.1049, 13.1069

Ga'ia: See Earth

Gan'ges: a major river of India, 2.272, 4.24, 5.58, 6.735

Gan'ymede: Trojan boy loved by Jupiter. Taken by the eagle of Jupiter to be the god's cupbearer, 10.163, 11.871

Gar'gaphië: a sacred Boeotian valley of Diana, 3.166

Ge'ryon: three-bodied, cattle-herding son of Medusa. Killed by Hercules, 9.209

Gi'ants: race of monsters, born of Earth and the blood of castrated Sky (Uranus), which failed in revolt against the Olympian gods after the Olympians unseated the Titans, 1.155, 1.159, 1.187, 5.374, 5.375, 10.157

Glau'cus: Euboean fisherman transformed into a sea god; pursues the nymph Scylla, 7.267, 13.1075, 13.1144, 14.1, 14.41, 14.73

Goat Stars: the Haedi within the constellation Auriga, the charioteer, 14.819

Ha'des: A Greek name for the underworld and the god of the underworld

Hae'mus: mountain in Thrace, associated with the ancient Thracian king Oeagrius, 2.239, 6.97

Harmo'nia: daughter of Mars and Venus; wife of Cadmus, 4.653, 4.662

Har'pies: creatures with the bodies of women and the heads and talons of birds, 7.5

He'be: cupbearer of the gods, associated with youth. Juno's fatherless daughter; Hercules' wife, 9.455

He'brus: a river in Thrace, 2.280, 11.53

Hec'ate: a goddess of the underworld and sorcery, 6.156, 7.90, 7.114, 7.203, 7.207, 7.276, 14.48, 14.472

Hec'tor: son of Priam and Hecuba; brother of Paris; husband of Andromache. Prominent warrior and leader of the Trojan troops. Killed by Achilles, 11.874, 11.876, 11.877, 12.3, 12.86, 12.87, 12.95, 12.5176, 12.518, 12.6310, 12.695, 13.8, 13.94, 13.211, 13.212, 13.304, 13.333, 13.338, 13.464, 13.502, 13.513, 13.584, 13.619, 13.802

Hec'uba: wife of Priam; mother of Hector, Paris, Polydorus, Helenus, Polyxena, and many others, 11.876, 13.487, 13.508, 13.579, 13.644, 13.651, 13.663, 13.670, 13.693, 13.695, 13.748

He'len: daughter of Jupiter and Leda; wife of Menelaus. Her abduction by Paris caused the Trojan War, 13.241, 14.771, 15.255

Hel'enus: prophet son of Priam and Hecuba; captured by Ulysses and Diomedes, 13.114, 13.866, 15.474, 15.488

He'liades: daughters of the sun god Helius by Clymene. Mourning their brother Phaëthon, the sisters were transformed into poplar trees with amber tears, 2.374, 10.95, 10.287

He'licon: Boeotian mountain, a site of the Muses, 2.238, 5.295, 5.769, 8.611

Hen'na: city in central Sicily, 5.447

Her'cules: son of Jupiter and Alcmena; completed twelve great labors under Eurystheus. Killed by the Hydra's poisonous blood and placed in the stars as a constellation, 7.406, 7.461, 8.220, 9.15, 9.21, 9.32, 9.55, 9.111, 9.119, 9.120, 9.147, 9.155, 9.184, 9.244 9.251, 9.287, 9.294, 9.307, 9.312, 9.321, 9.452, 9.454, 11.247, 11.253, 11.728, 12.365, 12.620, 12.621, 12.637, 12.649, 12.658, 13.26, 13.60, 13.483, 15.13, 15.25, 15.55, 15.254, 15.311

Hermaphrodi'tus: son of Mercury and Aphrodite; loved by the nymph Salmacis, becomes half man, half woman, 4.418

Her'se: one of the three daughters of Cecrops; loved by Mercury, 2.623, 2.805, 2.825, 2.834, 2.901

Hersi'lia: wife of Romulus; deified as Hora, 14.954, 14.966, 14.976

Hesper'ides: nymphs who guarded the garden of Juno's golden apples. Several apples were stolen by Hercules during his labors, 11.129

Hippodamei'a: wife of Pirithoüs. The Centaurs and Lapiths fought at her wedding, 12.248, 12.265, 14.771

Hippo'lytus: son of Theseus and the Amazon Hippolyte. Supernaturally restored to life and known as Virbius, 15.539, 15.593

Hippo'menes: husband of Atalanta; son of Megareus. Transformed with Atalanta into a lion for an act of sacrilege against Cybele, 10.644, 10.662, 10.675, 10.689, 10.699, 10.731, 10.736, 10.748, 10.755, 10.765, 10.788

Hippot'ades: a name for Aeolus, son of Hippotas, 15.782

Hyacin'thus: Spartan boy, accidentally killed by Apollo; a flower grows from his blood as a symbol of Apollo's grief, 10.170, 10.196, 10.205, 10.231, 10.233, 13.478

Hy'ades: nymph sisters mourning the death of their brother. Placed in the sky as a cluster of stars within the constellation Taurus, 3.653, 13.350

Hy'men: the god of marriage, 1.501, 4.851, 6.491, 9.877, 9.880, 9.914, 10.2

Hype'rion: a sun god and the Titan father of the sun god Helius by Theia. The name sometimes refers to Helius (who is himself sometimes identified with Phoebus), 4.215, 8.646, 15.443, 15.444

Ia'lysus: a city in Rhodes, 7.408

Ia'sion: son of Zeus and Electra; loved by Ceres, who bore her son Plutus by him, 9.483

Ica′rius: Athenian father of Erigone; occasionally identified as the constellation Boötes, 10.513

I′carus: son of Daedalus. Wearing wings of wax and feathers, he falls to his death as he flies too close to the sun, 8.234, 8.244, 8.274, 8.275, 8.276.

I′da: a mountain southeast of Troy, 2.237, 4.310, 4.325, 4.329, 7.401, 11.878, 12.598, 13.394, 13.621

Il′ium: another name for Troy, 6.106, 13.237, 13.490, 13.611, 13.629, 13.790

In′achus: river and river god of Argolis; father of Io, 1.619, 1.650, 1.694, 1.810, 4.806

I′no: daughter of Cadmus; aunt of Bacchus and Pentheus. Wife of Athamas, 3.340, 3.798, 4.456, 4.472, 4.538, 4.545, 4.555, 4.572, 4.584, 4.602, 4.611

I′o: daughter of Inachus, assaulted by Jupiter and transformed into a heifer. Called Isis in Egypt, 1.621, 1.716, 1.794, 2.585

Iola′us: nephew of Hercules; brought back to life as a youth by Hebe, 8.356, 9.452, 9.493

I′phis: (1) daughter of Ligdus and Telethusa; raised as a boy so as not to be killed by her father. When betrothed to Ianthe, transformed into a boy by Isis, 9.769, 9.818, 9.825, 9.834, 9.836, 9.858, 9.903, 9.912, 9.915; (2) Cyprian youth; hanged himself due to unrequited love for Anaxarete, 14.804, 14.826, 14.843, 14.869

I′ris: messenger goddess of Juno, associated with the rainbow; daughter of Thaumas, 1.282, 4.529, 11.681, 11.682, 11.687, 11.714, 11.723, 11.731, 11.747, 14.95, 14.955, 14.964

I′sis: Egyptian goddess, sister and wife of Osiris; the deified Io, 9.789, 9.797, 9.800, 9.888

Isma′ria: a region of southern Thrace, 9.736

Is′thmus: the Isthmus of Corinth, where the Peloponnesus meets Boeotia, 6.479, 6.480, 7.443, 7.455, 7.496

Ith′aca: an Ionian island, homeland of Ulysses, 13.113, 13.120, 13.618, 13.856, 14.196

Iu′lus: (See Ascanius) 14.673, 15.485, 15.854

I′xion: Lapith king, bound to a flaming and eternally revolving wheel as punishment for attempting to woo Juno. Father of Pirithoüs and the Centaurs, 4.508, 4.512, 8.455, 8.648, 8.693, 10.44, 12.582

Ja′nus: two-headed god of beginnings and thresholds. Husband of Venilia; father of Canens, 14.387, 14.441, 14.907, 14.911

Ja'son: son of Aeson; husband of Medea. Leader of the Argonauts, 7.6, 7.12, 7.33, 7.59, 7.69, 7.81, 7.92, 7.101, 7.103, 7.130, 7.135, 7.157, 7.163, 7.178, 7.205, 7.291, 7.334, 7.441, 7.446, 8.348, 8.398, 8.465, 8.472

Jove: (See Jupiter) 1.108, 1.116, 1.170, 1.210, 1.213, 1.286, 1.542, 1.627, 1.649, 2.66, 2.417, 2.431, 2.478, 2.487, 2.495, 2.536, 3.7, 3.30, 3.278, 3.283, 3.292, 3.305, 3.310, 3.361, 3.395, 4.316, 4.846, 5.428, 5.592, 5.603, 5.609, 5.616, 5.751, 6.82, 6.121, 6.595, 7.650, 8.116, 8.145, 8.184, 9.30, 9.150, 9.271, 9.291, 9.325, 9.459, 9.472, 10.240, 11.259, 11.266, 12.14, 12.647, 13.32, 13.105, 13.168, 13.169, 13.262, 13.323, 13.464, 13.692, 13.705, 13.850, 15.420, 15.964, 15.982

Ju'ba: a king of the Numidians, a Northern African people defeated by Caesar, 15.840

Ju'no (Satur'nia): wife/sister of Jupiter; patroness of women, marriage, and childbirth, 1.283, 1.639, 1.652, 1.656, 1.663, 1.727, 1.775, 2.486, 2.525, 2.568, 2.578, 2.586, 3.282, 3.301, 3.305, 3.307, 3.319, 3.347, 3.361, 3.394, 4.461, 4.467, 4.492, 4.501, 4.528, 4.578, 4.606, 4.608, 5.385, 6.101, 6.104, 6.237, 6.396, 6.490, 7.577, 8.262, 9.26, 9.148, 9.198, 9.290, 9.320, 9.325, 9.332, 9.348, 9.574, 9.877, 9.914, 10.168, 11.673, 11.686, 11.730, 12.582, 13.692, 14.96, 14.132, 14.672, 14.902, 14.955, 15.182, 15.419, 15.775, 15.861

Ju'piter (Jove): son of Saturn, husband/brother of Juno; ruler of the Olympian gods. Associated with the thunderbolt and its power, 1.118, 1.167, 1.257, 1.336, 1.624, 1.721, 1.788, 1.789, 1.805, 2.438, 2.469, 2.529, 2.545, 2.779, 2.809, 2.831, 3.272, 3.290, 3.301, 3.302, 3.345, 4.3, 4.675, 4.677, 4.710, 4.716, 4.721, 4.747, 4.783, 4.802, 5.13, 5.344, 5.382, 5.593, 6.59, 6.85, 6.106, 6.199, 7.409, 7.642, 7.671, 7.711, 7.888, 8.309, 8.708, 8.792, 9.17, 9.28, 9.223, 9.258, 9.296, 9.340, 9.474, 9.489, 10.155, 10.169, 11.335, 11.869, 11.872, 12.67, 13.7, 13.30, 13.172, 13.491, 13.723, 13.1002, 13.1003, 13.1020, 14.106, 14.684, 14.940, 15.81, 15.900, 15.965, 15.975

La'don: an Arcadian river, 1.755

La'ertes: king of Ithaca; father of Ulysses and father-in-law of Penelope, 8.361, 13.144, 13.171

Lao'medon: Trojan king; father of Priam and Hesione. Preceded by the Trojan king Ilus and Ilus' brother, Assaracus, 6.107, 11.224, 11.228, 11.237, 11.872

Lati'nus: king of Latium; father of Aeneas' wife, Lavinia, 14.522, 14.702, 14.704

La'tium: ancient area of Rome, 13.377, 14.491, 14.526, 15.639, 15.688

Lato'na (Le'to): Titaness daughter of Coeus; mother of Apollo and Diana by Jupiter, 6.178, 6.180, 6.192, 6.211, 6.212, 6.228, 6.310, 6.316, 6.3965, 7.430, 13.767

Lauren'tium: an ancient city of Latium, 14.395, 14.691

Le'da: mother of Castor, Pollux, and Helen; wife of Tyndareus. Jupiter came to her as a swan, 6.120, 8.346

Le'leges: a wandering people closely associated with the Carians, 9.740, 9.749

Lem'nos: island in the Aegean Sea; a sacred site of Vulcan, 13.54, 13.379, 13.481

Lenae'us: an epithet of Bacchus, honoring the god's association with the winepress, 11.149

Leo: zodiacal constellation of the Lion, representing the famous Nemean lion which Hercules killed in the course of his labors, 2.86

Les'bos: island in the Aegean Sea, off the coast of Asia Minor, 2.661, 11.58

Le'to: (See Latona) 1.746

Leuco'noë: daughter of Minyas; sister of Alcithoë. Narrator of "Mars and Venus," 4.188,

Leuco'thoë: daughter of Eurynome and Orchamus, king of Persia; loved by the Sun, 4.219, 4.232, 4.246, 4.265, 4.601

Lib'er: (See Bacchus) 3.573, 3.581, 3.705, 4.20

Li'bya: a country in northern Africa, 2.259, 4.684, 5.89

Li'chas: servant of Hercules, killed by the hero after unwittingly presenting him with the Hydra's fatal blood, 9.175, 9.237, 9.237, 9.240, 9.241, 9.251, 9.257

Ligu'ria: a region of northern Italy, 2.408

Liri'ope: water nymph and mother of Narcissus by Cephisus, 3.372

Luci'na: goddess of childbirth, 5.356, 9.330, 9.331, 9.349, 9.803, 10.581, 10.584

Lyca'on: early king of Arcadia; father of Callisto. When the disguised Jupiter visited Arcadia, Lycaon served him a meal of human flesh. Jupiter sent a flood as punishment, 1.168, 1.203, 1.227, 2.554, 2.587

Ly'cia: a region of southwestern Asia Minor, 4.332, 6.361, 6.389, 6.436, 9.741, 12.143

Lycur'gus: Thracian king, destroyed for resistance to the Bacchic cult, 4.25

Ly'dia: country in western Asia Minor, 6.15, 6.163, 11.110, 14.105

Mae'nalus: an Arcadian mountain range, 2.463, 2.493, 5.700

Maeo'nia: an old name for Lydia, 2.276, 3.642, 4.464, 6.7

Mareo'ta: a city of Lower Egypt, 9.889

Mars (A'res): god of war; son of Jupiter and Juno. Father of Romulus and Remus, legendary founders of Rome, 3.36, 3.142, 3.587, 4.192, 6.80, 6.487, 7.121, 8.494, 12.114, 14.929, 14.942, 14.949, 15.971

Mede'a: sorceress daughter of Aeëtes, Colchian king. Wife of Jason; kills their children in revenge when he deserts her, 7.16, 7.51, 7.83, 7.156, 7.192, 7.198, 7.212, 7.252, 7.272, 7.294, 7.320, 7.332, 7.333, 7.343, 7.372, 7.455, 7.471, 7.476

Medu'sa: one of the Gorgons, daughter of Phorcys and loved by Neptune; became a serpent-headed creature so hideous that at a glance she turned mortals into stone, 4.730, 4.834, 4.877, 4.880, 4.889, 5.82, 5.249, 5.285, 5.288, 5.299, 5.365, 10.23

Melea'ger: son of Oeneus and Althea; leader in the Calydonian boar hunt, 8.314, 8.344, 8.373, 8.435, 8.468, 8.480, 8.501, 8.513, 8.521, 8.588, 9.167

Mem'non: son of Aurora and Tithonus. Killed by Achilles at Troy, 13.697, 13.717, 13.723

Menela'us: younger brother of Agamemnon, Greek leader at Troy. Husband of Helen, 12.715, 13.246, 13.434, 15.181, 15.898

Mer'cury: son of Jupiter and the Pleiad Maia; father of Autolycus. Messenger god, guides souls to Hades. Known for his cleverness and thievery, 1.719, 1.752, 1.766, 2.766, 2.772, 2.786, 2.803, 2.827, 2.925, 4.324, 4.845, 5.203, 5.386, 8.709, 9.356, 9.360, 13.175, 14.334

Messe'ne: a primary city in the southwestern Peloponnesus, 2.761, 12.632

Mi'das: a Phrygian king; Bacchus granted the king's request for a golden touch, 11.102, 11.105, 11.161, 11.167, 11.186, 11.200

Miner'va (Pal'las, Trito'nia, Athe'na): virgin daughter of Jupiter, goddess of crafts, wisdom, and war. Patroness of Athens; 2.629, 2.657, 2.793, 2.836, 2.854, 2.859, 4.39, 4.847, 4.896, 5.350, 6.438, 8.294, 8.308, 13.408, 13.460, 13.789, 14.543, 14.552, 15.389, 15.785

Mi'nos: son of Jupiter and Europa; husband of Pasiphaë. King of Crete, 7.507, 7.525, 7.528, 7.532, 5.39, 8.26, 8.44, 8.48, 8.73, 8.102, 8.109,

8.117, 8.184, 8.189, 8.203, 8.210, 8.225, 9.500, 9.504, 9.505, 9.510, 15.543

Mi'notaur: child of Pasiphaë; born with the head of a bull. Killed by Theseus in the Labyrinth, 8.203

Min'yas: ancient ruler of Orchomenus in Boeotia; his daughters resisted Bacchus, 4.1, 4.37, 4.425, 4.466

Mithrida'tes: a king of Pontus in Asia Minor; involved in much conflict with the Romans near the end of the Republican period, 15.840

Mnemo'syne: (Memory) Titaness mother of the Muses, 6.125

Molos'sus: grandson of Achilles; ancestor of the Molossians of Epirus, 1.233, 13.862

Mop'sus: prophet son of Ampyx. Present at the Calydonian boar hunt and the battle of the Centaurs and the Lapiths, 8.363, 8.400, 12.527, 12.530, 12.601, 12.605

Mor'pheus: son of personified Sleep; brother of Icelos (Phobetor) and Phantasos. Assumes human forms, 11.736, 11.746, 11.751, 11.771

Muny'chia: port of Athens, 2.792

Muses: nine daughters of Jupiter and Mnemosyne; associated with the arts and memory, 5.295, 5.769, 6.2, 15.520, 15.683

Myce'nae: a city in Argolis; home of Agamemnon, 6.474, 12.45, 15.464

Mygdo'nian: a people of Phrygia, originally from Thrace, 2.269, 6.53

Myr'rha: daughter of Cinyras. Infatuated with her father; mother of his child Adonis, 10.347, 10.354, 10.398, 10.406, 10.421, 10.454, 10.458, 10.501, 10.510, 10.516, 10.546

My'scelus: an Argive man whom Hercules ordered to found the city Crotona, 15.23

Nabatae'a: a region in Arabia, 1.61

Narcis'sus: son of Cephisus and the raped nymph Liriope; beloved by Echo. His death fulfilled a prophecy of Tiresias, 3.376, 3.382, 3.403, 3.416, 3.438, 3.450, 3.535, 3.559

Nax'os: largest island of the Cyclades, 3.705, 3.709, 3.721, 3.764

Ne'leus: Pylian king and son of Neptune. Father of twelve sons, including Nestor, 2.770, 12.636, 12.640

Ne'mesis: goddess of righteous anger and retribution, 3.443, 14.799

Neoptol'emus: son of Achilles; present at the fall of Troy, 13.546

Nep'tune (Posei'don): god of the oceans and seas; brother of Jupiter, Juno, and Pluto, 1.294, 1.343, 2.293, 4.589, 4.597, 4.895, 6.126,

8.686, 8.960, 8.976, 10.695, 10.7120, 11.234, 12.32, 12.91, 12.232, 12.640, 13.1016

Ne'reus: a sea god who fathered fifty daughters, the Nereids, 1.191, 2.291, 11.423, 12.116, 12.117, 13.890

Nes'sus: Centaur son of Ixion; killed by Hercules for attempting to assault Deianeira, 9.108, 9.117, 9.120, 9.130, 9.132, 9.145, 9.173, 12.363, 12.526

Nes'tor: son of Neleus. Participates in the Calydonian boar hunt as a young man. In the *Iliad,* the elderly Nestor is a prominent warrior known for his wisdom, 8.359, 8.415, 12.199, 12.617, 12.624, 12.661, 13.73, 13.75

Ni'obe: daughter of Tantalus and the Pleiad Dione; wife of the Theban king Amphion. Apollo and Diana killed her fourteen children in vengeance for her boasts against Latona, 6.165, 6.172, 6.183, 6.309, 6.324

Ni'sus: Megaran king whose single strand of purple hair was vital to his country's survival. Betrayed by his daughter Scylla, 8.8, 8.18, 8.37, 8.96, 8.103, 8.149

Nu'ma: second king of Rome; husband of Egeria. Known for his wisdom, 15.3, 15.10, 15.516, 15.525

Nycti'mene: daughter of King Epopeus of Lesbos; turned into an owl, 2.658, 2.661

Oce'anus: Titan god of the oceans; refused to fight the Olympians. Fathered the nymphs by his sister Tethys, 9.573, 13.1126

Ocy'rhoë: prophetess daughter of Chiron and Chariclo, 2.715, 2.755

Odys'seus: Greek name for Ulysses, 12.716

Oecha'lia: a Euboean city whose king was killed by Hercules, 9.149, 9.374

Oed'ipus: Theban king; son of Laïus and Jocasta. Oedipus unwittingly killed his father, winning his mother as wife when he solved the Riddle of the Sphinx. Blinded himself in shame, 7.840, 15.465

Oe'ta: a mountain range between Thessaly and Aetolia, 2.237, 9.188, 9.231, 9.259, 9.279

Ol'enus: husband of Lethaea. After his wife was turned to stone for boasting of her beauty, Olenus chose to join her in her fate, 12.505

Olym'pus: Thessalian mountain considered the home of the gods, 1.157, 1.218, 2.65, 2.246, 7.258, 9.573, 13.720, 13.912, 14.375

Onches'tus: a Boeotian city, 10.694

Ophiu'chus: Serpent Holder constellation in the northeastern area of the sky, 8.220

Orcho'menos: (1) a city in Arcadia; (2) city in Boeotia, 6.476

Or'cus (Ha'des): the underworld; also a name for Pluto as god of the underworld, 14.134

O'read: a nymph of the mountains, 8.886

Ores'tean: epithet of Diana, whose image Orestes, Agamemnon's son, carried to Aricia, 15.528

O'rient: (1) place of rising, e.g., the Sun's, 1.838; (2) the East, referring to Eastern Asia, 4.66, 7.303, 10.354

Ori'on: constellation of the Hunter, a mighty giant placed in the sky by Diana. During a famine, his daughters sacrificed themselves for their people, 8.248, 13.356, 13.834

Or'pheus: Thracian musician, son of the Muse Calliope. Attempted to bring his wife, Eurydice, back from Hades. Killed by the Ciconian women of Thrace, 10.3, 10.53, 11.4, 11.22, 11.45, 11.70, 11.103

Ortyg'ia: early name for the island of Delos, birthplace of Diana, 1.745, 5.575, 5.739, 15.366

Osi'ris: Egyptian god of fertility; husband of Isis, 9.796

O'thrys: a Thessalian mountain, 2.242, 7.257, 7.395, 12.205, 12.590

Pa'chynus: a promontory of southeastern Sicily, 5.406

Pacto'lus: a Lydian river known for gold, 6.20, 11.95

Paeo'nia: a region of northern Macedonia, 5.355, 5.367

Pai'on: epithet for the god of healing and son of Apollo, Aesculapius, 15.582

Palae'mon: a mortal who was transformed into a sea god while a child, 4.602, 13.1094

Pal'atine: one of the seven hills of Rome; site of imperial palaces, 1.180, 14.387, 14.715, 14.947, 15.615

Palla'dium: a small statue of Pallas/Minerva, sacred to the Trojans. After Helenus foretold that Troy would not fall until the Palladium was taken outside of the city, Ulysses and Diomedes stole the image, 13.115

Pal'las: (See Minerva) 2.518, 2.634, 2.794, 2.927, 3.108, 3.136, 4.46, 5.54, 5.305, 5.391, 5.436, 5.745, 6.28, 6.32, 6.52, 6.80, 6.143, 6.152, 7.553, 7.728, 8.295, 8.320

Pan: half-goat god of shepherds and forests, originally Arcadian; played a reed pipe, 1.750, 1.753, 1.758, 8.230, 11.168, 11.173, 11.185, 11.187, 11.197, 14.599

Panchai'a: an island east of Arabia, 10.341, 10.549

Pandro'sos: daughter of Cecrops, sister of Herse and Aglauros, 2.623, 2.823

Pano'pe: a city in Phocis, 3.22

Pa'phos: a primary city of Cyprus, named for Pygmalion's son; birthplace of Venus, 10.330, 10.331, 10.609

Paraeto'nium: a northern African seaport, 9.889

Par'is: son of Priam and Hecuba; brother of Hector. Brought Helen to Troy, beginning the Trojan War. Killed Achilles, 12.5, 12.686, 13.240, 13.243, 13.603, 15.897

Parnas'sus: mountain in Phocis; site of Delphi and home to the nymphs of the Corycian cave, 1.329, 1.488, 2.241, 4.714, 5.324, 11.191, 11.397

Pa'ros: a Cycladean island known for its marble, 3.458, 7.517, 8.264

Parthe'nius: a mountain of eastern Arcadia, 9.213

Pasi'phaë: daughter of the Sun; wife of Minos. Mother of Ariadne and Phaedra. Stricken with love for a bull; mother of the Minotaur, 8.164, 9.850, 15.544

Pat'ara: wealthy city of the Lycian region in Turkey; site of a famous oracle of Apollo, 1.542

Pa'trae: an Achaean city, 6.477

Patro'clus: friend of Achilles. Wore Achilles' armor in battle; killed by Hector, 13.328

Pe'leus: son of Aeacus; father of Achilles and husband of Thetis. After he killed his half brother Phocus, Peleus sought support from Ceyx, 7.529, 7.732, 8.430, 11.255, 11.268, 11.283, 11.289, 11.296, 11.307, 11.314, 11.317, 11.322, 11.339, 11.407, 11.409, 11.410, 11.442, 11.454, 11.465, 11.477, 12.226, 12.426, 12.429, 12.432, 12.439, 12.444, 12.454, 12.691, 12.709, 13.181, 13.184, 15.962

Pe'lias: usurper of the Iolchian throne from his half brother Aeson; sends Jason on the quest for the golden fleece; killed by Medea, 7.334, 7.359

Pel'la: a Macedonian city, 5.354, 12.300

Pe'lops: ivory-shouldered son of Tantalus; brother of Niobe. Killed by his father and served as a feast to test the gods, 6.461, 6.471

Pena'tes: household deities. Aeneas rescued the Trojan Penates as he escaped Troy, 3.594, 15.488

Pe'neus: Thessalian river god; son of Oceanus and Tethys. Father of Daphne, 1.470, 1.527, 1.574, 1.604, 7.263

Pen'theus: son of Echion and Agave; Theban king killed for resisting Bacchus, 3.564, 3.585, 3.620, 3.636, 3.766, 3.776, 3.782, 3.786, 4.25

Per'gamum: the Trojan citadel, associated with Troy itself, 12.675, 15.479

Per'iphas: Attican king highly esteemed by his people. Jupiter transformed him into an eagle and his wife Phene into an osprey, 7.449, 12.520

Peri'phetes: son of Vulcan, living in Epidaurus. Slaughtered travelers with his iron club, 7.489

Perse'phone: Greek name for Proserpina, 5.543, 10.15, 10.835, 14.132

Per'seus: son of Jupiter and Danaë; slayer of Medusa. His rescue of Andromeda is memorialized in the stars, where he was placed as the constellation Perseus, 4.676, 4.709, 4.720, 4.723, 4.742, 4.750, 4.754, 4.782, 4.785, 4.812, 4.817, 4.827, 4.830, 4.844, 4.861, 4.864, 5.19, 5.36, 5.38, 5.40, 5.66, 5.80, 5.93, 5.99, 5.149, 5.158, 5.183, 5.193, 5.203, 5.211, 5.215, 5.228, 5.247, 5.271, 5.286

Per'sia: ancient empire in modern Iran, 1.62, 4.238

Phae'dra: wife of Theseus. Caused the exile of her stepson Hippolytus when he refused her advances, 15.543

Pha'ëthon: son of Apollo and Clymene. Killed attempting to drive his father's chariot across the sky, 1.808, 1.813, 1.835, 2.34, 2.36, 2.104, 2.108, 2.160, 2.194, 2.248, 2.350, 2.360, 2.406, 2.421, 4.277

Pha'sis: a river of Colchis, 7.8

Philam'mon: minstrel son of Apollo and Chione; half brother of Autolycus, 11.371

Phile'mon: elderly Phrygian; husband of Baucis. Humbly hosts Jupiter and Mercury, 8.714, 8.768, 8.795, 8.804, 8.805

Philocte'tes: Greek warrior given his friend Hercules' bow; marooned on the way to Troy. Since an oracle required the bow for Troy to be taken, Ulysses returned for Philoctetes, 9.254, 13.51, 13.376, 13.394, 13.478

Philome'la: daughter of Pandion; raped and mutilated by Tereus. Philomela and her sister Procne served Tereus his son for a meal, 6.517, 6.544, 6.556, 6.579, 6.589, 6.640, 6.662, 6.694, 6.699, 6.742, 6.757, 6.772

Phil'yra: mother of Chiron; a daughter of Oceanus and Tethys, 2.756

Phi'neus: blind Thracian prophet; king of Salmydessus. Aided Jason in the quest for the Golden Fleece, 5.8, 5.35, 5.41, 5.105, 5.109, 5.110, 5.127, 5.184, 5.240, 5.257, 5.265, 7.3.

Phleg'ethon: a river of the underworld, 5.729, 15.579

Phleg'yans: thieving tribe of marauders who raided the temple at Delphi, 11.488

Pho'cis: a country in Greece; adjacent to Boeotia, 1.324, 2.637

Pho'cus: son of Aeacus and the Nereid Psamathe. Killed by his half brothers Telamon and Peleus, perhaps at the instigation of their mother, 7.530, 7.731, 7.733, 5.736, 7.750, 7.809, 7.880, 11.314, 11.444

Phoe'be: Titaness mother of Latona and Asteria; grandmother of Apollo, Diana, and Hecate. Also a name used for Diana, 1.11, 6.248

Phoe'bus: an epithet of Apollo, referring to his association with the sun, 1.483, 2.23, 2.37, 2.117, 2.441, 2.681, 2.701, 3.10, 3.11, 3.162, 6.134, 6.245, 6.560, 7.361, 8.32, 10.137, 10.170, 10.189, 11.188, 11.190, 11.355, 11.370, 11.692, 13.774, 13.816, 14.163, 14.174, 15.213, 15.456, 15.693, 15.824

Phryg'ia: a region of Asia Minor known for the worship of Cybele, 6.164, 6.184, 6.200, 6.457, 8.703, 10.163, 11.99, 11.235, 12.50, 12.88, 13.52, 13.469, 14.634, 15.481

Phthi'a: Thesslian city where Achilles was born, 13.186

Pi'cus: son of Saturn; Latian king; husband of Canens. Rejected Circe's love, 14.369, 14.388, 14.395, 14.402, 14.418, 14.449, 14.460, 14.466

Pi'erus: king of Emathia; husband of Euippe. His nine daughters challenged the Muses, 5.353

Pin'dus: a Thessalian mountain range, 1.605, 2.246, 7.258, 11.643

Pirae'us: the port of Athens, 6.511

Piri'thoüs: son of Ixion; present at the Calydonian boar hunt with his friend Theseus. The battle of the Centaurs and the Lapiths took place at his wedding to Hippodameia, 8.349, 8.455, 8.649, 8.693, 12.257, 12.272, 12.387, 12.390, 12.391, 12.394, 12.396

Pisae'a: area between Arcadia and Elis; site of the city of Pisa, 5.474

Pi'sces: zodiacal constellation of the Fish; the two fish represent Venus and Cupid, 10.174

Pit'theus: son of Pelops and Hippodameia; king of Troezen, 8.703, 15.323

Plei'ades: the seven daughters of Atlas, represented by the cluster of seven stars found in the constellation of Taurus, 1.717, 2.933, 3.653, 6.196, 13.354

Pleu'ron: an Aetolian city, 7.428

Plu'to (Dis, Or'cus): god of the underworld. Son of Saturn; brother of Jupiter and Neptune, 4.561, 5.458, 5.479, 5.656

Pol′lux: son of Leda and Zeus; brother of Helen; half brother of Castor and Clytemnestra. The two brothers are associated with the constellation Gemini, 8.347, 8.423

Poly′damas: Trojan warrior and friend of Hector, 12.630

Polydo′rus: son of Priam and Hecuba; killed by the treacherous Thracian king Polymestor, 13.518, 13.641, 13.648, 13.761

Polyni′ces: son of Oedipus; exiled brother of Eteocles and Antigone. Killed in the battle of the Seven against Thebes, 9.460

Polyphe′mus: a Cyclops infatuated with Galatea. Killed Acis and members of Ulysses' crew, 13.915, 13.926, 14.194

Poly′xena: daughter of Priam and Hecuba. Sacrificed by the Greeks upon Achilles' tomb, 13.535, 13.538, 13.551, 13.620

Pomo′na: wood nymph of Latium; caretaker of fruit trees, 14.716, 14.885

Pompei′us, Sextus: son of Pompey the Great; defeated in naval battle by Augustus (then Octavian), 15.923

Posei′don: See Neptune

Pri′am: last Trojan king; son of Laomedon. Father of Hector and Paris, 11.873, 12.1, 12.695, 13.115, 13.242, 13.243, 13.518, 13.520, 13.564, 13.577, 13.620, 13.629, 13.718, 13.868, 14.551, 15.474

Pria′pus: a Phrygian god of fertility and gardens, 9.392, 14.735

Proc′ne: daughter of Pandion; wife of Tereus and sister of Philomela. Kills her son Itys and feeds the boy to his father, 6.489, 6.495, 6.503, 6.535, 6.538, 6.621, 6.651, 6.655, 6.670, 6.688, 6.696, 6.704, 6.715, 6.739, 6.745, 6.753, 6.773

Pro′cris: daughter of Erechtheus; wife of Cephalus. Accidentally killed by her husband during a hunt, 6.787, 7.760, 7.764, 7.778, 7.779, 7.782, 7.912, 7.933

Procrus′tes: barbaric host for travelers on the road to Athens, offering them a bed for the night. If guests were too short for the bed, he would stretch them; if they were too tall, he would lop off their legs, 7.492

Prome′theus: Titan son of Iapetus and Themis, brother of Atlas. Created humans from clay; stole Olympian fire and gave it to humans. Punished by being eternally bound to a rock with an eagle returning every day to eat his liver, 1.83, 1.405, 10.45

Proser′pina (Perseph′one): daughter of Ceres by Jupiter. Bride of Pluto; queen of the underworld, 5.455, 5.479, 5.582, 5.613, 5.627, 5.641

Pro'teus: prophetic sea god with the ability to change his form. Father of Thetis, 2.9, 8.825, 11.261, 11.295, 11.302, 13.1093

Pygma'lion: Cyprian sculptor of an ivory woman, which was brought to life by Venus. Father of Paphos, 10.266, 10.276, 10.300

Py'los: city in Elis; home of Nestor and Neleus, 2.766, 6.478, 7.415, 12.6323

Pyre'neus: Thracian king, attempted to assault the Muses, 5.319, 5.334

Pyr'rha: queen of Thessaly; wife of Deucalion and daughter of Epimetheus, 1.363, 1.397, 1.411

Pytha'goras: Greek philosopher from Samos; teacher of Numa. Tells of the ancient Golden Age and claims to be the reincarnate Euphorbus, 15.68

Py'thon: serpent who held Delphi as the oracle of his mother Earth before being killed by Apollo, 1.455, 1.472, 1.479

Quiri'nus: (1) name for the deified Romulus; (2) the Quirinal hill of Rome, 14.952, 14.960, 14.962, 14.981

Rhadaman'thus: son of Jupiter and Europa; brother of Minos. Known for his justice, he became a judge in the underworld, 9.499, 9.504

Rhe'sus: a Thracian king. Diomedes and Ulysses killed Rhesus and took his horses in a night raid, 13.114, 13.300

Rhodes: an island off the southwestern coast of Asia Minor, 7.407, 12.657

Rho'dope: Thracian mountain; once an arrogant mortal, 2.242, 6.97, 6.681

Ro'mulus: son of Mars and Ilia; twin brother of Remus. Founder of Rome; deified as Quirinus, 14.893, 14.902, 14.921, 14.928, 14.974, 15.613, 15.629, 15.970, 15.972

Ru'tuli: a Latian people, from the homeland of Turnus, 14.528, 14.614, 14.653

Sabae'a: a southern Arabian area, 10.551

Sa'bines: tribal peoples living east of Rome, 14.896, 14.919, 14.922, 15.5

Sagitta'rius: zodiacal constellation of the Archer, 2.85

Sal'amis: a city of Cyprus; founded by Teucer, 14.806, 14.876

Salma'cis: nymph of a pool in Caria; loved Hermaphroditus, 4.321, 4.341, 4.373, 15.348

Sa'mos: an island off the western coast of Asia Minor; sacred site of Juno and birthplace of Pythagoras, 8.262, 15.69, 15.70

Sar'dis: primary city of Lydia, 11.157, 11.172

Sarpe'don: son of Jupiter and Laodamia. Killed by Patroclus during the Trojan War, 13.309

Sa'turn (Cro'nos): god of agriculture. Titan son of Sky and Earth; father of Jupiter, Juno, Neptune, and Pluto. Doomed to Tartarus by Jupiter, 1.115, 3.291, 3.361, 3.398, 4.492, 5.486, 6.139, 9.198, 9.271, 9.572, 14.369, 15.964

Satur'nia: See Juno

Sci'ron: a well-known thief who pushed his victims over the seaside cliffs. Defeated by Theseus, 7.496, 7.499

Scor'pio: zodiacal constellation of the Scorpion, illustrating the scorpion which killed the hunter Orion, 2.86, 2.213

Scyl'la: (1) daughter of Nisus, the king of Megara. Betrayed her father and country to Minos, 8.103, 8.120; (2) once a girl, transformed by Circe into a sea monster, 7.78, 13.875, 13.878, 13.887, 13.893, 13.1071, 13.1079, 13.1085, 13.1143, 14.20, 14.43, 14.54, 14.62, 14.75, 14.82.

Scy'ros: Aegean island where Achilles spent part of his childhood, 13.186, 13.208

Scy'thia: a region northeast of the Black Sea, 1.65, 2.244, 5.750, 7.457, 8.888, 8.899, 10.677, 14.384, 15.312, 15.390

Sem'ele: mother of Bacchus by Jupiter; daughter of Cadmus, 3.278, 3.294, 3.300, 3.309, 3.315, 3.334, 3.572

Se'riphos: an island of the Cyclades, 5.279, 5.292

Sibyl: Cumaean prophetess, priestess of Apollo. Aeneas' guide through the underworld, 14.120, 14.122, 14.150, 14.178, 15.790

Sicily: largest Mediterranean island; southwest of Italy, 5.401, 8.329, 13.924, 14.8, 15.305

Si'don: a city of the Phoenicians, 2.934, 3.138, 4.633

Sige'um: Trojan promontory, 11.225, 12.90, 13.5

Sile'nus: elderly satyr; foster father of Bacchus, 11.99, 11.111

Simo'ïs: a Trojan river, 13.394

Sip'ylus: a mountain of Lydia, 6.166

Si'rens: the daughters of the river god Acheloüs; turned partly into birds. They entice sailors to a deathly island with their deceptively sweet songs, 5.642, 14.99

Si'syphus: thieving son of Aeolus. Sentenced to continually push a stone up a hill in Hades, only to have the stone roll back down, 4.506, 4.512, 10.46, 13.29, 13.36

Sitho'nia: a region in Thrace, 13.689

Sky: god and personification of the sky who is also called Uranus. Cousin of Earth and father by Earth of, among others, the Titans, the Cyclopes, and (by the blood of his own castration that fell to Earth) the Giants, 1.82

Smin'theus: epithet of Apollo as god of plague 12.669

Spar'ta: primary city of Laconia, 3.219, 3.234, 6.474, 10.179, 10.193, 15.60, 15.464

Sperchei'os: a river of Thessaly, 1.615, 2.273, 5.102, 7.264

Stro'phades: small island group in the Ionian Sea, 13.853

Stym'phalis: a region of Arcadia, 5.675

Styx: the main river of the underworld; often refers to the underworld, 1.141, 1.193, 1.793, 2.47, 2.107, 3.82, 3.292, 3.313, 3.553, 3.770, 4.4776, 4.480, 5.135, 5.582, 6.764, 10.13, 10.75, 10.348, 10.797, 11.582, 12.378, 13.559, 14.683, 15.172, 15.799

Sun, the: (See Hyperion and Phoebus) god and personification of the sun, variously identified with Hyperion, Helius (the son of Hyperion), and Phoebus, 1.10, 1.808, 1.829, 1.834, 2.1, 2.31, 2.124, 2.164, 4.189, 4.191, 4.240, 4.262, 4.268, 4.290, 4.301, 4.703, 6.501, 7.115, 7.241, 8.646, 10.185, 11.304, 13.1014–1015, 13.1145, 14.12, 14.31, 14.37, 14.399, 14.433, 15.443

Symple'gades: the "Clashing Rocks"; two islands that clashed into each other, hindering ships from entering the Black Sea, 15.368

Syr'ia: eastern coast of the Mediterranean Sea, area of the Phoenicians, 5.168

Sy'rinx: Arcadian nymph, pursued by Pan, 1.741, 1.758

Syr'tis: a bank of quicksand on the northern African coast, 8.144

Taen'arus: a southern Peloponnesian town, said to be an entrance to the underworld, 2.270, 10.13

Ta'gus: Spanish river known for its gold, 2.274

Tan'talus: son of Jupiter; father of Pelops and Niobe. Attempted to serve the gods his butchered son for a meal; sentenced to stand in a stream without the ability to quench his perpetual thirst, 4.505, 6.194, 6.273, 10.42

Tarpei′a: a Vestal virgin who betrayed Rome to the Sabines, who killed her, 14.897, 15.975

Tar′tarus: the underworld, the infernal regions beneath Hades, 1.115, 2.285, 5.430, 5.491, 6.782, 10.22, 11.770, 12.305, 12.601, 12.710

Tartes′sus: a Phoenician city in Spain, 14.484

Ta′tius: Sabine ruler; after a time of war, Tatius and Romulus ruled Italy together, 14.896, 14.927, 14.928

Tau′rus: (1) zodiacal constellation of the Bull, containing the Pleiades and Hyades. Represents the form that Jupiter assumed with Europa and Io, 2.85; (2) a mountain in Asia Minor, 2.236

Tel′amon: Argonaut, son of Aeacus; brother of Peleus and half brother of Phocus. Father of Ajax and Teucer, 7.529, 7.706, 7.732, 8.355, 8.429, 11.252, 12.716, 13.25, 13.142, 13.181, 13.319, 13.390

Tel′emus: seer son of Eurymus, 13.923, 13.924

Tem′pe: valley in Thessaly; site of the river Peneus, 1.603, 7.255, 7.414

Ten′edos: small island off the coast of Troy, 1.541, 12.134, 13.207

Te′reus: Thracian king; deceitful husband of Procne; father of Itys, 6.483, 6.495, 6.503, 6.509, 6.521, 6.542, 6.549, 6.571, 6.574, 6.591, 6.599, 6.636, 6.709, 6.733, 6.745, 6.750, 6.776, 6.790

Te′thys: sea goddess; wife of Oceanus. Preserved the life of Aesacus, 2.73, 2.167, 2.570, 9.573, 11.908, 13.1126

Teu′cer: (1) son of Telamon and Hesione; half brother of Ajax, 13.187; (2) the most ancient Trojan king, originally from Crete; 13.848, 14.806

Thebes: primary city of Boeotia; founded by Cadmus, 3.140, 3.606, 3.611, 3.620, 3.809, 4.36, 4.455, 4.602, 6.177, 6.181, 6.202, 6.204, 7.845, 9.342, 9.458, 13.206, 13.826, 15.465

The′mis: Greek goddess of law and justice; daughter of Uranus and Gaia, 1.333, 1.392, 4.714, 7.843, 9.458, 9.478

Thes′saly: region in northeastern Greece, 1.602, 2.606, 2.670, 7.187, 7.255, 7.302, 7.352, 8.915, 11.271, 12.103, 12.203, 12.204, 12.224, 12.246, 12.251, 12.416

The′tis: sea goddess daughter of Nereus and Doris, wife of Peleus; mother of Achilles, 11.262, 11.266, 11.281, 11.312, 11.469, 12.108, 13.193, 13.201, 13.347

The′seus: son of Aegeus; father of Hippolytus. Hero of the Isthmus of Corinth and of Athens. Killed the Minotaur, 7.453, 7.473, 7.486, 8.207, 8.307, 8.312, 8.349, 8.457, 8.626, 8.641, 8.647, 8.819, 9.1,

12.271, 12.281, 12.401, 12.404, 12.411, 12.415, 12.418, 15.532, 15.962

Thrace: a region northeast of Macedonia, 2.280, 6.98, 6.484, 6.497, 11.1, 13.760

Thyes'tes: son of Pelops. His brother Atreus killed Thyestes' sons and served them to him in a banquet, 15.501

Ti'ber: Italian river, runs through Rome, 2.282, 14.495, 14.502, 14.520, 15.469, 15.686, 15.807

Tire'sias: Theban son of the nymph Chariclo; father of Manto. A woman for seven years; given the ability of prophecy by Jupiter and blinded by Juno, 3.349, 3.366, 3.377, 3.567, 6.174

Tisi'phone: one of the Furies, 4.522, 4.530, 4.556

Ti'tans: first offspring of Earth and Sky. Led by Saturn, they successfully revolted against Sky (Uranus), castrating him, but were overthrown by the Olympian gods, led by Jupiter, 1.10, 1.83, 6.211, 6.501, 7.447, 10.185, 10.304, 14.17, 14.435, 14.442

Ti'tyos: a giant slain by Apollo and Diana for attempted rape of Latona. Doomed to the punishment of having his liver eternally preyed upon by eagles and snakes, 4.503

Tlepo'lemus: son of Hercules; king of Rhodes. Killed at Troy, 12.619

Tmo'lus: a mountain in Lydia; associated with the god of the same name, 2.237, 11.171, 11.178, 11.188, 11.197, 11.221

Tri'ton: sea god, son of Neptune. The sound of his horn calms or stirs up the sea, 1.345, 1.349, 2.9, 13.1093

Trito'nia: (See Minerva) 2.872, 2.885, 5.313, 6.1

Tro'ezen: a city of southeastern Argolis, 6.478, 8.650, 15.323, 15.552

Troy (I'lium): a city in northwestern Asia Minor; site of the Trojan War, 8.415, 9.262, 11.229, 11.241, 11.252, 11.873, 12.9, 12.24, 12.33, 12.176, 12.516, 12.671, 12.701, 13.26, 13.62, 13.201, 13.237, 13.267, 13.276, 13.297, 13.389, 13.395, 13.407, 13.411, 13.418, 13.422, 13.452, 13.454, 13.458, 13.486, 13.506, 13.516, 13.522, 13.601, 13.609, 13.695, 13.699, 13.752, 13.866, 14.543, 14.648, 15.460, 15.473, 15.477, 15.480, 15.857

Tur'nus: Rutulian king; suitor for the hand of Lavinia. Killed in combat with Aeneas, 14.524, 14.535, 14.616, 14.627, 14.661, 14.653, 15.860

Tus'cany: northwestern region of Italy, 3.693, 4.26, 14.255, 14.707

Typhoe'us: serpent-headed giant; son of Tartarus and Gaia. Destroyed by Jupiter's lightning while attempting to overthrow the gods and buried beneath Sicily, 3.329, 5.376, 5.380, 5.403, 5.408

Tyre: a well-known Phoenician city, 2.938, 3.40, 3.276, 3.593, 6.71, 6.255, 10.225, 10.293, 11.192, 15.314

Tyrrhe'nian: another name for Etruscans, 14.9, 15.605

Ulys'ses (Odys'seus): son of Laertes, king of Ithaca; husband of Penelope. Greek leader known for his cunning, 13.8, 13.16, 13.21, 13.56, 13.63, 13.66, 13.70, 13.72, 13.76, 13.96, 13.106, 13.129, 13.143, 13.368, 13.369, 13.415, 13.461, 13.467, 13.481, 13.511, 13.583, 13.856, 13.928, 14.77, 14.183, 14.186, 14.210, 14.222, 14.256, 14.276, 14.331, 14.342, 14.359, 14.650, 14.773

Uran'us: See Sky

Ve'nus: goddess of love. Born from the foam of the sea or daughter of Jupiter and Dione; wife of Vulcan. Mother of Cupid and Aeneas, 1.483, 3.142, 4.192, 4.193, 4.324, 4.587, 5.386, 5.421, 5.441, 7.890, 9.554, 9.914, 10.246, 10.260, 10.296, 10.306, 10.324, 10.600, 10.631, 13.753, 13.813, 13.909, 14.30, 14.93, 14.281, 14.554, 14.566, 14.660, 14.675, 14.677, 14.729, 14.798, 14.878, 14.904, 14.909, 15.421, 15.866, 15.96.

Vertum'nus: an Etruscan shape-changing god of fertility; wooed Pomona, 14.736, 14.781, 14.883

Ves'ta: goddess of the hearth fire; brought from Troy to Rome, 15.811, 15.865, 15.972, 15.974

Vul'can: god of fire and metalworking; lame son of Juno and husband of Venus, 2.6, 2.113, 2.845, 4.193, 4.194, 4.206, 9.281, 9.484

Xan'thus: river near Troy; burned by Vulcan when attempting to drown Achilles, 2.267, 9.742

Zeph'yrus: the West Wind, 1.64